THE CO... ...TH

Thomas ...cCarthy

THE COAST OF DEATH

by

Thomas McCarthy

SERVING HOUSE BOOKS

The Coast of Death

Copyright © 2010 Thomas McCarthy

All rights reserved.

No part of this book may be used or reproduced in any manner whatsoever without the prior written permission of the copyright holder except for brief quotations in critical articles or reviews.

Cover photo by Walter Cummins

Author photo by Lyn Clarke

Serving House Books logo by Barry Lereng Wilmont

ISBN: 978-0-9826921-1-0

Published by Serving House Books

www.servinghousebooks.com

First Serving House Books Edition 2010

To reign is worth ambition, though in hell:
Better to reign in hell than serve in heav'n
John Milton
Paradise Lost

– that mysterious arrangement of merciless logic
for a futile purpose.
Joseph Conrad

To Lyn

 Thomas McCarthy was born in Mallow, Co. Cork Ireland and educated there and in Dublin. He has lived there and now has his home in Peterborough, UK.

His stories have been published in *PEN New Fiction 1 & 2; Sunk Island Review; Paris Transcontinental; The Literary Review; Cimarron Review; New Irish Writing; The Irish Press; StoryQuarterly*. A collection of stories, *The Last Survivor*, was published in 1985. Citron Press published a novel *A Fine Country* in May 2000. A further collection of stories, *Finals Day & Other Stories*, was published in October 2002. His essay "At Least You'll Never Starve" is in the collection *Writers On The Job*, published by Hopewell Publications in the U.S. in 2008, and another esssay is to be included in an anthology due out from Serving House Books in 2010. At present, he is at work on a novel, *Flannery's World*, and a trilogy of linked stories called *Morning Has Broken*.

CHAPTER 1

His head aches and his mouth is dry. It is some while since he has been even slightly hung-over and he doesn't like the feeling; it takes him so much longer to get over it these days. And that sense of dread that always accompanies a hangover is reinforced by the job ahead of him. Come on, he tells himself, as he starts the car, it's nothing much. You know where you're going and all you have to do is leave a message. As the engine warms up, he opens the window for some air; he looks again at the map and checks the satellite navigation system is working. A couple of deep breaths and he is ready.

Once he is on the open road, he begins to feel better. After all, it isn't much to do, carry out a favour, not when he remembers how good the Boss is to him, how much he owes him. He might well have ended up like so many of those he knew had, who were still in Finsbury Park living in the hostel, spending all their time and money in the pubs and betting shops.

As he drives along the unfamiliar road, he thinks back to last night in the hotel bar. He had gone in planning to have his normal two pints and two whiskies, quite happy to sit by himself as he nursed his drink, not looking for or expecting any company, or any conversation. To his surprise, a couple of men began to chat away to him, nice and casual like, nothing heavy. He told them he was up looking for some places to fish, that he and his mate from England were planning a few days next year during the English close season. It transpired that one of them, Bob, was a keen angler, he boasted a little about the huge perch he caught last month, and he gave him a list of good fishing around the lakes. It seemed only decent to have a few more drinks, to end up staggering off to bed around midnight, knowing he was drunk and that if he didn't get to bed he was going to fall asleep at the bar.

Apart from feeling his heart thump a little more than usual, that and a slight headache and a thirst which he quenches with regular swigs from the bottle of Ballygowan water on the seat beside him, he feels okay really, better that he has a right to and for that he is grateful.

You have to be there before 10:30 at the latest, better if you can arrive about fifteen minutes beforehand.

He didn't question the instructions. He never does with the Boss.

The satellite navigation system tells him to turn right at the next junction, to head down the B road for one mile. He is pleased to be near the house, pleased also that it is nearly five past ten, so his timing is spot on. The rain, which has been intermittent but heavy during his two hour-journey, comes down again in a fierce burst so that he needs the windscreen wipers on full tilt. He wants to have a pee, he is feeling hot and he is sweating. It is as if his earlier euphoria about the slightness of his hangover is coming back to kick him for his presumption. He is relieved to see the drive to the house, to pull in and stop the car and try to get his breath.

He is panicking now. He is sure he has taken his pills this morning. So many of the bloody things, seven in all, but he prides himself on never forgetting them no matter what state he is in when he wakes up. His chest is painful, a bad dose of indigestion; he knows it was stupid of him to have eaten the huge fry for breakfast, but he is never able to resist a fry, particularly when he has a thick head. He winds the window down, struggling for breath. Despite the cold rain that swirls in through the open window, he is sweating heavily. With an effort, he manages to open the door, to swing his feet onto the grass.

The woman coming towards him is old. He sees she is fierce, that she is not scared of him and he thinks that is a good sign. He makes a huge effort to get out of the seat and he manages it by clinging to the door. By now the ground is spinning, he feels faint, as if he is in another place. He attempts to walk towards the woman and tries to speak to her as he feels another band of red-hot wire clamp itself around his chest and he starts to fall.

Mrs McGettigan looks forward to Monday mornings. She often chuckles to herself when she thinks about it. How many other people are happy like she is as they flog off to work after the weekend, often with hangovers and full of hatred of their jobs? In her lonely existence on the smallholding, a few miles from the nearest neighbours, with only her chickens and geese for company, it is a great comfort to have a regular visitor every Monday morning. She enjoys the preparations, laying out the rashers and white pudding and sausages alongside the two eggs she cooks for his breakfast each week, and checking her hens have laid enough eggs so she can give him the dozen fresh eggs for himself. It will never be enough to replace Paudie, dead these past twenty years, whom she thinks about for hours every single day since his murder, but she's grateful they look after her so well.

She straightens up as she comes out of the henhouse into the sudden drenching shower and covers the bowl of eggs that she has gathered with the old coat she wears in the garden, as she hurries back inside her cottage. The warmth of the kitchen is welcome as is the smell of the cakes of soda bread in the oven. She takes them out to test, decides they are ready and puts one to cool in the lean-to beside the kitchen where she grows her tomatoes and herbs. The rain hammers on the Perspex roof but she knows from other days like this it will soon ease off. She hopes so for she always likes to be outside to greet him each week. She prays it is him and not that strap of a wife, a young one with little breeding on her. Mrs McGettigan is convinced she is not good enough at all for him. She cannot understand what he sees in her, either. This weekly visit is good for her in other ways – it makes her clean and tidy the cottage, something she forgets to do, involved as she is with her garden and poultry. She glances up as she hears a car pull into the drive from the road, and is a little put out that he is early. She can feel the panic rising, the fluster she will be in because she has not started to fry his rashers and sausages.

The car comes to a halt. Through the rain, she peers at the car and thinks it is him, that he is early for once because usually he is late. It pleases her to see he is on his own. Rubbing her hands on her apron, she walks out to him, her old coat pulled over her head as the rain hammers down with an increased ferocity. As she approaches, he makes to open the car door, pushes it with an effort, she thinks, as he struggles to swing his legs to the ground. He stands up, sways, and manages with a great effort to remain upright. For a moment, she thinks he is drunk and he has perhaps fallen asleep in the car after a session somewhere. Is it somebody who is lost and from the looks of him, still drunk? But that can't be him, because she knows he rarely if ever takes a drink.

Very worried now, terrified that something has happened to him, Madge McGettigan walks over to the man. She is relieved, almost euphoric when she realises it is not him. Close up she sees his pasty white face, the sweat flecking his brow. He tries to speak.

'What is it? Are you all right? Will I get you a drink of water?' She can see the poor man is very sick.

'I need to speak with him…' He gets the words out with difficulty, as if he is choking. Before she can do anything else, the man starts to pitch forward; he tries to reach her for support, misses and falls on the wet grass in front of her.

'Jesus Mary and Joseph,' Madge McGettigan says, crossing herself. She kneels down to feel his pulse and is not able to find it. Bending towards him, she whispers an act of contrition in his ear, remembering poor Paudie, shot dead without a prayer said for him.

She goes back into the house and takes the mobile phone he gave her to call him in an emergency only.

He listens carefully. 'I'm nearly at your place. I'll call in in five minutes and collect my eggs and make sure you're all right.'

The rain has stopped and a weak sun appears now and then. Madge McGettigan goes into the house to get an old tablecloth to cover the man. As she kneels to spread it over the body, she hears the car, which he leaves on the road. She looks up as he walks quickly down the drive. When he reaches Mrs McGettigan, he puts his hand on her shoulder and gives it a squeeze. Then he squats down and looks closely at the body.

'Any idea who he is?'

'No. I never seen him before in my life.'

He thinks about this. 'What did he say exactly?'

'Something about he wanted to speak to him.' She is confused and can't remember exactly what the man said. He carefully checks the man's pockets, pats him as if he is looking for something. He stands up.

'You must call the PSNI,' he tells her.

This confuses her further. 'Call who?' she asks stupidly.

Patiently he says slowly, 'The police. Ring the police.'

Madge McGettigan flinches, hesitates. 'The RUC?'

'Just phone them,' he says gently but firmly. 'Just don't tell them I've been here.'

'You can be sure I will not,' she says firmly.

'Make the call now,' he says still gently but as firmly. 'Will you do that for me?'

Madge McGettigan nods and turns to go back to the cottage and as she moves away he slips the usual envelope in to her hand. He returns quickly to his car and it is only when she hears the noise as he pulls away that she realises she hasn't given him his eggs.

She hesitates. She is reluctant to have anything to do with police, who shot Paudie, and for whom Madge McGettigan has a visceral hatred and fear. She is still undecided until she looks out and sees the poor man lying on his back on the ground. She dials 999.

CHAPTER 2

Routine is important, he thinks as he watches the rain sluice down. After a weekend of warm, sunny, balmy August heat, he does not mind this change. It is Monday, and it ties in with the mood – the sullen acceptance of the start of the week and the return to work. Eamon sits in his car in the car park, waiting for the ferry, as he does most Mondays, after a weekend in the cottage. He watches it leave Magilligan, ploughing steadily across Lough Foyle. The sea is a brown sludge with flecks of white where the faint wind whips up small waves. Way back, he spent time in Magilligan Camp in the early days of the Troubles. A bleak miserable desolate spot, he recalls, accessible in those days only by road.

As the ferry nears Greencastle Harbour, Eamon flicks the wipers on as he plans his day. The wind has got up, the sea is choppy now and rain sweeps across, hiding the shore of Magilligan. He is booked to give a talk in Letterkenny the following evening, a standard introduction to classical music, how to begin – easy listening with the most popular melodic pieces. Of course, he is aware that his knowledge of music and his effective presentational skills are one reason for his popularity, why he is in such demand with women's groups in particular. The other, and probably greater, is his notoriety. During the question and answer session and when they break for tea and minerals, he is plied with questions about his spells as a prisoner, his time in the IRA. Was he really a member of the Army Council, the supreme ruling body of the IRA, some of the bolder, more curious, ask. These questions Eamon bats away, gently, with a smile. He has a number of anecdotes, humorous tales that he uses to lead his audience off that subject. Some persist. Sometimes a woman follows him out to his car at the end of the evening. There are hints, offers, and requests for sex. Eamon declines, politely, graciously. Long years of the secret life have given him an expertise, a veneer, the shield he uses to deflect such things.

Beside there is Mary, his wife, whom he loves deeply. Eamon is uxorious; the thought of hurting her in any way is repugnant. In any case, he thinks wryly, if she suspected anything she would not only be bitterly hurt, but probably would set about him physically. Her temper, mostly under control, can still flare when she is angry. Eamon listens to the nine o'clock news. Overnight there have been riots in Belfast. An Orange Order parade and march has been rerouted a couple of hundred yards away from a Nationalist street, and the Loyalists are kicking up. A muted, mealy-mouthed condemnation is all he hears from the Government in London. Eamon knows what the press reaction would be if such outbreaks of violence and damage – buses torched, shops burnt out, cars set alight – had been in a Nationalist area. The British media, accompanied by loud condemnations from the Loyalist politicians and their friends in London, would have castigated the Movement. But there is no word from the Loyalists. Silence for once, he thinks dryly, from the Reverend Paisley and his men.

Eamon resists the temptation to switch to a news channel. He is content with the introduction to Shostakovich's Eighth Symphony. How many times has he listened to it? He can remember the first time he heard it, when he was in Long Kesh. Over the years, he has caught parts, but only listened to the complete symphony, maybe five or six times, he calculates. His lower gums are sore where his denture rubs – he lost most of his teeth after being kicked during an interrogation – gingerly he runs his tongue over the tender area.

The ferry is full as it is most Mondays. He watches it berth. The ramp clanks down and the cars and vans drive off quickly. Once on board, Eamon fishes out some euros for the fare, and checks his pocket for the envelopes with the cash. This, too, is part of the routine. Each Monday he takes her pension from the Movement to Mrs McGettigan, the widowed mother of a volunteer killed by the British Army. For a moment, he wonders about the dead man in her drive last week. She has left messages for him, texted him also, and to his shame he has not phoned her back. Well he'll make it up to her this morning, spend a bit longer with her, and linger over the fry she insists on cooking for him.

How my days pass, Eamon reflects. Quietly, without much fuss or excitement, so unlike the past, but the better for it – these are the best sort of days. He gives his lectures when invited. Running the two B&Bs and café he owns with Mary take up his time. On Mondays, he doles out the pensions for the Movement, which come from the business. After he pays his fare, Eamon switches off the engine and allows the rain to obscure his view of the cars in front and on one side. This journey to Magilligan is not busy; the ferry traffic is one way at this time of day, there is nothing to see and the trip is short and familiar. Eamon closes his eyes and listens to Shostakovich.

And is startled, wide-awake and alert when the passenger door opens. Eamon reaches for the tyre lever he keeps beside his seat. A young man, collar turned up, baseball cap pulled low over his forehead gets in.

'Jesus, a hoor of a day,' he says. 'Turn that thing off.'

Eamon does not reply. He switches the radio off. Slowly he relaxes his grip on the tyre lever but retains hold of it for a bit longer until he realises what he is doing and lets go.

'Still quick enough,' Tom O'Connor says, watching Eamon's hand as he brings it up from the side of his seat.

'You should have told me you wanted a lift. I'd have picked you up.'

O'Connor does not answer. He drums his fingers on the dashboard. 'How's things?' he asks eventually.

Eamon is annoyed by the intrusion of O'Connor but also wary. He knows O'Connor has not dropped in for a chat. O'Connor has no talent, apart from his ability to inspire uneasiness, precisely why he holds the position he does. 'Fine,' he says eventually. 'Nothing to report. On my way to pay some pensions, like I do on Monday.'

'Good. How's the hotel business?'

'We just do B&B.' Eamon pauses. 'It's all right. We make a good living.'

'Yeah. Still it's a lot better than it used to be.'

Eamon nods in agreement. His mind is racing. What the hell is O'Connor doing here, creeping up on him? He is also annoyed with himself for being so lax, so open to an ambush. 'Sure, yeah it is.'

'How's Mary?'

'Fine. She's down in Limerick visiting her family; her niece has just had a baby.'

'Limerick,' O'Connor says slowly. 'Stab city. As the man says, they need some manners put on them down there. It wouldn't happen here.'

There have been a number of killings, a drug war, and an inter-family feud for control, which has led to tit-for-tat killings, and given Limerick a reputation for violence. That response is typical of O'Connor, who mouths whatever his boss Ignatius Davin proclaims. Davin who likes order and control.

Eamon wonders what Davin wants. He is certain O'Connor is here to take him to Davin. Iggy Davin, Eamon's mentor and former close ally on the Army Council, who is Chief of Staff and an iconic figure in the Movement. All-powerful and ruthless in his pursuit of those deemed to be a risk or threat, he is feared, a man to avoid, if possible. Davin is a powerful build, a massive man, deep-shouldered, broad-chested, yet agile, light on his feet, but he has put on weight over the years, or had, Eamon remembers, the last time he saw him.

Eamon is watching O'Connor, wondering and worrying. He has no desire to see Ignatius Davin, to have any dealings with him. Eamon knows Davin wants something. He does not know what, but he is certain Ignatius Davin is not concerned with his welfare. Eamon has accepted he is retired. In many ways he is grateful; he likes sleeping in his own bed most nights, unlike when he was on the Army Council and felt hunted and watched like an animal, so that he never slept anywhere more than two nights running. No, he does not want to return to that. Although at times he chaffs and gets restless, he is aware of how lucky he is, to be safe and sane: above all to have the bonus of Mary's love, this flowering of his late marriage.

'Well?' O'Connor prompts. 'It would not happen here, would it? No turf wars.'

'No.'

The landing stage is in view. The rain has stopped. Eamon sees there is another full load of cars and vans waiting to cross over into the Republic, people travelling to work there. Lots of that these days, more since the ferry went into service a few years ago. And the Celtic Tiger began to growl and roar, while the British Lion, at least in Northern Ireland, grew mangy and old and tired and did not make much noise.

'Pull in over here,' O'Connor says when they are clear of the ferry park and on the road. Eamon does so. O'Connor nods at the black camper van that is waiting in the lay-by. Another car pulls in behind Eamon's. O'Connor hands the keys to an unknown young man.

Eamon gets into the back of the camper van and sits on a bench seat that pulls down to make a bed. Opposite him, Ignatius Davin continues to chew a sausage roll, grey flecks of pastry spatter his shirt and open jacket. Eamon, who has not seen him for some months, thinks he is even fatter than when they last met.

Davin finishes the sausage roll. He wipes his mouth with a

handkerchief and brushes some crumbs off his jacket. 'We have a problem,' he says, looking straight at Eamon. They sway slightly as the van pulls out and accelerates. 'A problem that you need to sort out.'

Eamon feels his stomach contract and rumble, the symptoms of Irritable Bowel Syndrome, as his doctor insists on calling it. He takes a slow deep breath. 'We? Me? I was stood down years ago, Iggy. Remember? Pensioned off, put out to grass. "Go and read some books, Eamon," you said. "Do some thinking, write some policy papers."' Eamon hopes he has kept his tone neutral, that he has avoided any tinge of the bitterness he feels. He is not sure he succeeds. '"See the obstacles, the problems, as the paving stones on the path to success," someone told me. Maybe not you.'

Davin is silent. Eamon knows the technique. Let him speak without interruption and he will run out of things to say, let him vent his spleen and don't feed him anything.

'I didn't say that, Eamon,' Davin says quietly. 'I wouldn't insult you with that sort of bollocks.'

The camper van's windows are curtained. Eamon can't see where they are, but he guesses they have passed Magilligan prison by now, as they round a corner and pick up speed along the straight road to Benone. He knows the traffic is sparse along here, unlike across the border where the roads are busy, the prosperous towns clogged with new cars queuing for shopping centres. None of this calms his nerves or reduces the ache of his ulcer. He clenches his teeth and tries to take long slow breaths, the technique he uses when he is nervous before a talk.

'You remember Flash Gordon?' Davin says suddenly.

'Fernando Griffin?'

'Him.'

'A bit, yeah. Wasn't he in Cuba? Fluent Spanish speaker, liaison man with other groups in Latin America. Went out and set up the training camp.'

'Very good,' Davin says dryly, so that Eamon can't make out if he's being sarcastic or complimentary about his memory. 'He took to his heels before they picked up his squad in Colombia.'

Time to get a little retaliation in, Eamon decides. 'I didn't know, Iggy. I couldn't, could I? I'm no longer on the Council. I'm out of the loop.'

'Need to know, Eamon,' Davin says sharply.

But Eamon is not prepared to take it so easily. 'So now I need to know?'

Davin leaves his answer for a while. 'Now you need to know.'

They slow down as they go over some rough ground. Eamon can hear the faint crash of the sea; he feels the wind as it buffets the van. Davin, ever conscious of cover, has arranged to stop near the campsite, a natural place to see a camper van parked by the sea during the season.

'We'll have a cup of tea,' Davin says. He takes a thermos jug from a cupboard, puts tea bags in two mugs and adds hot water. 'Not perfect tea, but it will do.' He waits for the bags to infuse, prods them around with a spoon until he is satisfied, then fishes them out.

'Just milk,' Eamon says.

Always a careless dresser, Davin is wearing baggy corduroy trousers, a cheap jacket, over a grey pullover and shirt. He looks as if he has slept in the same clothes for a week. Davin sips his tea, grimaces and puts the mug on the table.

'Flash Gordon vanished. Nobody heard from him. Nothing. Never made contact. We sent people to try to find him. We left all the contact channels open. He may as well have been dead. Probably we accepted that he was. Latin America is pretty uncharted territory for us, Flash was the only expert we had on the place. Then we got a contact, a whisper that he was in Bogotá.' Davin stops. He leans against the sink opposite Eamon and looks at him, with the intense penetrating scrutiny Eamon knows so well. He says nothing, sips his tea and continues to stare. It is unnerving except that he is used to the technique over the years he worked closely with Davin. The wind rocks the van, the sea sucks and hisses and crashes over the pebbles.

'Another splinter group has appeared, taken some of our renegades, and suddenly they appear to be in funds.'

'I did hear something, not a lot. Just the usual whispers and rumours. I didn't pay much attention.'

'They call themselves the True IRA.' For a moment, Davin is lost in some other place, staring at the curtains, as though he can see through them. 'The money has to come from somewhere. None of it is from our sources. Okay, they can squeeze a bit here and there, but only enough to keep them in petty cash. Nothing like the sums they now have.

'So where is it coming from?' Davin puts the mug down. 'Question. Where does an organisation raise funds? Exclude the donations, the income from clubs and other legitimate businesses. Bank raids, sure, but there have been none, we know that. The big money has to be dirty money. Which means drugs, or hoors, or smuggling people into Europe. Slavery. Flash Gordon wouldn't do sex or slavery, not his style, too complicated. Drugs is much more his kind of business,' Davin growls. 'Small bundles, easily transported, a readymade market, dealing in cash. Just the job for Flash Gordon,'

'Proof?' Eamon says.

'There is, or there was, a sudden glut in the South. Prices dropped. The big boys didn't like it, so they come calling. What the fuck is going on? And we had to tell them we didn't know. Of course, they don't believe that. Why should they when we are supposed to have the ear to the ground and are always informed. But not this time. So we go to work to find out. A bit messy, as you'd expect, but then it usually is.'

Eamon tries to remember any beatings, anybody worked over with a baseball bat, kneecapped by a bullet through the legs, sent into exile in England, but he can't recall anything out of the ordinary.

'We did find out,' Davin says. 'A connection to London, to old friends of yours.' He stares at Eamon. 'Do I need to tell you?'

'No. I can guess. Michael Donnellan.'

'Him, yes. And your old protégée,' Davin does not sneer, he is matter-of-fact. 'Hugh O'Neill.'

Eamon nods slowly. None of this is a surprise, the resurrection of Michael Donnellan, the reappearance of Hugh O'Neill, after a gap of what? ten or eleven years. Sometimes that is how it is in their world. People disappear. Some stay lost, while others reappear.

'You know what this means if they get going? Another war, more bombs somewhere, and a perfect excuse for the Unionists to delay and prevaricate, to put us on the back foot by claiming we are not fit to take our place in the Assembly. Something that will stick to us. We take the blame, whatever we say or do. The mud, and maybe the blood, will stain us. The fucking Unionists will play it for all they can. All we've worked for will vanish. It will fuck the Good Friday Agreement. The Assembly, if it goes ahead, will exclude us. All that will be lost.'

Eamon has never seen Davin so animated, so passionate, unusually emotional for him. This is puzzling to Eamon. At the most, he would have put Ignatius Davin as ambiguous about the Good Friday Agreement, and all the concessions the Movement has made.

'Did you hear the news from Belfast?' Davin changes tack. 'It's them in the shit for a change, not that you'd know from the Brit's press. The way that is working out, we are getting the results we want. But it will all be like dust if Donnellan gets any momentum. We have enough people who don't like the way things have panned out and who only stay in the Movement because there is nowhere else for them to go. But Michael Donnellan with money…'

Eamon does see, all too clearly.

Davin says softly, 'Have you been away on your holidays yet?'

'No. We don't go away much. We like it here at the cottage. That suits us fine.'

'I think it's about time you took Mary away someplace else for a change.'

Eamon says nothing as Ignatius Davin makes himself a fresh mug of tea. He opens a cupboard where he selects a packet of biscuits. Eamon waits until Davin sits down.

'Why Mary and me? We've been out of operational work for years. I'm pushing sixty.'

'It is because you've been out of sight for years that you are the ideal choice, Eamon,' Davin slurps from his tea mug. He crams a biscuit in his mouth. 'Let's face it, you're so far below the radar, you are all but forgotten. Same with Mary. You don't know Flash Gordon, nor does Mary, and best of all he does not have an idea who you two are. That is what I need.'

Eamon is shaking. He hopes he is not showing just how scared he is.

'You'll go?' The question is rhetorical.

Eamon knows he does not have a choice. Once in never out. 'Where to?'

'You'll be briefed. What I need to know is that you'll do the job? Just go and take a peep at a few folk, confirm some things, that's all. A breeze really.' Davin takes another biscuit and chews as he continues his stare. The wind shakes the van, rain spatters on the roof.

Eamon nods. 'Okay, Iggy. Sure.' He stands up knowing the interview is over.

CHAPTER 3

Eamon and Mary board a Ryanair flight to Spain. Eamon wishes she were not here. He hates the possibility that Mary might be in danger. Then she takes his hand and squeezes it and he's enormously pleased to have her with him.

The flight is full, mostly of Spanish passengers. Eamon hears a steward ask for more lemon tea, which is in cans and chilled. Eamon returns to the guidebook and tries to memorise a few phrases in Spanish. How long is it since he has been out of Ireland? Must be ten years, he thinks – he does not count his few trips to the UK mainland as the same.

Mary has dozed off, her head on his shoulder. It has been a long day, an early start, a six a.m. departure from Dublin to London Stansted, where they got the flight. As she sleeps, Eamon goes back over his briefing.

Davin and his intelligence man, a young guy Eamon does not know, and whom he suspects would soon irritate him if had to spend any time with him, conduct the briefing. McAllister is in his twenties, a computer nerd, with all the latest technology.

They sit in a room in the one of the safe houses. Eamon guesses it is in the Gweedore, the remote north-western corner of Co Donegal, favoured by the Movement over the years for the ease of hiding and remaining undiscovered in the desolate, forbidding countryside. Could well be one he has been to for an Army Council meeting. He follows the same procedure. In the evening, at dusk, he drives from Derry to Letterkenny, where he leaves his car in a supermarket car park, and he goes into Tescos. He checks he is clear and nobody is following him, he buys sandwiches and some fruit, saunters out and across to the far side of the busy car park where he gets into a car, with a silent driver, and through the night is chauffeured deep into Co Donegal, by a circuitous route. At dawn, they stop at a remote cottage, more an outhouse than a home, with a camp bed to sleep on. Eamon has remembered to bring a flask. That evening when it is dark, there are further changes of vehicles and drivers, until a new one escorts him to the safe house at one in the morning.

McAllister has a large laptop, and on the screen, there is a list. 'Okay,' he begins, 'you travel to Spain, to take a short holiday and to investigate walking the pilgrimage – the *Camino* – the route to Santiago de Compostela. The walk is about 750 kilometres, you start in the Pyrenees and the walk takes about a month, depending on your ability. All of that is in the guidebook. In Santiago, you will stay in the best hotel, Hotel dos Reis Católicos. This is a former monastery, reputed to be the oldest hotel in the world, and is right beside the cathedral, on the great square…' At which point Davin snaps, 'Leave all that, he can read about it later.'

McAllister, who is dark-haired, and olive-skinned, as if he has some Spanish antecedents, takes the rebuke smoothly. 'Okay, I have some info on PowerPoint,' he says and clicks the mouse.

'This is the latest photo we have of Griffin, taken in Santiago de Compostela last month.'

Davin leans in to peer more closely at the photograph. 'Well named. Flash he is all right.'

Eamon sees a man with gelled black hair, a deep tan, very white prominent teeth. He can understand why the appearance of Fernando Griffin irritates Ignatius Davin.

McAllister resumes. 'We managed to find out he stays at the Reis Católicos, where he is a regular visitor, comes in for a couple of nights every month. A businessman is his cover, which I suppose is true. We're fairly sure he is the liaison, the treasurer. He checks the merchandise, pays the money, collects and then ships it over here.'

'He does all this himself?' Eamon asks.

'No. The drugs come in from Colombia by ship; they are collected by the local gangs, who store them someplace along the coast.' McAllister flashes a map on the screen. 'This is the northern coast of Galicia, the most western part of Spain, sticking out into the Atlantic. Here you have Finisterre, literally the end of the earth. This stretch of coast is known as *Costa da Morte*, the coast of death. It's well named. The coast is littered with submerged rocks and hidden coves and inlets. You need to know it like the back of your hand – otherwise you can soon be in the shite.

'We are fairly sure Griffin has a house somewhere along the coast, and a speedboat he uses to make his contacts. The drugs are shipped back here in different ways, by ship, by light aircraft, in trucks and cars. That is the easier part. The hinge is Griffin. He has a pilot's licence, so more than likely he flies the stuff in himself from time to time. As you know there are plenty of places along the coast of Ireland where he could drop them.'

Eamon nods. This makes sense. He remembers how he was piloted to and from the UK on clandestine visits.

'It's possible he uses a variety of networks to shift the stuff.'

'How long has he been there?'

Davin says, 'We're not sure. Maybe a year at the most. Our last contact with him was almost two years ago. He will have had to work his way back from Colombia.'

'Why does he use that coast all the time? It must be crawling with Spanish police and undercover people.'

'It is,' McAllister says. 'However, until recently Galicia was the poorest part of Spain. The Galicians were like the Irish, famous for the export of people. There are more Galicians in Havana than in Spain. They have a reputation for clannishness, for being tight-lipped. With all that poverty, the drugs money has bought silence. They use all sorts of scams. For example, furniture shops that only open for a few hours a month, where people go and "buy" a three-piece suite, or furnish a dining room for twenty euros. There is so much cash the police only capture a fraction of what gets through. In addition, there is a long history of smuggling in the area. What has happened is that drugs replaced tobacco, alcohol, white goods. And you also have the worst weather in Spain.' He puts a map of Spain on the screen. 'See how it sticks out into the Atlantic? It is very green, gets more rainfall than any other part of Spain. Given the coastline, unpredictable weather, and a close-knit community with a history of smuggling, it is difficult to police.'

McAllister clicks the mouse and Griffin's face reappears on the screen. 'The Galicians emigrated to the US, to Latin America, and a lot went to Cuba. We suspect Griffin made his connections there. So when the Colombians wanted to ship the drugs to Europe, they had an ideal dropping off point, a perfect set-up, as that part of Spain was more or less ignored by Madrid for years.'

'Strange,' Eamon says. 'Didn't Franco come from there?'

McAllister looks at him and seems surprised that Eamon knows this. 'Didn't make any difference. Like us, they were just dumped and left to get on with it.'

Eamon does not comment on this dubious interpretation of Irish history. He thinks, is this me getting old, or do these young guys really believe all this?

'*Costa da Morte* was made for smuggling. A tradition of seagoing, thousands of boats, little fishing boats, big fast speedboats, huge fishing trawlers, and a local population so impoverished, some of them were easily bought.'

'Griffin has fluent Spanish, as we know,' Davin says, 'and he also speaks galego, the local language, an even bigger advantage. As well, as can be seen, he looks Spanish, although he comes from Galway originally.'

'Any information about where he lives, what he does between collecting and paying out?'

'We think he has a place in Madrid as well as a holiday home on the coast. He flies into Santiago de Compostela, seems to arrive when there are flights from Madrid; usually he is with his wife, or some woman who says she is. They play the wealthy businessman and his indulged wife. They have a suite at the hotel; they eat in the best restaurants. He tips lavishly, drives a top-of-the range BMW while there. He makes no effort to be self-effacing; it's almost as if he is seeking to draw attention to himself.' McAllister clicks back to the map of Galicia. 'That location is ideal. From there he can strike out along the coast, be across the border into France by land. He may have a property there. He can be in Portugal in an hour or so, so it is possible he has a base in Lisbon as well.'

'Flash bloody Gordon, all right,' Davin growls again. And Eamon notes this antipathy in Davin, and is surprised because in the old days Davin was never personal. No matter who he was dealing with, it was always the job, work, the task in hand – nothing got in the way of Davin's cold ruthless logical deductions and analysis of the problem. Eamon wonders, as he has wondered all along since the visit, what Davin is really doing?

McAllister flicks another image on the screen. 'Here is the Illa de Arousa. It is not very developed, certainly less so than some other parts of the coast to the south. However, it is popular with Galicians; a lot use it for holidays. The accepted capital of the drug running is the port town of Vilagarcía, just before you cross to the Illa de Arousa. The trawlers from here pick the drugs up from ships off the African coast, the Cape Verde islands. When they get close to the coast, the local boatmen go out to collect from the various dropping places. We think, but cannot confirm, that Griffin has a house and his big speedboat somewhere along the coast, that his collection points are along here.' He indicates on the map. 'A bridge from the mainland reaches the island. The coast is sandy, lots of dunes and woods. There are holiday homes, many on the beaches. Big fast cars as well as speedboats. Griffin with his BMW and speedboat won't arouse any suspicion whatsoever there.' McAllister looks at Davin, who nods.

'All we have got is that he has been known to go there for a weekend. What we do know is he varies his departure from Santiago de Compostela. Sometimes he turns up for a flight to Madrid or Barcelona, some days he does not. But he always flies in.'

'Always?' Eamon queries.

This flusters McAllister. 'Well, we don't know that, actually. We do know he comes in on a flight at the beginning of every month.'

'It's a perfect set-up,' Davin interjects. Is he, Eamon thinks, trying to cover up something? Is some, or all, of what McAllister is telling me not right? 'As we know Flash speaks the local lingo as well as Spanish. He fits, blends in with the locals.'

They tell Eamon about Fernando Griffin's background.

'Spanish mother, who came from Vigo in Galicia. She met Sean Griffin, Fernando's father, who was a sailor in the British Merchant Navy. They married and after the boy was born, they used to come back to Galway on holidays, where his family lived. The father was killed in Galway. Got knocked over, hit his head on something and died. An accident. Fernando stayed on in Galway for some time, then went to live with his mother who was back in Vigo, where she worked as a teacher. Young Fernando spent every summer in Galway with his uncles, aunts and cousins; they are a big family, the Griffins. And in time he started to drift our way.'

'When?' Eamon asks.

'Late 80s,' Davin answers. 'Smart kid, took a degree in French and Spanish. But fond of the bright lights, women, wine.'

'And we took him?'

'Yes and no. He was a bit too obvious. On the other hand, he had languages, connections in Spain and he looked Spanish. We kept him in play, a reserve player. In time, he did some contact work with ETA in the Basque country. From there he was the obvious man to send to Cuba and Colombia.'

'Okay.' Eamon nods and wonders how much else went on he did not know about during his last years on the Army Council.

Then Davin tells him what he wants him to do in Galicia.

Mary stirs beside him, yawns and sits up. 'How long was I asleep?'

'About an hour. We are due to land in about thirty minutes.' Mary holds his hand, gives it a squeeze.

After he returned from the briefing, another night-time journey that took thirty-six hours, Mary was waiting for him in the house, frantic with worry, not convinced by his text message about having to go away for a few days. He knew that from the number of messages from her on his mobile when they handed it back in the car park in Lifford.

'Jesus Christ! Davin! Why can't he leave you alone?' Mary is furious, caught between fear and rage. 'How long is it since he made you retire, or threw you out to save his own rotten neck. The fucking bastard!'

'I know, I know,' Eamon says gently as he takes her in his arms.

But Mary is not ready to be comforted just yet. She pushes him away, pounding his chest with her fists. 'Leave me alone! We were supposed to be finished. No more. You told me. We promised each other that was it. We'd do our bit for the party at elections, run the business, pay our dues, and we always have. But no more operations, not after Golden Boy.'

'You know it's never as simple as that. We can't walk away.'

'You're too old for this, and my nerves are not what they were.'

Eamon is silent for a time, he stands looking out of the window of their third floor sitting room. He looks at the Walls of Derry, the spire of Saint Columb's Church, at the towering Apprentice Boys' Hall. He takes in, with his usual care, the recently dismantled British Army watchtower and listening post, from where they eavesdropped on the Creggan and the Bogside areas of the city. He can see the FREE DERRY wall and the Bloody Sunday Memorial. This room is insulated, as safe as he can make it from the probes and cameras of the British listeners and watchers on the closed circuit TV. He wonders if they really have stopped their surveillance and doubts it. Doubts it because he wouldn't do so in their position, he would continue to watch and listen but covertly.

'Did I tell you I bought the Andreas Scholl CD the other day? I'll put it on. He has the most incredible countertenor voice.'

Mary is calmer now. 'Okay.'

He puts the disc on, and as they listen, Eamon finds it peaceful, and notices the music has helped. Mary is calmer.

In the evening, a fine balmy one, they walk along by the sea in Greencastle, one of those times when they manage to get away for a night.

Eamon says, when he is sure they are clear of anybody or anything that might hear them, 'You mentioned Golden Boy. That was part of what Davin wanted me for. It seems Hugh O'Neill is alive, as is Michael Donnellan. Davin believes they are about to fund the next splinter group, the TIRA.'

Mary strides along, arms folded across her chest, lips pursed. 'Davin told you this?' Her face is set, suspicious. Eamon is not surprised. He tells her about the briefing. As he talks, he can see Mary's contempt for Davin has not diminished with the years – if anything, he thinks, it has grown. She blames Davin for Eamon's demise, believes that Eamon unfairly took the blame for the fiasco that was the Golden Boy operation. Eamon had tried to convince her that it was inevitable, that by then he did not really mind. He felt burnt-out, worn down by his years of living on his nerves. Being under cover, always on the move, like a hunted animal, had extracted a price. That he had come to believe his *idée fixe*, of a socialist republican island of Ireland, was just that. So when Davin came calling one day, with the wherewithal to set him up in business, as a front for money laundering, he had been relieved.

The famous, or depending on which side you took, the infamous, Operation Golden Boy.

In the end, Eamon missed it. Picked up at a roadblock, due to sloppy reconnaissance he was sure, although he never did discover why, despite the culprits' interrogation by Iggy Davin. Eamon got a four-year sentence in Long Kesh, where all he could do was sit and watch and await the outcome.

The attempt by Hugh O'Neill, a sleeper in London, who had Irish parents but who passed as a Londoner, which was no surprise, given that he was born and lived there all his life, apart from holidays spent on his grandfather's small farm in Kerry. Who was nicknamed the Golden Boy because of his blonde good looks. Eamon was part of the team who hatched the plot to assassinate Mrs Thatcher on the steps of Number 10 Downing Street. Back in those days, the public could still walk up the famous street and gaze at the entrance waiting for a politician to appear. Eamon had done the research, had slipped into England in disguise, and then spent time in and around London, had hung around in Downing Street; he had walked the streets, checked the escape route from Downing Street, down the steps to Horse Guards Road, timing everything. Eamon had taken Hugh to a safe house to test his suitability, his willingness to assassinate Mrs Thatcher, with the very definite possibility that he could lose his life doing it. He had attended the trials when they fired the poisoned dart fitted inside a camera on a couple of sheep, which it killed.

They transferred the control of the operation and of Hugh to another case officer. They trained Hugh in the use of the camera and sent him, one dank November morning down Whitehall and into Downing Street. There, waiting among the other tourists and press, Hugh stood on the pavement as Mrs Thatcher came out of Number 10 and approached some press photographers. Hugh aimed the camera and fired the dart. Without waiting to see if he had succeeded in killing the Prime Minister, he followed the plan, turned away immediately and made his escape. How he did so was a miracle of sorts. Raids on all the safe houses the Movement had set up followed, as the British began to roll up the escape route before Hugh left Downing Street, which convinced Davin and Eamon they had an informer. Despite Hugh's escape, the belief in the Army Council was that there was a traitor high in the ranks. The hunt for Hugh went on for months, his photograph plastered across the world's press and TV – but Hugh was away, hidden or dead. Within the Movement, Iggy Davin and the Internal Security Unit were searching for the London informer.

Some years later, one day, soon after Eamon's release from Long Kesh, Iggy Davin summonsed him to a meeting in a safe house, just the two of them. Where he told him they had located Hugh. Eamon can remember the disgust on Davin's face as he told him about Hugh, how he was living on a Greek island with an Englishman. 'Did you know,' Davin snarled, 'that your *Golden Boy* was a bloody queer? That he is living with another fucking queer? Can you imagine how the British press will play that if it ever gets out?'

Then Davin gave Eamon all the ins and outs, retracing the recent history of the Movement in London and in particular the career of Michel Donnellan, the long time Officer Commanding the London Brigade. He told him where Hugh was and he ordered Eamon to get him back. They intended to make a video of Hugh appearing unannounced at an Irish club run by Donnellan, where he would make a defiant appearance before slipping away again. Except that Davin did not want him to escape the second time. Hugh was to flush out Donnellan, who according to Davin was a long time informer for the British.

'You remember the end? When Hugh O'Neill escaped from the club in London?' Eamon says.

'Of course I fucking do,' Mary says savagely. 'I was standing at the side of the stage ready to escort him back to the safe flat to await instructions, when two of Donnellan's thugs grabbed me and locked me in a room. It was only with the arrival of the cleaners after the club closed for the evening that I got out. By then Hugh was long gone.'

'As was Fintan Flaherty until he blew himself up with the Englishman, Hugh's gay friend. "The love that dare not speak its name", as Davin mockingly called it – you know how uncomfortable Davin is about sex – when he told me Hugh was gay.' They reach the end of the path, turn around to retrace their steps. 'We reckon Hugh and he were about to meet up when Flaherty spotted them and he fought Flaherty while Hugh escaped and then Flaherty blew them up.'

'Did you arrange for Flaherty to carry a bomb?'

'No. We think that was Donnellan, that he wanted to create a diversion if things went wrong. He was no great fan of Flaherty's.'

'Well he wasn't alone there. Nobody had any time for him. We never understood why you picked him.'

Eamon sighs wearily. 'Because at the time he was about the only one who was so far out of the loop, nobody would recognise him. I needed somebody like that. You were both unknown, as far as we could tell. I wanted you, but I had to use him with you – he was all I had.'

'Like we are now,' Mary says sharply.

'Yes.'

'What happened to Hugh?'

'We never found out. Well I didn't. As he was always close to Michael Donnellan, I suspect he bankrolled him. They both vanished. And it seems as if they have been waiting ever since.'

Wait, as we all did, Eamon thinks. All the slow delicate moves away from the armed struggle to the political battlefield that in time led to the Good Friday Agreement, the cessation of violence, the ceasefire, the slow dawn of a sort of peace. To his surprise Davin had gone along with the peace process, had been instrumental in keeping the hotheads in line. Or so Eamon heard. If *An Fear Mór* says it's all right, that's good enough for me. *An Fear Mór*, the big man, Davin's nickname in the Movement, bestowed partly due to his bulk, mainly for his power, his charisma with the volunteers, perhaps too for his shadowy persona, unknown to the public, rarely photographed, never seen in public. But undeniably, the strong man of the Movement, who if he chose to do so could stop the political process when he wanted.

Now he has had time to digest the briefing, it makes sense to Eamon. Like so many of Davin's schemes do. Griffin, O'Neill, above all Donnellan, the man once tipped to take over from Davin. And if Eamon has doubts about what he has told him, it is that Davin still sees Michael Donnellan as a threat to his position. It is not as crazy as it seems, Eamon thinks. He knows how insecure he felt on the Army Council: the politics, the shifting alliances. Davin, for all his years as a member and Chief of Staff, is as wary of a fall as anybody else is. Eamon remembers how the closeness between Ignatius Davin and Michael Donnellan disintegrated into warfare as Davin became convinced that Donnellan was a British informer. Eamon has his doubts about it, he wonders if it is true. He knows how Iggy Davin sets his mind on something and once he has, he is difficult to shift. He also knows Michael Donnellan from his time in London and during the reconnaissance trips to the UK. He never had any suspicion about him, but then that would be part of Donnellan's skill at concealment. And he has never worked out how Hugh got away.

'If they aren't stopped,' he says to Mary, 'I can see the damage that will come. If Donnellan is pulling the strings, with O'Neill and Griffin doing the legwork, they are a threat.'

'What does he want you to do?'

'Help stop them. If they aren't stopped, they have the means to destabilise the Good Friday Agreement. They will bring it all down in order to continue sniping away at the Brits for years to come in the hope they will eventually get tired and withdraw. We know that is pointless now. We can't win by force. The Brits can't defeat us either. So if we believe we can succeed by the ballot box, we can't allow anything to stop it.'

Mary speeds up her walk. 'I know.'

Eamon, who is out of breath, struggles to keep pace with her, and takes that as her assent

CHAPTER 4

Hugh sips beer and nibbles an olive. They know him here, a bar he uses at least once a week, just south of Sol. It is almost ten, and the Madrileños are starting to make their way to restaurants, but he knows nowhere will get busy before eleven. He has been here for almost an hour and is no longer surprised that he has nursed a glass of San Miguel, where once he would have downed three or four. Besides, the Spanish way of life is not conducive to the suicidal drinking that had been so much part of his earlier life. Not that he misses it and he hates the after-effects of a hangover. Good job, I did kick the bloody booze, he thinks. The way I was going was just a long swallow to an early grave. He knows that part of the reason was the oblivion he sought, the hope that he could banish for even a short time the nightmares, the eternal fear he lived with when he was on the island. For a moment, he remembers Godfrey, God as he always called him. Dead too, gone, blown up trying to save his life. His mood changes again, darkens when he remembers that little fuckpig Flaherty and how he was the one who killed God. Just as well, he knows, because if he hadn't blown himself up as well, Hugh would have hunted him down.

    He pushes it down, and hopes that tonight is not going to be one of his bad nights, when he wakes in the early hours in terror, and is unable to get back to sleep. Come on, he tells himself, count the good things. Hugh at forty-nine is bald, inclined to put on weight. With his tanned features and his reasonable Spanish, he passes easily for a well-to-do middle-class Spaniard. Although he looks his age with his lived-in features, Hugh is still fit and tough, able to fend for himself in a fight, and is available as back-up muscle if required by his mentor and employer, Michael Donnellan. He likes the edge he gets working for Michael Donnellan, the need to keep alert all the time, these have given him a purpose where once he thought himself as, if not dead, just afloat on a stream of alcohol.

These weekly meetings with Michael are something he enjoys and looks forward to. They always eat in the same restaurant; Hugh relishes the *fabada madrileña*. Take away the chorizo, he thinks, and he could be eating one of his mother's dishes; a meal he also got a taste for when he stayed with his grandparents on their farm. All dead now, and for a moment he thinks of them with fondness, that familiar regret for all that he did not ask them, for their sheer absence.

He wonders what Michael wants to talk about tonight. Usually he gives him a list of jobs to be done the following week, trips to other Spanish cities, checking and meeting people, always as Donnellan's right-hand man, *el irlandés*. Hugh does not tell them otherwise, that although his parents were Irish, he was born and brought up in London, albeit within a close-knit Irish community, that he is an *anglosajón*. It was a schizophrenic life. At home, they might never have left Ireland, with the accents, newspapers, the church and the Irish priests. However, at school, away from his family, he was just another London boy. No wonder, he thinks, he took so easily to the secret life.

Hugh sees Donnellan approaching. He is still the same dapper man he was when he first met him all those years ago back in London. Michael Donnellan is one of those people who does not appear to age. He still has all his dark brown hair; has neither gained weight nor become lined and wrinkled. At seventy-two, he passes easily for a youthful fifty-year-old.

'*Hola*,' Michael says, as he joins him at the table. They always converse in Spanish when they are out and often also at work. Both are fluent speakers. Donnellan has the better accent but Hugh gets by. He speaks like an *extranjero*, a foreigner, but is no longer teased or mocked as a *guiri*, a funny foreigner. Donnellan orders mineral water.

As he waits, Hugh gives him an update on what he has done during the week. After a moment he notices that Michael is not paying the usual close attention, he nods, agrees, does not ask any of his usual precise questions. In a way, Hugh is relieved. He recently botched a job, was too brutal with the tenant of a bar in Toledo who is way behind with the rent. Donnellan has been explicit he is not to get involved with the physical side of the job. For the heavy stuff, he has a number of gypsies he calls on. Hugh tells him, is apologetic about losing his temper.

'Did you hit him?'

'No. Just got hold of him and threatened him that I might.'

'Still a frightening sight when you want to be.' Donnellan grins. He sips some water. 'All right. Tomorrow you'll need to go out to Vallecas. Get hold of Jesús and Manolo. You know, the usual deal. Half the money now, the balance when the job is done.'

Over dinner, Michael says, 'I have another job for you. For both of us. You remember Fernando?'

Despite himself, Hugh scowls. 'Him. Yeah I remember him.'

'I want us to go and pay him a visit.'

Hugh does not say anything, just eats, forking in mouthfuls of salad, while Donnellan picks at his.

'A one-off visit, I promise you.'

'Why?'

'Let's say there is the possibility of a bit of lucrative business coming this way.'

Hugh is suddenly weary; his temper rises. 'Look, you know I can't stand that arsehole. Why the hell do I have to do anything with him? He's got danger all over him. All that flash stuff, he's asking to get picked up.'

'It's just a simple visit. We have a few meetings, get things sorted out and we leave. And while we do so, we spend a few days at the seaside.'

'Big deal,' Hugh says savagely. 'I was on the Costa del Sol last week, stuck in a fucking traffic jam on the motorway.'

'Take the toll road.'

'I did. That is where I was stuck.'

Michael Donnellan does not reply. He finishes his salad, drinks some water, chats with Javier, the proprietor. The food is served and they eat in silence. As usual, Hugh eats twice as much as Donnellan, whose appetite is as slim as his figure.

'We need to take a trip to Galicia,' Michael says when he has cleared his plate. There is no longer the slightly jocular request in his tone, this is take it or leave it. Fed now, Hugh's mood is calmer; he slightly regrets his earlier outburst. After all, he owes a lot to Michael.

'Right,' he says.

Michael spends the next half an hour, while they drink a café solo each, explaining what he wants him to do. Hugh is to get as much done as possible next week, then prepare for their trip the following Monday.

After they part, Hugh wanders along the narrow streets until by chance he reaches the Plaza Mayor. He thinks about going home to his apartment in the northern suburbs, in one of the many tower blocks, featureless, anonymous, with the view from his windows of the brick wall of the next building. He puts it off, because he senses he may still be in for one of his bad nights. Maybe he will drift towards the Plaza Chueca, where he'll either meet somebody he knows or pick up a man. Hugh feels he has blended into life in Madrid, never more so than in the gay quarter. Here he is Antonio Marías Roland. For years he has not been Hugh O'Neill, son of Irish emigrants to London, who sent him 'home' as they always called it, every summer to spend part of the holiday with his grandparents. Where his grandfather instructed him in the republican history and folklore and groomed him as a recruit for the IRA. In this new life, Antonio is the offspring of parents who worked in restaurants in Lyon, his mother as a waitress, his father as the cellar man, not that any of it matters these days, as nobody asks. He is just Antonio, another regular in the gay scene in Madrid.

As he meanders, without any real idea of where he intends to go, but not to Plaza Chueca, he decides, he is thinking back to their conversation over coffee.

'Drugs? You're fucking joking, Michael, I hope.'

'No joke. I mean it.'

'For the money?'

'That is a big part of it.'

'You've not become a policeman in your old age.'

'Not that either.'

Mystified, Hugh listens as Donnellan gives him an outline of what he has in mind. 'It's a long shot, a gamble, I know. But if it comes off, we can retire.'

'So I need to become pals with Fernando Griffin.'

'For a while, yes, you do.'

Despite the evening's heat, Hugh shivers as he recalls those trips he made to Ireland over the last few years, to watch Michael's back, trips riddled with the fear of discovery. The flights into Dublin and Cork and Shannon, from different countries every time. Parts of overheard conversations come back to him, snatches he heard as he stood guard, in remote country houses, in hotel rooms, where they always took three or four rooms, so that they were secure on either side. He recalls the Irish voices inside one of Donnellan's many holiday apartments in Marbella and along the Costa del Sol. It was just business, as it always has been with Donnellan since he moved to Spain. Some of it is beginning to fit, to make a picture, and it is not one Hugh likes.

As he mooches along, Hugh is aware of just how near to danger Donnellan flies at times, how close he is to discovery. A millimetre further and he would be booked – except that this is not a football match, but their lives. Suppose he's wrong, or not telling me all the story, Hugh thinks. And the knot of doubt he has always had about Michael Donnellan since the trap in his club in London, the submerged, nagging fear about his, to use one of Godfrey's expressions, veracity grows again. Is Donnellan bent only on revenge? What if he is on the British payroll? Let's face it, Hugh reckons, we've been lucky here, we've had a clear run. Donnellan moves about with ease. An English expatriate, *Señor* James Rogers, always called Hams by his Spanish friends, who has lived in Spain for over twenty years. The insurance company, the property firm, the holiday apartments, the Irish pubs, which gave Hugh his nickname as *el irlandés*, all the successful businesses in the booming Spanish economy that has thrived since the country became a democracy after the death of Franco. Donnellan is part of that, with his fortified villa in the suburbs, where he is a neighbour of among others, los galacticos the millionaire stars of the Real Madrid football team.

For all their years together, which go back to the failed assassination attempt on Mrs Thatcher, Hugh does not know much about Donnellan. He has never been to his villa. When they meet, they do so in his office in an industrial zone, or as Spanish people do, in bars or restaurants. He knows Donnellan has always been a bachelor, has never had any inkling that he is gay, but neither has he shown any interest in women. Hugh assumes he is just one of those people happy with their own company. Or is the secrecy about his personal life more cover? Michael Donnellan, with his business empire and his long involvement with the Irish republican movement – could he also be a British agent, is that why he has been left alone? Hugh is certain if the Brits nail him, it will be a huge propaganda coup for them, one they will exploit before banging him up for life.

On the other hand, he thinks they may be playing a long game, have him in their sights and are just waiting to pull him when it suits them. He decides he needs a beer, he is unaccountably thirsty until he remembers all the bacon, ham and crubeens he has eaten. Inside he goes to a table, sits with his back to the wall where he gets a clear view of the door. The waiter gives him *La Razón* to read. Idly he flicks through the ads for prostitutes, is amused as always by the descriptions of what is available, as he tries to keep his mind clear. What Donnellan wants from him is one last job, he said. If it was only that, Hugh thinks, I'd do it with good grace. But he knows it won't be, that Donnellan is such a tenacious foe, so competitive, he always needs a fight, it is probably why he remains so sprightly, burning up his nervous energy. He looks up from his paper and feels the familiar tightening in his scrotum, he tenses across his shoulders, feels a cold sweat despite the bar's air conditioning. The two men who have slid into the adjoining table are speaking in English, which is unusual in this part of Madrid. And they are not loud and arrogant in the way of a lot of English tourists. They pay no attention to Hugh, talk quietly as one of them orders, '*dos cervezas*.' So what Hugh thinks, they're probably a couple of tourists who have lost their way, or a couple of guys here on business. But he can't just accept that, their arrival has disturbed him, set his alarm system running. He sips his beer and waits to catch the waiter's eye. When he does so, he indicates by sign language he wants to pay him. As soon as the waiter puts the saucer with the bill on the table, Hugh gives him five euros and goes casually through the entrance to the toilets. He sees a door marked Privado, tries the handle; it opens into a small kitchen and storeroom. Breathing quickly Hugh scrutinises the room, spots an open window, which looks down into a dark alley, lit only by a distant street light. He climbs through and pushes the window behind him.

    Outside, Hugh is relieved when he leaves the alley and then the rather dark side street, to be back in the bustle, the brighter lights. Maybe it's nothing, he thinks, I'm just jumpy because Donnellan wants to drag me back into something dangerous, when I don't want anything other than the life I have here. Staying alive and being alert at all times is enough, he knows that. He walks quickly heading along the Calle de Arenal towards Sol, where the crowds are thicker, the chances of following him become more difficult. Unless they are just the front guys, there to flush him out, while the rest of the team have him covered. He wonders who they are. Irish, British, maybe a couple of IRA men come to pay him a visit. He knows he is of value to the IRA dead or alive, either way they will milk his appearance for all they can. Or is

Donnellan having him tailed? Testing him in some way, to see if he is still able to look after himself.

At Sol, he crosses the road to the entrance of the Metro, passes by, then turns quickly into the small crowd and descends rapidly to the trains. He gets line 2 to Ventas. The carriage is busy. Hugh is the last to enter. He is fairly sure he is not being followed. Nevertheless, he is wary, watches as he adopts the weary glazed look of a Madrilèno going home. At Ventas, he is first off, walks quickly to line 5, and takes the train to Pueblo Nuevo. This carriage is not busy, and again he is certain nobody has followed him in to it. He changes to line 7 and gets off at Gregorio Marañón, and takes line 10 to Plaza de Castillo, where he takes a taxi. At the first bar he sees, he gets out, and uses a payphone.

'*Hola, Eduardo y Paco almorzaron.*'

Which is this week's code when he needs an emergency meeting with Donnellan. He suspects Donnellan is asleep, it takes him a moment before he says slowly, '*Vale. Ver es creer.*'

He walks from the bar, doubles back as if he has forgotten something, ducks into the forecourt of an apartment building, waits in the darkness of the shuttered shops, waits and listens – and hears nothing. There are no telltale footsteps, no rustle of clothing. Apart from the distant roar of the Madrid traffic, a twenty-four hour noise, he does not hear anything.

Another taxi, and he gets off in the Calle de Carmen, outside El Cortes Ingles, where he takes his time, still watching for any sign he is being followed. Hugh strolls now to Pasadizo de San Ginés, where still checking, he walks along and turns right before he turns back to retrace his steps. He is calmer when he sees Donnellan is waiting for him in the Chocolatería San Ginés, with a cup of chocolate and a churro in front of him.

'You're clear? Nobody on your back?' He looks worried, and this reinforces Hugh's belief that they are about to dive into something much bigger and far more dangerous than anything he has done over the past years.

'As far as I know,' Hugh says. 'Maybe I'm just jumpy.'

'Maybe. But better that than being jumped. Any idea where you might have been picked up?'

Hugh shakes his head. 'No. Didn't notice anything until I was in the bar. I was just mooching along. Not really paying attention.'

As he always is at moments like this, Donnellan is calm, thoughtful; composed again, the momentary panic has vanished. 'There may be nothing in it, might just be your imagination. Alternatively, if they picked you up in town, they tailed you until you lost them. Either way, we take no chances from now on. Full alert. It is enemy territory. We assume they are looking for you and me.'

'If that is so,' Hugh says slowly, 'who do you think it is?'

'It could be anybody. There are enough of them who'd like to find us.'

CHAPTER 5

As Eamon steps on the tarmac, the unaccustomed heat hits him. It seems to drill through his close-cropped hair and he starts to sweat. Slowly he looks around and notices the green hills of trees that surround the airport. Inside the terminal building, they walk slowly amongst the scurrying passengers, watching, and trying to get their bearings. The perfunctory customs check helps. Carrying their hand luggage, they walk through the luggage reclaim, past the scramble of people milling around the stationary carousel.

In the arrivals hall, small groups of families wait. A few chauffeurs hold name cards aloft. Eamon glances around; he is not sure who or what he is looking for, only that his senses are alert. He is very wary; he is treating this journey as a reconnaissance trip, like the visits he made years ago to survey potential targets in the UK. Back then, he assumed he was under surveillance all the time. The watchers did not know who or what they were looking for, but they were expecting somebody, and one slip, a hint or clue as to the purpose of his visit, would be enough to alert them.

Eamon hails a taxi from the rank. This weather is so much hotter than anything he has been used to, he is relieved to slide into the back seat and once they are moving, enjoy the breeze from the driver's open window. The driver is taciturn, does not speak after Eamon tells him he wants the Hotel dos Reis Católicos. Mary is silent also as they speed along the autopista. Through the trees and the new, high apartment blocks, Eamon sees briefly the famous bell towers of the cathedral of Santiago de Compostela. The taxi gathers speed downhill. Mary is not usually a nervous passenger; but she gasps as the driver overtakes a car on his left and gets a furious blast of the horn. He increases his speed and then cuts back to the right as they go around a bend, which earns him another, longer burst.

By now they are on the outskirts of the city, the taxi slows down at the bottom of another hill, past a market under a concrete roof that is open on all sides. Where is Griffin now? Eamon wonders about the accuracy of the information that Griffin is due at Santiago de Compostela over the next few days; why he bothers to come here. If he has a house near Vilagarcía, why not go straight there? Is it perhaps a precaution? To make sure his back is covered first?

Eamon is remembering Davin's words. 'You're on your own, Eamon. You want what is yours, the money Griffin owes you and you have come to get it. You're clean, retired, out of it. That's your story if they pick you up. This is a personal matter between you and Griffin, going back over the years.'

Eamon nods. 'If I'm in trouble, if for any reason your meticulous plans go wrong, Iggy. What then?'

Davin does not appear to notice the sarcasm. 'The usual legal help is available from Brannigan. You have his number. I've told him he might get a call from you. He will not be away, so contact him if there is a real need.'

After that Eamon tells Davin he is going to travel under his own name, he can't see the need to risk a false name and all that might go wrong if he is discovered. 'After all, Iggy,' Eamon says sweetly, 'if it's as innocent as you say, I have nothing to hide. What better cover than Mary and me going to find out about the pilgrimage?' And Davin does not demur. This again strikes Eamon as odd, to say the least, for Davin is used to getting his own way in operational matters. Eamon accedes to Mary's many hints that he changes to a new hairstyle, has it cut short, and sheds the mullet he has favoured over the years. He buys a pair of rimless specs, purchases new, casual clothes, chino trousers, a selection of shirts and a navy linen jacket, all so different from his usual drab outfit of sweater, old shirt and jeans.

They swing around to the left; the taxi slows to walking pace as they creep along by an old high stone wall, past pedestrians, families with kids in buggies. Eamon spots a pilgrim coming down the steps at the side of the cathedral, rucksack on his back, a stave in his hand. Despite all the careful preparations, the smooth trip, which began for him a few days earlier when he flew from Dublin to London, Eamon feels his stomach is rumbling and bloated, he has need of a loo. This is normal these days when he is tense. And it has been a week of high tension, his nerves stretched. In London, he met some old friends; he had his haircut, bought the new glasses at an optician's in Oxford Street, and his clothes from Aquascutum in Regent Street. Then he went with Dominic and a couple of his pals on what they call a booze cruise to Boulogne-sur-Mer in France. Except, they drove to Folkestone, put the car on the train that took them through the tunnel. While they stocked their car with cheap wine and spirits and beer and cigarettes in the supermarket, Eamon did his own business on the medieval walls of the old town. He has heard nothing since then; he just hopes everything he planned is in place. Davin's instructions stick in his mind. *Speed. Secrecy. Surprise.*

The taxi turns slowly into the Praza do Obradoiro, the great square that is the heart of Santiago de Compostela. On one side of the Praza, he sees the imposing Hotel dos Reis Católicos. As soon as their taxi stops, two uniformed porters come to take their cases. Reluctantly, Eamon lets go. It is an old ingrained habit, to hang on to his case, even though there is nothing in it apart from a change of clothes, a sponge bag and a couple of books. Everything that matters is in his jacket and trouser pockets or in Mary's large handbag.

It is busy at reception. Eamon pays off the taxi and waits. He looks at those checking in, wonders if Fernando Griffin is among the queue. He cannot see everybody; all he can hear is the rapid Spanish or Galician, galego, as Davin called it, the word sounding odd in Davin's Monaghan accent. He is unable to differentiate between them; they sound the same to him. As the guests leave the desk he realises these are all older couples, well dressed, with what look like permanent tans.

'There is a message for you, sir,' the receptionist says as he gives Eamon the room key and a folded slip of paper. 'It is from your car hire company.' Eamon nods as he takes the key and the paper.

The hotel retains a monastic atmosphere. They walk beneath an elaborate roodscreen, along cloisters, which open on to four courtyards, with trees and plants; there are benches along the walls. They take a lift to the fourth floor, the porter pushing their two small cases on a trolley ahead of them. The silence along with the dimly lit corridor is indeed ascetic, as is the darkened room to which he shows them, the curtains drawn against the hot afternoon sun.

'Notice anything?' Eamon asks once the porter has gone. Mary scans the room, while he glances inside the bathroom, searching for anything obvious, another old ingrained habit. Not that it matters. As a matter of operational security, they will not discuss anything in here.

'Just how wonderful this place is,' Mary says with a smile. 'And what a fantastic husband I have to bring me here.' She hugs him and kisses him full on the lips.

While Eamon reads the note, Mary unscrews the phone, checks it for bugs, puts it back together, then on her hands and knees locates the junction box, where she painstakingly unscrews it, inspects it, looks at Eamon and shakes her head.

The note is short and typewritten. Their car will be delivered to the hotel at six p.m. Will he please make himself available to meet their representative in the foyer? All this efficiency, Eamon thinks, is admirable.

Except he has not ordered a hire car.

Nor is it the message he was looking to receive.

Outside in the Praza do Obradoiro, they play at being tourists. They admire the looming spires of the cathedral that seem to hang from the sky, as though suspended by some mystical puppet master, towering over the huge expanse of the Praza do Obradoiro and the city. Swarms of visitors stand around open-mouthed, staring up. Others, in order to get a better photograph, lie on their backs near to the buildings of the Xunta de Galicia, the council of Galicia. Everybody wants to have their photograph taken standing before the great edifice.

Eamon smiles faintly, a shadow of a smile, as Mary takes a snap of him posed like all the other tourists with the cathedral in the background, but he is looking for minders, certain that Davin has not sent them here alone, he will have laid on somebody to watch and report back. He hopes that Davin has been responsible for getting a hire car for them. Eamon can't be sure there are not others who are also interested in their visit. How secure is Davin? Who was McAllister? Have the Garda Special Branch security picked him up in Dublin, alerted the British to follow him from Heathrow, and then again at Stansted airport? The French passport control waved them through when they drove into the tunnel at Folkestone, the car was not one of those pulled over and searched. On the return from Calais, they drove off the train and nobody asked for their passports. This run of good fortune does not reassure him, it brings all the fears that have beset him since his briefing to the surface, here, amidst the cacophony of voices and the four o'clock pealing of the bells. The foreignness of it all exacerbates Eamon's nerves.

Beside the cathedral, in the high afternoon heat, the human statues pose. A bronzed Roman centurion, whose only movement is to flick his eyes when a child stares up in astonishment wondering if he is real. He smiles and extends a hand and the child moves to take it and stand beside him. The photographs follow, payment, a note and some coins are pushed through the narrow slit of a circular receptacle. Beside him a fashion model from the 18th century, in long frock with yards of tulle and lace, and wearing a big wide hat. Next door, Fred Flintstone, a muscleman in a hairy bathing suit, holds a massive knobbly club aloft, as he perches precariously on a flimsy podium a couple of feet higher than anybody else. Further down a man dressed as a witch, with a large hooked nose, brandishes a long broomstick. He entices the visitors to straddle it. As they settle, there is a non-too-subtle lift of the stick causing squeals of surprise and of suppressed giggles from some women. When he has enough on 'board', the order is given. Eight right legs lift in unison, and bodies sway to the left as they simulate flight. 'Harry Potter!' a little girl screams in excitement.

Eamon and Mary walk slowly; they hold hands, very much the adoring couple. In between smiling at each other, they both search the crowds, looking for something familiar, a glimpse that will confirm what they are both sure of, that they are being watched.

Back again in front of the cathedral Eamon looks at the queue snaking along the double steps to the entrance. Over the beggars scattered deliberately apart, he is sure, and at the tour guides walking along, their umbrellas held aloft. And he sees nobody. And is not convinced. He wonders, not for the first time, if he is missing things. When he turns to Mary and asks how she is, she replies, fine, what a sight.

They retrace their steps to find a café in the small square just off the Praza. By now Eamon's stomach is so bloated, he feels almost ill. He selects a café with a view of the street and the square. The crush of people coming from and entering the Praza is continuous, a stream of humanity, young and old, of all nationalities. He orders a Coke and an ice cream for Mary. Although he normally never drinks Coke, he has discovered it is an effective palliative when his Irritable Bowel Syndrome is bad. At moments like this, it is difficult to believe his doctor's assurances that it is not life-threatening.

They do the usual tourist thing, of sitting and watching the crowds go by. Sometimes Eamon thinks he sees somebody, a face that passed by a few minutes earlier, now back with a woman on his arm. Others seem to come and go, but there is as yet no pattern, nothing he can be sure of.

The green Celtic baseball cap is pulled low over his forehead as he tracks past their table heading up one of the many dark, narrow streets that surround the cathedral. Eamon waits, looking ever so casually around as he says to Mary, 'Get him?'

'Yeah. Strange.'

'Sure is. Anything else?'

'No. Want me to take a look?'

'No. Now he's got us, he'll follow us.'

It is almost five-thirty when they make their way across the Praza da Quintana and walk up the steps and around the back of the cathedral to the Rúa Azabacaira. The pilgrims come down the hill, alone, in twos and threes, sometimes in larger groups, all of them in the uniform of rucksack, large floppy cap or hat, a stave. The click-clacking of the staves and sticks on the road is eerie, almost sinister; it reminds Eamon of Blind Pugh in the film of *Treasure Island*. Some shout and cheer, others are silent, and a few stop by the side door of the cathedral to bow their heads in silent prayer. Eamon walks down the steps, past the bagpipes playing an air that could be Irish, but he does not recognise it. He turns suddenly when he reaches the Praza do Obradoiro, and sees a second one, a young woman pilgrim, but he knows her, as he knew the guy in the Celtic cap.

'Wee Pádraig,' Mary muses, as they make for the hotel. 'I suppose it fits that he's here.'

'That's what I thought, it could be nothing. I know Pádraig comes over here a lot. Easy enough for Iggy to use him. But he has that young girl, Aileen, also.'

'It could just be he's keeping an eye on us, or it maybe is more complicated than Davin told you.'

Eamon laughs bitterly. 'You can be sure of that. Even if it is as he claims, he wouldn't leave us to get on with it. Trouble is young Pádraig is well known, has a bit of form. If he's here, who else is about? Anyway, let's see what the man has to say about the car.'

The foyer of the Hotel dos Reis Católicos is a tourist attraction. People wander in off the Praza do Obradoiro, look around the foyer and peek through the roodscreen at the cloisters and courtyards before returning by the lounge and bar and leaving that way. Eamon sits in a high-backed chair and watches the entrance. Mary strolls around reading the notices and flyers on the roodscreen and around the door of the hotel shop. Eamon admires her style, how she seems to concentrate on the notices, but he knows she will not miss anything.

A young couple come in; they seem absorbed in the surroundings, they stare at the dark oil painting on one wall, at the rich tapestry on another. He slips an arm around her waist. She already has her arm around him, now she hooks her fingers inside the waistband of his jeans. Without the Celtic cap, it takes Eamon a moment to recognise Pádraig Hanraghan again, to register that Aileen has changed from her hiker's shorts to jeans, and has shed her floppy sun hat. Pádraig does not look at Eamon. They continue their amble around, go past the roodscreen, then return and head off through the lounge, where they sit on one of the deep settees and watch the foyer. In between, they lean across to kiss, their arms entwined about each other. Eamon is trying to remember if Pádraig has been seeing Aileen, but he can't ever recall him with a girl, which makes this performance as the besotted young lover very believable.

Eamon sits and listens trying to understand a Spanish word. The rapid speech remains incomprehensible to him, increasing his sense of alienation. He thinks, I am lonely and apart from Mary, I am alone, and I am afraid. He tries to analyse what has brought this sense of dread, puts it down to the low spirits that accompany an attack of IBS, that and the uncertainty of their trip. He hears an American woman query something before her voice fades away. Still he watches the entrance and notices Mary has now moved to the hotel shop, where she is examining the rack of post cards. He wonders who buys anything from such places and supposes businessmen needing a last-minute gift to take home use it.

'Mr Healy? Mr James Healy?' A young woman in jeans and a blouse, a sweater draped over her shoulders stands by Eamon.

'No,' he says coldly. 'My name is Delaney.'

Quickly she shuffles through the papers on her clipboard. 'I am so sorry! You are Mr Delaney.' She smiles sweetly. 'I mean Mr Delaney.'

Eamon nods. He has to admire the speed, the dexterity which she changed the names. As he curses Davin, he wonders if this is deliberate. James Healey was the cover name Davin wanted him to use. Can Davin be slipping, or is this part of his plan, to unsettle Eamon, keep him on his toes, a ploy favoured by Ignatius Davin?

He goes outside with her to inspect the car. She hands him a folder with the details, takes an imprint of his credit card. Eamon listens carefully.

After she has left him, he stands, looks around the Praza, waiting and looking. A man walks past him, and says to the woman with him, '*Nil aon tinteán mar do thinteán féin.*' She laughs and they head for the queue at the bottom of the steps to the cathedral.

There is no fireplace like your own fireplace, Eamon thinks as he hears the familiar quotation in Irish. He breathes more easily and returns to Mary.

CHAPTER 6

What is that good-for-nothing Pádraig Hanraghan doing here? Is he working for Davin? One of those mindless kids she remembers so well from her own training, who could justify anything because they were at war. Mary knows he has been to Santiago de Compostela more than a few times. She has often wondered where Pádraig gets the money to pay for these trips. Not only to Santiago de Compostela, he has visited New York a couple of times. Could he be more than just Davin's eyes here? She is puzzled why Davin has dragged Eamon out of obscurity. It has all the hallmarks of one of those convoluted schemes he has had over the years. Some have worked but all of them have been high risk. Yet Eamon has told her – and she wants to believe him – there is little or no risk on this trip. If, as Davin claims, he is wholeheartedly in favour of the peace process, favours the Good Friday Agreement, then why the hell, Mary can't help wondering, are we so secretive, still mounting an undercover operation? If Fernando Griffin is running drugs, all they have to do is tip off the Brits through one of the back channels they use to convey secret information.

As she swivels the postcard rack, Mary fends off the offer of help from the bored shop assistant. There are views of the cathedral, of various seascapes and the countryside, which mean nothing to her. She is worried about Eamon, who suddenly seems to have aged; he looks old and tired. This shocks her, as she has always thought how fit he looks, at least ten years below his age. Maybe the new short haircut has contributed to his rather shrunken appearance.

Mary sees the young woman talking to Eamon. Her slim youthful body seems to highlight the decline in Eamon, how old and drawn he looks as he greets her, not very enthusiastically, she also notes. Pádraig has vanished from her view. She smiles at the shop assistant and takes another slow tour of the foyer, sees Pádraig entwined with young Aileen. Again she wonders where he gets the money for all these trips. Certainly not from what he earns, walking tourists on tours of the Walls of Derry with a quick look at the Bogside and the Bloody Sunday Memorial. Not at five pounds a tourist. She knows this because they have some of Pádraig's fliers and recommend him to those of their guests who enquire about such trips. It has to be Davin who funds him, probably as a courier, she guesses, that is one reason why he is able to travel so much. Nor can she figure out why Pádraig made himself so conspicuous in the square. The Celtic baseball cap is his trademark back home. Is he careless or has he been instructed to make himself known? She looks at some jewellery, then fingers the silk scarves and thinks they are all over-priced. By now, she is sure the woman is alone in the foyer. Eamon is signing a paper, she hands him a set of car keys, and they go outside. At which point she spots Pádraig and Aileen also leaving. Pádraig puts his cap on. She can't work this out, the blatant display by him, the use of Aileen, whom they both know.

Maybe I've been leading a normal life for too long, the return to secrecy and subterfuge is firing up my imagination. Maybe he is just here for a holiday. Aileen and he have come away to avoid the prying eyes and gossip back home. And Davin probably said, just let me know when you see the Delaneys, but don't let on you know them. He wouldn't need to say any more. Pádraig understands these things, as they all do. Besides he is a quiet lad, who does as he's told, has never been in trouble as far as Mary knows.

When Eamon returns he tells her he is going to the cathedral. 'Alone,' he says sharply, stalling the protest she is about to make. Eamon walks across and joins the queues at the bottom of the steps, and waits patiently to shuffle along and enter the cathedral.

Mary strolls around the hotel; she looks at her watch. Eamon wanted about half an hour alone in the cathedral. When he told her, she had bridled, had wanted to say, I want to see the cathedral as well as you. But she knows by now that Eamon has this need for solitude. She is used to it even though she resents it at times. She reminds herself sharply that this is no holiday. Alone in the gift shop, apart from the assistant who hovers nearby, fear sweeps over her, a dread she can't pin down of the unknown that lies ahead.

The cathedral is so crowded it is almost too full to move. She shuffles past the queue waiting to press their hands into the roots of the Tree of Jesse below the statue of Saint James. Mary looks for Eamon in the crowd. Down at the end of the cathedral, there is another lengthy queue of pilgrims who have completed the Camino, who snake along the side aisles and around the rear of the High Altar, waiting to climb behind the altar, to embrace the most sacred image of Saint James and kiss his bejewelled cape.

The crowds swell and push. Video and digital and mobile phone cameras flash, held aloft as though in adoration, to capture the best view of the ceiling, the pulpit, the choir stalls; it does not seem to matter what, they photograph everything. Mary is disconcerted, almost panicky as the ruck of tourists and pilgrims push and shove her. A young woman, in a short skirt and skimpy top, jaws rhythmically chewing gum, wanders in, her video camera running, looks for somewhere to point it and decides the High Altar is the place. Some priests sit in open confession boxes. A young man takes aim with his camera and the priest gestures angrily for him to desist. The man seems astonished, as though the chance to be photographed at all times is to be cherished.

Overcome by the crowds and the noise – there is a constant low murmur, a hum of conversation, broken now and then by a loud question – Mary sits in a pew in a side aisle. She looks at the huge thurible, the Botafumeiro, which requires eight priests to operate by ropes and pulleys, swinging it across the 30-metre ceiling of the transept. Once it was in use at every service, the clouds of incense sent out in the hope of fumigating the filthy pilgrims. She knows from her guidebook that nowadays they only operate it for a special Mass. As she observes the heaving scrum of people, Mary wishes she could fill the Botafumeiro with tear gas and clear the tourists out. She is constantly searching for Eamon and is worried she can't see him. Has he sent her inside the cathedral as a decoy, while he is off somewhere else? She still hasn't found out why he had to go to London four days ahead of their flight here and why he insisted on going by himself.

A young mother, ash blonde and fair-skinned, wanders along looking exhausted and dazed. Mary had seen her outside the main entrance, sitting on a ledge beside a beggar, breastfeeding her infant, while her son, a small boy with her very blond hair and colouring, clung to the hem of her short frock. Her husband, also young, blond, and fierce looking, is reading enthusiastically from a guidebook as his wife tries to follow, the baby in her arms; the little boy is scared, still clings to her skirt. The crowd is dense here, there is a danger a large man, who is so intent on admiring the carved pulpit, will knock her to the ground. Frantically she speaks to her husband. He looks up from the book, immediately thumps the man on the back, and shouts at him. The man turns, looks puzzled, as though an insect has buzzed around him, and moves on. The husband, duty done, returns to the guidebook and continues to recite the facts about the cathedral while his family follow, dazed, tired and bewildered. Mary wants to stand and shout: 'This is a place of worship, not a theme park!' Get hold of yourself woman, she thinks. Through a sudden gap in the crowd, she spots Eamon across an aisle from her. He is sitting bedside a couple who appear to be deep in prayer. They kneel for a time, then get up and leave. Eamon picks up his bag and follows them through the side door. Mary sits on, watching. Although she has seen nothing unusual, she has a sense of being followed, an eerie feeling of having shadows around her. She moves again, heading slowly for the same side door as Eamon.

Four musicians, a double bass, guitar, flute and mandolin, sit in a side street off the Rúa Azabaceira and play the adagio by Albinoni, followed by Rodrigo's Aranjuez. Mary sees that Eamon is not the only one to have left the noisy packed cathedral to sit in the cool air and listen to the quartet. They have CDs on display and when they take a rest, there are steady sales, with people asking the musicians to autograph the cover.

The pilgrims come down the hill in twos, threes, and larger groups, hikers and cyclists. Now a lone man, weighed down by his rucksack, with sleeping mat and bag, and a mug dangling from a strap, his brown legs encased in stout walking boots, his staff with the obligatory goatskin gourd attached to the top, walks slowly, obviously tired and overcome with emotion. By the side door of the cathedral, he stops, removes his baseball cap and bows his head as he prays. Mary realises there is a car behind him. Inside a TV camera records the scene. The actor moves on and stops. He lights a cigarette as the director hops from the car and they discuss the shot.

She finds Eamon alone on a stone bench, lost in thought as he gazes up at the cathedral. 'You're looking a bit better than earlier,' she says, she slips her arm through his.

'Things are starting to happen at last. He's due in at eight tonight on an Iberia flight from Madrid. Normally he picks up his BMW at the airport and drives in here.'

Eamon stops, looks around. Mary is relieved to see the lines of tiredness have lifted and he looks more like his usual self. 'I'd like you to go out to the airport, watch him arrive, then let me know, and I'll pick him up here.'

'Okay.' Mary finds she is pleased to have something to do. 'And the car?'

'It's available in ten minutes, just a phone call. No point in trying to find somewhere to park it. Let's go and have a drink, we have time before you go to the airport. What I'd like you to do is examine the map of the city and plot our route out to the autopista. We need to get on that, go down as far as the turn-off for Vilagarcía de Arousa.'

When they are sitting in a café in the Praza da Quintana, Mary studies the maps. Slowly, she thinks, she is getting back to an operational mode. She looks up as eight cyclists freewheel across the square, talking excitedly, almost reverentially. They have the look of relief after a long arduous task has been completed. Now she is doing something, she faintly mocks her earlier longing to be back in their cottage in Greencastle, sitting in the garden on a balmy evening, looking over Lough Foyle to Magilligan when the lights come on giving the prison the illusion of a village across the water. She picks out their route. 'The Isle of Arousal,' Mary laughs. And to her relief, Eamon does too. 'Later, wife, later.'

'Why are we going there?' Mary asks.

'We have to try and find out where he goes, follow the trail, see who he meets.'

'By ourselves?'

'No. We have a few helpers. The young woman and her boyfriend will be near at hand.'

She wonders why he does not mention the other couple he knelt beside in the cathedral, whose bag he picked up after they left and which he now has on his lap. Mary wonders about asking him if he also senses they are being watched, that a secret force surrounds them. Maybe he knows all that and has chosen not to tell her. Even after twelve years of marriage, he is still secretive, does not share everything with her.

'Have we anybody else looking after us? 'Mary asks him.

Eamon looks at her sharply. 'What have you seen?'

'Nothing, apart from you picking up a bag you don't own from those people sitting beside you in the pew. But I have a feeling we are being observed, almost like a guardian angel.' She laughs to cover her sense of the absurdity of her remark.

'Nice to see you haven't lost it,' Eamon murmurs returning for a moment to the sardonic tone he used to use with her. He pats the bag. 'I'll explain about this later. Just some things we'll need. See if anything seems odd on the way to and from the airport.'

Walking back across the Praza, Mary is conscious again of the unreality of the situation, the fog surrounding their trip. Will she recognise Fernando Griffin? What happens if he slips in and she misses him? At the hotel, she selects a taxi, sits in the back, and closes her eyes as they speed along the autopista towards the airport.

CHAPTER 7

After Mary leaves, Eamon sits on, listening to the music as the quartet of guitar, flute, mandolin and double bass resume playing. He decides to buy a CD, notes the name Cuarteto Saravani in his diary. The two Cokes seem to have settled his stomach, the rumbling has stopped, he is not bloated, and he has lost the urge to break wind every couple of seconds. Perhaps I need this, he thinks, as once more he eyes the crowd in the Praza, coming and going on the steps to the back of the cathedral. The idea of being retired and safe is no more than an illusion. After those years of operating at full stretch, on the run, living the secret life with his nerve ends stretched tight, the absence of so much work and tension from his life has brought not peace and calm but the opposite.

The return to teaching was what saved him, kept him sane. He renewed himself through literature and teaching; the lively students, who were not afraid to argue, to debate and disagree with him: being close to such energy, such vitality, so much young hope, with little thought of the failures ahead of them: that was his saviour from those twin dangers, the slow anger and fatigue.

A lot has happened since those grim early days back in the seventies. He sees in an English newspaper the death of Edward Heath, who was the British Prime Minister when the Troubles really erupted. So many dead, Eamon thinks, and we have survived. He wonders again, as he increasingly does, if they might have achieved their aims without the violence, and all those deaths. Could we have done as much through non-violent protests? Would we have been able to resist the brutal attacks, like that on the first peace march? Could we have held on to the peaceful ways? Intellectually he became convinced that it was impossible to have remained pacific. Reluctantly, he concluded that after Bloody Sunday in Derry, when British Paras shot thirteen people dead and wounded seventeen during a peaceful march against internment, they had reached the point of no return. Violence was inevitable. If they had not fought back, the old Unionist state, backed by the British, would have continued to crush and oppress them. But as he gets older and looks back on his life, he finds that he thinks more about the violence, whether it was the only way to make progress, although he knows that once unleashed, it acquires a momentum of its own and becomes extremely difficult to stop. The manner in which they used the young believers, with their fanatical belief in the Cause; the ignorant and slow-witted they threw into the fight, who often were no more than cannon-fodder for the British Army. The hard men, the snipers, the British Telecom-trained engineers who quickly learned to adapt their experience to the making of explosive devices. Against his nature and will, in his anger, despair and hopelessness on Bloody Sunday, he came to his belief that armed vigilance and violence was the only safeguard they had. Eamon cannot believe they would have achieved anything without it. Once we unleashed all that, the deranged, the stupid, the psychopaths, all came into their own – the toothpaste was out of the tube and there was no way to put it back. The spiral of violence grew and became a twisted force with its own momentum. Long before the first ceasefires, Eamon knew they had to negotiate, that the violence had to stop. What perplexed him, worried him, was how they were going to achieve that without splitting the Movement. Like all of the thinkers in the Movement, he was aware of the fate of Michael Collins, who led the war against the British in the South. One of the principals in the 1922 Treaty negotiations, he was killed by the anti-Treaty forces in the Civil War that followed.

Even now, he thinks, the Unionists will only give what they are forced to do and will dig in, remain entrenched as long as they can. Their intransigence has paid off for the eighty-odd years of the statelet that they have ruled so brutally for much of the time. Eamon can remember his childhood, how his father was in and out of work, the tiny house with five children and their parents, when there was no hope beyond getting enough to eat and at times Eamon went hungry. When getting a job was down to your father's contacts, the people he knew, that and luck and nothing else. How his father was the only person in their house allowed a vote for years. We are nearly there, he thinks, about to get our hands on real political power and if we had remained supine that would never have happened.

This leads him back to what has been his main preoccupation – what is Davin's game? The enforcer of the Good Friday Agreement.

Eamon sees that makes sense, he welcomed it and it went in some way to repair his sense of injustice at how Davin behaved towards him. We need somebody to hold things together, keep the rebels and the deranged in order, toeing the official line. He knows that this is something he wants to believe, as he is aware of how much money they need to maintain the elaborate support structure that underpins it.

The capital for their business. Your lump sum, Davin said, with a trace of a grin, the irony not lost on him. Make sure you do the right thing now, mind. With the help of the money, they had a deposit, they were able to afford the big house, to convert the bedrooms, build a kitchen and breakfast room in the extension, and meet the repayment of the mortgage every month. In time, this led to the accretion of profits from the B&B, a pile of money that grew, enabling them to invest in a second house. Eamon's offer of cash, a higher offer than any of those received, was accepted with alacrity, because Eamon knows, as the seller knew or believed, that to refuse would be damaging and costly, might well bring retribution. Over the next ten years, Eamon and Mary became wealthy. The two B&Bs, the three houses bought for rent, the café, leased off, with a share of the profits as part of the deal. Mary's accountancy training, along with her good business brain, helping their money to grow. How they achieved so much wealth with only a teacher's salary, is never questioned in public, not written about in the press, nor alluded to on the airwaves. Our perceived image, which is all that matters, Eamon thinks, is that we are shrewd business people. There may be a belief that with our connection with the Movement, it is better to deal with us, quickly and honestly, but that is no more than an acceptance of the reality.

The quartet finish playing Schubert's Ave Maria, they rest for a few moments before they begin the adagio by Albinoni.

The pensions and handouts are the interest paid, the Movement's money, the original properties held in perpetuity by the Movement. For a moment he thinks of Mrs McGettigan, how she will miss his visit this week as well. He wonders who her mystery caller was, the dead man, who had died of a heart attack, he read in the local paper.

Slowly but surely, as their income grows, he and Mary use it to invest for themselves and their families, with the cottage in Greencastle, the house in Limerick for Mary's niece, the other properties in the burgeoning economy of the Republic. Ignatius Davin's wealth has also grown exponentially; he is a man of property, with extensive investments, so Eamon has heard on the grapevine. Davin, who was always shrewd in financial matters, has used the small farm on the poor land he inherited as the basis for his secret fortune.

It has been well executed this accumulation of wealth, Eamon thinks as he finishes his Coke, catches the drip of condensation from the glass. Balzac had it spot on in *Old Goriot*, one of the novels Eamon used to teach. *The secret of great fortunes with no apparent source is a forgotten crime, forgotten because it was properly carried out.*

Eamon understands all this. He accepts the argument that they are clawing back what is theirs by right. But it is not something he has pursued with his normal intellectual rigour, this questioning of where they go to next.

Why this pursuit of Fernando Griffin, who seems to be no more than another lowlife, content to make his fortune through the misery of drugs? Is he really linked to the lost men, to Michael Donnellan and Hugh O'Neill? And if he is, why does Davin think their presence shadowing Griffin will be enough to bring Donnellan or O'Neill or ideally both of them running over here?

Is it because we are still locked in a war? The battle goes on to create the wealth, not simply for the enrichment of the High Command and those who serve them, but the necessary steady accumulation of funds, building up the war chest.

In essence, Eamon knows that what has been gnawing at him since Davin's messenger boy jumped him on the ferry, is whether Davin is lying. Suppose the pursuit of wealth has replaced running the war for Davin? Something else to use up that vast powerhouse of energy. This is a chance for Davin to secure a lucrative chunk of a drug-running cartel. Not that Davin would be found within a million miles of it. But he has the resources to control it, and, Eamon smiles wryly, to police it and then profit.

This dovetails. It has symmetry. It is simple. Davin and all in the Movement have been vehement in the denunciation of drugs. They have gained useful local knowledge, particularly in the south, on the Dublin estates, by clearing out the pushers and small-time dealers. This did not mean they were at war with the big money that ultimately controlled the drugs, merely they got them off the estates and gained the respect and votes they need to establish an electoral base. So when they come calling on Davin, look, the price on the streets is dropping, and it is coming from your people, Davin says yes, leave it to me, I'll get it sorted, and then he grabs control and feeds it back to them. It fits all right, has Davin's calculating mind all over it.

Eamon transfers the bag from his lap to his shoulder. That has been one less thing to worry about. The bag he had secreted in the car, sweated it would be found before they went through the tunnel to Calais, and which he had handed over to his cousin, Louise, when they met in Boulogne-sur-Mer. Louise, who has taught English in Paris for years, did odd jobs for him when he was on the Army Council. Louise had sent the bag to the Pyrenees where her friends conveyed it to Eamon. He wants to check that it has not been tampered with, booby-trapped, that all he needs is still there.

Eamon stops to buy a couple of CDs from the quartet. He walks slowly as the evening turns to night, the air is cooler and the crowds have thinned out. By now he knows they are being followed. He has seen a couple go past him, and then come by later on, wearing different clothes but the same shoes. They are good though, and if he didn't know what to look for, these telltale signs of a surveillance operation done with too few people, he would have missed them, taken them for another couple promenading in the evening, heading for an aperitif before dinner. Strange how Mary also has the sense they are being shadowed, watched over by somebody. This does not feel a malign presence to Eamon; he rather likes Mary's description of it as a Guardian Angel. But if it is there, who is it? Davin? Fernando Griffin, maybe Michael Donnellan if he is working with Griffin? Have the British picked them up? Are they running this surveillance? Is that what Davin really wants? Is he playing some double bluff with me, with Donnellan and Griffin? Eamon knows it is quite possible he and Mary are some sort of bait, that Davin has sprung this trap and is waiting for Michael Donnellan to walk into it. In which case, Eamon thinks grimly, it had better be watertight. Michael Donnellan is no fool. He escaped from London when they were sure they had him. In fact, Donnellan was several steps ahead of them. Because if he locked Fintan Flaherty to the bomb that killed him, and Eamon is sure that he did, Donnellan had worked it out well in advance. If he is involved here, he does not doubt he is just as formidable.

His mobile phone trills. 'Hi,' says Mary. 'I'm on my way back.'

*

At night, the floodlit cathedral draws the crowds. Under the arches of the Xunta de Galicia building, a band of singers and musicians entertains with Galician and Spanish music and songs. Across the Praza do Obradoiro, people lie flat on their backs to view the great twin spires, the huge bells, the steps and the locked gates of the weathered building.

Touts harass Eamon, trying to sell CDs, tours of the town, bus trips, and walks. They approach in polyglot fashion. '*English, Français, Deutsch.*'

'No thanks', Eamon says firmly to a man dressed in tights, knee-length trousers, a frilled shirt and a cloak, who exclaims in delight. 'You are Irish! We are fellow Celts!' he grins and takes Eamon's arm. 'Yes! Yes! You come with me. We make a special tour for you.' Eamon hesitates, waits for the code words he memorised on the plane and is terrified he will not remember the phrase. When it does not come, he realises the man is just another tourist tout. He shakes his arm free. 'Later, maybe later.'

Eamon walks on through the milling crowd. He munches some chocolate in the hope it will keep his stomach calm until they can get some food. He replays Mary's message from the airport in his head. *'I asked about the sun hat. They said nobody had handed one in but they will keep a note and if it turns up, we can collect it on the way back.'*

So, Griffin has landed and is on his way. He is worried because she has taken so long. While they went through the airport earlier in the afternoon, Eamon clocked the arrivals board, noted the flights by Iberia from Barcelona, Madrid and Lisbon, that they were all due in between seven and eight. Has she been picked up? Anxiously Eamon hangs around the entrance of the Hotel Reis Católicos, ignores the continual efforts to sell him things. The walking sticks and staves, with the ubiquitous clack-clack of their tips on the cobbles are fashion accessories. He hears the Galician bagpipes from the archway that leads to the side of the cathedral. He is watching and wondering why Pádraig seems to have vanished – he cannot spot a green Celtic baseball cap. Eamon knows Pádraig's job was to ensure they were in place and then make the contacts for the car. Davin will have planned to the last millimetre, last second, because that is how Davin works, how he always has done.

Eamon's suspicions about Davin's reasons for this trip keep growing.

He has access to people here. If all he needs are some photographs to authenticate the involvement of O'Neill and Donnellan, they can arrange that. Besides, Eamon reasons, they may well have altered so much as to be unrecognisable to him and Mary. There is plastic surgery to sort out an unhelpful appearance, let alone the ravages of time.

With relief he sees a taxi arrive, watches Mary, laughing and joking with the driver as she pays him, he marvels again at her ability to empathise with people. How fortunate he is that she loves him, loves him enough not to mind the fifteen-year age gap. That she is prepared to overcome her fear and loathing of Davin to join him, to work as hard and enthusiastically as she does at everything. He stands back for a minute, behind the people milling around a souvenir stall filled with an array of walking sticks, staves and a variety of hats, to see if she is alone. Nothing obvious. He can't spot the couple he had seen earlier. Maybe now they have them settled in the hotel, they have gone off duty, like Pádraig. He still can't figure out why Davin is having them checked. And if it is not Davin, who is it? He is banking – as he knows Davin has – on the fact that Eamon has been out of Republican circles for so long he is not considered a threat. Nevertheless, he continues to watch until Mary has gone inside the hotel. The trill of his mobile phone, 'Hi, I'm back.'

They sit in the spacious lounge at the side of the foyer, order drinks from a waiter and wait for the arrival of Fernando Griffin.

'What took so long?'

'He did the usual trick. Waited in a loo until all the flights had landed then walked through, so nobody could tell where he came from. Somebody met him in Arrivals. They were hugging each other, a lot of back-slapping, loud cries of welcome. And the guy palmed him something.'

'So he was the last through?'

'Yes.'

'Is he alone?'

'He was when he came through. After the man left, a woman, all glamour, very good-looking, came up, kissed him. Could be his wife, could be anybody, girlfriend. Hard to say, except she sort of fits him.'

'Flash?' Eamon chuckles slightly.

'Black hair slicked down, olive skin, gold dripping off him. One hundred percent carat pimp.' Mary shudders dramatically.

'So I have no worries there.'

'I'd almost prefer Iggy himself.'

Eamon is grateful for this brief levity. They sip their drinks, more Coke for Eamon. Mary has a glass of Ribeiro, the local speciality.

Two porters hurry to the entrance.

'*Señor* Griffin!' Griffin enters like a monarch, smiling regally, a hand extended, his jacket across his shoulders.

Eamon stands up and casually walks to the reception desk, past Fernando Griffin, who although he appears to be relaxed, welcoming the greetings of the staff, still has time to survey the foyer and beyond. For a nanosecond, his eyes flick over Eamon. Eamon notes Griffin's beautifully cut black chinos, tan loafers, the sky-blue polo shirt. The black thick hair is combed straight back, kept in place with a shiny gel. He flashes his fine white teeth as he approaches one of the receptionists, while Eamon waits to get the attention of the other man, where he asks for their room key. Mary joins him as they go through the roodscreen.

'That's Griffin's woman,' Mary confirms.

'So our birds have landed.'

They go separate ways. Eamon takes a few moments to look inside the old chapel of the monastery, now set up for a concert he would love to attend. He reads the programme. Mozart, Beethoven, Schubert. And all the time he is listening for the wheels of the porters' trolley and Griffin.

He has sent Mary back to the shop. Eamon watches the woman, who stands looking sulky, while Griffin is the centre of attention. He can't quite figure out if this is because she is bored or more used to being fawned over. Maybe it is just good cover, he thinks, because that is how beautiful women behave in public if they are not the centre of attention. When Griffin does join her, she talks rapidly, her eyes flashing angrily as she gives him a public telling-off. Griffin for a moment looks contrite, serious, almost worried before he runs a hand along her back and as he leans over to nuzzle her ear, she relents and laughs and they make their way, holding hands, following the two porters to the lifts. Eamon is relieved to see Mary moves quickly now, she is at the adjoining lift and waits as Griffin says *'Si, si.'* The two porters along with Griffin and the woman together with luggage squeeze into the one lift. As soon as it stops, Mary takes the lift to the first floor. Eamon sprints up the stairs. He waits in the corridor, is there when Mary comes out of the lift.

She takes a large brown envelope from her handbag. She sees a porter leaving a room. As she walks towards him, she smiles, waves the envelope, '*Señor* Griffin?' She continues to smile engagingly, as she holds the envelope in her hand and bends forward slightly, exposing her cleavage. '*Señor* Griffin?' she repeats. The porter eyes her breasts before smiling at her. 'Room 109, *señora*.'

It is not the room the porter has left; she passes room 103 and counts them off until she finds 109. The room is off a balcony that overlooks the chapel. Beyond the landing there is a lounge, with a settee and armchairs, the place decorated with heavy dark carved furniture and large portraits of Spanish noblemen and women. Mary checks it is not occupied. Moving quickly, silently, she looks along the corridor and nods to Eamon. As they walk back to the lounge, she indicates the door to Griffin's suite. 'I remember when I booked the hotel that there are large suites on the first floor overlooking the Praza do Obradoiro,' she whispers.

Now she uses the anti-bugging device to sweep around the landing outside Griffin's rooms. There is nothing. She shakes her head at Eamon and while she watches the corridor, Eamon slips a small button-like object beneath the rug outside the door. He crawls slowly, out of sight of the peephole in the door. Mary walks to the balcony to look into the chapel, watches the staff laying out the chairs in rows. Eamon taps her arm. Downstairs they find seats in the main lounge, where they wait for Fernando Griffin.

'That was in your bag, was it?'

'Yes. I suspected we'd need a few bits and pieces. I have also laid another car on. When we leave tomorrow, we'll switch cars. I don't want Davin's pals following us, which they will do if we use their car.'

He is relieved she does not press him further about how he got the stuff here, guesses she will have worked it out for herself. Eamon feels the compact Glock pistol in his jacket pocket, is reassured to have it.

'Is it all right if I have another glass of wine?' Mary asks. 'I feel the need of it.'

'I'm sure you do. Maybe I'll join you as well.' As he says this, the Spanish couple he spotted earlier saunter in, talking quietly, his arm through hers. They have both changed clothes again and the woman is wearing a wig of hennaed hair, or has discarded the black hair she sported earlier when Eamon first noticed them. This is interesting, he thinks, while his stomach knots again, his ulcer starts to throb painfully. Who are they watching now? Us or Griffin and his woman?

CHAPTER 8

Eamon watches as Griffin and the woman join two other couples, sees them greeted with loud cries of pleasure, there are hugs and kisses. Eamon and Mary wait for the Head Waiter to come and give them a table. When they are seated, it is as far from Griffin's party as is possible. However, he can see them and to check things, Eamon heads back out again and calculates he would have enough time to follow Griffin should he leave.

Mary looks up from the menu. 'I assume sir will be having huevos?'

'Correct,' Eamon says. It is a joke between them, his fondness for eggs, his refusal to accept the perceived opinion that too many are a health hazard. He is pleased to note there are several egg dishes, as well as the ubiquitous tortilla. As Eamon orders scrambled eggs with mushrooms, he recalls reading that eggs can cause an increase in cholesterol is no longer true. The arrival of soup starts to ease the gnawing in his stomach. He sips water as he watches Griffin holding court, laughing, talking loudly, and gesticulating. He has to admit there is an element of the showman about him, that in its own way this too is almost perfect cover.

They are downstairs in the morning when the button vibrates and he nods to Mary. Until now Griffin has not left his room, has not emerged from it since he returned there after dinner about one in the morning. He comes from the lift by himself and heads straight for the breakfast room. Eamon has already eaten, so Mary follows Griffin in for breakfast.

'Mr Delaney, your car is here,' a porter tells Eamon. Outside in the morning sun in the Praza do Obradoiro, a man and the young woman from the previous evening, stand beside a silver grey Opel.

The woman smiles. 'Good morning, Mr Delaney.'

Eamon decides to try his Spanish. '*Hola. Buenas días.*'

The man smiles, shakes his hand and replies, '*Mi hermana canta más fuerte que yo.*'

'I have no sisters,' Eamon says, relieved to meet his contact. 'Nobody sang in my family.'

'Here is your car,' the man smiles, he opens the door, and indicates that Eamon should take the driver's seat. He slips in beside him. 'You have driven a left-hand car before?'

Still checking, Eamon thinks. 'Only once, when I was last in Spain.'

'You have been before!' This said as though it brings him great pleasure. 'Where did you go?'

'I travelled to Sevilla and then to Cordoba to see the great Mezquita.'

'It is a marvel of all times.'

Still not sure, Eamon thinks, well maybe that is a good sign. 'As great a building as the cathedral in Sevilla.'

All the time, the man is pointing to the gears, where the lights are, he hands Eamon a plastic folder of maps. 'The car is clean, very clean. We clean it very carefully this morning.'

'I am sure you did.'

'When you sign for the car with my colleague, she will give you the papers with all the details. If you have any problems, you must be sure to call us. You will find the number is also on there.' Which means we are clear, time to go.

Outside, Eamon scribbles a signature and she hands him a folded sheet of paper. The woman says slowly, 'You will need to leave within a few minutes to be sure of arriving in time.'

Eamon waits for Mary, and as he does so, Griffin comes out from the hotel, mobile phone jammed to his ear. He talks loudly, and then is silent, listening. Slowly he glances around, spots Eamon, and ignores him as he continues his scrutiny of the Praza. So this is why I am pulled out here now, Eamon thinks. Show the dog the rabbit. He does not like this at all. For the present, he notes Griffin is alone, and Eamon wonders where the woman is, was she just cover for the night, is she still in bed, or is she off somewhere else watching his back? He is tempted to use his mobile to tell Mary to hurry up. Instead he silently prays, come on, for God's sake, he urges her, as he spreads a map of Galicia on the roof of the car. There is some congestion in front of the hotel. A tour bus arrives, some taxis are waiting, and there is a small queue of hire cars. He sees a blue BMW X5 pull up, notes Griffin's woman is behind the wheel. A big sturdy car, Eamon thinks, plenty of space for guns, and for concealing packets of drugs. He guesses it has been altered to accommodate Griffin's needs. She gets out, hands him the keys, as he continues to talk and listen. He has not looked at Eamon since his first glance, but Eamon knows he will have registered him from yesterday at reception, to their following him into dinner, to now. And Griffin will be on full alert. Not for a moment will he place Eamon as a tourist who has just happened to run across his path. These coincidences do not enter the equation when you are living as Griffin lives. Ignatius Davin knows all this, has set it up this way. Eamon is furious with himself for not being more aware, for going along with Davin's plans instead of doing what he always did, which was to loosely follow the plan, but get to the destination by his own route.

They make the autopista without incident. Mary's directions are clear, decisive. Apart from the directions, they have not spoken since Mary came from the hotel, put their bags in the boot and they drove out of the Praza, leaving Fernando Griffin still talking on his phone. As soon as they see a stopping place, Eamon pulls off. Mary uses the anti-bugging device to check the car.

'All clear,' she says. They get out and walk away from the car.

'Let's still keep it at the tourist level,' Eamon says. 'I don't know how effective that thing is. It may be all right, but they may also have something there it can't pick up.' He looks around to make sure they are alone. 'I have a gun for you,' he says and hands over the second Glock pistol. Mary hefts it, does so with ease and Eamon remembers how proficient she was with guns when she did her training. 'Let's hope we don't need them,' she says.

Eamon shrugs. 'Insurance.'

'This to do with our friend Iggy?'

'No. I organised all this.' He opens the boot and takes the bag, where he shows her the equipment, ammunition, torches, a balaclava mask, binoculars, a couple of fake passports one for each of them, some currency, sterling and dollars. 'As I say, just insurance.'

He drives back to the outskirts of Santiago de Compostela to the airport. They do not speak apart from Mary's curt directions, 'Left, next right,' until they drive into the airport car park. Eamon circles slowly, sees that Louise's friends are waiting in a parked Nissan Micra. Eamon stops, gets out and says slowly, not sure how much English they understand. 'You follow us, yes?'

'Where to?' The man's English is good. Eamon worries slightly at the faint grin, as if he finds all this something slightly comical, he decides it is more likely the man has one of those nervous smiles.

'We'll stop at Vilgarcía. Just stay in sight and whatever happens to us, don't stop.' The smile remains fixed on his face, Eamon sees. He goes back to their car and hopes he hasn't scared him so that he decides to leave them to it.

They turn off the autopista at Padron and head south towards the port. As they get closer to the coast, the wind is strong, Eamon is aware of how green the landscape is as he watches the trees bend and sway. He wonders if Mary thinks he is too obsessive with his fear of bugs in the car, if he has unnecessarily frightened her with his secret bag and decides, as he is the one with the years of experience, she'll have to accept it. They enter the town, drive slowly until they are through and on the coast road. On their left, he sees the wide bay; the sea is speckled with small boats, tiny one-man craft that remind him of coracles, on up to large speedboats and yachts. In the distance, he sees fishing smacks and trawlers.

'Let's stop here,' Mary says. 'I need to look at the map.'

Eamon has been checking the mirrors all the time. He is impressed with the driving of the other car. They keep their distance and never lose him. Now he indicates and pulls over to the seashore side of the road. Out of the car, the wind is strong and has a decided chill.

Mary walks away from the car, on to a small stretch of sand. There are a few people sitting, so well wrapped up, it could be an Irish beach, she thinks. 'Griffin usually calls at the hotel over there.' She points across the road to a modern building set back in the trees, between sand dunes. 'He has a coffee, makes a call or two before heading for his house.'

'That's all in there?'

'Yeah. A very detailed report on what he does from reaching here to going on to his holiday place on the Illa de Arousa.'

'Where is all this coming from? If Davin has this level of information, why the hell are we here?'

'I thought that when I read the paper in the car. You were right to maintain silence. Do you think we are being set up?'

Eamon gives a snort of laughter, dry, harsh, sardonic. 'We are that already. What else we're here for I don't know.' He sighs and stares out at the boats bobbing in the sea. A couple are packing up their towels and folding a windbreak. 'What next?'

Mary reads, '"Proceed to the Hotel Melusca" – which is there across the road – "en route to Villanova de Arousa. Your friend stops here for one café and he makes some calls on his cellular phone. If it is a normal trip, he then drives to the island and through Villanova to his house." There is a sketch map of the road and his place.'

'Let's go and have a coffee or something,' Eamon says. 'There is no point in trying to stay hidden from Griffin. He has seen us enough by now to be suspicious.'

He walks along the road with the map in his hand towards the Micra, parked in the next lay-by. As he leans in with his map, as though asking for directions, he says, 'We'll change cars when we make our next stop. Stay with the car, I'll come to you. All right by you?'

The man still has his silly nervous grin. He nods. Eamon prolongs his stay, as though taking instructions before he leaves them.

They sit in the lounge; they are the only people there apart from the receptionist at the other end. After some moments the receptionist notices them and calls, 'Rafael!' A young waiter emerges from the restaurant to take their order. The automatic front door opens and shuts, the wind howls through it, shrieking and whistling like wind in a ship's rigging. Eamon looks at the map of the region. He carefully reads the instructions that Mary gave him. They are detailed and precise and so far, they are exact.

'Here he is,' Mary says, as the blue BMW pulls on to the car park.

'Okay. Let's head for the next town and see what happens,' Eamon is calm now he has a plan, something positive to do over the next few hours.

They get in their car and he notices Griffin sitting in the driver's seat with the phone jammed against his ear. 'Your man might as well have that thing stuck to his head.'

Mary laughs, 'He's like a baby with his soother.' She looks again, 'I see his girlfriend is with him, too.'

As they leave Griffin glances up, he does not give any indication he recognises him. The road is not busy; it twists and turns, narrows in places, so Eamon has to slow down to let the few other vehicles pass. 'You'd never think it was August with so few holiday makers,' Mary says.

'I suppose it's the weather. It is pretty cold even for us. I imagine most Spaniards prefer it a lot hotter than this.'

The road winds through woods. Sand dunes flank the holiday homes, partially hidden in the trees. Some are big, and a lot have high walls and locked gates. Eamon notes the closed circuit TV cameras, he spots fences with razor wire strung across the top. McAllister's briefing seems accurate; many of these places are new, recently built, with a lot of money spent on the fortifications. He knows all about the need to make holiday houses secure – their own place in Greencastle was burgled soon after they bought the house. It would have continued, Eamon is sure, but for somebody putting the word around the local lowlife who the owner of the house was. Since then the village has been immune from the spate of break-ins and petty thieving which has continued around the countryside. This level of protection seems excessive, as though the inhabitants fear an attack. Eamon thinks it reminds him of Davin's home and fields, which are fortified as heavily as a British Army barracks or the old RUC police stations.

They swing in a wide arc as they cross the bridge to the island of Arousa. Here it is also quiet, not at all like a holiday resort at noon in late August. They see a long curving beach, the blue-grey Atlantic, the beach has just a few sun worshippers scattered on the vast empty expanse of white sand. Eamon whistles the March of the Toreadors from Carmen, a sign Mary knows that he is tense. As indeed, she is herself. She can't figure out why exactly as there does not appear to be any reason why Fernando Griffin should regard them as a threat, rather than a nuisance. Mary can't quite nail it down. It is like an idea she is slowly starting to understand but is not yet able to grasp.

'Keep straight on?' Eamon asks.

'Head down to the harbour. Be nice to get out and stretch our legs.' She looks again at the instructions and notes that after his stop at the hotel, Griffin drives to the harbour at Villanova where he sometimes buys fish. Do not be surprised if he abandons his drive here to return to Santiago de Compostela. Maybe they do not have the fish he requires. Perhaps there will have been delays with the catch.

The harbour is quiet; there are a few cafés and bars scattered around the square. They find somewhere to park easily – there are plenty of spaces. Some boats, mostly small rowing boats lie slanting to one side on the slipways, the tide is out and boats remain beached on the sand while others bob in the slow swell. A couple of men sit by their boats repairing nets. Mary walks alone along the sea front, selects a stone bench under an awning, and watches the road. In the hot sun, the square has few people; a trickle of cars comes along the coast road. Her heart is thudding, that familiar if somewhat forgotten mixture of fear and adrenalin, with the fear clawing at her. Now they are here and getting close to what they are looking for all she wants to do is return to the car, find a nice hotel, sit by the swimming pool with a good book, relax, be normal.

We are not normal, she thinks. And we never will be because of what we did in the past, what we do now.

We are marked for life.

She sits and watches, as she waits for Eamon. She is aware of the pistol in her jacket pocket. How long is it since she last held a gun, never mind used one? Who are the people he has met, who have followed them here from the airport? More mystery and Mary can't help thinking they are not like most married couples, that they keep many things secret from each other.

'I reckon his place is along here,' Eamon says. He points to the map of the island. 'That stretch of beach there, along the promontory, over that way.'

'There is a marina. I saw it when we passed along.'

'Well let's see if our friend buys any fish today.'

Mary can't see the blue BMW. She wonders if he has changed vehicles. There has been no sign of it on the coast road. Mary carefully checks all the cars, can't see one she has not noted.

When she looks back at the slipway Griffin is there talking to a fisherman. He has slipped into the town by a back street, moved slowly until he is happy his back is clear before coming along to one of the fishermen along the quay. He glances at them, but she knows by now it suits him to allow them along for this part of his trip. There is a handshake, a short conversation. For form's sake, she supposes, Griffin takes a parcel, passes over some money, before walking back across the square and vanishing.

Mary sips water from a bottle. 'I suppose we are going for a walk?'

'I'm afraid so. And wouldn't you know that the wind has died down, the sun is hot and we have to walk.' Eamon smiles, takes her hand and squeezes it tightly. 'Ok, let's get moving.'

Eamon is right. Out of the shade, sheltered here from the stiff Atlantic breeze, it is hot. Mary feels the sweat on her back, around her hairline and wishes she had worn a singlet instead of a blouse. They round a corner, where there is welcome shade under some trees. Slowly walking, looking around, they pass a couple of old villas, with large gardens, heavy with lush vegetation. Ahead the marina glistens, the azure water sparkling in the sunshine. On the beach they are in the open again, Eamon walks ahead of her, doing an excellent impression of a tourist, he looks suitably impressed at the scale and location of the large villas with their sea-view gardens and patios.

They locate Fernando Griffin's place. After all his flashiness, the upmarket BMW X5, the jewellery, the glamorous woman, they are surprised to find a small chalet, no more than a large beach hut. Odd, Mary thinks, and wonders aloud if they have the correct house.

'This be the spot,' Eamon says.

'You're sure?'

'The holiday home of our dreams that we might buy,' Eamon says, slipping into their cover story as laid down in the directions. 'Smart, very smart,' he adds, as he examines the tiny patio at the rear of the chalet. 'Well hidden from the road by the trees, and best of all, the boat can be reached in a couple of minutes.'

In the marina, the boats are moored in numbered berths. Among the yachts that vary from small family craft to large sea-going luxury boats, there are a number of big speedboats. Mary tries to imagine which one belongs to Griffin.

'Do you think they have two and three boat families around here?' Mary says trying to lighten things. She wonders what Griffin will do if he sees them now, for whatever he may have thought of his past sightings, to have tracked him down here can only mean they are after him for some reason.

'Let's take some photographs,' Eamon says. Mary stands on the narrow strip of sand between the marina and the cliff. Eamon takes a couple of shots with his digital camera, motions her back to take in the chalet. Mary takes a couple of Eamon posing before the marina. As she lines him up, he says, 'It looks as if our friend has brought the fish home.'

'Right.'

'Just keep snapping. He's spotted us, but he appears more interested in what he can see through the binoculars.'

'Which is probably us. How does he look?'

'Relaxed. As if he hasn't a care in the world.'

They walk back to the marina to admire the boats again and it is something of a shock to Mary to hear Griffin say in good English, 'You like boats?' He smiles wolfishly at Mary first, then at Eamon, then back to her, but his coal-black eyes are hard and they do not smile.

'Lovely spot to have a boat here, it must be magic,' Eamon says.

'You can hire a boat, or take a trip if you go to Villanova de Arousa. If you like, I fix it for you. My friend he has a boat business there.'

'Very kind of you,' Eamon says easily, and laughs. 'All I can do is admire boats. As soon as I set foot on one, I'm seasick.'

'And you?' Griffin turns to Mary. 'You also get seasick?'

'No. I'm fine.' Mary realises he is trying to place them by accent.

'On holiday, yes?'

'Yes, we are.'

'Where do you live?'

'London,' Eamon says, slipping into their cover story.

'Ah. Pretty different, I guess.' Griffin continues to smile at Mary, which she finds rather unnerving. 'What part of London? I used to work there.'

'North London,' Eamon says, still easy and relaxed.

'I live in Cricklewood.'

'Is that so,' Eamon says.

Griffin smiles at him but Mary sees the suspicion flit across his face before he manages to hide it behind his horse's grin. 'And where do you live?'

'Almost next door, in Willesden,' Eamon replies, still easy and relaxed.

This appears to satisfy Griffin, Mary thinks, probably because he has located Eamon's distinctive Derry accent.

'Maybe if you have time, I take you out in my boat. You permit me?' Griffin looks straight at Eamon.

'That would be lovely,' Mary says.

'Why not come with me now? I must go to the harbour to collect some lobster. My friend he saves some for me. You want to come? We are away for about half an hour.'

Mary's heart is thumping. She has difficulty breathing. Has he rumbled them? He can't be certain, she decides, he is very suspicious but he won't move at all until he is sure, there is no point in making trouble if there is nothing to worry him. She looks at Eamon, who smiles easily.

'If you'd like to go love, why not?'

Is Eamon ordering her to go? For a second she is furious that he has put her into this position, then she realises that for now he is not her husband but her commanding officer. What is Griffin after? What if he tries it on? Griffin is the sort to make a pass at her, try to go further in exchange for information. Come on, she tells herself, you know how to look after yourself, you are being paranoid again. She can't believe Eamon would drop her in like that, not without forewarning her, giving her the choice. But she remembers how he vanished and how he was on his return and she knows she can't rule out anything on a mission. Mary stalls, tries it out. 'Have we time?'

'If it's only half an hour, sure we do.'

'Okay,' says Fernando Griffin, 'let's go.' He speaks rapidly in Spanish on his mobile as they walk to the berth, to a very big speedboat. Griffin jumps down then holds a hand up to help Mary. He hands her a yellow hard hat. 'To be safe, we wear hats and jackets.' Mary removes her own jacket and slips the lifejacket on, squashes the hat over her thick hair. Griffin starts the engine and they move slowly out of the marina.

CHAPTER 9

As the big speedboat moves slowly out of the harbour, Eamon stands and waves to Mary. She turns back dressed in her hard hat and yellow life jacket. He tries to stay calm, to keep the smile fixed. Although he does not think she is at risk – he would never have allowed to her to go had he thought that – there is always the unexpected. However, it allows him to look around Griffin's chalet, and had Griffin not made the offer of a boat trip, Eamon intended to ask him for a tour of it anyway, in line with his cover of being interested in buying a holiday home around here. He doubts he will find anything, does not know what he is looking for, this is searching in the dark; he is taking the opportunity to get the lie of the land.

He hears the engine rev up as Griffin opens the throttle, the boat surges forward and is soon beyond his vision. He walks quickly, heading straight for the wooden steps from the beach that lead to the fence and gate, which is slightly ajar.

He moves around the side of the chalet, squeezing in the narrow gap between the wall and the wire fence. Round the front, the BMW X5 is facing the drive that runs down through the trees to a bend, where Eamon guesses it reaches the road. Quickly he tries the front door, he is not surprised to find it locked, as are the shutters over the windows, the chalet looks as if it has been shut up for a long time. He looks up at the roof, under the eaves, searching for TV cameras, he peers in the nearby trees, he can't spot any, but he guesses if there are cameras, they are well hidden; they are not there as a deterrent but to observe any visitors. The chalet is small, a large ground floor tapering up to the roof, like a triangle. Upstairs the front shutter is open. Eamon senses rather than sees that somebody is watching him, suspects it may be the woman. He continues round to the rear of the building. As he moves, he checks the shutters on each window, a gentle shove to see if any are open, before he returns to the beach. He walks quickly to the car. As he nears it, a man approaches him. Eamon is not surprised; he has been expecting somebody, possibly one of Griffin's friends who may have seen him poking around the chalet. '*Hola,*' Eamon says slowly, waiting, watching. He has his hand in his pocket, around the Glock pistol.

The man says slowly, '*¿Me das otra manzana?*'

Equally slowly, Eamon replies, '*Prefero el melocotón.*'

'We are here to help you.' He hands him an envelope. 'Instructions.' His English is hesitant, laboured, as if he has no knowledge of it but has memorised a few phrases, rather as Eamon has the Spanish.

Eamon nods. The man walks to a car, gets in and drives off. Eamon wonders how they found him, if in fact Davin knew they would come here, or have they tailed them from Santiago de Compestela and he has not spotted them? It does not matter why or how, he knows, but the fear comes over him again. It is as if Davin knows, or more likely, he guessed that Eamon would switch cars, would loop outside the plan.

As soon as the car is out of sight, Eamon gets into the Micra, he tries the gears, checks where reverse is and when he is familiar with the different car, he drives around until he finds a public phone booth. Inside he dials a Dublin number. There is a click, the answerphone says in English. 'Please leave your message.'

'We have had a look at the house; it is a wee bit small. The buyer seemed to be expecting us. This made our approach very uncomfortable. Please let me know how I am to proceed.'

He sits in the car and wonders if he can phone Davin on the emergency number and decides not. For all he knows Davin may be in Spain, although he doubts it; Davin does not travel: he sits at home in the centre, a spider in his web. Eamon leaves the car near the complex of shops and restaurants and walks back along the beach to the marina. While he waits for Mary, he reads the rest of the instructions.

Far from reassuring him, he finds they make him even more wary. Davin has sent them here, put them in this exposed position as the bait to lure Michael Donnellan out into view. He can't figure out why that is. If Davin wants to kill Michael Donnellan, he seems to have enough people here to do it. Eamon has read in the local paper about the murder of a suspected drug dealer, of the lack of progress by the police in finding his killers. It can't be that difficult for Davin to get a contract on Donnellan, to get him identified in order to kill him. He paces up and down the beach anxiously scanning the sea for the speedboat, listening intently for the roar of the engine. All he hears are the clacking of the metal burgees at the tops of the masts of the yachts, the hiss of the waves on the shingle, the raucous screeches and squawks of gulls. As he waits, Eamon decides that if Davin does not leave a satisfactory answer when he next calls in, he is going home and to hell with it. He sees a boat on the horizon; it grows as it comes nearer. Mary calls his mobile. 'Hi,' she shouts and he can barely hear her above the roar of the engine, the slapping of the sea against the hull. 'It's great! We're just coming into the harbour. See you.' Mary is convincing, sounds just the right note, excited and happy, keen to share it with him. 'Good for you,' he says, a little jealous, and even worried. It never quite leaves him, this fear that one day Mary will look at him, will tire of his old body, his bachelor habits, the need he has for long periods of solitude. Despite her snotty comments about Griffin, Eamon suspects he has some power over women, they like the whiff of danger he exudes, the lupine smile, the arrogance and swagger of the good looking man, even if he reminds Eamon of a pimp.

She waves energetically as the boat noses into the marina and slowly, neatly, Griffin brings her in to berth. As Eamon stretches his hand to help her out, he says humorously, 'Well, where's my lobster?'

Griffin shouts, Eamon doesn't catch it, then Griffin softens it with a smile that surprises Eamon with its generosity and warmth, he sees how Griffin has this other side, the one that was entertaining his friends last night at dinner, that makes him attractive to women.

Griffin picks up a plastic bucket and clambers on to the quay. Eamon sees the lobsters, black, immobile, as though asleep. 'My dinner,' he says, 'I could not get one for you, my friend.'

Eamon smiles, shrugs and asks, 'Is property expensive around here?'

Griffin waggles a hand. 'Depends where you go. For sure by the sea. But inland it is still possible to buy somewhere for not too much money.' He smiles again. 'Sorry about the lobster.' He takes Mary's hand, raises it to his lips, to kiss. 'Maybe you come out for a longer trip the next time, Mary?'

Eamon watches him very carefully. He moves slightly so he has a clear view of the chalet, where he has, he is sure, seen a movement, a movement Griffin does not want them to notice. Griffin makes a big thing of kissing Mary's hand, there is an element of clowning, of trying to distract his attention.

'I'll take a photo of you both.' Eamon smiles indulgently, points the digital camera, peers through the viewfinder, clicks, and is sure he has the figure who has been watching them from the back door of the chalet.

Griffin smiles again, puts an arm around Mary's waist, tries to squeeze her close, his hand is just below her breast. Eamon has to fight the urge to snap at him to back off and he is relieved when Mary dexterously eases herself out of Griffin's clutches. He suspects Griffin is probably trying to provoke him, to get their attention away from the activity at the chalet, where Eamon thinks he can now hear voices. Mary has sensed what this is about, she stays close to Griffin and they move sideways, giving Eamon a wider view of the chalet.

After Griffin has left them, with a kiss for Mary on both cheeks, a handshake for Eamon, they walk back. The beach has a few more people, couples, a number of women on their own, and a few kids, all spread out, well apart.

'What was all that about?'

'I'm not sure. He tried it on a couple of times. The old trick, did I want to steer the boat, he slowed down and stood behind me as he showed me how to operate the levers. Tried to fondle my tits, pressed himself up against me. Pretty crude and pointless really, the life jacket was thick and heavy.' Mary gives him a sharp jab with her elbow. 'He's a randy bastard. I reckon if I'd been agreeable, we'd have been in a bunk.' She pauses, watches Eamon carefully before she continues, 'I couldn't see there was anything to be gained by doing that. So I just laughed it off. Removed myself from his clutches and told him I am happily married. So he did the incredulous bit. "He is your husband?"' Eamon looks sharply at her, and he can see that she finds this gratifying, reassuring and she wishes now she had not thrown in Griffin's crack about his age.

'Yeah,' Eamon says and his spirits sink again. 'You're a very attractive woman.'

'But I'm a one-man woman. I don't think he's that sure of himself.'

'How so?'

'My guess is he is concerned, a bit worried maybe. He can't decide if we are following him, or if it is just a coincidence. Fishing, I'd say. It may have suited him to have me with him when he picked up his box, which I noticed he left in the cabin. His consignment of drugs, I assume.'

'Maybe. I think he also wanted to separate us, to see what I'd do. He knew I'd take a poke around the chalet.'

'Did you find anything?'

'No. It's a standard chalet, not much room around it, but a long drive and well hidden in the trees. I'm sure there was somebody inside and other folk arrived while you were canoodling with him on the beach. When we get to the car I'll see what the camera caught'.

'I suspect he spotted us, as you said. This was his way of checking us out. His groping me wasn't all sexual. He was searching me for a weapon, for a transmitter, anything suspicious that might hint we are not just tourists.'

'Anything else?'

'I thought I'd try him out. I told him we were touring but we had no particular route planned. Where would he recommend, somewhere we should see. He said it was all beautiful, along the coast towards the Portuguese border. They are some lovely towns, good hotels.'

Eamon sits in the car. He has parked at a picnic spot in the trees with a clear view of the entrance to Griffin's chalet. Since he returned from his boat trip, Griffin has been inside all day, apart from a brief visit to the local shop, where Mary observed him with a Spanish newspaper, a couple of litres of San Miguel, bottles of mineral water and some food which he put in the BMW. The picture of the chalet he took does not reveal anything, except a dim figure closing the back door. Eamon has taken the offer of help that was in the instructions. When he called the number, he said laboriously in Spanish, '*Tengo miedo de los perros.*' As he did so, he hoped that was the last time he has to remember an expression in Spanish. In good English, the man says, 'Do not worry, my dogs are locked up.' All this backup, Eamon thinks – Davin has good intelligence about Griffin's movements, when he collects a consignment.

Miguel is quiet, very competent. He has the hard cool demeanour of the seasoned professional that Eamon remembers from his best operatives. He has placed Miguel on the beach, with a woman known as Carlota, and they are walking up and down, arms around each other, while watching the access to the marina. Mary is at the end of the road, where the bend makes it obligatory for all cars to slow down as they begin to climb the hill up to the villas and chalets. Eamon has been looking for the others, the guardian angels, as they have called them. He is sure they are about – why else bother to shadow them in Santiago de Compostela? – but he has not seen a hint they are here. Am I cracking up, he asks himself as he watches the road, and feels fatigue creep up on him. I am not able to separate reality from my imagination. He realises he has not slept properly for a while now, since his meeting with Ignatius Davin, to be precise. He sips Coke and waits.

Eamon feels the sweat on his back, that cold sweat that always marked the arrival of fear, a fear he has not had so intensely for years. As he sweats, he sees a large car coming up the road at speed, then the lights turn off, he watches it going down the drive to Griffin's house. Eamon gets out of the car and runs to the bend on the drive as fast as he can. As he gets there, the car slows outside the chalet and there are no brake lights. The car is then reversed and parked beside Griffin's so both are ready for a fast getaway. Through the binoculars with night vision and the image stabilisers, he sees the hall light is switched off, as is the interior light in the car when a door opens. He can't make out how many are in the car, or even see more than an outline. A couple of figures, he guesses. It is dark where they park, beneath the trees. That tells him they are serious, they take no risks. When the chalet door opens, there is no sound of greetings, they file in, and he thinks there are two figures. The door closes. He gives it ten minutes. There is nothing, no sign of movement from the chalet, no lights, no noise, none of the babble of conversation.

On the beach, he walks with Mary. The sand here is soft and shifts under his feet, slipping inside his shoes. At sea, the lights come and go, flickering into view before vanishing. The breeze is sharp and chilly; Eamon feels it as his body cools. Miguel and Carlota walk towards them. In the dusk, arms around each other, they are perfect as the starry-eyed lovers. Miguel says quietly. 'Lights in the back, they open the shutters a little but is not possible to see anything.'

'Thank you.'

'Now we go.'

'Sure. Watch the front until we come to you.'

Eamon tells Mary about the car pulling into the drive.

'It was a Peugeot, a big silver one, with a Spanish number plate,' Mary says. 'A driver and passenger. That was all I saw.'

'Better than I did. Well done.' Eamon has the binoculars trained on the back of the chalet. He can see the lights, but Miguel is correct, the shutters are slightly open to give some ventilation but drawn so that they conceal the rooms.

'What do you think?'

'They know we're here, yet they still came. Either they don't think we are a threat, or else they feel secure enough to go ahead with us.'

'Maybe it's nothing.'

'Somehow I have a feeling this is all part of the plan.' Eamon hums tunelessly and almost silently. 'The trouble is – what is the plan?' He continues to look at the chalet.

When the movement comes it is fast, organised. The back door opens, two figures, barely visible in camouflage jackets and trousers, their faces blacked up, woollen hats pulled over their heads, come down the steps, walking rapidly, calmly, to the speedboat and within a few minutes the boat has vanished.

'How long?'

'Four minutes from leaving the house to going to sea from the marina.'

'Well drilled. So if you saw him collect a package today, why is he out again and at night?'

'Maybe that's how they deliver, in small packets.'

Eamon is not convinced. He stays a while longer watching the sea as the noise of Griffin's boat fades away. 'Okay. I'm going in to take a look. By the front door.'

Mary parks below the chalet, turns and before Eamon goes, she hugs him. 'For God's sake, be careful.'

'I always am.' He holds her for a moment. 'You have the phone signals? Good. If I let it ring, I'm in trouble; you leave as fast as you can. You have the numbers for the others. Get in touch with them, and then contact Davin.' He hands her two flash disks. 'Transfer the photos to that. Email it to the address, then transfer it to a flash disk, you post it to the safe house, and post the other disk to the other address.'

Beyond the entrance to the chalet, he goes sideways, at an oblique angle, through the trees. Eamon is sure there is closed circuit TV covering the drive that includes the edge of the tree line. He moves in a semicircle until he reaches the wire fence at the side of the chalet, he is hoping he has avoided the range of the lens. He crouches, bent double, he is panting and wishes he were fitter. At the fence, he thinks he is unobserved. Flat on his belly, he cuts the wire at the bottom, holding it to stop the strands whipping back as he crawls through the gap. He can't remember how long it is since he has done something like this, but he knows he is slower and stiffer; his breathing is heavy, almost laboured.

Once inside, he stands flush to the wall. He waits to get his breath back and allow his heart beat to return to normal as he wonders whether to go in at the front or the back. If there are two in the boat and two arrived by car, that leaves the woman and one man, unless the woman has gone with Griffin. Slowly, quietly, Eamon edges his way to the rear of the chalet. He tests the window he touched earlier, is surprised to find the top section is still unlocked. He opens it, searches for the handle and opens the lower window. He waits, listens, there is nothing but the sea and the odd car in the distance. He presses his mobile, one ring. I'm about to go in. He waits for the returning two vibes. Acknowledged. All clear here.

Slowly Eamon gropes along the window ledge, he finds a mirror, a mug with toothbrushes, a hairbrush, a jar, all of which he places in the washbasin, as he does this he memorises where they were on the ledge. With a pencil torch, he checks the sill is clear before he levers himself on to it and swings his legs over the basin to drop to the floor. He waits, hears nothing. When he has pulled the window to but left the catch off, he bends down and uses the torch, pointing it towards the centre of the door and he notes he is in a toilet, not a bathroom. He can see light underneath, wonders what is on the other side, is it a bedroom, or hall or passageway. Eamon stands by the door listening intently. There is no sound in the chalet, which seems peculiar if there is anybody here. Mary has not signalled anybody has left. He tenses his body, sure they have seen him on the TV, that the open window is deliberate, bait to get him inside. He dismisses this. If they wanted to grab him, they could have done so by now.

Time to move.

Cautiously he tries the round doorknob, stealthily turns it, and sees he is in a hall. Directly across is another room, to his left the front door, to his right a large open-plan room, a combined kitchen, dining area and sitting room. There are large glass sliding doors overlooking the small patio and beyond to the marina and sea. In a chair he sees a figure sitting, his feet up as he stares out to sea, talking volubly in Spanish on the phone.

Eamon waits. He holds the digital camera aloft. A mobile phone rings and the man holds the other phone to his chest and says, '*Digame*'. He pauses and speaks again, rapidly. Eamon finds it impossible to understand anything. The man pauses again. '*Si, si. Adios.*'

At that, Eamon slips back inside the toilet, closes the door, goes through the window, and stands outside as he rearranges the toothbrush mug, mirror, hairbrush and jar back on the shelf. He closes the window, reaches down through the small window to lock it, and then pushes the top one shut. On his knees he crawls to the gap in the fence and goes through.

He pulls the wire back in place. He hopes it will pass a cursory glance, even though he knows anybody checking it will know immediately it has been cut, will spot the flattened vegetation. He crawls back part of the way. When he gets to his feet, he presses his mobile phone, lets it ring twice. I'm out and on my way. Quietly, as quickly as he thinks prudent, he makes his way again at the angle through the trees.

In the car, Mary lets the brake off. They freewheel down the hill before she starts the engine. They do not speak. Mary reaches across to squeeze his hand. They drive in silence to the next village, where she parks near the shops and they get out and walk to a pizzeria. Mary waits until they have ordered.

'You okay?'

'Yeah,' Eamon grins and rubs his lower back. 'I'll be stiff for a few days.'

'So?'

Eamon glances around. The restaurant is not busy; they are well away from the nearest table. 'It's Michael Donnellan all right. I didn't see him, apart from the back of his head, but I heard him speak, recognised his voice immediately. He was by himself, talking on the house phone and then his mobile rang. All the time he was speaking Spanish. Didn't seem to be anybody else in, so I reckon whoever came with him went with Griffin.' Eamon pauses and shakes his head. 'I don't understand it. It was too easy. Unless Michael has gone gaga, he must have known I was in the room.'

'Do you think it was Hugh O'Neill who went out to the boat?'

Eamon shrugs. 'I don't know. But it's odd, because if Michael is there for what we think, why is he using a mobile, the Spanish police will have the area covered.'

'Maybe they don't know about Donnellan.'

'Even if they don't, it's a risk.'

Their pizzas arrive. Eamon has a mouthful of beer as they eat in silence. When he has finished, Eamon says, 'I can't decide if I was smart, foolhardy or just lucky. The old Michael Donnellan would never have left himself that vulnerable. Okay, he has been out of things for almost fifteen years; he's dropped right off the screen. Even so, he will always be on the edge, never taking a risk, particularly like that. Nobody seemed to be covering his back.'

'Yeah, I was thinking that. I'm sure somebody was watching him.'

Eamon drains his beer, signals to the waitress to bring a refill. 'So why did they let me in and out? That doesn't make sense either. Something is going on. I need to think this through.'

'What will you tell the big man?'

'I'll report what I saw. That is what I'm here to verify, that I have seen and heard Michael Donnellan sitting in a chalet belonging to Fernando Griffin.' He drinks some beer. 'Maybe now we can leave all this. Might be able to grab a few days' proper holiday.'

Mary looks at him as she empties her glass of Ribeiro, and then pours herself a refill. 'I wish, as they say.'

'Maybe I'm putting too much into this.'

'Or maybe you're too trusting. You know what I think of Davin. He terrifies me. He'll kill us if there is the slightest risk to him. You know that. Why else did you accept this job?'

The wine has made her bolder. Eamon is afraid her nerves are so stretched she is about to fly into a tantrum, which he knows is how she handles her fear; he reaches across to hold her hand. 'There is probably a simple answer, like so many things.' He tips some more wine into her glass. 'Come on. Let's see if we can find a hotel. To hell with Davin until tomorrow.'

'We could stay there,' Mary points to the map.

Eamon is not really listening. Forest fires have been sweeping through the north of Portugal and parts of Galicia. They sit in a service station restaurant on the autopista near Vigo and he watches the local news on the TV set in the corner.

'Baiona,' Mary goes on. 'It's quite close to the border. We can be in Portugal easily enough. It was where Columbus landed when he came back from discovering America.'

'Fine. Let's see if we can find a decent hotel.' Eamon grimaces remembering the motel room, which was all they could find late last night. 'That bed didn't have a mattress, more a plank of wood covered in cloth.'

Mary has been making notes. 'I've found another Parador in Baiona, the Conde de Gondomar. It's expensive, but it sounds wonderful. The hotel is an old fort, the one that guarded the port.'

'If it's as comfortable as the Reis Católicos, I'm happy. Let's go for it. We're officially on holiday. To hell with the expense.' Eamon orders from the *menu del dia*. By now, he is used to taking a flyer on his food. If he likes it, he eats it, if not to his taste he leaves it.

Mary goes outside to check if the Parador has a room. Eamon sits watching the car park below, shimmering in the midday heat. More and more he feels as though Davin is using them as bait, tethered goats in a tiger shoot. Last night was too easy. Griffin must know they are still in the area and that Eamon had looked around the chalet while he was out in the boat with Mary. Then he goes out in his speedboat with a certain amount of show, certainly not covertly, as darkness falls, leaving the chalet almost open. That open upper window in the toilet – was that deliberate or careless? From what he has seen of Griffin, he does not look the sort to make elementary errors like that. It is all too easy.

When he rang the next number in Athlone, he reported they had seen the sights of the town. They were exactly as he expected them. He rang again an hour later. The answerphone asks, 'Did you manage to see all the sights? Did you take any photos?' 'Yes, I saw the town hall and the council chamber.' Eamon waits, there is a clicking and the disembodied voice, like a speak-your-weight-machines, says, 'Go in peace, my son.'

Eamon picks at the casserole of minced meat and potatoes. His appetite has gone. He is trying to find a way into this.

He wonders about the reports that the Criminal Assets Bureau in Dublin, armed with enhanced legislative powers, has begun investigating certain new entrepreneurs in the south. Of course Davin is far too careful to be anywhere within miles of being linked to anything like that. However, Eamon remembers hearing a whisper that Davin was under investigation; he has read reports in the *Irish Times* about unnamed suspects, the details leaked by the CAB and the Garda Special Branch to selective people in the hope of creating panic. Maybe that is what Davin is seeking here, to create a diversion. It has to be that, or it is as Davin told Eamon, that he suspects Donnellan to be part of a drug-running cartel. Alternatively, Davin is setting up Donnellan. Eamon has a long drink of water. He can't believe he hasn't thought of it until now, that Davin might be setting him up. Suddenly the food is like ash in his mouth. How the hell has he let that possibility slide past? He feels his stomach rumble, he leaves the table almost at a run as he makes for the Gents.

When he returns, feeling marginally better, Mary is eating heartily as she waits to receive confirmation about the hotel. He is impressed with how quickly she has picked up some Spanish, while he has struggled to remember a few phrases and words.

Eamon tells her what he is trying to figure out. 'Am I putting too much into all of this, what do you think?'

'I don't think so. I have been thinking that our friend has other plans from what he told you. As you said, last evening was too easy. Almost as if Michael wanted you to recognise him. I'm sure there was somebody else in the house covering him.'

'I'm certain. Funny too how there was a set of wire cutters in the car, even though I'd brought my own. They left that and a torch for me. None of this fits. And if it doesn't fit, why is Davin not responding?'

'Have you told him how easy it was?'

'Yes. Said access was very simple, without a charge or any checks.'

'And all he said was go in peace.'

'Or rest in peace,' Eamon says grimly, and then regrets letting Mary know how concerned he is.

'Of course it might be true what Davin has told us. Michael always liked money. Wasn't he the money man in London?'

'He was. Known as that and the laundry man. He did very well all the time he was in charge. Used bank raid cash to fund his business.'

'Well if he liked the good life, he'll want to continue it over here. Why not drugs, if Galicia is the main entry point for Europe? He has all the experience; he has the right-hand man in Hugh. I can see,' Mary says earnestly, 'how that story fits neatly.' Her mobile phone rings, she answers then heads outside to take the call.

His *flan*, crème caramel really, arrives and he eats it with a semblance of appetite, hoping it will settle the rumbling in his stomach. Eamon tries again. Let us assume, he tells himself, that Davin is a British agent. If that is true, he would surely have told them what he was doing when he sent us out here. They in turn provide all the very impressive backup we have received. Cars, equipment, exact intelligence on Griffin's movements. Eamon knows how they can swamp an area when they want to do so. If that is a given, what is the purpose? Does somebody have suspicions, proof about Davin, conclusive proof? And this is his response? After all, he has done it before, when he was under pressure about the peace initiative, which collapsed once the Golden Boy operation was exposed. That might explain why he has not seen any signs they are being followed, apart from Pádraig, who was probably just there to light the torch, to provide a semblance of cover and let me know Davin has contacts with ETA, who are giving him the help. Are Miguel and Carlotta from ETA, doing a favour for Davin? Since the first day, he has not had a sight of Pádraig, so who is coordinating all this? If not Davin, who are the shadows, the Guardian Angels, that unseen presence they both feel around them? Are they here now? Eamon looks again down at the car park. The cars that pull in or drive out are families, middle-aged couples. Further below he sees the lorry park, and beyond that, through the heat haze, the sea and the port of Vigo. It is all normal, a typical late August day, hot, a cloudless sky. And yet he still senses there are people around them, more protective than predatory. At times he wonders if he is becoming paranoid. Last night, trying to sleep on the hard bed, he dozed off, and woke suddenly, convinced somebody was going through their belongings. He got up gun in hand to find the room empty with Mary asleep, snoring gently. If we are being tailed, he thinks, they are doing a damn good job. A professional operation. The only people with the expertise and resources to mount an operation like that are the British, no doubt helped by their Spanish counterparts. Eamon sips a *café solo* as he turns the problem around, sideways, upside down.

'Okey dokey,' Mary says. 'We are booked in from tonight. They will only take a three-night booking and we have to have dinner or lunch as well.'

Eamon enjoys the lack of traffic the further south they travel. He decides to stay on the autopista and not turn off for Baiona. If they are being followed, let the fuckers work for it, he thinks defiantly. There is no sign of a border control when they sweep into Portugal. Only the different spelling on the road signs, a bit like crossing the border from the North into the Republic back home, acknowledge they are in another country. The overhead clocks that tell them it is 1.30, he remembers the Portuguese keep their clocks on British time, no doubt to differentiate themselves from their much bigger neighbour. Ahead he sees smoke drifting slowly up from the forests on the mountains.

'Where to, bossman?' Mary says. She smiles and Eamon relaxes for the first time. Maybe he is being too complicated. He has been out of action for so long, the changes that have taken place since the ceasefire; things are different from when he was on the Army Council.

'Someplace on the coast. Anywhere. We'll stop and have a look around and we can say we've been to Portugal as well.'

As they approach the outskirts of Viana do Castelo, the smoke from the forest fires drifts down from the hills and is dense enough for the traffic to have headlights on, the air is acrid and smells of burnt wood and ash. They drive into the town on a straight road beside the sea, the tide is out, small boats lurch to the side on the mudflats, Eamon notices a stream of vehicles leaving to get away from the smoke and the possibility that the fires may sweep down from the hills. Now he wonders why he decided to take this pointless excursion. A detour will not throw off their followers. If they are the Brits, they will probably have picked up Mary's mobile calls to the hotel in Baiona, so they can hedge their bets as to their destination. They turn off and find a seaside café. The air is thick from the smoke, like a wood fire in a pub on a wet afternoon. Over coffee, they look at the map and plot a different route to Baiona.

Eamon takes a walk through the village, looking around. He can't find anything; there is nothing to rouse his suspicions. Nevertheless, when they are on a back road and still inside the Portuguese border, he parks off the road amidst some trees. He takes the anti-bugging device and checks the car, inside and out, underneath the chassis and in the boot, under the engine cover, searching carefully, minutely.

CHAPTER 10

The sun is hot, but too long in the shade, with the fresh breeze off the Atlantic, chills Eamon. There are about ten couples, some with children, lounging around the swimming pool, while others swim dutifully as though doing penance. He watches a middle-aged woman swimming a sedate breaststroke slowly, with grim determination up and down the length of the pool; she only stops when some youngsters cut across her. Eamon is impressed how well behaved the Spanish children are, in contrast with the three English kids who are running around shouting and yelling. Mary, who tans easily, is lying on her stomach, her bikini top undone, to get an even tan on her back. Eamon looks at her shapely figure, the coal-black long hair, which she has tied back into a ponytail: his love is so great it almost hurts him at times. He decides to take another spell around the pool. They have been in the Parador for three days and enjoyed it so much they have extended their stay until the end of the week.

As he strolls, Eamon listens intently. Most of the residents are Spanish, but he has seen a pink-skinned Irish family, heard the Dublin accents, watched them as they carefully lather themselves in sunblock, and cover up after a short period in the sun. The man says, 'Will we head for lunch, Breda?' The woman says lazily, 'I don't mind, love. Are you hungry, Colm?' she asks their young son. There are two British couples.

Somebody, he is sure, is watching them. Even after the days of quiet, where they have spoken only to the Spanish hotel staff, and nothing has happened to arouse Eamon's suspicions, he still feels the presence of the watchers he first noted in Santiago de Compostela.

Eamon had called a different number in case Davin had left further orders, but heard only the standard instruction to leave his name and number. At times he has relaxed, but never enough to ease his vigilance. It may be nothing. Or it could be he is being over-cautious. Nevertheless, he continues to be alert, to watch and observe. Mary, discreet, smiling, friendly, is looking for anything out of the ordinary, at who approaches their table or where they sit at the swimming pool. Every day they check the car and their bedroom with the anti-bugging device, and so far, there has been nothing. When Eamon searched the Nissan Micra on their way here, he removed the floor of the boot, checked the spare tyre where he found a small gizmo, which he thinks is a location tracker. He decided to leave it. If they have managed to follow them this closely, there is no point in trying to throw them off. Better, he decides, to let them think they do not suspect anything. He has not told Mary of his discovery.

Eamon nods to the young man on duty at the bar and storeroom, who hands out towels and cushions. He watches the visitors to the fort who stroll around the ramparts outside the hotel but are able to look in at the residents, as they do now.

'Okay?' Mary sounds sleepy.

'All is fine.' Eamon picks up his book. Perhaps, he thinks, this novel about Trujillo, the former dictator of the Dominican Republic, does not help my paranoia. He is finding too many unsettling similarities with Davin and the portrayal of Trujillo; how dangerous the lives of those closest to Trujillo were when they stepped just a millimetre over the line of his suspicions. Eamon cannot help but find parallels with Davin. They share the same sort of mind, the ability to burrow inside your head: they both have the aura of prescience, a more powerful protection than any bodyguard can provide. The novel has enthralled and horrified him. Along with his paranoia, it has triggered his dormant belief that the Movement has lost its *raison d'etre*. In the old days, when he was on active service, living a covert life, he was sustained by his *idée fixe*, as he thought of it. That their fight, their war, was not only for justice in the North, but also, more importantly, for a socialist republic for the whole island of Ireland. Eamon knows that is no longer possible. After the collapse of the Berlin Wall in 1989, that alternative was finished, dead. We are all neo-liberal capitalists now, he thinks. They will only achieve a socialist republic by force. The South does not want anything to do with it: after years of poverty, they are too interested in making money. The eighty plus years since partition has created two countries. That was why the Movement bought into the political process. After the Good Friday Agreement, what are we for now? To sustain a big machine in case we need it again? To gather cash to fund that and to have a war chest for elections and running the offices between times. To enrich the leadership.

For what other reason is Davin so intent on making so much money, other than to have enough to fund the next stage of whatever his plan is to gain control of the entire island of Ireland?

Eamon has been uncomfortable with this steady accumulation of cash for some time. Of simple tastes, apart from music, he has never understood why anybody should want more money than they needed to live on. He is uncomfortable with the emergence of a powerful materialist society in the South. Mary teases him, gives him lessons in economics, but none of that has changed his views. That undercurrent of unease, a sense of wrongdoing, is perhaps due to the comparative luxury of the Conde de Gondomar. The magnificent large public rooms, airy and cool in the heat of midday and early afternoon, the old stone walls of the fort, the polished wood floors, the paintings, the silver, the deep large furniture, the exquisite service. The sea is visible all around, as though the fort is located on an island connected to the mainland by a bridge. The sense of being pampered is reinforced, Eamon is sure, by the public walks around the fort, so that lying on a sunlounger, on towels brought to them by the young man on duty, he is aware of being inspected, envied probably by those not resident in the Parador, who stop to stare through the wire fence that separates them. To reach the swimming pool involves a trek along the hotel corridors before taking some steps to the swimming area. When he alludes about this unease to Mary, he tells her. 'We are becoming like the pigs in *Animal Farm*,' she laughs and tells him he is a hair-shirt puritan.

As he tries to settle, there are muffled explosions in the distance. On their first afternoon, sitting on the terrace overlooking the bay and public beaches, the sounds had both of them jumpy with nervous memories. Across the sea, puffs of smoke wafted slowly, from the mining of the mountain to build tunnels for the new motorway. He listens to the faint crack-crack. There is none of the ferocious ear-splitting bang of a car bomb, no twirling shower of glass shards, some of them as big as bayonets. Yet the sounds of the explosives make Eamon sweat again, that cold sweat of fear that has been absent from his life until the past week. He pulls a towelling robe around his shoulder as a gust of wind adds to the chill he feels.

Restless and chilly again, he goes on another circuit of the swimming area. He listens to the wind, the boom of the surf below, the faint voices of tourists on the walk, the continuing loud yelling of the

English children as they charge around, climbing in and out of their bedroom window. He thinks he has got Davin's plan. The tenterhooks of the Criminal Assets Bureau, and possibly those of the Garda Special Branch, probably aided and abetted by the RUC Special Branch, as he always thinks of them despite their change of title, and with some help from the Brits also, are so close to Davin, he needs something to divert and distract them. Above all, he wants to safeguard his position on the Army Council, because if he is arrested and charged, Davin, like every other member, loses his Council place.

Who can I tell about this? he frets. I can't expose Davin by myself if the others don't want him out of the way. For whatever reason, fear, respect – the belief he is the only man for the job. Maybe the answer is to do nothing. Let them close in on Davin and he will be out of contention anyway. But what if he survives? What if he has put Mary and me in the frame? Davin can easily pin misappropriating funds on Eamon. He walks to the other side of the pool, looking over the harbour, on the small marina, at the replica of Christopher Columbus's ship, the Pinta. Even this far away, Eamon can see how popular it is; there is a steady stream of people queuing to visit it.

Back on his sunlounger, he watches Mary as she does a fast crawl, churning the water. Maybe that is what I need, a swim in cold water to clear my brain he thinks. He tries to resume reading *The Feast of the Goat*. He is quite pleased he has managed to translate the title back into Spanish. *La Fiesta de la Cabra*. He thinks of Cabra, a district of Dublin. Did a returned priest, one schooled and ordained in Spain during the Penal Laws, name it? Do the residents know that cabra is Spanish for goat? Eamon allows his mind to go, one of the tricks he learned in prison, how to lose himself in something as ephemeral as this etymological quest. Fuck Davin, he thinks, at least for this next hour. There is a further series of cracks as the dynamiting resumes. He lies on his back and closes his eyes and still aware of the noises, although he is pleased the English kids have gone, he nods off.

He dreams about a housing estate close to the Phoenix Park in Dublin, where the drug dealers and pushers hold the population in a grip of terror. Despite the efforts of the police, local people, a vigilante group, nothing seems able to remove them from the streets. The rate of drug use is high, particularly amongst the young. Nothing tried is effective against the dealers and pushers. Eamon is dispatched to accompany the local man standing for a seat on Dublin Corporation at the next election. He listens to the terrified outraged complaints, the sense of hopelessness; he sees the wasted, lost lives. He reports back, draws up a plan to clean up the estate, to use muscle and organisation, but behind the newly reformed vigilante group of local residents. How well it works. How quickly they clear the estate of pushers, of addicts; how they keep the streets clean of needles, syringes, and the detritus of drug usage. They set up a local office to provide help for drug users. How the media approves. How easily their candidate sweeps into his seat on the Dublin Corporation, on a tide of number one votes. This is a good time. What they should be doing all the time. He dreams on, mixing truth with fanciful thinking, until he opens his eyes and realises he was not dreaming but remembering what had happened.

When we believed we had something to offer, that we could make a difference to people's lives in the South, to show there was hope and help for those not able to fight back. Eamon thinks, maybe I'm being romantic, I've gone soft under the love of Mary, the comforts of married life, the slow orderly days, when nothing much happens, when we slide into bed at night, tired after a day of honest work, without fear or terror snapping at our unconscious.

If cleaning up that estate was the good side of it, then the shitty bits are these trips, the hunting down of men and sometimes women. Which is what they are here for, have probably signed their death warrants by confirming the presence of Michael Donnellan with Fernando Griffin. He can't get away from wondering what the reasons are for Ignatius Davin handling it this way. There has always been the belief, fuelled by Ignatius Davin, that Donnellan was an informer, on the British payroll, that they were the people who got him out of London after Golden Boy. Eamon always had his doubts about that. Donnellan was resourceful, a shrewd businessman. Impossible that he hadn't made plans for every eventuality.

Is it Davin who is on the Brits' payroll? Why not, he thinks. They have managed to infiltrate the movement at all levels. Why not Davin? After all, we've all had the offers, covert, overt, slyly, openly, sold with all the seductive guile of the British officer class, as well as its counterpoint, the brutal threats and tactics of their NCOs. The threats of blackmail. So why not Davin?

If he analyses Davin, he is cold-blooded, hungry, ambitious, and madly energetic, an introvert extrovert as he read somewhere, a description of a personality that fitted somebody like Davin. Power is what drives Davin. The hoarding of so much money being a manifestation of that power, particularly in periods of calm, like now. If holding power is his game, why not be the ultimate power broker? Turn the movement inside out, divert the hounds away from the problem, to not only save his life but also just for the hell of it, for what greater power can there be?

Eamon does not say anything to Mary as they move to the terrace for some lunch, a tortilla for him, a salad for Mary. They watch the faint clouds of smoke rising from the mountains, like an engineering version of a Papal election, he thinks. The terrace is not busy; most of the Spanish seem to lunch in one of the two restaurants. They sit by the stone balustrade that separates them from the lawn.

'Any news?' Mary asks.

'I've not checked since yesterday. I suppose I better. You know how Iggy can change his mind.'

Mary laughs. 'How long can you risk his mood if you're not in regular contact?'

'It's not easy to find a public call box, not since mobile phones became so popular.'

'We've done what he asked us to do. He signed us off.'

'That was a few days ago. I can't believe he sent us just for that. I'll phone this afternoon and leave another message. He put us at a big risk, if what he claims about Griffin is true. Griffin might have decided not to take a risk. It would have been easy enough to kill us and dump us out at sea. That must happen around here.' Eamon sips some water. His stomach has settled down, the bloated feeling has gone, as have the cramps, a sign he is over the strain, for now. 'I don't want to keep going over the whys and wherefores, except that he is on to something and I don't think he has told me the whole story. I've looked at it sideways, back, front, upside down.'

'He has a reason, though.'

'There is always a reason where he's concerned. Nothing is ever done without purpose.'

'It's not unusual us not being put in the picture. Remember the need-to-know basis? It didn't bother you then.'

'I'm not alone in my doubts, am I?'

'No,' Mary admits.

'When that happened in the past, I was in the loop. I knew the background. I don't this time, and I suppose that fuels my apprehension, my suspicions. In those days, even if I wasn't aware, I had a pretty shrewd notion why we were doing something. But none of this adds up. Unless he wants to muscle in and take over the whole operation.'

Mary is shocked. 'You can't mean that.'

'Why not?' Eamon tells her how he thinks it might be, that Davin will have control, but it will be a franchise operation, where he retains the business but subs out the running of it for a share of the profits. While Mary digests this, Eamon becomes aware of how refulgent the sea is and puts his dark glasses on. 'Why not?' he repeats. 'Where else would he go? Why not, I guess is what he thought. We are amassing as much cash as quickly as we can. He has plenty of experience and the right people to enforce it for him to run a deal like that at arms length. We're not getting anything like what we used to get from the States. I know we don't have the expenditure, at least not as much anyway on the arms. We run intelligence on people, keep the troops happy, or happier anyway by keeping them busy. We plan, and we extract cash from every legitimate area and continue to seek funds where we can. Knock out banks. What's the difference between that and running a franchise for a drug runner? I mean, it's not a moral question any more, is it?'

Mary is silent as their food is served. She thanks the waiter in Spanish and is rewarded with a smile of devotion, Eamon notices. As she eats her salad, a breeze whips around them bringing the now familiar coolness to the afternoon heat, matching Eamon's sombre, brooding mood.

'Let me try to understand you,' Mary says. 'He has sent us here to confirm what he has heard. There is a racket run by Fernando Griffin. He reports to Michael Donnellan, who has Hugh O'Neill working for him. All three have a very good reason for upsetting things, all have a motive for revenge. Fernando probably feels he was let down, left on his own in Cuba and had to make his way back. So he's pissed off, for a whole load of reasons, going back to when he was kept hanging around. I know what that feels like,' Mary says with a flash of anger. 'Anyway, these three have excellent reasons for using the money to fund TIRA.

They have a political motive in that they don't like the concessions made in the Good Friday Agreement, and they are not the only people in the Movement to think like that. As well, they see the release of prisoners and must feel they have been left out to dry. No amnesty for them, they are still on the wanted list. Above all, they feel betrayed by Iggy. They hate his guts, belong to the very long list of those who have every reason to want him locked up or killed.'

'So far, so good. All plausible,' Eamon concedes.

'Why then is there anything odd in what we've done? We have confirmed what he suspected, haven't we? From time to time, we've gone outside of the box on operations. After all, you did exactly that when you sent me off with Flaherty because you didn't know who else to trust. Maybe that is all he is doing this time.'

'Maybe.'

'I think you should make contact.'

'You're right. I am probably letting my imagination get the better of me.'

Early evening they walk through the gardens of the Parador and descend to the seafront below the battlements, on to the path around the fort that runs beside the sea. The walk is popular, with men and women walking briskly.

'Tell me,' Mary says, linking her arm through his, 'how far back you and Iggy go. You never have told me.'

'I met up with him when we were in Magilligan Camp. Both of us were lifted under the internment. I don't know much about his private life. He keeps it very secret, he's married and he has two daughters, I think. We made our way through the ranks in the mid 70s, but I could never say I was close to Iggy, never knew what made him tick. I reported directly to him. To be fair, when you worked for him, he gave you all the support you needed.'

'I'll bet he did,' Mary says angrily.

Eamon ignores this. 'Even when he told me he was going to get me bounced off unless I wanted to resign first, he made it convincing. For all that I worked closely with him for the best part of ten years, there was always a niggle in the back of my mind. Nothing I could put my finger on, but a doubt that would never go away entirely. Maybe because I'm never sure where I stand with him. I read somewhere that is the hallmark of a good leader. Iggy was never the man to inspire devotion, not his way, always kept people edgy, uncomfortable. Fear is his weapon, oh yes, in buckets.'

They pass the seawater swimming pools with the damp sandy floors, the tiny strips of sand between the rocks still wet from the sea. The sun worshippers have reclaimed the tiny beaches now the tide is out, 'Well,' Mary says briskly, 'you must have done an audit, a trail check on him. We do it for everybody, don't we?'

They pause as a couple of men round the point walking rapidly. Eamon waits until they are well past them. They stop to sit on the wall and look down on another seawater pool beside the sea, where an elderly woman in swimsuit and cap, sits on the edge and dangles her feet in the water.

'We do.' Eamon pauses. 'But nobody has ever done one on Davin, or if they have it has stayed well hidden. He was always at the centre of the things, the enforcer of security. It just did not cross anybody's radar. Something about belling the cat, I suppose. The old conundrum – who spies on the spies?'

'I can't believe that.'

'Unless it has happened during the past ten years. It never did in my day, mainly because there never seemed to be time. Those audits were always instigated at Iggy's behest.'

'I think we are in serious trouble,' Mary says calmly. 'We're wide open. He can pin Griffin's dirty racket on us.'

'And a lot more.'

CHAPTER 11

They decide to have dinner in the trattoria, a separate building in the hotel grounds. While Mary reserves a table, Eamon walks by himself. At seven in the evening, the heat bounces off the walls of the fort, even in the shade he finds he is sweating. Going down the hill, he walks slowly, casual but alert; by now he has decided their watchers are as much babysitters as jailers, depending on how you want to look at it. Past the beach, still crowded even though it is in shade now the sun has gone behind the fort. He crosses the street, ambles past a café crowded with aperitif drinkers, goes on and turns left towards a shopping area where he had registered a public phone box a few days ago. Inside, with a pocketful of coins, he dials the emergency number in Ireland.

An answerphone clicks, a woman who sounds old, Eamon guesses, says in a broad accent, 'Are ye having gas? I knew I'd miss ye if ye rang and I only after going to town. Anyway, let me know when ye'll be back. All well here. Don't forget my postcard!'

Under the shower in the hotel, Eamon plays the message over again. He can't find anything in it, the signal is clear. Just stay in touch and let me know when you'll be back. Not that it does anything to reassure him. When he comes from the bathroom, drying himself, Mary puts her arms around him and kisses him. 'We're supposed to be on holiday,' she says, letting the silk sarong fall from her body, as her hand reaches down to fondle him.

The evening is glorious; the red globe of the sun sinks slowly, lighting up the mountains opposite and glistening on the beach below, crowded with late bathers. Their table in the trattoria is by a window. As they take their seats, Eamon has the peaceful wondrous feeling he has whenever they make love. He reaches for her hand, holds it a little tightly and strokes it. Across on the mountains, an explosion is rapidly followed by two others. They watch the smoke float slowly, lazily to the sky. At the mouth of the harbour, before the open sea, there is a small island, like a traffic sleeper, he thinks, as the boats full of tourists returning from trips along the coast skirt around it. A couple of speedboats roar across the aquamarine water, the trail of churned sea as white as jet streams across the sky. It is so tranquil, so calm, yet despite their lovemaking, for a moment he feels the tension return. Let it be, whatever it is, and enjoy this evening. I can do nothing now, he thinks. Events are out of my control.

Mary finishes ordering in her halting Spanish, although it pleases the waitress, who compliments her on her command of the language. 'I ordered a bottle of the *Alberiño,* the local wine. And we are having a fish dinner.'

'Fine. I like this, ordering food I don't know about. Like those cockles the other evening. I would never have ordered them, but I enjoyed them, much more than I thought I would.'

Slowly the trattoria begins to fill up. A table of three English people dominate the place with their loud voices, and one of them, an overweight red-faced man tries his Spanish on a waitress, who smiles politely as he attempts to make her understand him by raising his voice. Eamon thinks of the noisy kids at the swimming pool, wonders what it is about the English, why they are so loud, a relic of their days of Empire, perhaps. In time the food and drink makes the English table soporific and quieter. Eamon and Mary smile across the table. They swap part of their dishes, the delicious orange mussels, and what Eamon learns are called *anguillas*, little tiny eels. He tastes some of the octopus Mary ordered. He savours the local white wine, which is crisp and dry. Eamon had rarely drunk any alcohol, until Mary introduced him to the delights of wine. Or knew anything of women until Mary, he remembers. And allows himself a wry smile.

Mary pours the last of the bottle into their glasses. 'Will I order another one, or will we settle for a glass?'

'Whatever you like, I'm in your hands,' Eamon says, smiling fondly, so relaxed with the delicious food, the setting of the darkening harbour, the flashing of lights as the boats come and go, that he wonders why he was so het up only half an hour ago.

He manages to retain the smile, to keep eating as Fernando Griffin and another man, whom he can't see clearly, as he is behind Griffin, stand in the entrance of the trattoria waiting to be seated. Griffin looks at Eamon, nods and smiles faintly. After a brief discussion, the manager leads them to the far side of the trattoria, away from the sea view, to seats at a table on the mezzanine floor. Clever, Eamon thinks, with a clear view of the entrance and quick access to the emergency exit. He now sees the other man is middle-aged, bald, tanned. Maybe it is a coincidence, he thinks. To cover his confusion, he resumes telling Mary about the *The Feast of the Goat.*

As he does so, he keeps an eye on the far table. If Mary has spotted Griffin, she is not letting on. He can't see him properly as the table is partially obscured by a pillar. They order coffee while Griffin and his companion talk and eat very slowly. There is a bottle of wine on their table, but little is drunk.

'All right,' Mary says eventually, 'who do you think is with my admirer Fernando?'

'Not sure. It's like being flung back into a London Particular. The more I see, the less I understand.'

'Do you think you should let Iggy know?'

'I don't know. I suspect he already knows. Let's get out of here.'

They walk along the battlement, looking down on where they walked earlier. In the dark, weak lights faintly illuminate the path. The harbour mouth is dotted with small boats, they drift around the island, their lights flashing and vanishing. Floodlit, the fort is magnificent, towering in the surrounding dark. A boat rounds the island, and then stops, the lights go out. Is there any significance Eamon wonders, or has it dropped anchor for the night? They stroll on as he tries to figure out what the arrival of Griffin means.

'It might not be anything,' Mary says. 'He likes luxury. It's on the coast and he probably comes here to get away from his shitty little chalet.'

'Not as often as he does the Reis Católicos. They didn't know him in the trattoria, he wasn't fawned over.'

'Let's walk to the top of the fort and look out to sea.' Mary takes his hand. They stroll to the top of the grounds, to the original fort, the battlement lined with cannon facing the sea. Eamon wishes he had his iPod; he needs music now to help him to think. Some Mozart, possibly the Piano Concerto Number 9. Mary is silent as they walk on; they stop to look down over the moonlit bay, the peace of the night broken only by the game of basketball under the floodlights in the court beside the fort, as the players call the moves and encourage each other. Eamon is thinking they should leave now, get in the car and go, but where to? And if Griffin and his mob want them, they have them trapped – all they need to do is block the entrance to the Parador car park.

'So is this a holiday or are you here on business?' The voice from behind him is familiar. He is stopped from turning around by a hand, firm rather than forceful, on his shoulder. 'Better stay facing the sea and admire the view. You too, Mary.'

'Fernando Griffin,' Mary spits it out.

'I don't think you would ever forget me,' Griffin says cockily. Eamon finds his stomach knots in fear. 'Tell me, *señor*, while you both hand over your mobiles, have you been looking for me?'

The hand on his shoulder tightens perceptibly. 'No. We're on holidays, as I told you when we met up a few days ago. Look, what the hell is going on?' Eamon says angrily, hoping he has hidden the fear.

There is a rapid exchange of Spanish, none of which Eamon understands. He passes his mobile over, Mary hers. Another voice says in heavily accented English, 'Spread your legs, and put your hands on the guard rail.' Two hands frisk him, calmly, expertly. Eamon hands over the room and car keys, the loose coins, standard practice to remove anything that might be useful as a weapon. He has left the guns hidden in their suitcases, but he's sure they have been found.

'Well now you've got all that,' Eamon says, still angry, protesting. 'Maybe you'll tell me what this is all about?' He tries to sound angry as well as worried.

'What is going on indeed,' Fernando Griffin says rapidly. 'Maybe we go somewhere more appropriate, where we can talk in private.'

The hand turns Eamon around. He sees two figures in front, glances over his shoulder and sees Griffin, flanked by another man in a leather jacket with his hair tied in a ponytail, spots a shadowy figure behind them. Five in all, he thinks, with God knows how many others in reserve. He feels a gun prod the small of his back.

They walk back towards the Parador, slowly, while Griffin and ponytail chat in Spanish. It looks very normal, a group of people walking and talking. In front in the clearer light, Eamon sees two women emerge from the darkness and join them. Seven, he thinks and his fear grows into terror. He is cursing himself for being so lax, for being lulled into taking a holiday when they should have got the hell out of Spain as soon as they sighted Michael Donnellan. They make their way across the car park, up the steps of the entrance, into the foyer. The receptionists are busy. A porter nods. Griffin speaks to him in Spanish. They mount the stone stairs and at the top are ushered into a large sitting room, part of a suite, with a bedroom off it.

A figure sits in an armchair. Eamon can't see who it is.

'Right,' says Michael Donnellan, casually as though they are old friends meeting again after a long time, 'Take a seat, Eamon.'

In the large room, with views over the grounds of the Parador and the harbour beyond, Eamon and Mary are directed to two upright chairs. Once they are seated, the curtains and windows are closed; two lamps are switched on, angled so they can't see clearly who is behind the light. Eamon has recognised Donnellan and Griffin, he hears other people moving about.

'You still like the high life I see, Michael,' Eamon says lightly. He wonders if their hands will be bound behind them. The chairs lend themselves to it; he assumes that is why they have been ordered to sit in them.

'While I bow to no man in my belief in a Republican Socialist Ireland, Eamon, I can see no reason to go about the task in tatters and half-starved.'

'This is business,' Fernando Griffin snaps. He is very edgy, tense, unlike Donnellan, who appears very much at his ease.

CHAPTER 12

Michael Donnellan moves into the arc of light. He takes a seat in a comfortable chair, places his hands on the arms, and smiles. Eamon looks at him, is surprised to discover that he looks no different to the last time he saw him in London almost twenty years ago. He is slim, dapper, and has all his brown hair; he does not seem wrinkled or even lined.

'Okay, Eamon, tell me about yourself and about Mary, whom I have not seen since she abused my hospitality way back when.'

'If your idea of hospitality is locking someone up in a storeroom, then you deserve to have it abused,' Mary retorts, evenly, calmly, to Eamon's relief.

Donnellan smiles, puts his fingers together under his chin and says slowly, 'I hear you took the rap for all that, Eamon. You were the man fingered when Flaherty blew himself up and Hugh vanished.'

'I was. Yes.'

'What did you do? It can't have been easy, not after all you had given to the Cause.'

'Change is never easy, Michael. But it had to be done. I went back to teaching. In time, Mary and I got to know one another and got married. We bought a house and to help pay the mortgage, started to do B&B, and we made something of a success. That's about it.'

'Put out to grass. Or in your case put out to campus, I suppose. You're very modest, Eamon. I hear you've become a successful businessman, not to mention scooping the pool by marrying Mary.'

Eamon says nothing. He is not sure if Donnellan is trying to goad him.

'Of course the salary of a lecturer is not that much is it? Despite that, you have bought not one but two B&Bs, a couple of other houses, as well as a delightful – so I am told – holiday home in county Donegal. Some of you guys who retired early did very well.'

Eamon is impassive. He is remembering the interrogation training.

Never offer anything, remain silent when provoked, and speak only when there is no choice.

'Some of us did not get treated at all well, Eamon,' Michael Donnellan says slowly, with a wide generous smile, so disarming, Eamon thinks, it almost makes you want to put your hand in your pocket and give him all you have got. 'And none of us, not even you with your portfolio of property, your thriving business, no doubt a generous pension from your former employers, can match the wealth of our old friend and comrade in arms, one Ignatius Leo Davin, Piggy Iggy himself. Who, from all I hear, is a multimillionaire and goes on coining it legally, as well as illegally, from all the nefarious methods he continues to employ. Still running people on covert operations, intelligence gathering, despite all the bullshit about "a cessation of violence," as I believe it's called.' Donnellan leans forward slightly. 'Anyway, enough of that. Tell me Eamon, why are you here?'

'We're on our holidays, Michael, that's all. Nothing sinister. I'm no longer involved in anything, nor is Mary. We are just a couple of hard working people.'

'Not involved at all? Never in touch with Iggy?'

'Not often. I bump into him very occasionally. Our paths rarely cross these days.'

'Why did you come to Santiago de Compostela?'

'The same reason most people do. To see it, and to enquire about walking the *Camino*, maybe next year. To have a look around Galicia.'

'I see. Just a couple of tourists?'

'That's right.'

'That isn't how you look to my friend Fernando over there. He's convinced that you are anything but tourists. Everywhere he goes, there you are. From the moment he checks into his hotel in Santiago, you are with him all the time.'

'We happened to bump into Fernando a couple of times. I don't know if you have been in the hotel in Santiago when he's there. If you have been, you'll know it's hard not to notice his arrival and his presence about the place. The rest was just coincidence.'

Donnellan does not answer for a moment, shrugs his shoulders slightly and smiles. 'You'll understand why I was curious when you and Mary arrive in Santiago de Compostela, book into the Hotel Reis Católicos. Why you then make some very obvious efforts to follow

Fernando. In fact you were so amateurish, you almost lured him into believing that is what you are, a couple of innocent tourists. Even when you turned up at the hotel in Villagarcía, he was inclined to think it was just a coincidence. Then you are there on the beach behind his house, looking at his speedboat. He takes Mary out on his boat, and he knows you are not tourists when she refuses him, when we all know that Mary never says no to a man.'

Eamon pats Mary's arm, is relieved to sense she is aware that Donnellan is seeking to provoke either or both of them. Eamon listens very carefully. After a few moments, when the room is silent, Donnellan says in his bantering tone, 'Well, you can imagine how much Fernando's *amour propre* is bruised by Mary's rejection. He starts to think that she only likes gay men, as he has heard about her fling with Hugh O'Neill when she was supposed to guard him in the safe house in London. Then he finds out that you're her husband, Eamon, and he just gives up, shakes his head, says this is one crazy woman, who likes only gays and old men.'

Again, there is a pause as Michael Donnellan surveys them, his face wreathed in a friendly smile. Mary and Eamon say nothing. Donnellan lets the silence hang for a while.

'No little tryst with Fernando on the boat, which would have been one method of maybe getting something from him. So, when Fernando tells me all this, when he says you took photographs of his chalet, Eamon, while he very generously gave Mary a trip around the bay, you went and looked around his property. Of course, he's suspicious. Then he thinks, well maybe you are no more than curious. You do the right thing, asking about the price of property along the coast. Last thing he sees you walking along the beach and that seems to be it, at least for the next few hours.

'However, Eamon, when you break into somebody's house, just to take a brief peek, and leave without any signs of disturbance, apart from the cut in the wire fence and the path through the woods you took to get to the house, that suggests somebody with an interest that is more than the normal curiosity about property. You turning up on the closed circuit, well, it gives Fernando a shock, a big shock. Then you have gone! Not a sight of you anywhere. When he tells me all this, I have to agree with him, it is strange. But as you seemed to have disappeared, well we'll leave it alone and just be more careful in future.' Donnellan sits back; he pours a glass of water and drinks lightly.

'Next thing you are here. Fernando remembers that Mary has asked him plenty of questions about where else you might go on holiday, that he has told her go along the coast. You can imagine his shock when he goes for dinner tonight and finds the pair of you sitting almost on guard duty by the entrance.'

'There is nothing in it, just coincidence and curiosity,' Eamon says. He is sweating now. He knows all he is doing is trying to buy some time before they kill both of them. That the only reason it hasn't happened already is because Michael Donnellan wants to find out as much as he can, if this trip has other implications – are they from the Movement, or the Brits.

'You seemed to have a lot of help while you were in Santiago de Compostela. And other people at Arousa. A bit much that, to tell me it is a coincidence, Eamon.' Michael Donnellan continues to smile.

'Let me have him. I make him talk,' Griffin snaps.

'I don't think we need to come to that – well not yet.'

'Okay, it was not right to take a look around the chalet. Just that old habits die hard, Michael.'

'Christ almighty! No wonder Iggy wanted you out if that's the best you can come up with, Eamon.' Donnellan crosses his legs and smiles again. 'Now I wouldn't like anybody to be treated as I was, tried and convicted in my absence, without a chance to argue my case. To be forced like I am, to run and hide for the rest of my days, assuming I can stay out of the way of the hit squads sent after me.'

Eamon says quickly. 'I'm not here to try to find you Michael.'

'That is a relief. Isn't it, Fernando?' Donnellan says sarcastically.

'Give him to me. I have had enough of this crap and bullshit.'

Donnellan ignores Griffin. Eamon suspects this is part of their method, agreed before they picked them up. 'Now we can do this in one of two ways, Eamon, you know that. We have, shall we say, the Fernando route, or my gentler way. I have some acquaintances around here, who if they think, let alone discover, that you have been sniffing around trying to find out about matters they consider to be their business and nobody else's, won't hesitate to remove the threat.' He smiles again and says in a chatty friendly tone, 'Or we can proceed by you telling me why you're here.'

The room is very quiet. All Eamon can hear is the muffled slam of a car door down in the car park. He is trying to decide how much he can get away with telling Donnellan. And even if he tells him all he knows, will it be enough to save them? Maybe he can save Mary.

'We're here on holidays, Michael,' he says quietly. 'Hard to believe but that is it.' He is sweating. Cold slimy perspiration runs down from his armpits, it is across the back of his neck up into his hairline, he can feel it on his forehead and upper lip, the palms of his hands are clammy, slippery. He has an urge to urinate, that inconvenient pressure in his bladder that comes from time to time, is intense. Not that, he prays, don't let me piss myself. Not in here.

'Eamon, I don't have the patience I once had. Do I really need to show you the CCTV footage? To tell you about the changes of cars, the couple who were watching from the beach while you did your spot of breaking and entering? If Mary is also on her holidays, then why was she sitting in a car to pick you up when you left the house? Or is that some sacred ritual, part of your married life?' Donnellan pauses. 'Come on, Eamon! Who sent you?'

'If you want to talk to me alone, I may be able to help you.'

'Good man, Eamon. I thought you would see it my way.' Donnellan is suddenly affable again. 'Tell all now, mind.'

Eamon looks at Mary. He peers into the light, sees Griffin and a couple of figures standing behind him. 'I'll talk to you on my own. Mary is not involved.'

'Eamon,' Michael Donnellan says with infinite courtesy, 'I am the one in charge. You don't have a choice. Now start talking. Mary has been with you all the way.'

Eamon takes a deep breath, tries to control his voice, feels the increasing urge to piss but refuses to ask if he can use the bathroom. He says, and is relieved how calm he sounds, 'Davin asked me to see if I could take a look over here. You know we have zero tolerance on drugs. He told me the supply in the South had grown exponentially, was exceeding demand, prices are dropping and he hears it is because there is a new player on the scene. This is affecting things, the stability is threatened. We, being the guardians of such matters, are losing our credibility with the electorate. We are supposed to keep the lid on that can of shit. I don't know how close you keep in touch with politics back home. Sinn Fein is growing in strength. An increase in drugs could affect our electoral chances. He told me he had information that Fernando Griffin was the link.'

'Why Fernando?'

'He has been missing since he was in Colombia.' Eamon notices Donnellan raise a hand as if to tell Griffin to stay silent. 'No word or sign from him. Then suddenly he is rumoured to be running Colombian drugs into the country.'

'And your conclusion is?'

'It's fairly obvious he is involved in some way. How big or small I can't say.'

Donnellan smiles again, nods his head in agreement. Eamon thinks, he's very relaxed, he is not really probing. He already knows all of this.

'Let me get this straight, Eamon. You've been retired for what, about fifteen years. No involvement at all?'

'Nothing active, no. I work at election time, deliver leaflets, stuff envelopes, drive the old folk to the polling station, and put posters up. That's all.'

'And Mary?'

'I'm the same,' Mary says firmly.

Eamon holds her hand, grips it briefly, and gets a squeeze in return. He thinks, I wouldn't give any odds on our getting out of here.

'You haven't been doing anything else?'

'Some research, writing some policy papers, on finance, social policy.'

'That is what I do also,' Mary chips in.

'No doubt you are a great help with investment advice,' Donnellan says evenly, with a hint of sarcasm.

The door opens after a light double knock. Eamon briefly sees the dim light from the corridor, and notes one figure slip in.

'Let's recap then,' says Donnellan. 'You're both out of it. Not involved at all, not in the political scene, out of the public gaze. All you two are is a couple of policy wonks. Just quietly getting on with your new lives. Suddenly, fairly recently, up pops Iggy and he says, "Eamon, old stock, I have a little job for you. I want you to come out of retirement, go back in the field and find out if Fernando Griffin, who has been missing for a few years, is somehow involved in running drugs through Spain." Have I got that right?'

'Yes.'

'Did it not strike you as a bit odd? That you would be rusty – as we saw only too clearly a few nights ago – not fit, not very able at all. Did it not occur to you that your old friend Iggy must have had plenty of better-trained people he could use?'

Eamon does not answer.

'So what did Piggy Iggy tell you?' Donnellan says slowly.

'That he wanted somebody not known to Griffin. As I have never had any dealings with him, nor has Mary, we stood a good chance of having a look without being spotted.'

'Was it only Fernando you were to look for? Nobody else?'

'Only Fernando Griffin,' Eamon says. 'You know why. Because of his Spanish background, he speaks the language like a native. There are the connections in Cuba and Colombia. I could see his reasoning, why he linked him to the drug running.'

'Did he want to know if he was on his own, a renegade?'

'He didn't say as much, but the inference was that he would have other folk with him.' Eamon says as casually as he can. 'I mean, he has a nickname, Flash Gordon, known as a big spender, very ostentatious with his money.'

'On that basis, there must be a hell of a lot of drug runners, Eamon,' Michael Donnellan says easily. He hasn't batted an eyelid, Eamon sees, and again he has the distinctly uncomfortable feeling that Michael Donnellan knows all they have done. This has the feel of a show trial. Is this something Davin has set up? Some link between Donnellan and him? He can find no obvious reason, nor anything obscure.

'Who else knows about this operation? Who authorised it?'

'I was briefed by Iggy. I report only to him.'

'Come on, Eamon!' Donnellan says sharply, all affability gone. 'Operations like this have to be sanctioned by the Army Council. Even Piggy Iggy knows that.'

'It's as I've told you. Davin briefed me, he funded it. I report to him and him only.'

Donnellan digests this, takes his time, he sips some more water. 'Were you briefed by Davin himself? Who came calling with his message?'

Eamon thinks this bit is okay. I can tell him what happened. Which he does, starting from Davin's legman jumping him on the ferry, to the briefing in the safe house conducted by the anorak McAllister.

Donnellan listens intently. 'Did it not occur to you that Davin might be on a flier? Trying his luck, chancing his arm? Doing it off his own back?'

Eamon does not answer. He has thought of little else since his meeting with Davin.

'If it did, Eamon,' his tone is soft again, 'if it crossed your mind, and I'd bet my last euro on that being the case. We all knew that Eamon Delaney was the Philosopher King, the brains who masterminded so many of the best propaganda campaigns, who brought a razor-sharp intellect to our thinking. Always very efficient and clinical, the consummate operator is Eamon Delaney, who always covers every eventuality in his preparations. The thing that is troubling me, Eamon, is that having worked out that this must be a little scheme for the benefit of Iggy and nobody else, why you went along with it?'

'Iggy and I go back a long way.' Eamon is groping his way now, trying to gauge what Donnellan wants to hear, how he can divert him. He clings to a smidgen of hope that because they have survived this long, they are somehow more valuable alive – at least for now.

From behind the lights a man says, 'You were always the one for personal favours, weren't you, Eamon?'

For a moment, it does not register with Eamon who is speaking.

But Mary says, 'Hugh O'Neill. So it was you in the restaurant.'

'Well done, girl,' Hugh says in his London accent. He comes into the arc of the light and Eamon sees the big bald man who had come in with Griffin. 'After all these years and without my hair, you still recognise me.'

'Hard to forget an ex-lover, isn't it?' Michael Donnellan says slyly.

Eamon sees he is watching them both, waiting for a reaction. He wonders why he has brought Hugh into the interrogation now, and decides Donnellan just wants to keep them on the hop, an old inquisitor's tactic.

'Eamon,' says Michael Donnellan very quietly, seriously, 'you know the rules, for all I know, you wrote most of them. They explicitly state that nobody can embark on a solo mission, or any type of operation for any reason, without Army Council approval. Personal favours do not come into it.' He sits back, and again he lets the silence linger. There are muffled voices in the corridor that vanish. Otherwise, there is only the faint hum of the air conditioning, a nervous clearing of a throat. Eamon wonders how much longer he can stave off the needs of his bladder.

'I don't think you're telling me the truth, Eamon. Quite the opposite in fact. You're trying to lead me away from it.'

'I've answered all your questions, Michael. What I have told you is what happened. It is unorthodox. I accept that. But we are in an unorthodox period. We have a ceasefire. There have been no operations for a long time. The old rules are maybe not as applicable now.'

'Eamon, you have the mind of a Jesuit, full of sophistry, a casuist to your fingertips. You have done what we all do, told me some of what happened, but not all of it. We don't have the time to bat this around all night. So either you tell me everything, or I'll have to suggest to some of them that we discuss this with you and Mary, but in separate rooms. It's about time she and Hugh renewed their old relationship, I think.'

Donnellan stands up. 'You come with me, Eamon. Let's see if Mary will be more reasonable with Hugh, and if not with him, perhaps Fernando. In their ways, both of them can be very persuasive.'

Eamon feels the resistance drain away from him. He stands up, takes hold of Mary's hand for a second, before he is ushered into the adjoining bedroom. Inside the door, he cannot help himself. Piss streams down his trouser leg, cascades into his sock and shoe as the stain spreads quickly across his stone coloured chinos.

'Messy fucker,' Griffin snarls. 'Why didn't you ask to use the john?' He shoves Eamon roughly into the bathroom. 'Use the fucking thing, take a crap while you're at it. I don't want to wipe up your shit as well.'

In the bathroom, he looks for a window, but knows there is not one. Quickly he removes his shoes and socks, his trousers and underpants, rinses them, sponges himself and dresses himself in the wet shoes, trousers and underwear. He finds he is shaking. He barely makes it to the lavatory in time to void his bowels. Griffin has kept the door slightly ajar.

Eamon tries to think, to put together enough to buy some time. He decides all that matters is to save Mary. He counts the few positives, is relieved that Griffin is in here. He has no doubt that Griffin would torture, maybe rape Mary if he wanted to, if he thought it would serve his purposes. He does not know if what they said about her and Hugh is true, he thinks it is just a tactic, as he is sure they have no secrets. In any case, this is not the immediate problem. He cleans himself as best he can.

It is a large square bedroom, with two double beds at the far end. The wooden floor is polished to a high gleam, the furniture heavy and solid.

Michael Donnellan surveys him, looks at the piss-stained trousers. 'The joys of old age, Eamon,' he says slowly. 'You'll have to stay like that. None of my trousers will fit you.'

'I have a spare pair in my bedroom. While you're turning that over, one of your guys could bring me back some.'

Donnellan nods, speaks in Spanish, one of the men leaves. From the speed of his Spanish and his pronunciation, Eamon surmises Donnellan speaks it fluently, which suggests he has lived here for some time.

'We better make you comfortable, Eamon. We might be here for a long time,' Donnellan says. He goes to the window, peeks through the side of the heavy curtain. 'You are alone here?'

'As far as I know, we are.'

'What about the people in Santiago and Arousa? Who are they?'

'I don't know. Somebody Iggy was able to use.'

'His reach is a long one, it seems.' Donnellan closes the curtain. 'You're not bullshitting me, are you? Iggy has got somebody watching your back? Babysitting you for Iggy?'

'If they are, I haven't seen them. There has not been contact with anybody since we left Arousa.'

This seems to satisfy Donnellan. 'Eamon, we'll start again, and this time I want the lot, from the beginning. One chance only. If you fuck around…'

Eamon nods. He clenches his hands, his buttocks, his legs, in case he betrays his fear.

CHAPTER 13

'We change places this time, Mary.' Hugh O'Neill takes her into a small bedroom just along the corridor. This is a man's room, she sees, with trousers and shirts scattered on the bed. She notices Hugh's expression of mild distaste, remembers how tidy he was, neat, fastidious almost. 'Sorry about this, it's not my room.' He picks up an armful of clothes and puts them in a wardrobe. 'Sit there, please.'

Mary says calmly, although she is not at all calm, 'I often wondered what happened to you, Hugh. That was a terrible mess, wasn't it? Eamon was very concerned about you too.'

Hugh shrugs, he seems indifferent. 'It was a long time ago. You just have to get on with things. Like now. You tell me why you're here. If you do, I can keep you safe and away from our mate, Flash, as you call him. Bloody name suits him.'

'Flash Gordon,' Mary says helpfully. She detects the note of disdain about Griffin. She thinks they could not be more different. The puritan Hugh, the garish Griffin.

'You need to tell me everything, Mary,' Hugh says seriously. 'These jokers won't mess around. I have not forgotten what you did for me in London. Without it, I wouldn't have been able to get away. I'm on your side, my love, but I must have the lot.'

Mary tries to gauge him, she decides he is serious, he is scared – and why wouldn't he be as he's been on the run for what, the last twenty-five years? She has no idea what they will do to Eamon, except she knows how the Movement treats informers, and she is in no doubt that Donnellan and Hugh will behave in the same way.

'I can't add much to what Eamon told you. I am sure Iggy has some other plans, we're here because he needs us to get to you and Michael.'

'So what about Davin?' Hugh says suddenly, sharply.

Mary decides there is no point in hiding anything from them. She tells him how Eamon simply vanished one Monday while she was down with her niece in Limerick, of how she had no word of him for three or more days, how frantic she was with worry.

Hugh digests this for a moment and says quickly, 'Why do you think Davin wanted to find Griffin? Does he think Michael and me are in it as well?'

'Yes.'

Hugh is silent, does another length of the bedroom, his rubber-soled shoes flapping and squeaking slightly on the wooden floor. 'How do you know this?'

'Because Eamon told me. Iggy believes you and Michael and Flash Gordon are using the drug money to fund the True IRA. That is what this is all about.'

'Why didn't Eamon tell us that?'

'I don't know. Maybe he thought he could get away without doing so. You know he's loyal to people, Hugh.' She pauses, trying to see if it affects him, if it is something he remembers about Eamon. Carefully she says, 'If he had done what Iggy wanted him to do, you would have been killed as soon as you had come offstage.'

'I nearly fucking was. Some bastard came at me.'

'Eamon never sent me the message to put the plan in action. Iggy wanted you dead. He was going to make a martyr of you. As Iggy saw it, you were an embarrassment. He put Eamon under a hell of a lot of pressure to kill you. Eamon didn't do it. So it isn't just me you owe, Hugh. Eamon saved your life as well.'

Hugh laughs, a short sardonic laugh. 'Sure I do. He sent me on the suicide mission to top Mrs T.'

'As I understood it, Hugh, you volunteered.'

'That's enough. We're here to find out what this is all about, Mary. Now tell me everything about you, from when you left London to now. If you convince me, we can stay here, just you and me.' His face sets, she sees the hardness, the coldness in his eyes. 'Or Flash bloody Gordon will take over. And I won't stop him.' Hugh stares at her as he lets the silence build up.

Mary tells him all she knows while Hugh listens impassively; a tape recorder is running all the time. When she has finished, he asks her a few more questions, and then he goes back over it again before he summarises what she has told him, checking he has all the salient points. 'Okay. Okay.' He opens the door, admits a couple, he speaks rapidly in Spanish, so fast Mary can't catch more than a word. He leaves them there, the man at the door, the woman sitting in the chair, both of them still, watchful, good at guarding people because they're used to it, she thinks.

When he returns, Hugh paces up and down the small bedroom, like a caged animal. She remembers how he was famous on the Greek island for his murderously fast hikes across the mountains in the heat of the day and she sees the same restless, pent-up energy.

'Did you really recognise me when I came into the trattoria?' he says unexpectedly.

'Not immediately. There was something about you that struck a bell. When you walked past our table, your gait seemed very familiar, and then I watched you eat, and I was sure it was you. I suppose when you spend three of four days closeted with somebody you notice things.'

Mary remembers he was inclined to silence. That he was a drinker, near enough an alcoholic. She sees no sign of it now, nor is he sucking cigarette smoke deep down into his lungs, as though he could not get enough. He is tubbier and bald of course, yet as soon as she looked up and saw him following Griffin across the restaurant, she knew it was Hugh. She hadn't told Eamon. Had not told him because she suddenly knew they were in a trap, there was no way out. She feared that if they left immediately, tried to get away in the car, they would not get very far. She knows this is Griffin's patch. If they meant to get them, they would have covered all the exits, the possible ways of escape.

'Did you ever think of me, Hugh?'

'Sometimes.' He is curt, not unkind, preoccupied. 'Of course I did. I had a lot to think about. Mostly I thought about God. Poor Godfrey.' He is silent.

Mary says nothing, she realises how naïve she was back then, wanting to believe that Hugh only stayed with God, as he always called him, because he was protecting him. She knows now that Hugh loved him.

'He tackled Flaherty to protect me. I should have done more. I might have saved him.'

'What happened?' Mary says gently.

Hugh stops pacing up and down and sits beside her on the bed. 'After I got out of the club, after I flattened that gorilla, I made it into town. I knew my way about the place. I mean London is my manor, as we used to say. God always liked to plan everything. "Let's have plan A, old love," he'd say, "And plan B. And just in case we end up in the merde, old love, we better stick plan C up our sleeve as well." Although I never told him anything about my past, he guessed. So we had a number of fall-backs if ever things went pear-shaped. I had a couple of numbers to call, messages he left with his friends. One of them was we would meet up by the Royal Festival Hall. He'd park by the old Shell building about nine in the evening.' Hugh stops, is silent. He stares ahead at the abstract painting on the wall, a series of shades of black and grey that mean nothing to Mary.

'Well I got there, and hung around with the beggars, the down-and-outs and winos under the bridge. I had been living rough, in a squat, moving on every few hours. I fitted in with them, one more scruffy bastard made no difference. I had been there the previous night and he hadn't shown up. I didn't even know if he'd got my message. Anyway, I'd decided to give it one more go because I didn't want to become known as a regular. I hung around, watching the arguments and the fights. But God, bless his good heart, turned up. He had a new motor, had managed to get some cash together. Had arranged somewhere to stay, a flat in Eastbourne. We were all set to lie low then make our way back to Europe.' Hugh pauses, shakes his head. 'Then I made a stupid mistake. That was the worst thing. I was a heavy smoker, so was God. Neither of us had any cigarettes left. So I nipped across to Waterloo station to buy some fags. When I came out and got to the steps, I saw God wrestling with a man. He shouted to me, "Run Hugh! Run!" I panicked. I mean, I didn't know who it was. It could have been the Old Bill for all I knew. I'd just got back to the station, was about to jump on a train, when the bomb went off. Next day I found out it was Flaherty. Strange thing is I've never had a smoke since that evening. Never wanted one. In fact the thought of it makes me sick, makes me want to throw up.'

Mary says nothing. She takes his hand and gently strokes it.

'Well, I got out of Waterloo. The first train I could get on. Got off at the second station, doubled around, laid low. By then I was good at that. I got some work as a tyre fitter – you could always get a job in that trade. Worked in Basingstoke and Southampton to get some dosh, all I had was the twenty quid God gave me for the fags, I'd spent my emergency cash that you never found. I was skint.'

'And then you met Michael again.'

But Hugh has come out of his reverie. 'You sure you told me

everything? Not forgotten anything?'

'No. It's okay, Hugh. I know how it works.' Mary finds her mouth is dry. Her stomach gripes are bad. 'I need to use the loo. Woman's trouble.' She is grateful they left her small bag, where she keeps her emergency tampons.

Hugh says nothing. Goes to the bathroom to check it and emerges with a razor and towels, the glasses, anything she might fashion as a weapon to use on herself or him.

'I've left one small towel. I'll leave the door open. Sorry about the lack of privacy, but I can't take any chances.'

When she comes back to the bedroom, Mary says, softly. 'Thank you. It is very embarrassing.'

'Sure, sure,' Hugh says coldly. He resets a miniature tape recorder. 'From the beginning, Mary. How did you get out of London?' he pauses for a moment. 'And while we're there, how come you and Eamon got together?'

How indeed, Mary thinks, as she tries to sort out her emotions, disentangle the fear and worry about Eamon.

'They never gave me anything to do after your escape. After a few months, I became involved in Sinn Fein down in Limerick, where I was working. Eamon and I met during a by-election in Kerry. By then I'd heard that he was out on his ear. Like me. Anyway, we sort of fell in together. I found him much more fun than when I reported to him, I saw the man rather than the operator.'

Hugh laughs. 'We used to call Eamon the monk. He was never known to have been near a woman.'

Mary knows this is true, that she is the only woman Eamon has known, and that she had to initiate him. For a moment she forgets the danger, as she remembers his awkwardness, his innocence almost, that it was that vulnerability of his she liked so much, that and being able to reach him where once she had believed him beyond such things.

'Go on,' Hugh urges gently.

'We started to see more of one another. You know he likes classical music, so we met in Dublin, went to some concerts there. It was a slow thing, nothing fast. After a time it sort of felt right.' She says slightly archly, 'You know, probably like you and God.' It was that, she thinks, as well as the lonely life she led, still single at twenty-nine. Besides, she knew that her previous life, her involvement with the Movement, precluded a number of men, who if they had known of her background would have been understandably cautious, and if they did not, would have most likely felt cheated, deceived when they did discover the secrets of her past life. With Eamon, there was none of that baggage to worry about. They were in accord.

'We decided to take the plunge. We bought a house together, and because we couldn't afford the mortgage on what Eamon earned, we ran it as a B&B. We settled down, Hugh,' she says softly, 'in so far as people like us can ever go back to a normal life.'

'Yeah,' he says with feeling. 'Yeah, I can imagine.' His mobile trills, he speaks in Spanish and abruptly leaves the room.

Mary sits trying to ignore the stomach cramps that always come with her period. She wonders if they have any codeine, hers is in their bedroom in the toilet bag she uses for their medical travel pack.

Hugh comes back in. 'Okay Mary, Michael and Eamon have a lot to discuss, it's going to be a long night.' He hands her a small bottle of water. 'I want you to take a couple of these, they'll help you sleep.'

'I'll be all right. Just get me some codeine, I have cramps. There is a tube in our bedroom.'

'These won't do you any harm, Mary. All they do is send you to sleep for a few hours.' He sits beside her, puts the pills on the bed beside her. 'Just take them. Or else we'll be forced to make you.' He shrugs indifferently. 'It's up to you. We do it the easy way or the hard.'

Put like that, she thinks, there is no choice. She swallows the pills.

CHAPTER 14

Eamon sits on a couple of towels. Michael Donnellan says nothing for a long time, just stares, as though he is making up his mind what to do with him.

'How is Piggy Iggy these days, Eamon?' Donnellan says at last, casually, as if they are chatting about an old friend not seen for some time.

'Like I said, I have little to do with him. From what I hear, he is much the same, charging around. He holds the Movement together, Michael, keeps the wild men under control.'

'Not a man to cross, as we know.' He pauses. 'The only people who like Iggy are those who've never met him.'

Eamon shrugs. He watches Donnellan for a sign, a hint. 'Life is a little quieter now, he's had to adapt to that – we all have.'

'You know Iggy as well as anybody, Eamon. Both of you escaped from Magilligan, one of the more spectacular escapades, I recall. You swam out into Lough Foyle, where a boat picked you up and brought the pair of you ashore in Donegal, outside British waters. It had the press almost wetting themselves, not knowing whether to applaud the daredevil cheek or condemn the escape of dangerous terrorists. His closest ally on the Army Council, his counsellor; the one person to whom he always talked; you knew everything when Iggy was Chief of Staff.'

'No one knew everything, Michael. It doesn't work like that.'

Donnellan waves an impatient hand. 'Sure, sure. But you were the one he trusted. Your judgement was very important to him.'

Eamon does not contradict him a second time. He thinks Donnellan is not as certain as he was earlier, when he knew the answers before he asked the questions. There is a knock, a man enters, whispers to Griffin, who conveys the news to Donnellan in voluble Spanish.

Donnellan nods. 'It seems Mary does not have your conscience about talking. She says you are here to find if Hugh and myself are in cahoots with Fernando. That we are bankrolling the dissidents. Is that the case?'

Eamon says, 'Yes.'

Donnellan shrugs impatiently, a gesture of irritation. 'You see,' he says to Griffin, 'I told you they had your number.' He switches to Spanish, and Griffin replies angrily, before he leaves them alone.

'I want to put a hypothesis to you, Eamon,' he says after another lengthy pause, when the only sound is Fernando Griffin talking loudly to somebody guarding the door on the other side. 'That Iggy Davin has sent you and Mary over here for a reason, possibly a couple of reasons, and none of them are to do with what he told you he wanted. That he is doing what he has always done when a crisis erupts. He takes control, acts off his own bat. Invariably this action causes more trouble, but these problems never land at his door.

'When you decided I was the informer in London, blowing all our operations, you acted secretly, independently of the Council. That is correct?'

'Yes.'

'But Iggy knew, didn't he? He came to you and said we have a problem in London.'

'We all knew that, Michael,' Eamon says sharply. 'It didn't need a genius to work out that we had informers.'

'Of course. But it was Iggy who suggested that only you could finger the informer in London. He made the pretence that he didn't know who it was.

'Let's go back further, to the assassination attempt on Mrs Thatcher that very nearly came off. What happened to Hugh?'

'He was blown, somebody found out. We were paralysed, we couldn't move,' Eamon says.

'The London Brigade, much derided, leaking like a sieve at the top, that's who got him out. Under the noses of the Brits. So how come we are to blame?'

By now, Eamon is more uneasy, uncomfortable and terrified than he has been for a very long time. Since the time he escaped a British Army ambush in the countryside, and ran, stumbling and twisting, out of breath, aching, until he found cover beneath a culvert, where he squatted up to his nose in freezing water while the soldiers drove past, halted, got out and started to search the area. Eamon knew that if they found him they would have tried to turn him, if that failed, they would have tortured him, and maybe killed him. That freezing night, his body numb with cold and fear, his jaw locked tightly to stop his teeth from chattering, he waited for the end. Now he has the same foreboding.

'To look at Iggy Davin,' Donnellan resumes, 'he is both terrifying and yet a bit comical. That squat body, the comb-over hairstyle, those thick cheap specs, the terrible scarecrow's clothes – he looks a joke. Maybe that is how he does it.' He pauses. 'You know the medical term for somebody like Davin is a psychopathic personality. They are highly intelligent, personable, quite charming when they need to be – and completely amoral.'

Eamon's throat is painfully dry. He indicates he would like some water. Donnellan nods. As he drinks, he senses Griffin is still impatient with all this, he can hear him patrolling next door, that he wants to work him over, he resents being out of the room.

'Tell me something, Eamon. Did you really believe I'd sold out in London? That I was responsible for letting Hugh's escape route go to the Brits?'

'The evidence seemed clear enough.'

'Oh I'm sure it was. Who put it together? Who was judge and jury? Ignatius Davin.' Donnellan pauses for a second. 'Who is never questioned, never checked. Who in my time, never, ever had his trail checked. He always escaped that. The big cat, too valuable, not to mention dangerous, to examine.' He pauses again. 'Can you remember the original plan for Hugh to get out of Downing Street?'

'It's a long time ago, Michael. If you remember, I was in Long Kesh.'

'I know. Let me refresh your mind. Once he'd fired the shot, he was to leave Downing Street by the steps down to Horse Guards Road, go along to Admiralty Arch, to Charing Cross, and get on the Underground there. And the reason I can recall it is that I never knew what it was until Hugh told me.

'He didn't do that, he didn't do it because it seemed obvious to me, to Hugh also, that if the Brits were going to throw a ring around Whitehall, the last place you'd go to was to one of the three nearest Underground stations. So unknown to the Army Council, and therefore Iggy Davin, I suggested to Hugh that he ignore that plan and get out of the immediate zone as fast as he could.

'By then I knew something wasn't right, the whole thing stank. Why, for example, was it that none of us who lived in London and who knew our way around, had any input in the planning? They asked us to provide safe houses before and after. That was all. Funny how every one of those houses was raided within hours of the attempt.'

'Not surprising if somebody was talking.'

'Sure, Eamon, sure. But the two safe houses I laid on for Hugh were never touched. He stayed in both of them until we got him away from the UK. And I didn't know where the safe houses were. We provided information, suggested different areas of the city, and gave them a list of estate agents to contact. Beyond that, I knew nothing. Davin sent a team of sleepers, unknown to me. They rented houses. I had no idea where Hugh was supposed to go.'

'That was standard practice by then, Michael. You know we worked in cells.'

'Of course I know that. And one of Iggy's henchmen, the late lamented Pascal Clancy, took over running Hugh for the last month. He worked only to him. So they knew where he was going as well.'

Donnellan gets up and paces around the room. He goes again to the window, which is in semi-darkness, and peers out through a slit at the side of the curtains. Reassured, he resumes. 'The only people who knew where Hugh was headed, what his escape route was, were Pascal as his handler and Ignatius Davin who knew the entire plan. We provided some backup, briefing on times, when to get to Downing Street, all that sort of logistical information. We gave him the weapon. This is where Iggy was very clever, Eamon. He left enough of the operation open to others. Part of it was down to us so he would be able to put the heat on when it suited him.'

Donnellan sits down slowly, wearily. 'We had nothing to do with it. I couldn't have blown any of it because I did not know what the escape plans were. They briefed Hugh by written instructions, sent by Ignatius Davin.'

Eamon finds he has pissed his trousers again. He was not even aware of it. Now he shifts uncomfortably, his thighs chaff. The only relief is that he is still sitting on the two towels. He thinks back to the aftermath of the attempt to assassinate Mrs Thatcher, by the use of a dart, the tip coated in ricin, concealed in a camera, fired by Hugh as he took a photograph of Mrs Thatcher as she came out of the Prime Minister's residence in Downing Street. The dart missed her by a few millimetres. How they used it as proof of the ingenuity of the Movement, of their ability to get right inside the apparatus of the British security system, to the heart of the government, with impunity.

'What did you know about Fintan Flaherty? Your choice to accompany Mary to somehow pull Hugh back to London,' Donnellan asks.

'That he was a loudmouth. He wasn't very good. Iggy said he'd been tried out on a few small jobs and hadn't shown much judgement, had a fiery temper that got the better of him. I worked him over, told him that if he once stepped out of line that was it.'

'Strange that Iggy wanted him.' And Donnellan tells him about Flaherty's arrest for harassing a woman in a London pub. 'What would he have done with anybody who behaved like that on active service?'

'At best a bad beating, otherwise a bullet in the back of the neck and a label of informer.'

'Sure. And thrown out of the Movement forever. Instead, Flaherty goes back to Co Cork, resumes his job as a teacher and becomes active again in the Movement, and starts climbing the ladder in the Munster Brigade.'

'Maybe Iggy didn't know?' Eamon says. He is trying to pick any holes in Donnellan's story, to test it as best he can for any weakness, to see if he is stretching the truth, leading the argument towards his version.

'Iggy knew all right, Eamon. I made bloody sure of that. I arranged for the court case details to be sent to him. I was there when he read them.'

'It isn't an offence to be picked up and questioned by the law. That happens to most of us at one time or another. It could be Flaherty did no more than was said. Lost his head over a woman. We know what he was like with women.'

'Sure we do. He was cunt-struck. Another reason for not having him within a million miles of anything. Instead Iggy agrees with you that he is to go with Mary, a young, very attractive woman. From what I know about that trip, Flaherty could hardly keep his hands off Mary, that trying to screw her was more important than getting Hugh back to London.'

'I know what happened, Michael,' Eamon says firmly. 'They did get Hugh to London, to your club.'

Donnellan patrols the room, silent, deep in thought. Eamon

wonders about asking if he can change out of his stinking trousers. He senses that Donnellan wants him on his side, that he no longer fears him – why else would he dismiss Griffin and do without a minder.

'You spot the pattern, Eamon? After the Golden Boy fiasco, I'm the bad guy. I have to get away and fast. This buys Iggy more time. He is still the genius, the enforcer, who always gets the informers. All those who might be able to pin something on him, or worse, because this is something Iggy fears above all – that some of us get together to compare notes. We are named, blamed, and if he can get away with it, killed. Failing that, we go on the run, or like you, are put out to grass. Even as devious a mind as Piggy Iggy would not try to hang a thing on Saint Eamon. So instead he compromises you, he buys you.'

'All this is very plausible, Michael. Like all good cover stories, it has more than enough truth in it to make it so. I don't know what you are getting at. That Iggy is adept at the power politics on the Army Council? Of course he is. He wouldn't have been there for as long as he has been if he didn't know how the game is played.'

'Eamon, in a minute you can go in there and use the bidet and change. Then we'll sit down and I want to take you on a very interesting trip over the years. I want to show you what I have discovered.'

'What does the Movement fear above all else, Eamon?' Donnellan is impatient now, his former calmness, the relaxed mien of earlier, is gone. He does not wait for his answer. 'The split. Going right back to the pro and anti-treaty forces in 1922.'

'Yes.'

'What evidence is there for the new group?'

'Word on the street. Gossip, rumour, a few guys who are usually in the know. Certain people have not been seen for some time.'

'And Iggy's confirmation to you, right?'

'Yes.' Eamon is sweating again. I'm far too slow these days, he thinks. All I have for this is Iggy's word, nothing else. There have been rumours, but then there always are such whisperings and fantastical conspiracies.

Donnellan says, 'You have a sharp mind. You always ask the questions; get straight to the heart of an argument. You know what I'm driving at – I'm sure you arrived at the same conclusion quite some time ago.' He pauses, deliberately, Eamon thinks, he wants to make his point. 'Unlike Iggy Davin, you were always capable of using complexity in your reasoning, of avoiding simplicity. You never bought into the idea of the purity of the Cause. That we have to hate one thing to achieve our aims. That it is as simple as that.

'But not so of late, it seems. Instead of reasoning, calculating, thinking things through in the way you always did, you leave your conscience in bed every morning when you get up, safe in the knowledge that the political moves are going our way. That we can't get any further by force. Instead, as we breach the political barrier, we can be patient, we can wait, move on slowly. All right, you say to yourself, Ignatius Davin has become a greedy pig. He is a thug who has been responsible for killing more people than I believe is necessary but your instinct is to believe him.

'Let me ask you something. When did you last see a dead man?' Another lengthy pause until there is a knock on the door.

'*Dos cafés solo, señor*,' a porter says.

'Well?' Donnellan says when the porter has put the tray down and left.

'A few weeks ago.'

Donnellan says softly. 'Tell me about it.'

Eamon tells him about the panicky call from Mrs McGettigan.

'Would that be that old woman you conscientiously visit each week to pay her pension?'

Eamon starts, the cold prickly sweat is back, and he is relieved that Donnellan has his back to him as he pours coffee.

'Describe what happened.'

Eamon tells him what Mrs McGettigan has told him.

'I sent him. Somebody got to him en route. He was poisoned. The autopsy claimed it was due to the medication he was taking for epilepsy, that he had had an overdose of Phenobarbital, enough to kill him. Which is total bullshit. He had that condition for some time. He knew all about his dosage. Somebody forced an overdose down him.'

Eamon can't think, can't move for a moment. 'Why did you want to contact me?'

'I wanted to meet you, and some other people, who do not believe that Ignatius Davin is the saviour of the Movement, who in fact regard him as the opposite. Now tell me exactly what Davin told you.'

Eamon sees the dawn light faintly coming under the curtains. He sips the sweet strong coffee, grateful for the caffeine and the boost to his blood sugar level. He is not sure what to tell Donnellan, whether to believe him or not.

'Come on, Eamon!' Michael Donnellan snaps impatiently. 'Let me get you started. Iggy takes you off to a safe house in the Gweedore. Does it with all the usual security checks, switch of cars, takes up to three days to get there, travelling in the small hours, hiding up in daylight. You arrive exhausted at two in the morning and find Iggy as bright and fresh as if he's just got up. And Iggy is well briefed, he knows his stuff. He has read all the papers, and some more, as he always does. Correct?'

'Yes,'

'You're not really in a position to question what you're told by then, are you? You're disorientated, as if you had just got off a twenty-four hour flight. No need for that any more surely, Eamon. The Brits have dismantled their lookout towers and listening posts. Besides, what Iggy has to say to you could have been done on a walk somewhere remote. But that's not his way, is it? Not if he can make it dramatic, heighten the tension. If he can cast himself as the man who saves the Movement from a split. Again.'

Eamon is shocked, almost stunned, not by the revelations but by his own blindness.

Donnellan takes the laptop again. 'Let's take a look. Check a few things.'

When he has finished, Eamon says sharply, 'That was ten years earlier. There is an awful lot of hypotheses, Michael. My dictionary defines a hypothesis as a provisional supposition which accounts for known facts, serves as a starting point for further investigation by which they may be proved or disapproved.'

'Ever the teacher, the pedantic Eamon. Let me give you my definition: the facts are there but the proof is lacking. I prefer my version.'

Outside, the morning air is cold. There is no wind and the tide is out. In the distance, Eamon sees waves languidly breaking on the semi-submerged rocks that lie across the mouth of the natural harbour like spread-out teeth. Donnellan is silent. He walks alongside him, with minders fore and aft.

Who else knows about this? That Donnellan stayed in contact with other enemies of Davin is no surprise. Does Michael Donnellan have a back-channel contact, and if he has, to whom? The Brits, or the Irish, to somebody in the Movement who has the same suspicions about Ignatius Davin?

He knows Ignatius Davin does have contact with the British and Irish governments, if not directly, then using the back channel that has always existed, the line of communication kept open even during the bleakest of times, when either side wished to pass a message in secret to the other. And it could be Davin. Why not? At one time or another, the Brits and Irish approached everybody.

So why not Ignatius Davin?

Reasons?

He considers them.

Money. A Swiss bank account, might appeal to somebody as in need of the constant reassurance that money gives Davin.

Revenge? For what? He is in the position to exact revenge on anybody he wants to punish.

Power. If he is an informer, the one long suspected by all of them to be at the heart of the Movement, then the reason can only be that. Power is what drives Iggy, money and all the other bits and pieces being no more than the means required to obtain and hold it. And it was usually Iggy, in those private off-the-record meetings, who hinted that a member of the Army Council was an informer.

Eamon thinks of Milton.

To reign is worth ambition, though in hell:/Better to reign in hell than serve in heav'n.

By the time they have completed the walk around the fort, Eamon is tired and his eyes are full of grit. Wearily he climbs the steps back to the fort walls.

Donnellan resumes his seat and looks steadily at Eamon. 'I'm not the only one who has gone down this track. There are others looking carefully around Iggy Davin's murky past. We were not alone in our suspicions. This dossier,' he holds a small flash drive in his hand, 'has been passed on. If anything happens to me, the probe will continue, it won't stop with me. We won't be deflected. We've learnt our lessons.'

'Others have seen the dossier?'

'Of course. You're not the only one. After they saw it, you were named as the man in the best position to put it to good use.'

Eamon says dryly, 'Whoever recommended me is as out of touch as I am.'

Donnellan leans forward. 'After Paddy's death I went to Ireland a couple of times. I took a hell of a risk, but I knew it was the only way. I couldn't pursue this myself; almost certainly I would be killed if Iggy got to know of it. As soon as he has a sniff, or sees a chance to get at me and continue to divert attention away from his activities, he does so.'

'So how does Iggy put two and three together and get you linked with funding TIRA? He won't have done that without being fairly sure he can prove it.'

'I send money back. I look after some of the old London brigade, a few of whom have gone home to see out their days. But that is all I do.'

'You're telling me there is nothing going from you in the way of funds?'

'That's right. I wouldn't know where to send it anyway. Does TIRA exist apart from in Davin's imagination?'

Breathing in the stale air of Michael Donnellan's suite, Eamon wonders what he will do once he gets home. He explores the possibilities, the few people he might be able to talk to in the Movement and realises with a sickening sense of inevitability how much of a grip Ignatius Davin holds.

Michael Donnellan, showered, shaved and changed into a lightweight suit comes in from the bedroom. His zingy cleanliness seems to Eamon to be a deliberate reminder that he remains an unshaven, grubby prisoner. There is a knock on the door. 'Ah,' Donnellan says appreciatively, '*desayuno*.' A waitress puts a tray on the table, and gives him the bill to sign.

Michael Donnellan finishes his bowl of fresh fruit; he delicately wipes his mouth, has a sip of coffee. 'Eamon, there is more.'

Eamon looks at him and he wonders what other revelation Donnellan is about to spring on him.

'You know what Operation Armageddon is?'

'Yes.'

'Tell me,' Donnellan says seriously, leaning forward intently, 'what it means to you.'

Eamon hesitates. He wonders if Donnellan is testing him in some way, is probing because he doesn't know. Donnellan sits and waits and says gently. 'I know what it is, Eamon. Remember I was on the Army Council when we formulated the plan.'

'Then why the hell are you asking me, Michael,' Eamon can't help himself snapping.

'Because I need to know if it means the same now.'

'The protection by all possible means of the Reverend Paisley and his family. Keeping him alive is of vital importance to the Movement.'

'Because…'

'Because, after internment, he is the finest propaganda weapon we have, the Movement's *raison d'être* in many ways.'

'Sure. And now as he moves towards a power-sharing government, we face the real possibility of him becoming First Minister with Martin McGuinness as Deputy First Minister. Quite a shift from the *über* hard-line Loyalist, whose many slogans include *Not An Inch, Never In My Lifetime*, as regards having anything to do with the Movement. A man who has built his career on not doing any deals that might dilute the purity of Loyalism and Protestantism. Now he is about to do just that and with a man whose hard-line Republican beliefs are as strong as his Unionist ones.'

'I guess that's politics,' Eamon says. 'They have both outflanked the other parties.' Eamon is puzzled. He can't quite see where Donnellan is heading. Donnellan takes a deep breath, as though he is not at all sure about how he is going to proceed. Eamon watches him; he notices the faint tan on his hands, the manicured nails, the light grey suit with matching cotton socks, the black expensive loafers: when Donnellan crosses his legs, the crease in his trousers is clear, delineated – it seems to define him. As he talks, Eamon finds that he is absorbed in this study of Michael Donnellan, of how sensitive his hands are, and as he notes this, he recalls that Michael once killed a man with his hands, which makes the sight of them even stranger, such danger in that delicacy. And he listens, because he knows what is coming.

'Let us then roll this on and assume they reach an agreement, pushed into it by the Brits, the Irish and the Yanks working on both sides. Where does that leave Iggy?' He sips his coffee, grimaces at the taste.

Eamon shrugs. 'Doing what he does now but with a lot more time to make money, which seems to be his main occupation these days.'

'You have heard of the Nuclear Option?'

Suddenly Eamon finds himself going cold as he realises exactly where Donnellan is heading. 'It is the opposite of Armageddon, the assassination of Paisley and his colleagues.'

'Yes. Just that.'

Eamon carries on. 'A contingency plan only, nobody ever seriously believed it might be used.'

'You know the saying there is no such thing as an accident. If the Nuclear Option was planned, it was *precisely because* somebody thought that one day it would be needed. Time to think again, Eamon. That is what the TIRA are planning to do.' He pauses. 'And the paymaster for this operation is…Do I need to spell it out?'

Eamon shakes his head. He feels nausea rising. This seems too much, as he wonders again if Donnellan's mind is so warped by his hatred for Davin, he has slid into a fantasy world.

'Why the hell would Iggy want to do that? Him, the enforcer of the GFA. The man who puts manners on anyone who steps out of line?'

'But perfect cover. Who has interrogated all of the dissidents? Who has an encyclopaedic knowledge of people? Who knows people's abilities, who can do what job?'

Stupidly, like a child Eamon hears himself asking, 'But why? And why now?'

'Power, what else? It's all starting to slip away from Iggy. Once they start to decommission seriously, begin to stand down the volunteers, as more and more of them go into politics – where does that leave Iggy? Where he does not want to be.'

Eamon is lost in deep thought. Donnellan leaves him as he does a tour of the room. He goes to the window and opens it and looks over the car park and the grounds of the Parador, out towards the sea. The sunshine is brilliant, an azure sky and sea. Eventually Eamon says, 'Is this another one of your hypothesises, Michael. Or do you have some means of proving it?'

'Oh I can prove it, Eamon. What I'm not sure is what I or we can do to stop it.'

'It will be a bloodbath. Nobody will give them any support.'

'That won't be how Iggy sees things. He will allow the Loyalist backlash to go ahead, to get the world media to be at least neutral once the atrocities start. Above all, Iggy will be top dog, in charge. The saviour of the Movement. The man who kept the Republican purity intact. He will bet that British public opinion gets so fed up and quickly, it will force the British to pull out, leaving the mad Paddies to sort it out themselves. If the British are in Iraq and Afghanistan, it is debatable that they will have the troops to deploy enough men in the North as well. Oh, it can work all right.'

Eamon looks closely at Michael Donnellan. He decides this has the air of authenticity; it is very plausible and it has all the marks of one of Davin's plots. Now he understands why Davin sent him on what he has until now considered a wild goose chase.

'So the True IRA exists?'

Donnellan shrugs his shoulders. 'Who knows? It might be Davin's code name for the Nuclear Option. What he is trying to do again is to create confusion, throw smoke up, anything to take the spotlight off him to allow him time to get organised.'

'How much information do you have?'

'We know there have always been rogue elements in British Security, who believe only the Loyalists, working with the Brits, should rule the North.' Donnellan prowls around the room before he sits down. Eamon is aware again how sharp the creases in his shirt are, there is no sign of a wrinkle: Dandy Donnellan still.

'It isn't only on our side we have those who regard the GFA as a sell-out. All those members of Paisley's Free Presbyterian church who want nothing to do with Catholics. They saw him as their bulwark against the Papists hordes hammering at the citadel gates. They have always been against the GFA. If Paisley is murdered, it will be the final proof to them that the Republican side can never be trusted not to resort to violence. You've considered the Loyalist reaction if Paisley is assassinated in the contingency plan. Well, if it happens now, after the moves he has made you can treble the reaction. They will go on a rampage, resurrect the war in full, and we have a civil war.'

'How are they going to do it? A suicide bomber?'

'No. Not our way is it? No. A sniper. I have information about inquiries regarding a rifle with a distance of over 800 metres equipped with the latest US laser sights. We have a couple of good snipers who would do the job. If the money was right, he could hire one. There are enough hit men wandering around willing to do a job if the reward is worth it. From 800 metres, they have a good chance of getting away with it.'

'That is a hell of a distance to be that accurate.'

Donnellan opens a folder, puts on a pair of reading glasses. 'There are a number of rifles designed specifically for snipers. One of the best is the Lapua Magnum .338. It has a night vision device. More importantly, they guarantee a first hit at six hundred metres. In addition, there are all sorts of controls to allow for strong winds. There are bullets, special sniper ammunition, including some plastic bullets capable of being accurate up to a thousand metres, special lightweight bullets that will carry extra distance, and armour-piercing bullets.' Michael Donnellan closes the folder and removes his spectacles. 'A calm day, even on a windy one, using a good marksman. It is more than possible, Eamon. We know nobody can be entirely protected against an attack.'

Eamon stands up. Suddenly he is dog-tired. He is so exhausted he just wants to lie on the floor and sleep, to put the last twelve hours from his mind.

'We are pretty certain there is covert information about Paisley's movements that is passed to Iggy. There is an Englishman, Richard Gimson, once of MI5, believed to have been Iggy's case officer for a time, who after he was kicked out of MI5 went native, threw in his lot with the UDA. It's possible he is the conduit. Iggy's web of connections, his links with British security have not all been one-way traffic.'

'Where is the rifle coming from?'

'The old Soviet bloc. Lot of disaffected security people who have lost pensions and all the perks, and have set up as arms dealers, security firms, mercenaries. The Movement has some contacts there I'm sure. Does Sean O'Dowd mean anything to you?'

'A former Adjutant-General and Iggy's number two until he fell out of favour.'

'It seems they are friends again. With his contacts, O'Dowd will know where to source the rifle and all they need for it.' Donnellan pauses. 'We have the plan. We have the armourer, O'Dowd. What we don't have is the sniper and the time and place.'

Eamon takes his time as he always does with a complex problem. He works through the whys, the logic – if he can call it that – of Davin's plans. Donnellan lets him do so.

'It's the doomsday scenario.' Eamon says it flatly. 'I do know this much,' he concedes. 'Iggy has little concept of the limits of power. I do, you do. For sure Adams, McGuinness and Paisley do. But Iggy? No. He does not.'

'No,' Donnellan says softly. 'He does not.'

Eamon lets his breath out slowly. 'Jesus Christ Michael, if Iggy gets wind of this we are dead men.'

CHAPTER 15

'What you think? She is happy with her old man?' Fernando Griffin says. He holds up a hand and the surly waiter responds immediately. Hugh wonders what it is about Fernando, that he can always attract the attention of waiters. He decides he has the aura of success, the promise of big tips. He snaps out an order for two beers. 'You think he is still able to fuck her, eh?' Griffin grins. 'She looks like she needs a lot of fucking, that one.'

Hugh shrugs indifferently. He finds Griffin even more hateful than he had thought possible. If Hugh wasn't under orders, he would like to sort him out, knock the arrogant smirk off his face; despite the difference in their ages, he still fancies his chances. To restrain himself, he massages the knuckles of his left hand.

They are sitting in a café across the street, opposite the entrance to the Parador. Michael Donnellan has instructed Hugh to wait until Eamon and Mary have left. To make it look as normal as possible, and to try and see if there is anybody else in Baiona who might be looking for them or for Eamon, Donnellan has deployed his gypsies, Jésus, Carlos and María-José around the street. Carmen strolls by arm-in-arm with her friend Mirna, smiling, laughing and chattering. Twice they have been past them, changing their dresses for bright skirts and tops and then back to dresses. They are so good, Hugh wonders if they really are part of the gang that Jésus leads. He supposes surveillance is part of their job.

Hugh finishes his beer and eats the *pulpo Gallego* and the *patas bravas*. He stands to shake hands with Griffin, two old friends saying goodbye at the end of their vacation. Hugh drives away in his silver Peugeot 607, fast, powerful and, most importantly for him, anonymous, unlike the flashy mid-navy BMW X5 favoured by Griffin here in Galicia. Hugh knows he also has cars in Barcelona and Lisbon. Unlike Griffin, Hugh enjoys driving, he does not feel comfortable on flights, probably, he realises, because he has only flown a few times, always on a dangerous assignment, or the time he was escorted back from Greece by Mary and her little sidekick. Griffin hops on and off Iberia flights with the regularity of an executive.

Once clear of Baiona, Hugh heads for Ourense and the autopista and the long haul back to Madrid. He wants to settle things, let his emotions calm down, because seeing Mary again, spending almost eight hours alone with her in the bedroom has brought back those days in London, days when by subtle hints and nudges, she gave him the few clues and hints about where he was being held that enabled him to make his escape. To his surprise, he found himself at one point during the night, as he sat watching Mary, longing for her, that if she had woken up and smiled at him, in the way she had done, he would have climbed into bed with her. That in itself, this rare spurt of heterosexual carnality, is astonishing to him. He puts it down to no more than the sight of Mary, all those intense days brought back. She is still vivacious, twenty-odd years on.

When Michael first contacted him in Madrid, told him he wanted him to do a special job, Hugh assumed at first he was planning another trip to London or Ireland. There have been a few over the past years. London is okay for Hugh. Like Madrid, it is big and sprawling and cosmopolitan, and he finds it easy to mingle with the crowds and vanish. After all, London is his native city, where he lived and grew up, where he worked as a tyre fitter, doing breakdowns in and around the city. Ireland, however, feels alien now, particularly in the countryside, with the sprawling estates of white bungalows, so unlike the desolate landscape of his childhood. When Michael told him what they would be doing in Galicia, Hugh was blunt. He replays their conversation again.

'Drugs? You are fucking joking, Michael, I hope.'
'No joke. I mean it.'
'For the money?'
'No, not really. No.'
'You've not become a copper in your old age?'
'Not that either.'

So they had driven south out of Madrid, with Hugh at the wheel because he is a terrible passenger, a nervous wreck, who drives every centimetre of the journey, braking at imagined dangers, cursing the slowness of the decision to overtake. They motored down to Toledo, where Donnellan owns a bar and a restaurant. The tenant of the bar, after a visit from Jésus and his friend, has quickly found the back rent. Donnellan sat in a café opposite to look at the place, while he told Hugh what he has unearthed, and the reason for the visits to Ireland and London became clear.

'It has been a long difficult search, Hugh. A very lengthy hunt. He's clever, cunning and he has a nose for any danger to himself. But I think I can get him.' At which point, rare for Michael Donnellan, he smacks his hand hard on the café table.

Hugh listens. It is convincing. Hugh tries to filter out his own hatred of Davin, his obsession with revenge for what happened to Godfrey. To think, as God urged him to do. *Be objective, old love; spend time in a period of ratiocination.* To use one of his favoured phrases. By then they are in the small office Donnellan uses off the Plaza de Zocódover, in the towering shadow of the Alcázar.

'Okay, suppose you're correct,' Hugh says, 'friend Davin is bound to have built plenty of traps and moats around him. In fact, I'd say it is probably easier to attack the Alcázar. If he is in the pockets of the Brits or the Irish, they will have him ring-fenced as well.'

'There is no such thing as complete security, Hugh. You can always find a chink somewhere. I think I have found it. Oh, I agree, Iggy will have a tight firewall around him. However, I have a few ideas.'

Hugh pulls off the autopista for petrol. He stands by as the attendant fills the car, cleans the windscreen and headlights, then takes the euros in payment. Inside the café, Hugh orders a *café solo* and stands at the counter to drink it. Is Donnellan being straight with him? He trusts him – as far as he trusts anybody. He remembers again God's dictum about having more than one plan. Surely Michael Donnellan has something else in mind if Eamon and Mary do nothing, or worse, decide to believe Davin, or ignore it because they do not want any trouble? From what he hears and from Mary's answers to his questions about her life over the last few years, she and Delaney are wealthy. Why risk all that? Hugh is angry at being pulled back in to all this as well. He long ago accepted he was not going to get a pardon – how could he when he has never been put on trial and convicted. He guesses even a failed assassination attempt on a Prime Minister probably does not count under the amnesty for prisoners in the Good Friday Agreement, a matter of anger and bitterness for Michael Donnellan also. What Hugh wants is out. Maybe it is time to move on, rethink things. If Michael has not considered anything else, well Hugh is not planning to hang around. In one sense, he suspects he is tempting him with the chance to get at Davin for betraying him, and indirectly for killing God.

Hugh has been careful with his cash, has lived on his wits for so long, he knows he can get by without Michael Donnellan. Time to look at his escape routes, those he has always kept updated, secret, and ready for use once he sniffs any danger. Despite the comparative ease of life in Madrid over the past ten years, the fear of discovery has never left Hugh: it is there like a nagging tooth that responds to a slight prod.

Back on the road, he sets the cruise control at one hundred and twenty kilometres an hour. The traffic is sparse and he makes good time to the outskirts of Madrid.

That day in Toledo Michael explains that they will be going to Galicia to meet Fernando Griffin. To have, in Michael's euphemism, a breath of sea air, a little break by the ocean. That he needs Hugh to visit Jésus and get him to bring as many of his people as he can, that he wants them to stake out Griffin first, to make sure the road is clear, and that Griffin, who Michael does not trust, has kept his side of the deal. Which is to allow Michael and Hugh to pose as his partners in the drug-running Griffin does.

Hugh is still not sure that Michael does not have an investment in Griffin. After all, he has no scruples about making money where he can, the only proviso being that personal risk is non-existent. Why not invest in drug-running? It is what he has always been good at, spotting an opportunity before other people, getting in early, and, as important, getting out while the stock is still high, even on the rise. 'Never take the top brick off the chimney,' is a favourite saying of his.

Hugh went with Jésus, took his reports from Santiago de Compostela airport where he picked up Griffin on his last two visits, trailed him into the hotel, followed him down to the coast. They watched him as he went through his procedures, which varied on each trip so that he did not leave footprints to follow, the only indication of what he was doing were the louring presence of his bodyguards. Because, 'my friend, these are some dangerous fuckers, these pigs,' Jésus spat out, not from repugnance at the availability of drugs, which Hugh knows Jésus uses himself, just the recognition of one professional for another.

When Michael told him that Eamon Delaney and Mary were

coming to Santiago de Compostela, that he is sure that Davin has fallen for the bait, the whole operation swung into being. Michael threw money and men at it. Jésús somehow produced more of his people; they posted them around Santiago de Compostela, watching both the Delaneys and Griffin. How they avoided tripping over the guys used by Davin, particularly the night they staked out Griffin's chalet by the beach, is something Hugh still does not know.

Perversely, it is because of all this activity that he does not believe Michael when he tells him that it is only to lure Eamon out here, to enable him to get him on his own patch, where he knows his security is not in danger. After three days of watching Eamon and Mary in the Parador, they are convinced they are alone, there is nobody riding shotgun for them. The local muscle that Davin has procured, whom Jésús identifies as members of ETA, have not been seen in Baiona, have dropped out after the stake-out of Griffin's chalet in Arousa. Michael gives the nod to move in. So Hugh has to swallow hard, endure dinner with Griffin, as he listens to his boasts about all the women he has fucked, will fuck in the future. Griffin is good, he gives him that. Women like him. The waitress almost wets herself when he asks if he can see her later. Hugh has the further ignominy of standing guard outside Griffin's bedroom while he takes the waitress inside, 'to fuck her brains out, *amigo*.'

When Michael gives Hugh the same presentation that he later shows Eamon, Hugh remembers the trips back to London, to Ireland, the meetings in remote houses and in hotels, where they booked adjoining rooms, four in a row, so the security is as tight as they can make it. Hugh has the sweats, his hands shake, he grips the steering wheel tightly as he thinks of the risks, one slip and that would have been it, nicked, banged up in Portlaoise jail for the rest of his days, or somewhere in England.

These meetings were not all in Ireland. Some were in the complex of holiday apartments, part of Michael's properties on the Costa del Sol, in and around Marbella. Hugh has been there, as Michael's bodyguard, riding shotgun. The holiday apartments were used to entertain those Michael wanted information from or to impress with the veracity of his plans. Hugh has driven him to meetings in the mountains north of Malaga, where few tourists venture. There he continued his slow, painstaking accumulation of scraps of information, personal accounts of failed operations, secret briefings, spells in prison, debriefings. He put together the apparently random series of coincidences that on their own could be missed, passed over, but when put together, linked with dates and set down, side by side, cross-referenced, provide a pattern so distinct, vivid, it almost took Hugh's breath away.

'You better be sure,' Hugh remembers a strong Irish accent, Kerry as he discovered later, saying in a hard tone, a mixture of shock, suspicion and dismay. There followed a silence, so long and threatening, that Hugh fingered his Uzi pistol and thought he would have to use it.

'You better be *fucking* right. Jesus Christ! This will blow us apart.'

Slowly Hugh understands what Michael Donnellan did, by building his group of intimates. And of course, he thinks, Davin got wind of it, knew something was stirring up the waters, muddying his views. Because, presumably, he could not get more information. To express too much interest would confirm what those who had seen the Donnellan Dossier suspected. Clever, Hugh thinks, very clever, the way Michael does it. Davin will not risk too much, so he drags Eamon out of retirement, persuades him to go with Mary. The question is how much of it Eamon believes.

He comes off the A52, joins the NVI, which takes him to Madrid. He is aware again how close Donnellan is flying, too much so for Hugh's liking. Suppose he's not right. That knot of doubt he's had about Michael Donnellan since the trap in his London club, the suspicion that it was Michael who rigged up Flaherty with the bomb that killed him and God. The ease with which he got away once Michael located him on the south coast of England. Suppose this is no more than Michael looking to avenge all the defeats and humiliations from Davin. Or is he just after Davin's death, so he can see his years out in some sort of security?

Let's face it, Hugh thinks again, we've had an easy enough time of it here, a free run of things. Michael moves around the country, as he wants. The English expat who goes by the name of James Rogers, who has been here for the past twenty years. So why the fuck, he says to himself in exasperation, is he putting all this at risk? An old man with a few scores to settle.

This is madness. Hugh's paranoia, fuelled by the past week's events, is intense. Besides, Fernando Griffin worries him. He does not trust him. There is nothing to stop Griffin legging it to Ireland and for a few favours over there, letting Davin know what has taken place. He has his doubts as well about Michael's explanation, his partial defence of Griffin. That he worked for the Movement in Cuba and Colombia and just escaped arrest. What if the people Griffin deals with hear about his role as cover for Michael's plan? Hugh thinks they will not be happy with some other folk knowing about their operations. Flash Gordon with his glamorous women and extravagant lifestyle to maintain, will surely sell what he knows about Michael to Davin as insurance; the life expectancy of drug runners is not known for longevity.

Back in his apartment on the seventh floor, Hugh opens the balcony doors to look at the brown blocks of apartments that make up most of his view. He watches the aircraft coming in and leaving Barajas airport to the north of Madrid.

Restless, he goes back inside to open other windows and get some air into the stale atmosphere. There is a litre bottle of San Miguel in the fridge. Hugh hesitates. He has a binge now and then when things get bad, when he locks the apartment, drinks himself senseless, and then spends a week recovering. The temptation to blur the edge of his restlessness and fear is strong and he hesitates before closing the fridge because he knows getting drunk will only exacerbate the problem. He takes his laundry and loads the washing machine; then he tidies and cleans the already neat and spotless apartment. That done, he sits to watch the TV, flicks through a bullfight, flicks again through a chat show, an old black and white movie.

He leafs through his notebook, checks his false passports, his set of Spanish papers, work permit, identity card. He goes to his laptop to look at his bank balance, he counts the cash he keeps hidden in a safe disguised under the floor in the kitchen, where he has euros and dollars and a little sterling. One of his plans is to take the train to Barcelona and from there go to France and maybe head back for Greece. He has kept up his Greek over the years in Spain, by talking with one of his Greek mates.

His mobile rings. 'Just checking that you got back all right,' Michael says. 'Good trip?'

'Yeah. Fine. Listen there are a few problems that have happened. We need to meet up and talk about them.'

There is a short intake of breath. Good, Hugh thinks, you have not been expecting that. 'Can they wait until our meeting tomorrow?'

'No, I need to get them sorted out now.'

They arrange to meet in the hotel off the Teatro Real that Donnellan uses for his meetings when he does not want people in his office.

The weather has changed as Hugh emerges from the Metro at Opera. In the heavy downpour, he hurries past the closed and shuttered Teatro Real, the banners flapping damply, to the hotel. Inside he waits in the foyer listening to the rain on the glass dome.

'What now, Michael?'

'We wait.'

'And Griffin?'

'Griffin is in Lisbon in a safe place. With Jésus and a few of his pals for company.' Donnellan pauses. 'We will meet him in Lisbon in three days, when I give him the final payment.' He smiles and leans across to pat Hugh's knee. The gesture, like his smile, is avuncular. 'No, I don't think he will be going to see Iggy with any tittle-tattle, either.' He leans back in the settee and is almost swallowed up amidst the deep cushions. 'How have things been since you returned? Any visitors to the apartment?'

'If I have had they are bloody good. Nothing. Everything as I left it.'

'And outside? On the way here?'

'Nothing I could see.'

Michael Donnellan nods. And Hugh feels foolish, silly for doubting him, for thinking he had not covered all the exits.

'Don't relax. We need to keep in contact a couple of times every day. We phone at eleven tonight and twelve tomorrow. Then move it forward by five minutes each morning, back by five every night, until further notice. We still have our meeting in the morning. I want you to fly to Lisbon. Make the payment to Griffin.' He leans forward again. 'I know it's hard, Hugh, but we have to be patient. Eamon was the last building block to be put in place. It's a matter of allowing the concrete to dry now.' He pauses. 'With our friend out of the way, we can relax. Because if we don't get to him first, he'll take us.'

CHAPTER 16

Eamon resists the temptation to drive fast. Mary sees this by the manner in which he clenches the steering wheel, the rough grinding of gears once or twice. He reaches the autopista and takes the turn for Portugal. Since leaving the Parador, he has not said more than a few words to Mary. She knows there is no point in talking to him, trying to elicit anything from him when he is like this. All she can do is sit in silence, ask only rudimentary questions. 'Water?' She proffers a bottle. Eamon nods and drinks. The road is clear; there is little traffic, the odd car, one truck. They speed on, as they did a week ago, on the vast empty road into Portugal. Ahead she sees the faint haze of smoke from the forest fires that have continued to blaze.

Mary feels sluggish, her face is drawn and lined, her eyes puffy. I feel like shit, as well, she thinks. She knows it is the after-effects of the sleeping pill. Eamon also looks dreadful, haggard, as bad as he was when he returned from his meeting with Davin, so she is sure he has had another night without sleep. Twice she has suggested that she drives and all the thanks I get, she thinks bitterly, is to have my head bitten off. This is so unlike Eamon's normal behaviour, she knows something is eating at him. After all, she says to herself in a vain effort to lighten her mood, I'm the one with the fast temper, Eamon who is always cool, calm and collected.

From what she can remember of her conversation with Hugh before she fell asleep, there is something going on that has put the frighteners on him, a tension, exacerbated whenever he is with Griffin. She sensed he is quite happy with his life, secret as it is, that he has learned to live with the constant risk of exposure and betrayal, that whatever the reason that brought him to Galicia, he came reluctantly, from necessity. She noted how his antipathy towards Griffin almost led to a fight when Griffin came and sat on the bed, put an arm around her shoulders, smiled and despite herself, she sensed again how attractive he could be, the same response she had on his boat. Her fear made her shrug him off angrily. This was enough for Hugh to speak harshly to Griffin in Spanish. She guesses from Griffin's reply, equally snappy and fast, he resented Hugh's interference. Griffin left the room and she did not see him again until they were leaving the hotel.

When they are well inside Portugal, she says as calmly as she can, 'Eamon, I need to know what is going on. And why we are heading back into Portugal instead of going to Santiago de Compostela and getting on our flight home today.'

Eamon says nothing for a while, then as they encounter some traffic, he slows down, gets in the inside lane, and tells her briefly what Michael Donnellan has told him during the night.

Mary listens, her heart goes south through her stomach and feels as if it has plunged through the floor of the car. All her nightmares about Davin made reality in a couple of sharp, concise sentences.

'I called the emergency number. Message to phone Aunt Vera back home. Where there was a message from Iggy to get back and report in. I left a message to say that was not possible, that you had been ill in the night and could not travel, that I didn't know how long we would be, that I am not able to leave you and I'll be in touch as soon as we are ready to leave.'

'Does he believe you?'

Eamon shrugs. 'I don't know. I reckon we have a few days before he gets his pals in ETA to check it out – that is assuming they are prepared to do that for him.'

'So what are we going to do?'

'That's what I'm trying to figure out. First, buy some time. I want to put as much distance as I can between Davin and us. I don't know if he has any backup in Portugal. I suspect not as there was never any mention of the place. I hope to God I'm right, otherwise we are going to be in trouble.' He pauses. 'I'm counting that he won't be sure where we are right now, so if he has Pádraig on standby he won't know where to send him. I reckon we have about forty-eight hours before Iggy decides to set the dogs on us.'

Mary's mouth and throat is dry, she swigs water to ease it, hands the bottle to Eamon. 'If you tell me where we're heading, I can look for a hotel. You need to stop and sleep for a while, you look shagged out.'

'I'm all right for now. I thought if we could get to Porto or Lisbon and get a flight from there. I need some time before reporting to Iggy.

Above all I need to clear my head, cobble together what I'm going to say to him when we meet.'

'You believe Donnellan?'

'Yes. It only confirms what I've long suspected but refused to believe because I didn't want to do so. Not Iggy – I wanted to think that. Anybody but Iggy. It could not be him. Jesus! What a fool I've been.' He bangs the flat of his hand on the steering wheel and causes the car to swerve into another lane, where they get the angry blast of a horn.

'Right, that's enough,' Mary says firmly. 'Next stop, we change over. I'll drive while you think.'

Eamon nods, stays in the slower lane. They see a sign for Porto. Eamon pulls over to the hard shoulder. They slide across each other. 'Head for there?' Mary says.

'No. I think it is too close to Baiona. Let's go on to Lisbon. We should be there early afternoon.'

Mary drives, keeping to the inside lane. She is nervous, not used to motorway driving. Eamon, she is relieved to see, has put the seat in the reclining position and is already asleep; he snores softly, starts now and then when she brakes. Mary thinks: I must drive as I was told to drive once: as fast and as carefully as possible, as if I was taking a pregnant woman to give birth. She does this, is glad of the responsibility of the driving because for short moments it takes her mind off the enormity of what Eamon has told her. To try to topple Davin. She can't imagine how they are going to go about that. Who can they tell without the information being relayed to Davin, who has informants everywhere, who hears everything, misses nothing? She worries about her niece in Limerick, about the house she and Eamon bought for her because they feared that her husband was a messer and would one day leave her or kick her out. That hasn't happened so far, but Bobby is in and out of jobs, is too fond of the jar, and Mary suspects, although she cannot prove it, at times he is violent towards Charlotte. Just the sort who is vulnerable to Davin, and she suspects that Davin already has his eye on Bobby – it's the sort of minor detail at which he excels.

Further south, past Braga, the traffic on the E1 is heavy as she approaches Porto. Now she wishes Eamon would wake up and take over the driving. Mary feels vulnerable as the massive lorries roar past her while she is forced to dawdle in the inside lane too scared to risk overtaking. There is a sudden violent shower of rain, she feels the tyres begin to lose their grip and slows down until she sees a sign for a service area ahead, where she pulls off. By now, Eamon is in a deep sleep. Reluctant to disturb him, she does not want to leave him in the car in case he wakes and panics if she is not with him.

It is past one, the heat quickly dries off the rain. Gently Mary brushes her lips across Eamon's forehead. 'Are you all right, love?'

Eamon struggles to waken. He looks at her, eyes full of sleep. 'Where are we?'

'In a service station, south of Porto. I need a break and some food, and so do you.'

They find a table in the cafeteria. Mary goes to the self-service counter, loads a tray with some salads and cold meats, hard-boiled eggs in mayonnaise, which she adds to Eamon's plate, bottles of water, some fruit and a flan for Eamon. They eat in silence. After Eamon returns with two espressos, he sits and looks at the red Michelin map. 'I think we should go to Lisbon. We can lose ourselves better in a big city. Try to find somewhere to stay tonight. Tomorrow I'll check flights.'

Eamon seems refreshed and alert after his sleep and food. He drives with speed and determination; they make good time on the E1, on past Coimbra. Nearer to Lisbon the traffic is heavier; she spots the sign for Fatima and remembers how as a devout child she was due to go on the diocesan pilgrimage there and stricken by some childhood illness, had to miss it. She wonders if she will ever get to visit it, a place that exists only in her memory of a child's bitter disappointment. She busies herself with the guidebook, finds hotels in Lisbon, she writes a list with telephone numbers and is about to punch numbers in her mobile when Eamon says sharply. 'Don't use it. I don't want any risks, no possible clues where we are. I don't know if it's doctored in any way.' He pauses, shrugs. 'I can't be sure that Michael hasn't bugged it. I may be nuts, but from now on it's red alert all the way. We'll use a phone box.' He is relieved he removed the bug in the spare wheel.

They find a hotel in the city centre, at the edge of the Parque Eduardo VII. It is small, the rooms are basic, and it has the look of a transit stop. Eamon pays in cash for two nights.

'I'm going out,' he tells her. 'I need to make some calls and I want to make sure I'm clear. Give me fifteen minutes, and then take a taxi down to Avenida da Liberade. Get out just past the turn for Alexandre Herculano and walk back up the hill towards the statue of Pombal. Wait there and watch my back as I play the tourist.' He looks at her critically. 'You're almost as dark as a native of Lisbon. Buy a local paper, if anybody talks to you in English play dumb.'

'How come you know all this?'

'I had a few days here years ago, a short holiday, when I spent my time sightseeing. Good to be able to put it to use.'

By now it is past five. A breeze blowing up from the sea tempers the heat. Mary has changed, put on a dress, which enhances her dark colour. She pays off the taxi, and then strolls purposefully under the shade of the trees as the traffic tears up and down the hill of Avenida da Liberdade. She sees Eamon studying a map in the Praça de Pombal. There is a bench on the Avenida, where she sits, watches idly, glancing now and then in the direction of the Praça de Pombal. It is busy, young men and some women crowd around smoking, chatting, amidst the tourists and backpackers. Eamon takes his time, pours over his guidebook, examines the statue, and resumes his perusal of the book, as if he has no other interest. When he has completed his inspection of the giant statue, he saunters down the Avenida. Mary raises her copy of *Público*, she hears Eamon's footsteps as he walks past. She lowers the paper as she turns the pages. There are people walking by, and she watches carefully looking for a pattern, for somebody who does not appear to be following Eamon, a couple engrossed in each other but whose eyes are on him. She sees a small man, so thin he seems skeletal, dressed in jeans with a white T-shirt advertising John Smiths Extra Smooth. A mobile phone hangs from his belt, strapped on his hip like a cowboy's six-shooter. Behind him a fat, blowsy woman, who is suffering in the heat, struggles to keep up with him as he walks ahead of her. Mary wonders if they are watchers, the man being so obvious he is beyond suspicion, likewise the woman. She notes the slogan on the back of his T-shirt: NO NONSENSE. Then she realises the man is drunk, he staggers as he calls to his wife in English, before weaving his way into a bar. Mary sits flicking through the paper but sees nothing. A car pulls in further down. She looks for the other three or four cars driving up and down, for a motorcycle outrider. Two men sit and talk as Eamon goes past them. One gets out, slams the door, he follows Eamon and Mary's fingers twitch until he vanishes inside a fast food place.

Strolling down the Avenida da Liberdade, she is glad of the shade from the trees. She has Eamon in her sights, notes how he stops from time to time to look in shop windows, before he turns abruptly into a side street. In particular, she is on the lookout for some surveillance on foot. The street is too narrow, with cars parked tightly, for the use of cars or a motorbike. She checks for anybody close to Eamon, then a back-up further behind, almost out of Eamon's sight, and a third on the opposite side of the street, with a wider view, probably with a radio control. Still she cannot spot anybody. For a time she loses sight of him, then picks him up again when he reappears in the Praça dos Restauradores. Slowly, methodically, they continue in tandem, Mary some way back from Eamon, through the streets and squares of central Lisbon, past the hawkers, the shoeshine men, the Africans selling toys and jewellery and leather goods laid out on large rugs. There are drug dealers in doorways. Prostitutes, gaudily dressed in high heels, some in shorts that end at the top of their thighs, hiss at the passing men. She strolls by Rossio Station, watches Eamon cross the Praça da Figueira and notes he goes into the Rua da Madalena. She takes the opposite side of the street to Eamon and although she is very careful, she finds nothing suspicious. In the Praça do Comércio, she is aware of the immensity of water, of the river and the sea, the glare under the bright sun. Dazzled for a moment, Eamon is lost to her sight in the vast square of land and water, until she picks him up turning off for the cathedral. They start climbing up the steep hill in the evening heat.

Cathedrals, Mary thinks, she will always remember this trip for the cathedral in Santiago de Compostela and here in Lisbon. The road bends around, an ancient tram clanks down the hill, and she steps back on the narrow pavement. Ahead Eamon toils up the steep incline, his back bent. A motorbike tears up the hill, a woman clinging to the man who is driving it. Is that one of them? However, they speed past Eamon. Once more Mary stops, as if to admire the cathedral. She notes the souvenir stall, the beggars by the main doors, the few people who wander in and out, unlike the throng in Santiago. Still there is nothing untoward. If we are being watched, she thinks, they are very good. She shivers despite the heat and the beads of perspiration just beneath her hairline.

The street to the castle is steep; Mary stops from time to time to catch her breath, to look around, and there is nothing. For a moment, she is entranced by an area of blue tiles, a balcony where there are views across the river. She rests for a moment, is about to go on when she hears a familiar voice. Fernando Griffin deep in conversation in Spanish with a man she does not know, rounds the corner. Mary sinks back, turns and looks at her newspaper. Griffin, still talking rapidly, murmuring, goes on up the hill. She lets him go, out of her sight.

Why is Griffin here? Just what the hell have they jumped into? She resists the urge to hurry, to get to Eamon as soon as possible. Instead, she forces herself to loiter, to observe Griffin out in front until she loses them again to another bend.

When she climbs the last steps, she sees Eamon leaning on the parapet near a cannon looking out across the city toward the River Tagus and the harbour and port, the bridge and on the far side the statue of Christ, arms outstretched. A shimmer of her lapsed faith comes to Mary as she finds herself praying for Eamon, for her family, for herself.

She stands back, moves to the side of Eamon. Tourists come and go, take photos, digital cameras held aloft. A tall German in shorts and open-toed sandals takes a picture of his girlfriend then approaches Mary. 'Please? You take of us?'

Mary is so relieved she nods, unable to speak. The German man gently shows her how to focus the camera and what to press. As she does so, she sees that Fernando Griffin is coming around the corner in conversation with a different man. Her heart is in her mouth or in the pit of her stomach, she cannot decide. She turns slightly, hoping Griffin will not notice her. She walks towards the couple, away from Griffin, and talks to them, asking about the city.

'For sure you must go to Belém, see the tower and the Monument to the Discoveries. But do not miss the Mosterio dos Jerónimos. That is a most wonderful place.' His enthusiasm is infectious, she is glad of it, she takes the opportunity to move closer to them, as Griffin continues his walk and still talking, goes past her, past Eamon who has his back to him as he looks over the city.

'Thank you,' she says.

'No,' the man insists gently. 'It is we who must thank you.' He stares at the pictures in the camera. 'Such beautiful pictures. Thank you.'

At last, she feels able to join Eamon.

'Well?' He does not turn to look at her.

'Nothing, until a second ago, when Griffin came past with another guy. I don't think he saw me.'

'Fuck it! If he's here, the other two won't be far behind him. Come on, let's move.'

For the next hour, Eamon takes her around the city at a smart pace. Down to the docks, back across the expanse of the Praça do Comércio, by the river edge, where she sees a couple of rats sniffing around calmly searching for food, she supposes, before they scurry out of sight. They board a tram to Belém. As soon as the tram leaves the Praça, Eamon looks at her, nods and they get off at a stop near the telephone exchange. They continue through back streets at the same rapid clip, up hills, down again and she is glad she put on sensible walking shoes. At last, he stops at a bar on a side street off the Avenida da Liberade, where they sit and order beer.

'Okay,' Eamon says coolly and she can only marvel again at how well he handles the pressure. 'I think Griffin uses Lisbon as one of his bases. They have a big drug scene here, as they do everywhere. Did you spot the pushers along the way?' He does not wait for her reply. 'I suspect Donnellan and Hugh will be after him. They aren't going to let him out of their sight until Davin is sorted out.'

'I don't think he saw us.'

'He saw us all right. He just does not need to do anything for now. Griffin hasn't survived this long by missing anything that might be dangerous.'

Mary drinks her beer, she finds her throat has a rock in it, has closed over, the beer will not go down, she coughs and splutters and almost chokes.

'Michael has given me a week to get something moving. If I don't use it, he is going to give the information he has elsewhere.' Eamon pauses, 'where it will do the Movement far more damage.' Eamon gulps his beer, orders another and a brandy for Mary. 'Okay. I think we're clear, apart from Griffin. We'll have to risk that. I'm taking a flight to London, the first I can get. You stay here for two days, then follow me. By that time I hope to have things moving.'

'No,' Mary says firmly. 'I'm coming with you.'

Eamon considers this for a moment, and then he smiles thinly. 'I'm sorry. I forgot for a second that you are my wife and not a volunteer. We will travel on the same flight, but not together. You'll have to look sickly. For sure Davin will have people watching all flights into Ireland from Spain and maybe Portugal.'

They get seats on an EasyJet flight to Luton the next afternoon. The flight is not full. They sit apart and take it in turns to scrutinise the other passengers but see nothing to concern them. When they land in a windy, wet Luton, Eamon and Mary split up, make their own way through the arrivals, passport control, to the train station. On the way, Eamon stops at a pay phone to call the emergency number. He tells Mary, when they are sitting on the train to London, he has left a message that they expect to be back home by Thursday.

They have a day left.

On the train to Kings Cross, Eamon makes notes in a tiny black notebook. Mary has time to sit, to think through what is about to unfold. She will remain with him for today before catching a flight to Shannon and staying with her niece. Eamon tells her what he wants her to do, his instructions are precise, exact, brook no argument, he is like the Eamon of old when he briefed her before the trip to Skiathos with Flaherty. Over the years, since his return to normal life, she has almost forgotten this side of him, austere, rigid, forbidding, very much in control of himself. It scares her a little although she understands why he is like it.

They book into a hotel near Russell Square. From here, Eamon vanishes almost immediately, leaving Mary to brood and wait. She rings her niece from the hotel to tell her she was taken ill on holiday, that they missed their flight from Santiago and could not get another one, hence the trip to Lisbon and London. By now, Mary has secured a seat on a flight to Shannon the next day.

'Great, I'll meet you at the airport.' Charlotte is always pleased to see her aunt, who is just a few years older and is more like a big sister. 'Bobby is away playing golf in Mayo for a few days.' Mary wonders how Charlotte puts up with the feckless Bobby, who always has funds for his drinking and golf and anything else that takes his fancy. She thinks of how much money she and Eamon have given them to furnish the house, help with the emergency bills when they happen. However, she controls her temper and says, 'Oh good. We can have a few days of girl talk and enjoy ourselves.'

CHAPTER 17

Eamon relaxes a little more when he is sure that Davin does not know where he is. He called the safe numbers, and despite hints from Auntie Vera that he let her know where they are so she can call them directly when she is back in the house, he has not done so. On the last call the answerphone clicked in without a message, so he guesses Davin accepts he is going to have to wait.

'Where were you, boy?' says Donal Crowley in his loud fashion. 'Spain! Jaysus I hear 'tis fierce hot out there, it would have you roasted in next to no time. Listen to me, we must meet up some time. Wouldn't you think of getting yourself and the missus down here soon for a few days? I'd say ye must be worn out working fierce hard the way ye do, the pair of ye.'

All this, Eamon knows, standing in a phone box outside the British Museum, is Donal's country bluffness, which hides a shrewd intelligence. Like Eamon he has taken a back seat, but unlike Eamon went into politics, becoming a Sinn Fein councillor and in time mayor of his home town in Co Cork, the first ever Sinn Fein member to hold the position.

'We will, Donal. But I have some business to see to first.'

'Good man yourself, never the one to let things wait. Listen here to me, I have to go now. Will you give a ring a bit later on?'

Which is Donal saying, I understand, and I don't know if this phone is safe. So wait and call me on the number kept for very special occasions, a number he changes regularly. One of his men, who works in Eirecom, gives him a temporary number from time to time for his various businesses.

Eamon drifts down Charing Cross Road, enjoying the walk in the blustery dampness of a September day. He turns into Northumberland Avenue, glad to be out of the bustle of the tourists who crowd around Trafalgar Square. There are builders at work down one side of the street and he wonders what the former Metropole Building with the boarded up windows is going to be, if it is to be another building to house the many agents of the British security service. He walks to the Embankment, where he takes the Bakerloo line south. He gets off at the Elephant and Castle and makes a point of studying the Underground map as if he has missed his station. He crosses the platform and takes the next train back to Waterloo. He moves around the main line station concourse, he can't spot anybody following or watching, but he needs to be doubly sure before he goes down to the Underground and gets the Northern line to Tooting Broadway. From there he locates a phone box and rings Donal's special number.

'Right, boy,' says Donal, only this time he is restrained, subdued.

Concisely, quickly, Eamon briefs him. 'The investigation was very thorough. They went back over all the invoices for a number of jobs. Whenever our friend was involved, the invoices were loaded in his favour. When he was absent, on holiday or sick, the margins were what we expected. At first, I had my doubts. Now I have seen the report, and it is very very thorough, I have no doubt that the company has been taken to the cleaners.'

Donal listens without interrupting him. When Eamon finishes, he says, 'You're sure of this?'

'Yes.'

There is a long pause. 'And you have it all on a file?'

'Yes.'

'Get it to me.' Donal gives him an email address. 'Can you do that now, without too much bother to yourself?'

'Yes. I'll call you back in two hours and ten.'

'Good man yourself,' Donal says. However, he does so quietly, as if the enormity of what Eamon has just told him has only now registered fully.

Eamon heads back on the Northern line to Kings Cross. Again, he is watching, checking nobody is following him and is as certain as he can be that he is alone, one of the millions who trek across London every day and night. He goes to the Victoria line and rattles along in an almost empty carriage to Highbury and Islington station. Outside, he walks briskly towards Upper Street, cuts back into a square, doubles round. He is alone; nobody else is in the square. When he is sure he is clear, he heads back to the main road where earlier he spotted an Internet café beneath a greengrocer. He goes down the steps to the basement. It is busy, mostly Middle Eastern and African men in front of screens, he notes, which suits him. At the counter, he waits while the woman has an argument on her mobile phone. Reluctantly she says, 'I have to go now.' He asks the rate. The woman tells him, she seems distracted, as she writes a password on a form and hands it to him. 'Over there love, that machine.' She points to a row of PCs along a wall. The vacant one is at the end of the room, away from the counter. Eamon takes a seat, he inspects the PC, is relieved to note the USB port is on the front of the machine. He logs on, then hunches forward over the keyboard and inserts the flash drive in the port. The woman who served him is back on the phone, is so engrossed in her call she is not watching the room. All the other users sit staring at their screen. Quick as he can he types in Donal's email address, clicks on the attachment sign, locates the file TRAINING POLICY. He presses send, waits as the message vanishes from the outbox. He sends a note to a hotmail address he has used before. When he clicks back to check incoming mail, the hotmail message has been bounced, which he expected as the account has been closed for some weeks. The email to Donal has gone through. Eamon removes the flash drive, surreptitiously slips it in his shirt pocket, logs off, takes his time sheet to the desk, and waits while the woman, who is having some sort of a row on the phone, says loudly, 'I can't be doing with this!' She flings the mobile on the desk behind her, takes his form, and he pays her.

Outside he crosses the road, jumps on the first bus that is going south, stays on it until they reach the river, where he gets off and walks rapidly across Waterloo Bridge. He is tempted to go down to the Royal Festival Hall to find out what concerts are on but he avoids the temptation because he knows he will not be here. Eamon walks back through Covent Garden, past the scrum of people watching the live acts, doubling back now and then, always on the lookout, until he reaches Regent's Park, where he sits on a bench. There is five minutes to wait before he can phone Donal. He thinks of the lines from Macbeth. *If it were done when 'tis done, then 'twere well/It were done quickly.* Done quickly it has to be. He watches a little girl wobbling past on her bike, anxious father jogging beside her, his hand on the saddle. Eamon thinks, I hope to Christ that Donal believes me, and he does not go straight to Iggy Davin. Because if he does, Mary and I are dead.

He hasn't told Donal about the Nuclear Option. Nor Mary. It will be time to do that once they accept that Davin is the long time informer. When he thinks of it – and it's with him all the time – he feels the terror crawling up inside his belly, forcing the nausea into his mouth so much that he has to fight the urge to vomit.

By slow stages, Eamon makes his way home. He flies into Dublin airport, where Paudie, who owns a taxi and makes a living driving to and from Derry airport, and who acts as a driver for Eamon when he needs one, collects him. Paudie, once he senses Eamon is not in a chatty mood, stays silent as they drive across the midlands of Ireland taking the road into the north to Enniskillen and on to Derry. They arrive late in the afternoon. Eamon lets himself in and waits for the summons to Iggy Davin.

Without Mary, the house feels strange. He has spoken to Noreen who looks after the two B&Bs when they are away. There is nothing to report, as she tells him how many bookings they have. Eamon wanders around, he keeps out of sight of the guests, as he usually does, not wanting to either frighten them off or become an object of curiosity should his former life come out. The plan they agreed in London before they went their separate ways, was to behave as normally as they could. Eamon will return and wait for the call to report to Davin. Mary will stay with Charlotte for a few days. What could be more normal than looking after her niece and young baby when she is having problems with her husband? He longs to ring Mary in Limerick, to see if she is all right, to find out if Davin has gone after her. With difficulty, Eamon resists the temptation.

He waits and in the early evening, as dusk falls, he knows they will come for him any time now.

CHAPTER 18

'So,' Ignatius Davin says. He sits in an office chair behind a desk, in a room converted into an office. He is jovial, relaxed even. 'How is Mary?' They are alone.

'Much better. I think it was a touch of food poisoning.'

Eamon is aware of Davin's calmness, the inscrutability on his bland face, the large wodge of fat that seems to support his chin, the crumbs from whatever he has just eaten scattered on his grey pullover, the incongruity of the tie knotted so carefully amidst the disarray of the rest of his clothing. Eamon tries to match Davin's steady gaze as evenly as possible but it is not very long until he feels the return of the familiar panic he suffers in Iggy's presence. How much does he know? How much will he be seeking to tease out? He tells himself that Ignatius Davin is not omnipotent, despite his almost successful efforts to convey otherwise.

In his own time, when he has finished giving Eamon the evil eye, Davin shifts his bulk in the chair, causing it to squeak. 'What's the news?'

Eamon tells him what he has rehearsed, which is that he picked up Flash Gordon – and he always calls him by his soubriquet – as planned, and then followed him to his chalet by the sea. He has pushed down all he knows about the plan to assassinate Paisley. He has to do so if he is to have a chance of surviving this interrogation.

'Describe it,' Davin says.

'I can do better than that. I have some photos on my digital camera.' Eamon shows him, then resumes with his search of the chalet. He is careful not to omit anything, being sure that Ignatius Davin has already received details from his Spanish contacts. When Eamon concludes, Davin says nothing, he leans back in the chair, hands folded across the vast expanse of his belly; the only sign of agitation is the twiddling of his thumbs frantically chasing each other in rotation. Eventually he says, 'That was too easy. It was a set-up.'

Eamon agrees. He notes the early easiness of Davin has gone: the ballistic screening seems to have a new, fiercer intensity. He swivels the chair around. The room is curtained, the lights, one on the desk, a smaller lamp placed on a shelf between box files and neat stacks of printing paper, cast shadows. Eamon wonders if Davin ever sees daylight, so much of his life is nocturnal, most of his day spent in darkness.

'What happened after you saw Michael Donnellan?'

'I left immediately, went back the way I had come in. Mary had the car waiting for me on the road. I waved goodbye to your Spanish friends, and as you stood me down, we went off for our few days on holidays.'

'This place you went to, Baiona?'

Eamon nods. He places the bills from the two Paradors on the desk.

Ignatius Davin gives them a cursory look. 'Why there?'

'Chance, that's all. Mary picked it out of the guidebook.'

'Did it occur to you that Michael might have seen you in the chalet?'

Now Eamon slips into his story, rehearsed, written down, redrafted several times, a tale he has told himself so often, he believes it. 'Of course I did. I couldn't be sure but I'm fairly certain there was CCTV. I blacked up, wore something to hide my face. If he did pick me up, they won't have recognised me. I don't think Donnellan was interested in me. Flash will have briefed him that we were about, but he'll know what my position is in the Movement these days. As you said yourself, Iggy, I am way under the radar. There was nothing taken, or touched in the chalet. I don't imagine there is much of value kept there anyway. Flash uses it solely as a base, because it gives him good cover, just another holiday home not used very often. He's just like anybody else there, with the speedboat registered in its own berth, the house locked and shut up most of the time. He has a smart set-up. I don't think they calculated I'd go in for a poke around.'

'Hmm. You're sure it was wee Michael himself?' Davin grunts; the gaze is unremitting.

But by now Eamon has become used to it, is so far into his act he is not that aware of it. 'I knew it was him as soon as I heard him speak. His voice hasn't changed at all.'

'And what about his nancy boy, Hugh, the Golden Boy?'

'I never saw him. I'm guessing here, but I suspect it was probably

Hugh who went out in the boat with Flash Gordon.'

'That Hugh O'Neill has more lives than a fucking cat. How come he wasn't executed in London?'

'The order was given, Iggy. It was to have happened right after he came off stage,' Eamon says evenly. 'But as you no doubt remember from the debriefing afterwards, he got away.'

'One of the unresolved mysteries,' Davin says calmly. His eyes have never left Eamon's. Now Eamon starts to sweat, his stomach is straining, he wonders just how much Davin knows, how much is calculated speculation.

After a further period, while it seems to Eamon as though Ignatius Davin is seeking to test his nerve through the brooding silence, he says snappily, 'Well, at least we have the evidence, that Flash Gordon and wee Michael work together. You say you have photos of them together?'

'No. But I can do better than that.' Eamon plays what he hopes is his trump. 'I've not only got the photo of the back of Michael's head. I also have his voice on the video.' Davin looks sceptical. Eamon clicks on the video link, plays the shot of the back of Michael Donnellan's head, the view of the sea, of him speaking in Spanish.

Eamon says, 'I got a student of mine to translate it. He tells me all he said is, *'Nothing to report. How long will you be? Okay. I'll see you there.'*

Davin listens intently. 'I'll get this transferred to a computer.'

Eamon nods. Ignatius Davin pockets the camera. Again, there is the silence. 'This sickness Mary had, what was it?'

'As I told you, it was probably food poisoning; we ate a lot of fish, most likely something there.' Eamon is still sweating heavily, he fights to keep control of his bladder; he thinks that is Iggy all over, he relaxes you before hitting you.

'And you were all right?'

'Fine. Just as well really, as she wasn't able to move for a few days.'

'Where was this?'

'In the Parador in Baiona. She was either in bed or in the toilet throwing up. I was nursemaid for a couple of days.'

'So why the return from Lisbon?'

'Because it was closer to Baiona than anywhere in Spain. There were no seats on flights to London from Santiago de Compostela. I managed to find seats to London, and then on here.'

'You took your time in London.'

'Again it was getting seats.'

'You can always get a seat if it's an emergency.'

'I didn't know that it was, Iggy. You told us to have a few days holiday. I don't believe in throwing money away.'

Davin digests this, then stands up. He questions Eamon about the business he manages for the Movement, he tells him to put in a bid to purchase a building, a disused shop that is about to come on the market, on behalf of the Movement. 'You have the know-how. We'll make the usual arrangements about finance.'

'Okay,' Eamon says.

'Right. I'll be seeing you,' Davin says. The interview is over. Eamon leaves, wondering if this is it. He and Mary keep a close eye on the local commercial market. They have not heard of this one, so is this Iggy's way of signing him off? Is he standing him down for now? Or is he hoping to lull him, relax him enough to let something slip?

Outside in the dark, another van waits for Eamon. He climbs into the back, hears the doors locked, he looks at the wooden partition that blocks off the driver and passenger seats as he tries to analyse the meeting. He can interpret the brevity of their meeting either way. Davin is so much in need of the evidence linking Donnellan and Griffin, he just grabbed it, the rest was standard, to make it look as if he was doing the usual debriefing. Alternatively, and this, Eamon thinks, is the more plausible, he is now busily checking back. He will dispatch Pádraig and possibly others to find out if Eamon and Mary did indeed stay in the Parador in Baiona; and while he waits for the information Iggy will go over Eamon's story, to trawl through it, search it for any inconsistencies.

The ride back is bumpier than when they came out. Eamon perches on a bag of tools, clings to the wooden slat on the side. The van smells of oil, he surmises it belongs to an engineer, a mechanic of some sort. He guesses they are going by another route, all of which is standard practice. And if he wonders at Iggy's obsessive need to continue to follow best security practice when they should not have the need to do so, then it reinforces his sense that Iggy is a damn sight more concerned than he is letting on, he tempers it with the knowledge he would do the same. It is instinctive by now. There is a stop, a switch to another van and a shorter ride. Eamon is sweating; he is thrown around as the van picks up speed. Alone in the noisy darkness, he wonders and worries how much

Iggy really knows, if Donal Crowley has told him, if Donal believes the evidence on the file. After all, he may decide to leave well alone. In many ways, the last thing they need is the revelation they have another informer, never mind somebody as revered within the Movement as Ignatius Davin. As they tear around, Eamon wonders if Iggy is having him transported to a further interrogation, the information about the property being just a sop, something to make him relax. Past one, they drop him off in a lay-by near the airport. As if on cue, a taxi swings out of the entrance and glides to a halt. Eamon recognises the driver, one of the older volunteers, now retired, who helps out his son by driving the taxi for him a couple of nights a week.

'Your car is back home, Eamon.' Francie is soft-spoken, but the softness hides a hard vicious streak. Francie had been one of Ignatius Davin's interrogators, brutal and controlled, merciless. Eamon looks at him.

'How's tricks, Francie?'

'Okay. Health not what I'd like it to be, but I make the best of it.'

Eamon looks at the clock in the cab, realises he has been away over seven hours, all for a forty minute interview. He switches his mobile phone on, handed back to him with his other possessions when he got out of the van. There is a message from Mrs McGettigan, who since she discovered texting is in the habit of sending him messages about whatever takes her fancy. There is nothing from Mary, not even her 'Luv u,' that she sends him when they are apart.

'Drop me here, Francie,' he says, at the top of his road. 'I want to stretch my legs before bed.' He puts his hand in his pocket. 'What's the damage?'

Francie says half-indignantly. 'There's no charge for you, Eamon. Anyway, I was on my way home.'

Nevertheless, Eamon stuffs a fiver into his shirt pocket. 'Well buy the new grandson a wee present.'

After the taxi drives off, Eamon waits until his hearing and eyesight adjust to the street. He looks down the hill at his house, at the other side of the street. There is the usual line of parked vehicles. A car passes going up the hill. Two men come out of Buck Mulligan's pub talking quietly then their voices fade away as they walk home.

Satisfied the house is not under an obvious guard, Eamon slips down the side road, turns into the alley that runs along by the back of his house. Quietly as he can, he unlocks the yard door, slips inside and waits. Nothing, not a sound. He looks up at their bedroom on the third floor. There is no light.

Inside the house is deadly quiet. The three downstairs bedrooms are occupied; both B&Bs are full tonight. He goes upstairs to their apartment on the third floor. He moves from room to room, the bedroom, the sitting room and bathroom, his study-cum-office. There is no sign of Mary. He checks the answerphone; the cold distant voice says he has no messages. He does the same with the business line, where there are a few calls from suppliers, an inquiry about a booking for next month. Mary was leaving Limerick about lunchtime. The last call he'd had before he was summonsed to see Davin had been from her, telling him she was about to set out.

To try to calm himself, he sits at his desk and looks down on the street, which is deserted, it is almost one-thirty, the pub has closed, and being a midweek night, there is little happening. He stares, peering into the doorways for anybody lurking, looks for a parked car or van that is occupied, all he notes are the cars and two vans, the usual ones that park overnight. Eamon closes the curtains, switches on the lamp over his desk. It comforts him that he has Donal Crowley's assurances they are continuing to evaluate the file; the initial assessment is that it is dynamite, that it confirms what has long been suspected about Ignatius Davin. It does something to assuage his fear that Davin has hauled in Mary, about the same time he was. Easy enough for him to know her movements, to have her picked up and taken to another safe house. Still trying to remain calm and not panic, he lists on the paper what he thinks Davin knows about Mary.

Is Iggy aware that she slept with Hugh when they were in London? He tries to hide the pain this causes him by telling himself that was how she coped with the intolerable strain, that how people behave on operations is not always normal, besides he was not involved with her then, he regarded her as he did any volunteer. He is sure Iggy does not know, if he did, he's sure Davin would have ordered Mary's execution. The only way he might have found out is if Griffin has talked to him. On that, he has Donnellan's promise that Griffin is under his control. When Eamon contacted him using the emergency phone number, after they saw Griffin in Lisbon, Michael is calm and soothing. 'Yes, we let him go to meet a contact about his business. We had to do so otherwise there would have been complications. However, he was with other members of the company all the time, he was never alone. Believe me, these are very good people, the best, *señor*. We do not employ cowboys. Now he is on holiday, at our staff resort, until I hear from you that the deal is on.'

Suppose Iggy knows anyway, that he has kept it quiet, as he often does when he has information. Mary is tough, though. She stood up to the three weeks of interrogation by the Internal Security Unit after Hugh's escape and the fiasco of the Golden Boy operation. This means, he tries to console himself, that Ignatius Davin is not sure. He wants to believe that there is a connection between Griffin and Michael. Eamon has given him enough evidence. What Iggy is doing now is double-checking. Eamon is thankful they forced Mary to take a dose of sleeping pills, blocking out her memory of most of the long night he spent with Michael. The night of the pissed trousers, as he privately thinks of it.

Sitting there after he switches the light off, he knows his mind is not at rest and will not be until Mary is back. A void inside that opens up whenever he contemplates losing Mary. Of course, Iggy will be very careful. He won't want to take any risks by harming her if he can avoid it. He knows Mary's fiery spirit saved her a couple of times during her grilling, but he is also aware of how she seemed to goad one of the women, who would have beaten Mary to death if they hadn't stopped her.

CHAPTER 19

'We went there for a few days' holiday. I found the hotel by looking in the guidebook,' Mary says calmly. She sits on a hard kitchen chair, in a room bare of any other furniture apart from an old worn-out armchair and settee. There are two men and a woman she does not know. The woman, she assumes, is there to offer some respectability to the proceedings, to give the puritanical side of Ignatius Davin the veneer of probity he always needs when he is questioning a woman. He paces up and down slowly. He has removed his jacket and flung it on the armchair. She notices the back of his pullover is rucked, exposing his shirt, as he hitches up his trousers.

'Go on,' he says.

'I called them up and they had a room but they would only let us have it if we stayed for a minimum of three nights' half board.'

Davin shrugs impatiently. 'Why did you pick there?'

'We'd gone south after we left Arousa, went into Portugal, Eamon thought we might go to Porto and stay there.' Mary is on autopilot; her story is mostly the truth with a few embellishments. 'But there were forest fires in Portugal, so we decided to head back into Spain.'

'What happened to you to make you sick?'

'Something I ate, I assume. All I know is I was suddenly violently sick. I had no strength at all; all I could do was stay in bed. I don't remember much for a couple of days, apart from vomiting and sleeping and drinking water.'

'Did you see a doctor?'

'No.' Mary manages to control a jerk in her leg. She hasn't thought of that. Is there anything else? She watches him as she wonders if Eamon has told Davin she did see a doctor, but decides she can risk getting away without knowing if she had or had not. 'I never thought about it, it just seemed like an upset stomach, the sort of thing that can happen on holiday, particularly when you eat a lot of different food.'

Ignatius Davin appears to be considering this as he does another tour of the room. In that he reminds her a little of Hugh O'Neill, they both have this restlessness, the need to walk as they think.

'After you recovered, you went to Portugal again. Were the forest fires over by then?'

'No, but they were in the north of the country. Once we were past them, it was normal. We had to go somewhere other than Santiago to get flights back. There's only one flight a day from there.' The video camera points straight at her, and she sees the woman is taking notes. Mary wriggles in the seat where she has become stiff as she waited over an hour for Ignatius Davin. 'It was only a matter of sorting out what flights were available. We ended up in Lisbon, it being an international airport, the chances were better for getting flights.'

Ignatius Davin sits behind the video camera, stares at Mary while he digests what she has told him. Mary hates and fears the stare. Davin's mind, when he wants something is like the tide coming in; it creeps and rushes, probing, seeking the weakest part of the defence. Beat me up, she thinks, anything is better than the look. The sweats, that cold clammy feeling; the difficulty as she tries to control her bladder, at least a beating is simple; you just curl inside yourself and wait for it to end. To distract herself, she wonders if he has already pulled Eamon in and suspects he has, that was why they brought her here and held her, forced to sit on the hard kitchen chair as she waited.

'Did you see Flash Gordon again?'

'No. The last time I saw him was when he dropped me off after giving me a spin in his speedboat.'

'Oh. And when was this?' Mary thinks she can hear a hint of surprise; it gives her some hope, a bit of confidence until she wonders what Eamon has told him.

'We were looking around the marina. He came up and offered to give us a trip around the bay in his boat.' Mary tells him how it came about, tells him exactly what happened, including how Griffin tried it on when she was aboard. And here Mary uses her previous knowledge of Ignatius Davin. 'He put his hands on my breasts; he tried to get his hand down inside my pants. He had a hard-on. I could feel his mickey pressing into me. I had to fight him off to stop him trying to strip me naked.'

165

Davin grunts and Mary thinks, good, I hope that makes your puritanical side cringe.

Davin says eventually, 'You were always mad for the men, I'm told.'

'Well you were told wrong,' Mary snaps back. 'You asked what happened and I told you. How was I to know Griffin is a sex maniac? I can't stand him. He makes my skin crawl. I only went on the boat because I was ordered to, so Eamon could find out what we were sent to…'

'All right,' Davin is peremptory. He nods at the guards who leave. 'And Michael Donnellan, what did you make of him?' The question is sudden and almost throws her for a second.

Mary shrugs. 'Nothing. I haven't seen him since he had me locked up in his club in London.'

Davin stares and she can't tell if he believes her, or if he knows the truth. 'I hear from a little birdie that wee Michael and your husband are planning to set up a rival organisation, that Eamon is to be the new Chief of Staff,' he says it softly. 'What did he offer you, Mary? A seat on the Army Council?'

'I was offered nothing. I never saw anybody apart from that sleazebag, Flash Gordon.'

Heavily he says, 'You better be telling me the truth, Mary Delaney…you wouldn't want me to get Francie to persuade you if you're lying.'

'Why would I lie, Iggy? I told you how it was.'

Despite her outward calmness, Mary is tense. Is this it or is it just the hors d'oeuvre? She remembers how in the three weeks of debriefing they had started like this, a short sharp interview, the first session. They left her then for a few hours, waited until she had fallen asleep when they dragged her awake and began a fresh interrogation. She realises she is alone now, apart from the woman, a fat lump with a right bitch's face, Mary thinks. However, she does not take her for granted – if Iggy Davin has chosen her as a guard it is because she can handle any trouble. Terrible doubts fire through her, about Eamon, about Michael Donnellan. What did they talk about during that long night of talks? Is Eamon telling her the truth or just part of it, about the treachery of Ignatius Davin?

Mary has not been offered water and although she is thirsty, she does not ask for any, she does not want to give them a weakness they could play on. She tries to stay focused on the interrogation. Will they rough her up? They did a little of it the last time, slapped her across the face a few times, yanked her hair to pull her head back. They denied her the use of the toilet, forced her to urinate and defecate in the corner of the shed. She was strip-searched, her insides probed by a woman whose only remark was, 'It's all right, I'm a nurse,' as she pulled off a pair of rubber gloves. After that, they left her naked apart from a blanket for three days. That was her punishment for swearing at the guard who beat her up badly. As her backside goes numb, Mary psyches herself up for more of that treatment, because the longer she is here, the more certain she is that it will happen. She supposes they are watching the video, analysing it for anything to indicate her story is not true, monitoring her body language, listening intently to every word, comparing what she has told them to Eamon's account.

After a time, despite her struggle to remain awake, she finds herself nodding off. She has not had much sleep of late, waking early, unable to get back to sleep. Then the terror when her car was forced off the road soon after she left Limerick, outside Newmarket-on-Fergus, a man got in her car and she was bundled out and into another car, where she was blindfolded and did not see light again until she was brought here a few hours later. Mary finds she has dropped off to sleep, but the uncomfortable angle of her neck snaps her awake from time to time. She is aware of her guard changing; for a time both men replace the woman. When the woman returns, Mary asks to use the toilet; she escorts her to a bathroom. She notes the old bath and toilet fittings, the long chain hanging from the cistern. The woman closes the door and stands with her back against it, watching as Mary squats over the toilet.

They take her back to the room, where they give her a blanket and indicate she can use the old lumpy settee. Mary sleeps intermittently. In the morning, she is shaken awake with a silent offer of a mug of tea and some biscuits, which she takes. They allow her to use the bathroom, again under the supervision of her female guard. As there is soap and a towel, she washes her face and hands, and feels a little fresher, more alert. Back in the room, with the curtains closed but not enough to stop the daylight seeping underneath, she says to the woman, 'How long is this going on for?'

The woman shrugs, and does not speak. Mary has not heard her utter a word, when she wants to get her to do anything she indicates.

Mary tries again. 'Let me speak to Iggy, or ask him how long I'm to be kept here. I have a job to go to.'

She knows there is no point in trying to find out anything. The woman remains tight-lipped, silent. The only change in the monotony is when the two men relieve the woman, but they are also silent, do not respond to any of her questions, or even to her mild flirting. Mary decides they are holding her in the hope she will reveal something, or else they are coming back for another more brutal session of interrogation. She guesses it is around midday when the woman hands her a supermarket ham and salad sandwich. Her appetite is not good, she picks at the food, is unable to taste what it is. When it is dark, the woman leaves her for an hour and returns with a plate of sausages and beans and bread, and a mug of tea.

All the time she is terrified of what they might be doing to Eamon, what if they break him and he tells them about the long night in Baiona, when Michael Donnellan laid out so calmly and concisely the details of the treachery of Ignatius Davin. She cannot rid herself of the suspicion that perhaps Eamon has reverted to his old ways of secrecy, that he and Donnellan are planning a new organisation. Alternatively, maybe Donal Crowley has decided for his own reasons to tell Iggy what Eamon has told him. All these fears torment her during the long hours of the day and most of the night; all that sustains her is that she is not being questioned, and if that is so, maybe Iggy Davin is just holding her as a sort of insurance. She can't imagine what for, but that is the only hope she has. Every time the door opens, or she hears movement outside the room, she tenses, wondering if this is it. If Iggy has found out, she knows her death is only a matter of time.

After two days, she has calculated they are in a farmhouse. There is no traffic, little activity apart from the coming and going of the guards. She tries again to engage the woman in small talk, asks if she can have some fresh underwear, maybe a bath. All she receives is a shake of the head.

She is suddenly shaken awake from a deep sleep. She is hauled to her feet, While she slips her shoes on, they blindfold her again and bundle her outside and into the back of a van.

CHAPTER 20

Eamon sits, stands, walks, dozes, because there is nothing else he can do, as he waits through the long night. He hears Isabella, the woman who cooks breakfast for the guests, arrive and he knows without looking at a clock it is six-thirty. After he has said hello, he takes a mug of milky tea, refuses an offer of some toast and goes back upstairs. He waits until seven to phone Mary's niece.

The phone is answered on the second ring, as if Charlotte has been waiting for a call. 'Eamon,' she says and he thinks she is a little downcast as he suspects she is expecting a call from her husband, Bobby, who is probably off on another golf trip. She recovers quickly and says brightly, 'So, how were the holidays?'

'Great, lovely place. Listen Charlie, is Mary up yet?'

'She's not here. She left for home after lunch yesterday.' Charlotte is worried. 'My God, I hope she's all right.'

Despite the fear that seems to have put an icy grip around his heart and invaded his stomach, Eamon is reassuring, at his avuncular best. 'I'm sure she's fine. She said she might call in to see her pal Linda in Sligo. You know what they'll be like when they get together. She probably spent the night with her,' he laughs easily, hopes he has disguised the fear.

'Did you try her mobile?'

Eamon laughs again. 'You might as well ring the Pope himself. When she's out with the pals, she always has it at the bottom of that big bag of hers and she hardly ever hears it ring.'

Charlotte, he can tell, is not convinced. 'Will I give Linda a call?'

'No, no. She'll only get mad if she thinks I'm fussing. I have to go out and do some business. I'll ring later and I'll text her.'

'Tell her to be sure to give me a ring as soon as you speak to her.'

'I will.' Eamon remembers the proprieties. 'How's my favourite godchild?'

'Liam is fine. We're just getting ready to go to the day nursery.'

'Give him a big kiss from me.' Eamon pauses, 'How's Bobby?'

'He's away in Wales. The Munster team have a match in Cardiff tonight,' Charlotte says flatly, without emotion.

For the next few hours, Eamon is busy with his work. Normally Mary does the bills, says goodbye to the guests who are departing, in line with their policy of keeping Eamon out of sight. He makes the bills out, takes cash and cheques and credit cards; he hands out fliers to those who want to see the city. When he gets a request for a tour of the city walls and the Bogside, he offers to book the tour for them and rings Pádraig's mobile phone. After a delay, the connection clicks in. 'Hello…' Pádraig is cautious.

'Pádraig!' Eamon is all bonhomie. 'Eamon here. I have two people with me who want to do the tour of the walls with you. Is that possible?' He listens carefully, notes the slight hesitation as Pádraig decides what to do.

'I can't manage it right now, I'm busy,' he says brusquely.

Eamon chuckles indulgently. 'You're not still on holidays in Spain, are you?'

'Goodbye now.' The phone is switched off. Eamon smiles at the two English visitors, says, 'It must be great to be young,' as he finds another tour and makes the appointment for them.

When he has finished the morning's business, he checks the two mobile phones he and Mary keep for emergencies, those they buy at random in supermarkets and discard once they are used. After that, he checks the office phone and their private line again for any messages. He rings the cottage in Greencastle and lets it ring out until the answerphone clicks in. He does not leave a message. What did you expect, he asks himself? Just accept it. Iggy was always going to haul Mary in for questioning. If she had gone into hiding that would have made him even more suspicious. He will hold her until he is satisfied she is telling him the truth. Eamon goes to his car, he pockets his gun and when he is back in the office, he checks it over. Next, he walks up the hill around the park at the top to a phone box, where he rings Donal Crowley. There is no reply from the special number, so he takes a chance and contacts him on his office phone.

'I'm sorry we are going to be a bit delayed getting down to you,' he says. 'Mary is still away with her friend. She should have been home last night, but she must have decided to stay on for a bit longer.'

Donal, on the surface, is reassuring. 'I know, boy. Women would have you driven to distraction. Yerra, you know what they're like; they come back from the pals when it suits them. As you know, the spare room here is always available. Just let me know when she's back from her travels and we'll have the sheets aired. We could do with seeing all of ye soon. As you well know the missus would be fierce friendly with Mary.'

This is Donal saying he understands. If Mary is not home by the end of the day, they will do something about it, for now, we wait and see, but if we have to move, we're ready to do so.

At least, Eamon thinks, as he walks around the park, they are ready to confront Iggy Davin. By now, Donal knows that there is more than the file about Davin. They have arranged to meet as soon as Eamon is free of Davin. In the meantime, he has written the details of the plot down, sent it in code in an email to Donal, a detailed account of what Michael Donnellan told him. He had finished his message with a stark sentence. *I must ask that this is conveyed to the other members of the club immediately.*

They verified the other file. And there was no effort to cover it up, to accept it and leave Davin unmasked. I can't panic now, he tells himself, I must be rational. All that Iggy is doing is having our story checked while he puts Mary through the hoops, looking for any inconsistencies between what I have told him and what she does. If it is all okay, he will let Mary go. He knows Iggy might hold Mary hostage, in order to squeeze him. He wonders what false information they are feeding Mary, how she is reacting. Stop it, he rebukes himself, it's out of your hands for the day. If not, they will come for him very quickly. Either way, Eamon reckons he will know by the end of the day.

Eamon has a meeting with their accountant in Lifford. Normally Mary deals with him, but he goes in order to keep the appointment and to occupy himself. John Joe is with another client. As he waits in the outer office, he phones Michael Donnellan.

'*Hola, dígame.*' A woman's voice he has not heard before answers.

Eamon is alone in the office. '*Señor Rogers por favor.*'

'One moment please,' the woman says in perfect English.

'There is a problem,' Eamon says quickly. 'The customer is not satisfied – the samples do not appear to be what he is looking for.'

'That is not surprising,' Michael Donnellan says evenly. 'After all, they are extremely delicate bits of merchandise; it will take time to have them evaluated to ensure they meet the high requirements of our client.' He pauses. 'How long have they had the samples?'

'Since yesterday.'

'I don't think that need concern you at this stage. However, if there is not a response by tomorrow, I will arrange to send further samples, to augment the first batch. Rest assured. We value your business and the worth to our company. We will do all in our power to protect your investment.'

You fucking better do that, Michael Donnellan, Eamon swears silently, because if anything happens to Mary, it won't be only Iggy Davin I'll be after.

Michael Donnellan continues. 'What about the other client? How did he find the goods?'

'Favourable. I understand he is in discussions with other members of the board. Once we know how the other samples are received, we'll be in a position to set up the deal.'

One of the accountants employed by John Joe has come into the office while Eamon is on the phone. Eamon smiles, motions to him to return to his desk. He wonders if he is one of Davin's ears, as they call them. John Joe has no connection with the Movement; they use him solely to deal with their own business affairs. But Eamon knows you can never be sure. He replaces the phone and says, 'How's Eddie?'

Eddie, like many in his profession, is not gifted with the social graces. 'Grand,' he says sharply, staring intently at his shoes. 'He'll be out to you in a sec,' and sits before his computer without another glance.

Eamon finds it difficult to concentrate as John Joe reels off figures. Normally Mary is with him when they meet John Joe; he relies on her skill with figures to help him grasp the accounts if they get too complex. John Joe is talking about some tax exemption they are entitled to on their properties in the Republic, but Eamon cannot keep his mind on what he is saying. He tries to focus, anything to keep his mind from worrying and fretting, his imagination from going into overdrive.

When he gets back home, there is a call from Charlotte. 'Any word from Mary?' she asks without any of her normal friendly greetings.

'She's fine. She called me earlier, she met up with some other friend and they made a night of it in Bundoran,' Eamon contrives to chuckle through the lie and it works as Charlotte says, 'Oh good, thanks be to God she's all right. Tell her to give me a ring tonight.'

Eamon knows he has another long restless night ahead. He hears the guests come in for the night. He locks all the downstairs doors, puts the NO VACANCIES sign in the window and goes up to their bedroom; it startles him not to find Mary in bed, propped up reading, as she is most nights. He does not even consider going to bed, although he is tired. Instead, he settles himself in his deep armchair in the living room. He puts a Vivaldi concerto on the CD player, the music goes unheard, and he dozes but never for more than a few minutes. He wonders where they picked up Mary, where they have taken her, has she cracked yet? Because he knows nobody stays silent forever. Is this part of some huge plan, with Michael Donnellan and Iggy Davin using him and Mary while they work together? Is it some devious scheme by British security to compromise the Movement again? Round and round he goes, wrestling with every possibility he can think of, virtually paralysed with fear. And all the time, while he is preoccupied with Mary, with her safety, he is trying to grasp the enormity of Davin's plan.

Before Mary came into his life, he had faced death a few times – he expected to die, prepared himself for it – but then he did not have Mary. He had only himself to worry about. Mary has made him vulnerable in a way he never considered possible. His love for her holds him back from doing what he should, which is to grab hold of one of Davin's legmen and demand to be taken to Iggy. He is half-asleep when the ringing of the front door bell wakes him. He opens the door, a young man hidden in shadow says, 'He wants to see you.'

They do not blindfold him; he recognises the road as they drive over the border into Donegal, to a caravan park that is almost empty, they continue through it into some trees where they escort him into Davin's camper van. Davin sits at the table, with several cartons of Chinese food in front of him. He looks up but does not stop eating, wielding chopsticks with skill and speed.

'Where is she?' Eamon can't help it, he shouts at Davin.

Davin raises an eyebrow, continues eating, and when the cartons are empty, places the chopsticks in one of them. He sucks his teeth, before he says calmly, 'She's under my protection. We are checking her story. You know how it goes.'

'What's there to check, Iggy? We did what you asked. In fact I'd say we did better than that.' Eamon is aware of the frowsty smell of food as the remains congeal in the cartons.

Ignatius Davin does not take his eyes off him as he burps, then swigs some tea. 'You should know by now what high stakes there are here. Let me remind you again what will happen if the True IRA are successful. They will bring another group into play. We are stretched already trying to watch the INLA, Continuity IRA, the Real IRA, not to mention all the other low life who need manners put on them.'

'What the hell are you trying to tell me, Iggy, that I don't know already? I have always been loyal to the Movement. It has been my life, as it has yours. Mary did no more than carry out my orders, she did her usual thorough, professional job. We've done the business like you asked us to do.'

'Sure, Eamon, sure. But there are a few things I'm not too happy about. Those couple of days in London, and then you come back on separate flights. So where has Mary been since she returned?'

'She's been to stay with her niece in Limerick, as I'm sure she has already told you.'

Davin does not blink nor betray any emotion. 'Tell me again what you got up to in London,' he says quietly as he sips some more tea.

'We got in from Lisbon, found somewhere to stay, and then looked for flights. Mary was still feeling under the weather so we decided she should go directly to Shannon, where her niece could pick her up and look after her for a few days until she got her strength back.'

Davin nods, 'So why did you need two days in London?'

'I told you, the flights were busy and expensive. I have a cousin in London so I took the chance to look them up while I was there.'

'You refused to tell us where you were,' Iggy Davin says abruptly. 'Despite being asked a few times, you refused to reveal your whereabouts.'

Eamon looks at him and he thinks he is on a flier here, he smells something but he can't pin any of it down; he suspects Iggy is trying to make him panic. He says calmly, 'Operational security, Iggy. Don't give any information over the phone unless it is essential. I didn't know if Auntie Vera was acting off her own or not. At no stage did she use the emergency code, so I just passed on the bare minimum, as we were always instructed to do. And by waiting for a few days, I got a cheap flight as well.' He decides to press Iggy. 'There was no urgency! You said so. If there was why did you tell us to do our own thing after I confirmed that Michael and Flash Gordon were working together?'

'Where did you fly to?'

'Dublin, as I have already told you. From there I was picked up, came home, made contact and was hauled out to see you almost immediately.'

Ignatius Davin stands up and moves around the camper van, his ursine bulk filling most of the space, like a bear in a small circus ring. He turns back to stare at Eamon. 'Eamon, I've never been convinced we got to the bottom of the London Particular. Somehow I know there is unfinished business there, that it is tied in with this.'

'Sure there is, Iggy. Michael Donnellan and Hugh O'Neill, that's the connection.'

'That's part of the connection, Eamon. The other part is you and Mary.'

Eamon is silent, rigid. Has Mary cracked? Donal Crowley lied to him, strung him along while he and Iggy made their plans to snare him? Alternatively, is Michael Donnellan involved with Iggy in setting up a drug running business? Is he the man behind the sniper?

He says and is surprised at how even he manages to keep his voice, 'Of course, we were part of it then. However, we are not now. And if you hadn't come calling at my door, Iggy, and told me to go to Spain, I would not have met Griffin, or seen Michael Donnellan again, so even that tenuous connection won't hold up.'

'It would not surprise me, Eamon,' Ignatius Davin says quietly but his voice is full of menace, 'if you were tempted to join your old buddy, wee Michael.' He resumes his seat. 'After all, you must have felt you'd had a raw deal. I fought for you all the way, but in the end I had to accept the majority on the Council wanted your head, wanted you out of things. So I'd understand that if one fine day Michael Donnellan comes calling and he says, "Eamon, some of us think the direction the Movement is going in is all wrong. This is just another sell-out to the British and their soulmates, the Unionists, their lackeys in Dublin. That in almost every way I can imagine, all the struggle, all those sacrifices, the deaths and the wounded ruined lives, have been in vain. What have we got for it? A cat's cradle of promises, all strings and loopholes, tricks to keep the boys and girls mesmerised while those at the top get the fame and above all the fortune, nice ministerial salaries and perks in the Northern Ireland Assembly. Some of us believe we have to continue with the armed struggle. It will never end until the British have left all Ireland." That is what I think Michael Donnellan said to you in Spain.

That is why you went into the chalet, why you stayed there and met him and then he spoke to you and sold you the deal.' Davin looks straight at him. 'What did he offer you, Eamon? Chief of Staff of the TIRA Army Council? Wee Michael and you were big buddies once upon a time. You were in charge of Hugh O'Neill. You had the Council order to execute him, capture wee Michael and bring him to trial. But nothing happened, they both escaped. That was why you took so long to return from Spain, why you went to Lisbon and then you go AWOL in London.'

Although inside he is shaking, the sweat drips down his back, he feel his neck is damp, and his stomach is a knot of suppressed wind, Eamon manages to sound sharp and offended 'That is complete bollocks, Iggy. I voted for the Good Friday Agreement. I bought in. I'm sure it's settled. I believe the best way forward is through the ballot box. We don't any longer need to be at war, in a fight we can't win. It's a stalemate.'

'Sure, Eamon. We all believed that in the early days, until the Reverend Paisley took over as the leader of the Prods and began to string us out with his one more demand and when we concede that one, the next one comes along pat. For every step forward, he tries to make us take three backwards.'

'That is all part of the process, Iggy. We can get there because we have time and we are right. I can live with the delaying tactics. And I'll tell you again. Michael Donnellan or anybody else has not made me any such proposition. If they had, I'd have told him what to do with it. If you hadn't ordered me to go to Spain, I wouldn't have known Michael is still alive.'

Ignatius Davin leans back against the wall of the camper van. 'But you did meet Donnellan, didn't you, in that fancy hotel you stayed at in Baiona?'

Eamon stays calm; he sees what Davin is seeking to do. 'No Iggy. I did not meet him there or anywhere else. Apart from the staff, I spoke only to Mary when we were away.'

'You've been making some phone calls though.' He waits as though he expects Eamon to confess all his calls, and when Eamon does not answer him says, 'You rang Pádraig today.'

'Yes I did, as I often do to give him some business for his tours. He's still in Spain from the sounds of it. I suppose you have got him checking up on where Mary and myself stayed.'

Davin does not answer. He nods and Eamon feels a hand on his shoulder. Eamon does not move. 'I want Mary, Iggy. You have no right to hold her.'

Ignatius Davin looks at him in surprise. 'I have every damn right. If there is any possible risk to the Movement, I will hold who I need to for as long as they are required. Don't forget that, Eamon.'

It is almost dawn. Eamon is dropped off on a deserted stretch of road. He walks on to the entrance to a dilapidated rundown bungalow, where he finds his own car. He drives home and is back at the house in twenty minutes. He goes in quietly, finds Isabella in the kitchen, says hello and goes to the apartment. Which is still empty. There are no messages on phones, no texts on mobiles.

CHAPTER 21

To Hugh's surprise, Griffin does not kick up much when Michael Donnellan holds him under house arrest, until Eamon has passed on the information about Davin. All he demands is the freedom to meet some of his contacts in Madrid, alone. When Michael agrees, but sets a time limit for his return, Hugh begins to fret, until Michael Donnellan tells him he is sending Carlos and Mirna to follow Griffin and when Hugh raises an eyebrow, Michael smiles and says, 'They passed you twice half an hour ago and you never blinked. Griffin won't recognise them.'

At Michael's insistence, Jésus accompanies Griffin, trails him, aided by the unobtrusive Carlos and Mirna, both of whom speak fluent Portuguese. Hugh knows how much Jésus loathes Griffin. He shares Hugh's suspicion that all the flashy behaviour brings unnecessary attention, is stupid and dangerous: he wonders how much it is costing Michael to have Griffin under guard in Lisbon, where Griffin demands more time alone to meet his contacts and again Michael agrees.

Hugh sits in the square watching the entrance to the Monument to the Discoveries. In the distance, the white Tower of Belém stands like a lonely sentinel at the mouth of the Tagus. That is me, he thinks glumly, stuck out there and guarding what exactly? Hugh checks his watch. He is early, but absurdly he also expects Griffin to be early. He is nervous, so much so he has been tempted to have a couple of drinks, and is, in a way, pleased to be at work. His mobile trills. 'Hola,' but it is Michael checking he is in place. He tells him that Jésus and Griffin are driving out to meet him.

'Clear about the agreement?'
'Yeah. No problems.'
'Good. Catch you later.'

Since they left Galicia, Hugh has been restless, nervous; he wakes at the slightest noise. More than once, despite Michael's reassurances, he looks at his plans and thinks seriously about getting out of it. All that stops him, he knows, is the sense of loss. At least in Spain he has people around him. There is Michael, of course. Jésus, who he fancies, but knows it is not reciprocated because Jésus is a lover of women, is hardly a mate, but he knows they work well together, they understand one another. The desolation strikes him when he tries to imagine what life would be like if he was to start over again. He thinks of the nick, of being banged up, as they used to call it when he was growing up in London. He knows he has been lucky not to do time, while recognising that since he joined the Movement thirty years ago, he has lived a life that in many ways is as restricted as that of a prisoner.

Come on, he tells himself. Concentrate on the job in hand. He stands and strolls around the square, past the tourists, who are not yet here in numbers this early in the morning. Although he comes to Lisbon regularly, he has never had time to get to know the city. It is always straight in, check into the hotel, sit and watch Michael as he wheels and deals and then he drops him at the airport to fly back to Madrid while Hugh sets out on another of his long drives. He likes these journeys, enjoys picking guys up in the service areas, these fleeting moments of excitement, the whiff of danger, the narrow escapes he's had on a couple of occasions. The guy who was bait for the other two of them who jumped him as he was with the man. Hugh still shakes at the memory, of his own carelessness, of how lucky he was to escape, and only after he had knifed one man, scaring the others away. There is a body buried in a wood outside Elvas close to the Spanish border. As far as Hugh knows, nobody has discovered the corpse that he buried far in the woods, in a deep grave. Since that time, he avoids that route out of the country.

It was another close escape, one he could have avoided, should have done. However, he cannot do that; he needs the smell of danger. That thrill he gets in taking a risk. Maybe I am trying to make it up to poor old God. He never realised when he was alive how he relied on him. Hugh thinks of Godfrey with his tight shorts, the thinning hair combed so carefully and held in place with hair spray, the slightly campy way he talked, his little vanities about his appearance. I did love you, God, only I never realised until you were dead. Where would we be now if Godfrey were still alive? Not doing this he thinks, that's for sure.

From the sea, he walks back towards the centre of the square, wondering why it is taking Griffin and Jésus so long to get here. He knows the traffic along Avenida 24 de Julho often crawls and guesses they are stuck somewhere in it. Unless Griffin has somehow escaped from Jésus, but he is certain Griffin is not going to risk losing whatever vast lump of cash Michael has agreed to pay him. Hugh fingers the packet in his jacket pocket, a squat jiffy bag well sealed with brown sticky tape.

Jésus, driving Griffin's Porsche, parks at the pavement. Hugh walks across slowly, looking for anybody taking an interest in them and gets in the back seat. He and Jésus exchange high fives, their standard greeting. Jésus pulls back into the traffic.

'Okay, where is the man?' Griffin is edgy; he fiddles with his wristwatch strap.

'Waiting for you, we have a little drive first,' Hugh says.

'Fuck that! The deal was we would meet here, in Lisbon, after Baiona. You got what you wanted. I want my money. Now hand over.' Griffin has a head cold, he sniffs, blows his nose on a tissue, which he crumples into a ball and tosses out of the window.

'Shut up,' Hugh says as he slides the snub of his Uzi pistol against the back of Griffin's neck. 'Just do as I tell you.' He has to control the urge to smash Griffin's head open.

'*Joder, que no nos toquen los cojones!*'

'Nobody wants to fuck with you,' Hugh says calmly. 'And I have part of your package.' He shows the sealed jiffy bag to Griffin. 'There has been a change of plan, that's all.' He presses the barrel a little harder against his neck. 'Instead of meeting here, we have a change of venue.'

In the underground car park, Griffin gets out reluctantly, while Jésus escorts him to the rented Renault Espace. 'Round to the back,' Jésus snaps. 'I don't want no trouble. Nothing.'

They stand Griffin against the car, legs spread, arms outstretched on the roof. Hugh searches him, removes his mobile phone, his keys, his gun, a black compact Glock 9mm. Hugh does not recognise it, weighs it in his hand for a moment before transferring it to his rucksack. He leaves him a packet of tissues. In the car, Jésus sits beside Griffin.

'Here,' Hugh tosses the sealed jiffy bag to Griffin, 'check that. You'll see, we keep our word. The balance is when we get to Michael.'

He pays the attendant, while Griffin tears the tape off the jiffy bag. Hugh drives slowly in the heavy traffic out of Lisbon, across the Tagus Bridge, and takes the Sintra road. When they are clear of the city, Jésus says calmly to Griffin. 'Okay, *amigo*, now we have to get you covered up.'

'What the fuck is this? I do a fucking job, I carry out my side of the deal and now this shit!' Griffin is not so much indignant as terrified, Hugh thinks. For a moment, he has a wisp of sympathy for him. He says calmly. 'Come on, Fernando, you know how the Movement operates. Strictly need to know. There is no way you will learn where we are having the meeting. Once Michael has finished, you'll be delivered safely back to where you came from.'

Griffin, he sees in the mirror, carefully puts the cash inside his jacket; he guesses he has a secret secure pocket there. He blows his nose heavily, sniffs and coughs, he takes another tissue and when he has finished throws both from the window. Very skilfully, almost without a perceptible movement, Jésus slips a hood over Griffin's head. He pulls the draw cord and retains the cord in his hands.

'Listen to me, *amigo*, there are air holes for you, but no funny business or I choke you.'

'Yeah, yeah,' Griffin says, his voice full of venom.

Jésus nods at Hugh. 'And just this, *amigo*.' He puts handcuffs on Griffin, moves across and puts the seat in the horizontal position.

As soon as Griffin is hooded, Hugh turns off and loops around the Lisbon ring road until he is on the N3 heading north. They drive in silence for a while. Jésus leans over the passenger seat and says softly to Hugh, *'Mucho luido y pocas nueces.'* Hugh laughs. It is a sign that Jésus is relaxed now, his saying, 'a lot of noise but no walnuts,' being how he expresses relief. Despite that, Hugh is watching the mirrors of the Renault all the time. He is sure Griffin has not come alone; he will have arranged to be followed. By whom it is hard to say, as he has been very careful in keeping any of his associates out of sight, he likes to give the impression that he is a lone operator. Hugh suspects the Santiago woman is somewhere nearby, that Griffin will have suspected they would not meet in Lisbon, because nobody would seriously give advance notice of a location.

'All okay?' Hugh asks.

'Sure.'

He takes the road to Tomar, drives steadily, watching his mirrors and any cars that overtake and then slow down. It does not take him long to reach the outskirts of the town, where he drives steadily into the centre. Griffin is lying beside Jésus, he has not moved or spoken, he may be asleep, or trying to lull them into thinking that. Hugh is uneasy. He can't accept that Griffin has been that trusting, certainly not naïve enough to allow them to spirit him away. But they have not been followed, he is quite sure of that. He wonders if they missed a bug, something secreted that allows him to be located at a safe distance. He mentally goes through the contents of Griffin's pockets. Hugh found nothing during his search – unless Griffin has hidden it inside himself.

When they are close to the entrance to the Parque do Mouchão, Hugh does not slow down but continues past. He holds a hand up to silence Jésús. He goes round a traffic island and drives back into the Praça da República. They pass a taxi rank. He nods at Jésús.

'Okay, *amigo*,' Jésús says as he removes the hood. He handcuffs Griffin and folds his jacket over Griffin's hands. 'Now you come with me.' He has a firm grip on Griffin's arm as he emerges from the car, takes him straight to a taxi and bundles him inside. Hugh accelerates away immediately and heads out of town. Once he has left Tomar, he turns off, parks the car and climbs up to the edge of the old Roman aqueduct, from where he has a clear view of the road. He phones Donnellan.

'They are on their way by taxi. I'm just checking that he came alone.'

'And?'

'Not sure yet. I'll be surprised if he has. I'll be in touch.'

Hugh crouches down behind a pillar so that he isn't visible at ground level; he is out of sight unless he moves suddenly or somebody climbs up the stone steps and sees him there. As he waits, he finds he is longing for a drink: the thirst is as bad as any he had when he drank all day until he fell into bed and temporary oblivion for a few hours. There is nobody, no tourists or other visitors. He knows this is a popular place at nights for lovers, has been here himself once with a man he picked up. Hugh gives it a further fifteen minutes, squats down where he is able to see the road, his hearing alert to the sound of any approaching vehicle. He has to fight the urge to nod off. He has not had much sleep the previous night, no more than three or four hours, and those were restless, full of fearful dreams. The day is hot, the sun beats down, and there is a lack of air. He can see the Renault where he has parked it in the makeshift car park, openly, as though he is a visitor. Then he sees a car approaching, a blue Alfa Romeo, and finds it strange to imagine an acquaintance of Fernando Griffin driving such a modest car. The car pulls in, sees the Renault and stops. Hugh recognises the woman from

Santiago, her coal black hair, the short skirt, the dark almost black skin. She is with a man he does not know. They get out and walk to the car, peer inside. She takes her mobile phone and when Griffin's phone trills in the Renault, they get back in the car, she reverses, turns and shoots back on the road.

'He has company,' Hugh tells Donnellan. 'His bit of skirt from Santiago and another bloke.'

'That it?'

'Here, yes. Want me to take a look, follow them?'

'No. Get back here. Bury his phone somewhere on the way. He's got a location guider in there, I'll bet.'

Hugh wraps Griffin's mobile phone in a plastic bag, ties the bag by the handles then flings it as far as he can into the undergrowth beside the car park. He drives at speed back to Tomar, slowing only to go through the open gates of the Parque do Mouchão and continues to the Estalagem de Santa Iria hotel. After he has parked, he looks carefully around the hotel car park at all the cars, checking for the Alfa Romeo. There is nothing until he spots it outside, parked on a side street. He wonders why they have left it in such a conspicuous place. Maybe they want him to know they are there and waiting for Fernando Griffin. Hugh does not like this at all. If they left the car there, do they know where Michael is staying? That he spends a few days each month in the hotel? How come they know so much about Michael's habits, he thinks, and if they do, then for sure Davin will, even if Griffin has kept quiet, which he doubts. The chance to play off Davin and Donnellan is too great a temptation to somebody like Griffin.

By the time Hugh gets to Donnellan's suite on the third floor, with the views over the Parque do Mouchão and the river, he is breathing heavily. He knocks once, waits, and then quickly gives three single distinct raps. Michael answers the door himself, they go through the small hall into the living room where Griffin sits in a chair, his arms handcuffed behind him, a look of wary rage on his face.

Michael Donnellan says nothing, takes a chair opposite Griffin. 'Now, Fernando, my friend, who was your visitor in Santiago de Compostela? The one who paid a call to your room one evening?'

'It's none of your fucking business. I meet a lot of people.'

'Sure you do. And at peculiar times. But this was at four in the morning, when you had seen somebody out at two and gone to bed. You were asleep when your visitor turned up. An Irish visitor.'

'So what? There are a lot of Irish in Santiago these days. They do the *camino* like anybody else, and they also like to enjoy themselves.' He sneers. 'Or do you still think the only pleasure the Irish have is getting drunk?'

Donnellan nods. Hugh grabs Griffin by the ear and hauls him to his feet. Griffin shuffles. Hugh nods at Jésus. As he does so, Jésus, with the skill of a garrotter, inserts a thin gag in his mouth, which he yanks tight, stifling any further cries from Griffin.

'Drop his trousers,' Donnellan says calmly.

Hugh does so; he sees the terror in Griffin's eye and laughs. 'Your arsehole is safe with me, Fernando. We have a better way.' Without warning, he grabs hold of Griffin's testicles, he twists, squeezes and tugs viciously. Griffin, despite the gag, manages a muffled screech and sinks to his knees.

'Okay, Fernando,' Hugh says. 'That's what we call foreplay. My very good friend here,' he nods towards Jésus, 'he does not believe in such fripperies. He tells me they have a simple custom of dealing with those who betray them. More direct. They pay with their *cojones*. That piece of skirt who has been following you would not like it too much if you go back to her minus that part of your tackle, would she?'

Griffin is not able to speak; he is on his knees, bent over, his head almost on the ground as he tries to regain some strength. Hugh bends down. 'Okay fuckface, start to speak. This is a nice hotel. We don't want to make a mess in the bathroom if we can help it.'

Griffin, ashen-faced, struggles to get up, Hugh takes an elbow, aids him to his feet. Griffin shuffles, his trousers around his ankles. He nods at Jésus, who removes the gag but remains behind Griffin ready to reinsert it.

'Right,' Hugh says, 'who is with your tart from Santiago, the one driving the Alfa Romeo?'

Griffin is about to deny it then changes his mind. 'He works for me. Two other guys are following them.'

'Describe them, and their car.'

'Average height, one is a bit tubby, both have dark hair. They usually wear jeans and shirts. They will be in a silver Toyota. They both wear shades.'

'What are their instructions?'

'To make sure I come out, collect me on a signal. If I don't report in by,' he looks at the clock on the wall, 'two this afternoon, they are to come and find me.'

'How is that to happen?'

Griffin shrugs uneasily. 'We have long established plans.'

'Like a direction finder locked in your mobile phone?'

Griffin shrugs again.

'Because if that is it, they are going to have a long wait,' Hugh says. 'You haven't stuck something where the sun don't shine, have you? Do I have to do a search?'

'You'd like that,' Griffin snaps.

Hugh squeezes his throat, the heel of his hand hard against Griffin's windpipe. 'You better be a bit more helpful or I'll let him sharpen his knife, or maybe I'll let him do it with the blunt one.' To emphasise his point he makes to grab Griffin by the testicles again. Griffin cowers, twists his legs sideways in an effort to protect himself. He takes a moment to recover his speech.

'There was a direction finder in my car. And I had one in my cellular phone. They followed the phone.'

'So how come now the phone is miles from here, your friends are sitting in the car down the road? If they are here, your two goons won't be far behind.'

'I just use the phone. They are hoping you'll be here.'

Again Hugh thinks this smacks too much of advance knowledge, that somebody has done their homework on Michael Donnellan's habits. He signals Donnellan to follow him into the bathroom.

'I don't like this,' he says when they have closed the door. 'I can't believe he has brought only that amount of protection.'

'Why not?' Donnellan says calmly. 'He thinks he'll have Davin's protection as well. Besides, if we do cheat him, he'll reckon to get back at us. No. This is what I suspected would happen. It is to our advantage to have him with us than not. You know the old saying; better have him inside the tent pissing out, than outside pissing in. I let him know I come here now and again. Fernando is a smart boy, he worked it out we might bring him here.'

Hugh shakes his head, unconvinced, as he often is by Michael's thinking.

Back in the room Donnellan says, 'Time to talk, Fernando. What did your visitors in Santiago want?'

'I told them we did some business together, Michael, you and me, that was it. They wanted to know if I'd seen Eamon and Mary, they showed me photos of them. I said I'd never seen them before.'

'All right,' Donnellan says slowly. 'Describe them.'

Griffin giggles nervously. 'That was strange. They were just a couple of kids, a young couple. He was so nervous he was almost shitting his pants. Small thin kid, silly fucker running around Santiago in a Celtic baseball cap.' He has recovered somewhat since his testicles were squeezed but still looks uneasy, wan. 'She was all right, big tits,' he says. 'She looked like she knew what she was doing.'

'So you gave them a little of the story in the hope they would be satisfied with that.'

'They bought it, for sure.'

'Really.' Donnellan says calmly, reasonably. 'And did you find out who they were?'

'Sure. They were from Davin, they said. I believed them.'

'They left you after that?'

'No. They wanted some details of my dealings, where I go to in Ireland.'

'And what about your escapades in Cuba and Colombia?'

'Nothing.' Griffin shrugs. 'It surprised me. I was sure they had come for me, that you were part of the plan. That you had led them to me.'

'So what else did they want to know from you, Fernando? They confirm the link between the three of us, which was not difficult to do. They want some information about where you have your deals in Ireland? I am sure you sold them old contacts, banged up or dead. They don't question you about anything else?'

'A few things, chicken-feed most of it. I thought they were going through the motions for the sake of it. What they wanted to know was if I did business with you.' He shifts uneasily.

'They believed you when you said you did not know Mary or Eamon?'

'How would I know them? I never heard of them until they start following me in Santiago two weeks later and you tell me what you want from me. I agree,' he warms to his valedictory little speech, 'to help you. We have a deal. You pay me when you have finished with them. Well, you finish and now you want to fuck with me.'

'Fernando,' Michael Donnellan says with what seems like infinite patience, 'I want to know what you told them.'

In the large bathroom, Hugh goes to work on Griffin. Jésus inserts the gag, and forces him to bend over the edge of the bath. While Jésus holds Griffin, Hugh pummels his kidneys and ribcage with the small club he carries for such events. He belts it across his shins, hits his toes and ankles. He is starting to think he will have to get serious, when Griffin, who is screaming – there are muffled strangled cries though the gag – indicates he is willing to talk.

'You'd better mean business this time, Mr Flash Gordon,' Hugh says, 'because if I start again I won't stop.'

Griffin doubles up in pain, the welts and bruises on his legs and back and ribcage are angry-looking. He still has his trousers around his ankles. Hugh notices how shrunken his penis is. He moves him out of the bathroom.

Michael Donnellan looks up from reading a magazine, as though they have just returned from a walk. 'Right, Fernando, let's hear it all.'

After Fernando finishes, Hugh hands him a mobile phone. 'Call your mates. Set up a meeting back in Lisbon for a week's time. Let them know you are all right. And speak in Castilian, not Galician.'

By then Donnellan has packed his bag. 'Let's move on it,' he tells Hugh and Jésus.

Later, when Hugh thought about it, as he and Jésus drove over the border, heading to Seville, he was surprised how easy it was to break Griffin. When he says as much, Jésus just spits out of the window and shrugs. 'He is nothing. Always this show, he is hiding his fear.'

Griffin is trussed up, asleep on the back seat. After they had his confession, that two men, posing as drug users, had approached him in Santiago. They wanted to know his connection to Michael Donnellan and Hugh O'Neill. That he had promised to meet them in Santiago in a week after he collected his money from Donnellan, that he had agreed to tell them exactly what had taken place. Hugh, who has some experience of what people withhold under torture, and Jésus, who is even more expert in this dark art, agree that Griffin has told them the truth, or most of it, that he wouldn't risk the money Michael promised for the possibility of a pay-off from Davin.

They drive to Las Tres Mil, the slum on the road outside Seville, between the Guadalquivir River and the main railway line. Hugh has been here before with Jésus, to leave various things with some of his friends among the *chabolistas*, the shantytown inhabitants. In the afternoon heat, even the dogs are no more than idly interested. An emaciated mangy mongrel lifts its head, looks at the car driving slowly past them before dropping its head back to the ground. There is almost no movement at this time of the siesta. Hugh is glad of the air conditioning as he sees the outside temperature is hovering at 39 degrees.

'Over there,' Jésus points to a dilapidated four-story block of flats. 'Go to the back.' Hugh parks among some battered almost wrecked cars, a couple of worn out buggies, three scooters, a rusty bicycle, a football; a tyre on a rope hangs as a makeshift swing in the open doorway.

Hugh stays in the car and watches the elegant figure of Jésus, his black hair tied back in his customary ponytail, the gold neck chain swinging outside his shirt, as his lithe body moves casually, languidly. He picks his way in his soft leather boots through the detritus of the parking area, avoids the potholes and delicately steps through and over the ordure, to check they are expected.

'Okay, it is all right, they wait for us.' He looks at Griffin with contempt; he is obviously reluctant to have to touch him as Hugh grabs him under the arms and hauls Griffin from the car. He is half-asleep from the injection of Tamazepam they gave him before leaving Tomar, as they escort him in through the hall where the smell of dogs and urine is almost overpowering. Slowly they drag, half-carry him up the three flights of stairs to the top floor, where Jésus enters an apartment without knocking. A large man and an equally big woman noisily embrace him. By the open door to the balcony, a donkey tethered to the outside railings looks at them dully, placidly. Hugh is not surprised to see the donkey, he knows that animals are transported up and down in the lift. As Hugh watches, the donkey drops a turd. Fernando Griffin is slowly waking up. He looks at the shitting donkey, at the filthy room; the stench and the heat are intense despite the shade and open windows and the fan blowing the hot air.

'Okay, Fernando, you'll be staying here for the time being. It ain't the Parador, but no harm in roughing it now and then, eh? Now just behave and you'll be fine,' Hugh says evenly and pinches Griffin's cheek.

Griffin looks at him with venom. He is still groggy from the injection but is coming around. 'I want to see Donnellan! This was no part of the deal, fuck this, I'm out of here!'

Jésus has a knife at his neck. 'Don't insult my friends. They will take care of you better than you deserve.'

'Sure they will, Fernando,' Hugh says. He can't help himself, he laughs at the idea of the lover of luxury captive here in squalor, with a shitting donkey for company.

CHAPTER 22

With Mary back from her interrogation, Eamon moves with circumspection. He immerses himself in the business, tidies up all the jobs that need to be done, like visiting Mrs McGettigan and eating another large fry to make up for the one he missed a month or so earlier. As instructed by Ignatius Davin, he puts in a bid for the large commercial property, an old family drapery business that has closed down: he is not surprised when his offer is accepted without any attempt to drive up the price or to delay giving him an answer while other bids are considered. He goes about his life as it was until a month ago when Ignatius Davin hauled him in and everything changed again.

By the end of the week, they are nearing the end of their busy season, the bookings taper off and he and Mary are able to get away to Greencastle for a few days. Although they are unobtrusive, Eamon knows they are under constant surveillance by Ignatius Davin's people. He spots a few familiar faces, recognises the inexperience of some of their watchers but does not let on. He takes it as a given their phones are tapped, that it is also quite probable that Davin has bugged their living quarters. They sweep the cottage with an anti-bugging device and discover a small listening bug high in the ceiling. Eamon decides to leave it, to let Davin think he has him bugged: it is easier to do that than arouse his suspicions by disconnecting it. All it means is they will continue to be careful in their conversation. When they talk on the phone, he and Mary confine their conversations to daily matters, the business, the cottage, the state of Charlotte and Bobby's marriage. Charlotte and their son Liam are coming to stay with them in Greencastle, while she decides if the marriage can be saved. Bobby, who never holds down a job for very long, has been fired from his job driving a delivery van. He is full of indignation, spitting with anger and demands that Eamon, 'sort those fuckers out,' so they will reinstate him. In an effort to calm Bobby, because he cannot afford any sort of disruption at present, he promises to have a word with a friend who has a haulage business in Limerick, although he wonders who in their right mind would want to employ the unreliable Bobby.

While he does all this, he establishes his cover. Donal Crowley heads a task force with all the resources available; it has total power. To attend the meetings, Eamon deploys all the skills he honed in his years on the run. He drives, or others drive him, to remote parts of the country, often secreted in the boot of a car or under the seats of a 4x4. He uses the breakdown of Charlotte's marriage to travel to Limerick to offer comfort and advice and while there or en route, slips away to meetings. The pack, as Eamon privately calls this group, has now examined the evidence against Ignatius Davin, code-named Training File. They have agreed that Ignatius Davin for so long the iconic figure within the Movement – *An Feár Mór*, the Big Man – is the mole on the Army Council. Tracing back, trawling through the details so painstakingly compiled and computed by Michael Donnellan, they have concluded that Davin's involvement with the British Security Services stretches back to his early days in the Movement, probably from when he was elected to the Army Executive before becoming a member of the Army Council, over twenty-five years ago.

Eamon, walking alone one morning in late October along the banks of Lough Foyle, while Mary is talking to Charlotte, trying to help her over her infatuation with the feckless Bobby, thinks the unmasking of Iggy should not be such a seismic event to the four of them who examined the evidence. After all, we are an organisation with a long history of betrayal, of informers at all levels from the part-timers to those at the top of the Movement. For some of his years of active service, Eamon sat as a judge in courts, as a member of the team who decided the sentences of those found guilty – who was given a beating or any of the other punishments deemed to fit the crime. He has condemned men and one woman to death for the most heinous crime in the Republican code, that of informer. He is sure they have been wrong at times in some of their convictions, that innocent men and women were put to death. Other people were sentenced who should never have been exposed to the dangers of their work, too weak to resist the blandishments or blackmail, whatever it was that made them turn over information detrimental to the safety of the Movement and its members, the secret known only to themselves and temptation. However, to have confirmed at this stage of their long journey that the most respected, revered figure is not what they believed, is indeed responsible for the most odious crime in their world, is still almost unbelievable for some. Head down against the stiff breeze sweeping across Balbane Head, Eamon is thinking about how they are going to take Iggy Davin out of circulation. Killing him is relatively easy, despite the many layers of protection he has around him. His movements, though secret and at times unpredictable, nevertheless have to follow certain procedures, he adheres to timetables; as Chief of Staff, he has to attend and chair meetings of the Army Council. Simple enough there to take him outside and put a bullet through the back of his neck. Here the four members of the pack have arrived at a consensus, without any discussion, namely that they will confront Iggy, accuse him, give him a chance to explain what led him to betray so many people over his years in the highest echelons of the Movement. There are important pieces of information to prise out of him. For example, is he alone? Is there within the ranks somebody who acts as his messenger boy? Who does he report to, the British or the Irish security? Who runs him? Who is his controller; is there more than one? There are the ways and means he uses to get in contact, to hold meetings. How he presses the panic button. Not least, there are his reasons, his gains, financial and others.

That night, after Charlotte and Liam have gone to bed, when Mary is alone in their double bed, Eamon slips out through the back garden. He makes his way in the black squally night, with the wind gusting and soughing through the hedges and trees, to a back lane where Donal Crowley's nephew, Ciaran, waits to drive him to the safe house they have brought into use over the past few weeks. An old derelict cottage that Eamon and Mary purchased some time ago and which they have been restoring themselves whenever they have some time. Eamon has made it secure, fitted blackout panels, new double locks. The only approach is along a path, too narrow to take a car or van, a route that is easily watched. Donal has brought along Ciaran and gathered a squad of six guards who stake out the area, augmented by three of Eamon's locals, men he knows are personally loyal to him, which is not to say he did not think very hard about recruiting them for the job. After the unmasking of Ignatius Davin, it is difficult to know who to trust. Ciaran is a bright young man, who impresses Eamon with his coolness: there is the same deceptive chatter that his uncle uses to hide the steel, the quiet patient determination.

'How are we doing, Ciaran?'

'Grand so far. No bother. We have the area covered. It's a good spot, well concealed. You'd want to have very good local knowledge to find it. Your own lads know the countryside, so I've deployed them in the outer ring. They also have the advantage of knowing local people and if they have to talk they won't give themselves away by their accents.' He is silent as they bump along a small boreen. 'To be doubly sure the cottage is safe and secure, a couple of us went over it again today. As well, we have a couple of good dogs in the caravan. If somebody does turn up, it will only be because they have had a tip-off.'

Eamon nods. It is the constant fear. Who knows who the informers are, who will have dropped a hint, maybe inadvertently or through that sense of false pride let slip that they are privy to certain information? Again, Eamon checks his own men. He can't imagine any of them being other than tight-lipped, their dourness is normal and accepted.

They come to the meeting singly, at gaps of between ten and twenty minutes. Eamon is the last to arrive. Inside the cottage they sit at a table Eamon and Mary bought at an auction in Beleek, which he is in the early stages of restoring. Before they begin, Eamon covers the table with a cloth. They sit on plastic garden chairs. There is little else in the room, apart from the lights, which are supplied by a generator.

Eamon surveys the others. Even though this is the sixth time they have met, he still finds himself speculating, wondering and fearing if anybody is an ally of Davin. How many committees have met over the years without Davin? As they shuffle papers, he looks slowly around the table. At least I am sure of Donal Crowley, he thinks.

Eoin McDonagh, one of the bright guys in the Belfast brigade, a muscular, heavily built man, whose body looks beefed up from long sessions on the weights, sits beside Donal. His shaven head and thick neck give him a slightly simian appearance. Eoin was serving fifteen years in the Maze, where he was the Officer Commanding of the Republican prisoners, and was one of those released early from the Maze as part of the Good Friday Agreement. Despite his reputation as a hardliner and a militant, he has accepted the Agreement as the best the Movement would get and he helped the leadership to sell it to those of the members who saw only an endless war as the way to rid the island of the British. Eamon knows he has always been close to Davin, that once he was a protégée of his: now he is a member of the committee that is about to set in motion the plan to capture and interrogate Davin. So far, Eamon has to admit, he has appeared impartial, examining the evidence with a forensic attention to detail.

Breda Kelly is from a family with deep roots in the Movement; her father was a former Chief of Staff of the Army Council, her uncles and grandfather were also long-time IRA members. Breda is a small woman, with pretty, photogenic features, often used by the Movement for TV interviews. Eamon knows that beneath the feminine exterior, she is as hard as nails, an interrogator with a fearsome reputation. Breda was one of those who interrogated him and Mary after Golden Boy and he knows Mary hates her guts. In private, she is a nail biter and a chain smoker. Eamon has no knowledge of where she stands in Davin's estimation, not very high he suspects, given Davin's antipathy to the rise of women in the ranks of the Movement. How secure is Breda? Could her atavistic instincts be against the Agreement? Eamon realises he still does not believe that Davin has thrown his support behind it, he is doing what he always does, he supports the present leadership's policy while keeping in contact with those who oppose it and is willing to abandon any position if he can do so with credibility in order to gain further influence.

Eamon and Donal, who is there in his own right as a member of the IRA executive council, make up the pack.

Donal looks slowly around the table and ends with Eamon. 'We are agreed, so? The evidence is compelling. We have no choice but to act.'

There is a nodding of heads.

'We have approached the politicals, I take it?' Eoin McDonagh asks. He knows they would not be at this stage without the agreement of the leadership of the Movement at all levels. Eamon is briefly puzzled why he has asked that question. He glances quickly at Donal, who says calmly, 'Yes, it's all cleared.' Eamon wonders who else knows and he decides McDonagh is as nervous as the rest of them, that the obvious question is just a way of opening his contribution to the discussion, a loosener to ease the tension.

'Right folks,' Donal says, as the wind whistles around the roof and shakes the hardboard nailed over the window frames, 'We need a timetable. Then we need to decide on ways and means. It will have to be as tight as anything we have ever done. I think we all know the risks involved if we don't get this right. There will not be any second chance.'

'What arrangements have you with himself, for a panic meeting?' Breda asks Eamon.

'I make a call to a landline and leave a message, which changes every three days. The message is usually that I need a plumber or an electrician, some domestic emergency.'

'Then what happens?' Eoin asks.

'I go to one of three pick-up points all outside the city, they tell me in their reply. I drive and wait and get collected.'

'How many pick you up?' Breda is short and stocky with cropped red hair. Eamon notices her fingernails, bitten back almost to the cuticles. She has already stubbed out three cigarettes while waiting for the meeting to begin.

'A plain van, sealed off from the driver. There are always two when I'm picked up, sometimes one on the return journey. Well that's what happens when I am summonsed. I have never had to use the panic button. I get in the back, the door is locked and I'm driven off. Sometimes we change vans, sometimes not. The length of the journey varies, from twenty minutes to a couple of hours. We've met in safe houses in the Gweedore, I'm fairly sure. When I got back this time I was debriefed in what looked like a bungalow, near to his own place, I think, from the little I saw. It was almost dusk when I got there.'

'If he had you brought to his own place he must have been anxious to see you,' Breda says.

Eamon ignores her. 'We also meet in a big camper van he uses. I've been in that twice.'

'He's been buying and selling those for a while. Easy enough to change vans whenever he wants,' Eoin McDonagh says. He pauses for a moment. 'Tell me, Eamon, what your assessment would be if you pushed the panic button. What do you think he's likely to do? Surely to God he wouldn't wait for a day or two, have you brought by a long route to the safe house. Not if it's an emergency.'

Eamon has been thinking along the same lines. 'I suppose not. But you never know with him, he is unpredictable. He has a sixth sense where danger is concerned. One of the points that hit me in the report, as I'm sure it did to everybody else, was how close he was to being exposed a few years ago, and what happens? He suddenly has a heart bypass. Goes out of circulation for the best part of a year. Comes back when there is a lot of doubt, unease over the Good Friday Agreement. Does his bit of calming down the lads, reins in the doubters, gets the whip out against the recalcitrants and becomes the hero of the hour.'

'Puts manners on them, you mean,' Eoin says, and Eamon thinks it is a sign of how serious they are there is not even a smile at this mocking of Iggy's catchphrase.

'What are you getting at, boy?' Donal says. 'Would you ever tell us what you mean?'

'That he reminds me of a deer. He stands there and the first whiff of a scent he's gone. We have to be very careful and when we move we have to be very fast, because he'll bolt, like a deer does, at the slightest hint. I mean, he'll not be complacent, he must know how close people have been to him over the years, he must be expecting another probe at any time.' He pauses, 'Now maybe it would suit us if the Brits got him away quickly, I'm sure the plans are there, they won't want to lose somebody who is as important to them as he's been, they will soon have him kitted up with a new identity, a hefty pay-off and pension, a new life in Australia or the States. But we don't want that, as we agreed. He is to be brought to trial, made accountable, his crimes made public.' Eamon looks at them individually. 'This will have to be baited carefully, and above all the net has to be secure.'

'Agreed,' Donal says and the other two nod in confirmation. 'Suggestions?'

'I know I can get a meeting with him very quickly. I am pretty sure he's satisfied himself that Mary and myself have brought him back what he wanted, which is evidence to stick the drug running on to Michael Donnellan and with it the funding of TIRA. We can say something along the lines that Donnellan has contacted me, wants a meeting here, maybe in the South. That is the easy bit. It's what comes next that we need to sort out now.'

There are individual bottles of mineral water in front of them. Eamon sips and listens to the wind, he wonders again how secure they are here, if Mary and Charlotte are all right, although he has posted a further two of his men to watch the cottage, in case Bobby turns up drunk, or in the remote chance of a raid by Iggy's men. If Iggy does suspect, he can let the Irish government know, a hint, a nod from his

British minders will be enough for them to try to lift them all and hold them, even kill them – it is easy to claim they resisted arrest. Alternatively, they could stake the place out and pick them up one by one as they left. He dismisses it. He has made the location as secure as he can, he has had guards watching the place for over a week and there have been no reports of anybody in the vicinity, not even a hiker or two, whose curiosity might take them down this almost concealed boreen.

Breda is first to speak. 'You're right. It has to be something to do with Donnellan trying to recruit you. Give him details of what you've been offered, tell him you're waiting for the meeting, or should we give a time and place for that as well?'

'All that matters,' Eoin says calmly, 'is that he agrees to see you. That's when we move in.'

Donal has a sheet of paper with some notes in his tidy tiny handwriting. He says in his deliberate way, 'Before we dangle the carrot in front of the horse, we need to be sure we can get the halter around his neck long enough to lead him to our horsebox.'

'Have we the resources?' Eamon asks.

'That's not the problem. We have the numbers. It's who is best for the job.' Breda says.

'And who we can trust,' Eoin says sharply. 'You know how he's regarded among the lads. I'll admit to you now, I had to force myself almost when I read it through. So what some of his loyal followers will believe is going to be a big, big problem.'

Eamon grimaces. 'How many can we muster?' He looks at the three of them. 'We cannot risk anybody from the Internal Security Unit. We have to keep them in the dark.'

'We can do that all right,' Eoin says calmly. 'They are too busy doing Iggy's work, they only listen to him. A lot of that group are not popular. They are a bit of a law to themselves. But we will need to have them watched as well.'

The wind has died down, only the drumbeats of rain on the roof break the silence as they sit and make notes and calculate. Eamon gets up to stretch his legs. They resume and begin to put teams together. They lay out a grid, a timetable, appoint leaders and assign tasks to different groups, decide on who will do the recruiting.

'Okay,' Eamon says when he has looked at the grid, checked over the plans and cast an eye over the names of the groups. 'Most important of all. Who is going to follow me when I'm picked up by Iggy's men?'

'I have just the man,' Donal says. 'A driver we call Shadow. You can never find him.'

'If he's not local, he'll stick out,' Breda says.

'He won't stick out, not this man, I promise you that,' Donal says firmly. He writes a name on his sheet of paper and pushes it in front of Eamon. 'That do you?'

Eamon glances at the name. 'He'll do,' he says, and knows he says that because that is all he can say, they don't have anybody else. He remembers Shadow from way back and wonders if he can still be as good behind the wheel of a car as he was in his prime. But that is what we are down to, he thinks, none of us are any longer at our best.

They resume the planning. When they draw up rosters, they settle on call signs, they agree codes on mobile phones; the phones will be purchased individually and will not be used until the operation. There is agreement on complete secrecy, nobody outside the four of them here, and Shadow and Ciaran, will know the details of who is to be snatched.

By the time they have done all this, it is gone five in the morning.

Donal Crowley yawns nervously, hiding it behind his hand. 'So what message will you give himself, Eamon?'

'That Michael has made contact. He is ready to start recruiting heavily. He is willing to make funds available and he wants me to become Chief of Staff.' He pauses, 'Which is what Iggy accused me of accepting already. I'll tell him how I admire his prescience.' He pauses again. 'You will have to be right in after me, because if he doesn't believe me, or if he has different information, I'm not going to be seeing any of you again.'

'We know what's needed,' Eoin says quietly, firmly.

'I'll wait to hear from you. How long before we're ready to go?'

'No more than thirty-six hours. If we can get things sooner, I'll let you know,' Donal says. 'We are all aware of how little time we have.'

Donal is the last to leave. Before he goes, Eamon says, 'That offer of staying with you…' Donal nods. 'I want Mary out of all this.' Briefly, he tells him about Charlotte and her problems with Bobby.

'Leave that to me, boy. Send her down to the missus. I'll make the arrangements to have her met and driven to my place. You need have no fear of her there, boy. My lads have me well guarded all the time. Greta will look after Mary and Charlotte.'

'I know that, Donal. Thanks. Okay. Here are the keys for the cottage. By the time you call in later this morning, I'll be gone, so just settle in. They all know you from your last visit, so I don't anticipate any problems.'

'Good,' Donal says pocketing the bunch. He pauses for a minute. 'Her husband, what's his name, Bobby? – maybe we should take him out of the way for a few days as well?'

'Good idea. It wouldn't surprise me if Iggy does know about Bobby.'

'Better not take any chances. Leave that to me.'

'And the other matter?'

'O'Dowd, our former Adjutant-General, is under surveillance, we're ready to pick him up as soon as we have Iggy.' Donal sighs and for a minute his usual mask of geniality falls away. 'As you can imagine that was the clincher all right. If word ever gets out…'

Eamon puts his hand on Donal's shoulder and squeezes it.

Eamon is the last to go. He stacks the garden chairs in a corner, checks the room carefully as he removes any trace of the meeting, he puts the empty water bottles in a plastic bag, along with the cigarette stubs and ash left by Breda. He double-checks the building until he is satisfied there is nothing left to indicate there has been a meeting, that it looks as innocent of anything apart from some restoration work. After he switches the lights off, he opens the doors to let the air blow through and remove the smell of smoke.

Ciaran has driven Donal away. A man materialises from the darkness. 'Hello, Eamon,' he says. 'Shadow,' Eamon says grimly. He gives him exact directions about where to park and wait. Shadow gives Eamon a number. 'Three rings when you leave the house, and I'm with you.'

'Okay.'

When he gets back to the cottage, Mary is sitting in her dressing gown at the kitchen table. He can tell she has not been to sleep. They do not speak for a moment. Eamon sits down and Mary pours him tea from the pot. Eamon looks at her and then perceptibly towards the ceiling and the bug.

Briefly, he tells her what she is to do.

'I want to stay here, be near to you. Surely Charlotte will be all right on her own for a little longer?' Mary says.

'I know you do. But Charlotte is vulnerable. Bobby boy is trouble. And wee Liam as well, we can't risk them. I don't want to be away from you any longer than I have to. But we must look after Charlotte and Liam.' Eamon holds her tightly. 'You know how we'd never forgive ourselves if anything happened to them. All we struggled to help them could be undone.'

He has wrestled with telling her about Davin's plan, and in the end the old operating rule took over: tell only those that have to know.

Mary nods against his chest; they hold each other for a long time.

CHAPTER 23

Eamon goes the following day to examine the property he has purchased on behalf of the Movement. The deal is all but done; he is waiting for the exchange of contracts, the completion of the legal arrangements. He tours the premises, the offices upstairs and the small cashier's cubbyhole overlooking the shop area. He can remember as a small boy being fascinated by the pneumatic tubes snapping and whooshing into place sending bills, documents, money and change to and fro from the counter to the cubbyhole and back. Not that they came here very often, money was always tight; he thinks it must have been for his First Communion suit. He attempts to control his nerves, to banish the icy dread in his stomach, by trying to envisage the premises as a café and restaurant: there are plans for an internet café in the basement and function rooms on the upper floors. Another part of his mind is checking what is in place and what is left to do. Only now and then is he aware of Chabrior's España coming through from his IPod. Donal, Eoin and Breda have put their units in place, deployed them as close as they dare to Davin's home, around Eamon, and over the border ready to spirit Davin away to a safe house. Shadow, true to his soubriquet, has faded into the streets around the B&B where Eamon and Mary live. Eamon thought he had spotted him driving an aged battered Ford Escort, parking it outside the chemist's shop opposite in the afternoon after he returned from Greencastle. When he came out to walk down to inspect the premises there was no sign of Shadow or his car. I hope to Christ Shadow is as good as he claims to be, he thinks. He knows from his long experience that even the most meticulously planned operations can be blown off course by a slight thing, something unforeseen, a haphazard event that was not taken into account. How long will he have after he tells Iggy that Michael Donnellan has contacted him, before Iggy's formidable antennae start to twitch, to send signals so that his penetrating mind confirms he is in danger? Not long, Eamon knows. His story that he is about to be offered the job of Chief of Staff of the TIRA, the job Davin has already accused him of taking, will have to be good enough to hold

Davin back for as long as it takes to come and get him. This is shit or bust, Eamon knows.

Mary phones at nine to tell him that she is with Charlotte and Liam at Donal's house in Co Cork. For the sake of any listeners, she asks Eamon about Donal, does he have all he needs for his fishing holiday while staying in their cottage, which is also her code if Eamon is all right. He assures her all is well. He asks about Bobby, if he has been pestering her, to which Mary says no, she hasn't heard from him all day, which indicates Donal's men are hiding him for the next twenty-four hours. All in place so far, Eamon thinks as he paces around his study, wondering what else he can do; something is bound to go wrong, because there is always the unknown, the unexpected, the fluke. At nine-thirty, he sends a text to Donal. 'Mary says tanx.' Which is his message that he is about to press the panic button.

He walks down to the town, sauntering, nodding and saying hello to a few people. He passes a phone box littered with empty cigarette packets and crumbled newspapers, the grey walls scratched with obscenities. Eamon hesitates, he goes through the motions of patting his jacket as though searching for his mobile phone. He goes in, picks up the phone and dials, gets through and lets it ring out. Which means use the next number.

By now, his hands are clammy and his legs feel weak, he breathes with difficulty. However, when he exits from the phone box, he shakes his head as though in disgust, and continues his evening stroll. The weather is mild, there is no wind, and people walk around without jackets.

In the City Hotel, the foyer is crowded with American tourists drinking their after-dinner coffee. Eamon makes for the Gents where he rinses his hands. Back in the foyer, he heads for the public phone. This time the answerphone clicks on after four rings. There is no message. Eamon says slowly and clearly, 'The water tank in the loft is leaking. I need a plumber to fix it by tomorrow. For now I've switched off the water.'

Outside, he walks slowly back up the hill to the house, looking neither left nor right. By the time he is back in their living room, his mobile has a text. 'Wit u ASAP.' This means he is to go out to the Buncranna Road and wait in the second lay-by, so it is to be a fast meeting, he will not be going very far to meet Iggy Davin. As he drives away, he resists the temptation to check his mirrors to see if Shadow is following, if he picked up the three rings Eamon did a few minutes earlier. I'm off and running now, he thinks, I can't stop. He drives slowly until he is outside the town. There is no sign of the Ford Escort and in a way, he is not surprised because if Shadow is as good as his reputation, he won't be obvious. A couple of cars overtake him, otherwise he is alone. He wonders if Donal received his second text. 'Fishing ok tomorrow.' He can't resist drumming his fingers on the steering wheel, any more than he is able to stop humming the March of the Toreadors. He alternates between that and touching the cold tyre lever beside his seat. His gun is in the usual cache hidden in the left hand side of the driver's seat. He knows there is no point in taking it with him. All he will have on him is his money, mobile phone, a set of keys, his pocket diary, all of which he will hand over before he gets in the van or car. He thinks he could be wrong about it being a quick meeting, going to the Buncranna Road may not mean anything; it could still be a long circuitous trip to a safe house or a short one to Iggy's camper van. Conjecture about his destination is pointless: Iggy will have decided on this meeting place well in advance in case it ever happens.

Eamon sees a van waiting in the lay-by. A man stands outside smoking, a mobile phone pressed to his ear. Eamon takes a deep breath and parks behind the van. In the darkness he can't make out who he is.

'Are you the fella who knows a plumber?' Eamon says.

The man nods. 'Empty your pockets.' He takes the car keys. 'Have you locked it?'

'Yes.' Eamon hands over his money, phone, house keys and diary. When he has done so the man frisks him quickly, expertly. 'Okay, in the back.' Eamon climbs into a van he does not recognise. 'Let me have your shoes,' the man says. Eamon does not ask why, as he is handed a pair of trainers without laces. 'You can wear those.' Eamon feels a shiver of real fear. They had discussed fitting something in the heel of one of his shoes, then dismissed it as too dangerous, too risky, because if it were discovered Eamon would be dead within minutes. In the end, it was Donal's advocacy of Shadow's skill as a tracker that clinched the argument. But Eamon can't help wondering if somehow Davin has heard part of their discussion. He pulls the trainers on, the door is locked, the engine starts and they move off.

Eamon finds he is thinking back to his early days in the Movement. Both his parents were staunch Republicans, at a time when not many were. It meant his father was suspect to many employers and was forced to take whatever work he could. Despite that, Eamon and his sisters were well educated, Eamon going on to teacher training college. Then everything changed when he went on the Peace March, the infamous day when the RUC and B Specials, the auxiliary police force, attacked the marchers at Burntollet Bridge. Eamon had been batoned to the ground. He was lying there, bleeding from a head wound, when Ignatius Davin hauled him to safety. He has never forgotten the sentence Iggy spoke before he left him, 'We can't put up with this any longer.' Eamon, along with other marchers, had been expecting the march to be disrupted, and then rerouted. With the attention from the world media, he assumed there would not be any violence from the RUC or B Specials. Up to then he considered himself a moderate, who believed they could achieve their rights, be treated as equals and not second-class citizens, through peaceful means. The Civil Rights movement in the States seemed to be achieving their aims in that manner. That day it all changed for him as the first rocks and stones began to shower down on them and his belief in peaceful means evaporated when the RUC baton-charged the march: not discriminating who they clubbed to the ground, young and old, women and men, the famous and the ordinary, were left senseless and bleeding. He thinks of the words of William O'Brien: *Violence is the only way of ensuring a hearing for moderation.* How, reluctantly, he came to believe that was true.

 The van bumps along. By now, he is used to jerking from side to side, as he hangs on to the wheel hub, bracing himself as best he can. He tries to remember when the imposing figure of Ignatius Davin next came into his life. Both of them lifted in the round-up of IRA suspects. We started together then, he thinks, Iggy and me, interned in Magilligan Camp. From where we escaped, the plan hatched by Iggy, by swimming across Lough Foyle, to a motor boat, which ferried us to the relative safety of Irish coastal waters. The leadership, anxious to garner as much publicity as possible, pushed them hard to give a press conference, go on TV, which Iggy and Eamon refused to do. Their escape, as Michael Donnellan had reminded him, had the British press alternating between admiration at the daring plan and outrage at the lax security that allowed it to take place. No credit given for the ingenuity of Iggy's plan.

 That was Iggy Davin, a bull of a man, who then went his own

way for some years, until they came together, the Young Turks on the Army Council. We go back a long way, Iggy and me, he thinks. The van stops, Eamon tenses, but they move off again, as if at a traffic light. He wonders where they are, calculates they have been on the move for about half an hour. He repeats his opening statement for Iggy. It will have to be convincing, he knows, like the first sentence in a novel, good enough to hold his attention, rouse his curiosity, make him fearful, while keeping dormant his suspicions about Eamon.

When they stop, Eamon clambers out. 'Okay boss,' says one of the men, 'I have to put this on you here.' He blindfolds Eamon. 'I'm supposed to cuff you as well, just in case you get too restless.' This is said half-apologetically.

'I know the rules,' Eamon says evenly. 'Do what you've been told to do.' He feels the hard metal on his wrists. They take an arm each and lead him across some uneven land, transfer him to what he guesses is a 4x4, due to the height from the ground. They move off, twisting and turning down boreens and lanes, he hears bushes and trees scrape on the windows.

He is surprised when they stop again that there is no further change of vehicle, calculates they have been driving for a further thirty minutes or so. Still blindfolded and cuffed, they steer him over rough ground for another ten minutes, he suspects to disorientate him as he stumbles in the loose trainers and feels the wet grass soaking his socks. Eamon sniffs deeply, he tries to locate the whiff of the sea, the smells of farm slurry, or animals or silo feed, but the swirling breeze defeats him. They take him indoors, he senses light through the blindfold, the building is warm, they manoeuvre him towards a chair. Once he sits, somebody removes the cuffs and blindfold.

'Right, Eamon,' Ignatius Davin says, 'to business.'

Eamon blinks, he shields his eyes with his hand, the lamp points directly into his face, and he tries to accustom his eyes to the blinding light. He sees a plastic bottle of water on a table and helps himself to a drink. 'I've had a message from Michael. He wants to meet me in a day or so. He has a proposition he thinks I will find impossible to ignore.' He massages his wrists where the cuffs have rubbed.

'What is it?' Davin's voice is close. Eamon can just make out his bulk on the other side of the light. 'What does he want?'

'I don't know. It could be he wants to involve me in one of his deals. He was always in business of some sort or other. Or else you were right and he wants to persuade me to join him in the True IRA.'

Davin is silent. Eamon know he is the object of his basilisk stare, he can almost feel Davin's suspicions, hear his mind rehearsing the arguments, balancing all Eamon and Mary told him when he questioned them. When he eventually speaks, he says quietly, 'So what do you think Eamon? Is he trying to make mischief?'

Eamon is aware of his wet feet, of how he can't judge the effect he is having on Iggy because he is unable to see his face. 'I don't know, Iggy. It might be business, after all the economy in the Republic is booming.'

'A good way of getting money into circulation, to recruit for his private army.' He stops again. Eamon strains for any other noise; he can't tell if he is alone with Iggy or if there are others in the room. 'How did you get this message?'

'A phone call to the office line, the one we use for bookings in the B&B. It was left about 2am. We were in Greencastle that night, it was on the answerphone when I got back.'

'Have you kept it?'

'No, I haven't. I erased it.' He is aware of Iggy's heavy breathing, as if he is trying to control his temper.

'Let me have the message word for word, Eamon. I want that famous memory to give it to me verbatim.'

The cold and damp, his wet feet, are forgotten. Eamon is sweating. How far away are Donal and Ciaran and the others, Eoin, Breda? Did Shadow succeed in following him? If he did, was he able to do so without being observed. He has not heard any sounds of a fight, no gunshots, screaming and shouting, the clamour of a raid. Eamon takes a deep breath. '"I wish to enquire about doing some business with you. This would be over a long time. I am calling you from Spain. I have a business proposition I think would be of great interest to you and maybe some friends. I will call you again in a few days. If you are interested, fax me an answer on 915392076."' Eamon takes a deep breath. 'That's it exactly.'

Ignatius Davin moves slowly, dragging a chair, and sits almost face-to-face. Eamon smells his coffee breath and his sweat; he sees the beads across his face until Iggy mops them away with a handkerchief. He watches him intently as he sits in the kitchen chair. Iggy crams the handkerchief back into a pocket, places his hands to rest on his stomach, his thumbs twiddle rapidly. He says nothing. The silence adds, as Eamon knows it is meant to do, to his unease. He has a sudden intuition that Davin does not believe a word he has said, that he is allowing him this time while he decides what to do with him, the survivor's instinct in Iggy calculating what the safest route is for him. Just as suddenly he gets up from the chair and walks out of the light. Eamon sees him standing with his back to him. There is no word, no motion. The house is silent. Outside there is nothing. They could be anywhere, in the depths of the countryside, in a town, snug in suburbia.

'You're in constant touch with wee Michael, Eamon,' Davin says coldly, calmly, a voice that brooks no argument, is confident, certain. 'You had a long meeting with him in Spain or Portugal, maybe even in London when you went missing.' He speaks with a deadly authority. Eamon does not answer. He tries and hopes he succeeds in looking quizzical, worried, as if he thinks Iggy Davin has suddenly lost it. 'That is so, isn't it, Eamon?' Davin returns to his seat.

'No, it isn't.' Eamon hopes he sounds firm, calm. 'I've told you what happened. I saw the back of Michael's head, heard him speak and took a photo, that's all.' Despite his even tone, by now Eamon is certain Davin does not believe him, that he knows about the all-night meeting with Michael Donnellan. He should never have gone for that early morning walk with Michael and Griffin and Hugh. God knows who saw them, photographed them together.

'Come on, Eamon, that won't do. This is all part of the plan to set up a separate organisation, to tap into the discontent there is around. Wee Michael knows that on his own he won't get the recruits. He's been out of things for too long. But with you and Mary, as well as a few of your friends like Donal Crowley, now that is something very different. With that sort of support, wee Michael has something he can use. Set up your own Army Council, write your own constitution?'

'Iggy, this is madness.' Eamon knows he is fighting for time, that Davin will kill him now because he does not want to risk the possibility he may be right about Eamon; he will have Eamon shot, brand him as an informer, it is easy enough to plant the evidence. 'I've no idea what he wants. If I was going to become involved with him, why would I tell you as soon as I heard from him?'

Davin raises his hands in a who-knows gesture, then drops them on his knees. 'Eamon, you were never as simple, as straightforward, as you like people to believe. You need me out of the way, then you can move in to pick up the reins, steer the Movement in another direction. I have the proof that you and wee Michael are as thick as thieves.'

Eamon waits, he is certain now that despite all Michael Donnellan's assurances, his assertion that he has Griffin in a safe house, that somehow Griffin got the information to Ignatius Davin and all Davin has done is to sit back and wait to see what they would do. Griffin was not there in the room in the Parador when Michael Donnellan gave Eamon the details about Davin's treachery. But Griffin does know that Davin wants to buy arms from Serbian dissidents. So although Davin knows they met, he maybe does not know why, has arrived at his own conclusion, has decided to milk it as another attempt to split the Movement. Maybe that accounts for the relatively easy interrogations that he and Mary received on their return. Eamon is sweating, it runs down his face, he is about to deny it, to keep talking, he tries to say something but nothing emerges. Iggy Davin stands and leans close to Eamon's face. Softly, as though stroking him verbally he says, 'That was it, wasn't it, Eamon? You were always the advocate of the long game. Time solves most problems, was one of your sayings. And I think that is what you have been doing, you and Michael. Waiting for the right moment, planning, and hoping to get your timing right.' His face is so close Eamon feels his hot breath. Davin puts a hand around his jaw. 'Are we going to hear everything Eamon, eh? The whole thing from the start? You know I'm going to get it one way or the other. Do you want me to drag Mary in as well, get her in here for some more interrogation?' The pressure on his jaw intensifies.

The silence is broken as the door opens and four figures, faces hidden in balaclavas, come in and spread quickly around the room with guns pointing.

'One move and you're dead,' Ciaran says.

Ignatius Davin does nothing, he retains his hold of Eamon's jaw, he continues to stare at Eamon. 'I was right,' he says to Eamon.

'Yes and no, Iggy,' Eamon says. Two of the figures haul Davin off, pull his arms behind his back and slip handcuffs on him. Eamon massages his wrists as much to hide the shaking as to relieve the chafing from the tight handcuffs. 'You were correct about my meeting with Michael, but wrong about the motive, the aims.' He stands up. There will be time for this later on. Now it is imperative they move Iggy Davin out of here as fast as they can. They gag him and wind tape around his eyes, then hustle him outside.

'We need to be gone,' Ciaran says. He does not remove his balaclava. Eamon follows him to the outside where a soft rain is falling. Eamon sees they are on a smallholding, beside a large bungalow, another piece of Davin's vast property empire, he supposes.

Shadow is waiting in his Ford Escort. 'I bet you thought I'd lost you,' he says.

'You took your time about it,' Eamon says sharply. 'I don't think I'd have survived for much longer.'

'We gave them time to relax, make them think nobody was following. They have had it a bit easy lately. They were not expecting anybody. It wasn't difficult to get in.'

Eamon does not say anything, as Ciaran joins them in the car. 'Okay, he's on his way to the safe house.' He pulls the balaclava off his head, smoothes his hair back into place. 'Donal and the interrogators are waiting for him.'

'Who is with Donal?'

'Eoin and Breda. They have an Internal Security Unit lined up waiting.'

Eamon feels the panic hit him again. 'Are you fucking mad? They are all Iggy's men, hand-picked, loyal to him.'

'Not any longer. While this was going on, Eoin and Breda recruited a new Unit, our people. They don't owe Iggy anything, except maybe a good kicking for all the harm he's done to people over the years.'

'I hope we don't descend to that. We need a good professional job done on him, get him to tell us everything.'

Ciaran shrugs. 'I have no influence over that. My job is to get you away from here and over to Donal. Do you want to go home first to change?'

'Where are we anyway?' Eamon asks, removing the trainers.

'Not far. Your driver took Shadow on a good run around all right. We're just outside Strabane. Iggy has a place near here, or he has access to it, probably he leases the farm to one of his pals.'

'Who was guarding him? What happened to them?'

'There were only four around the bungalow and the driver. We got all of them, it wasn't too difficult, nobody was killed, one guy has a broken nose. The driver of the van got away but was stopped about a mile from the house. She put up more of a fight than any of the others. They were not really expecting anybody. They seemed to be there almost for show.'

'Has Donal any other message for me?'

'No.' Ciaran says, 'that was it.'

Eamon is sweating again. Where the hell is O'Dowd? Why hasn't he been picked up? If he even sniffs that Davin is under interrogation, God alone knows how he will react. He knows he can do nothing, that he is in Donal's hands, or whoever it is Donal has deputed to capture O'Dowd.

'What about his British controller?'

'No sign of anybody, it seemed like you and Iggy and his four guards.' Ciaran looks at his watch. 'He's over the border now, well on the way.'

'We're not using any of his safe houses?'

'No. They will all be booby-trapped and watched. Donal and myself set a few places up over the last few weeks. Iggy was not as popular as we thought. Made a lot of enemies over the years. This place is safe, there are three rings surrounding it. We are just inside the outer one now.'

Eamon sits back in the seat. It's over now, he thinks, apart from the interrogation of Ignatius Davin, Chief of Staff of the IRA Army Council – and long-time spy for the British. He can visualise the headlines, the media coverage when the story breaks.

He sends a text to Mary. *Fishing good tonight.*

And one to Donal. *Good catch?*

Then he waits.

CHAPTER 24

Eamon decides to go home and change. As well as some shoes, he needs a shower, he feels dirty, guilty almost, as though he has done something wrong, that capturing Iggy alive is somehow not right, that he deserves a quick death. The feeling of loss, of an innocence betrayed, surprises him. In the shower, he lingers under the hot water much longer than he usually does. He is reluctant to go to the interrogation of Ignatius Davin, although he knows he has to do it.

While he changes, Eamon asks Ciaran, who has been on the phone, talking in a code. 'Who knows we have him?'

'Donal has told the politicals. There is an emergency meeting of the Army Council being called. That's all I know for now.'

'What's the reaction been?'

'A few were surprised, I think, but nobody was that shocked, there have been too many exposed as informers over the last few years. It's got so bad you don't know who will be next.'

'Aye, well we had our suspicions about somebody at the top table for many a long year,' Eamon says reflectively. 'The Brits pulled their usual trick. They've been at that long enough, it's second nature to them, to get us chasing our tails. We don't know who is enemy, who can be trusted.' Eamon pauses, 'But then that is always the way. You never know what turns somebody into a traitor. In the end it's down to them and their conscience.' He shakes his head. 'Even when we are so careful.'

'Well not this time. We got our man, and more importantly, we have him wrapped up,' Ciaran says with conviction. And Eamon looks at him, at the certainty of his youth and he hopes there is no need for Ciaran to spend twenty-five years of his life as he has done, scrapping and fighting and living on his wits. That was what the war was about; to make sure they were never in that position again.

'Have they got anything out of Iggy?'

'Nothing,' Ciaran says flatly. 'He is refusing to talk, to speak even. They took him to the first house, and while they changed cars and drivers, Seamus Hegarty did the formal charging, asked if he had anything to say. He hit him a few belts. That was only to be expected, I mean Seamus lost a brother in one of those raids set up by Iggy. But not a word from your man. He's a tough hoor, all right.'

'I'm not surprised. It will take time to break Iggy. Anything else?'

'No. I've told you all I know.'

When he is dressed and has had a cup of coffee, he phones Mary, even though it is past midnight. 'We got the deal through. The old site is ours. Now we have the big job of gutting it and refurbishing it.'

Mary's reply is wary. 'It won't be dangerous, will it? How will it affect the foundations?'

'The foundations are solid. They have been in place for a long time. The surveyor is happy.' He pauses. 'It will take some time to get it all organised, but we have the deal. That is all that matters for now.'

He checks his other mobile. There is nothing. This absence of news about Sean O'Dowd's whereabouts gnaws at him. His stomach churns – so much of the plan hinges on picking up O'Dowd as soon as they had hold of Iggy.

By two in the morning, he is on his way to the safe house. At the door, Donal meets him and takes him to one side. 'He's in a bit of a mess, boy,' he says. 'We have shown him the files, shown him the details and the evidence.'

'Did he show any reaction?'

'Nothing. Just sat there like a big sullen bear. Yerra, you know Iggy better than anybody, he is always like that, the deadpan face. You couldn't get as much as a breath out of him if he doesn't want to, so of course some of the lads were frustrated.'

'That won't do any good. You can beat the shit out of Iggy before he'll talk.' Eamon is worried. 'Anyway, it never works. All you get is what they think you want to hear. You know my opinion about torture.' He pauses, aware of his worries and concern of the pressure he feels at the task of interrogating Iggy Davin. 'How long have we got before we have to move him again?'

'Take as long as you need, boy. I don't think the British will come after him. Why bother? He's finished anyway. And the Garda won't get within miles of here without us being warned, even if they knew we're here.'

'But the Brits will leak the fact that he's missing. It makes good mischief. We'd do it, so they will.' Eamon is worried.

'I agree. There has to be something that will maybe make him talk, that might make him open his gob.' Donal says. 'It's finding what it is, that's the tricky part.'

'O'Dowd?'

Donal shakes his head. 'The house was empty. When they went for him he was gone and for some time by the looks of it. I don't know how. He was under observation all the time. We're after him. We'll get him.'

'Yeah, but will we get him in time.'

'Iggy will have had some plan to keep O'Dowd safe. Maybe he told him to get lost every time he had you and Mary in for questioning.'

Eamon concedes. 'That would be Iggy's form all right.'

'We better make a start,' Donal says and there is an urgency in his tone that is usually absent.

Eamon follows him into the room. Ignatius Davin is tied to a chair. There is blood around his mouth and nose, his upper lip is swollen, as is one eye, which is almost closed. Without his cheap glasses, his face seems naked. He looks vacant, almost simple-minded. They have removed his shirt; he sits with his great belly sprawling over his thighs. He stares at Eamon blankly and gives no indication he recognises him.

Eamon sits down and looks at him and speaks softly, almost gently, 'I'm sorry about this, Iggy. Some of the lads got carried away. We'll get you cleaned up in a while.' He waits and when there is no response, he says conversationally. 'I can understand why you did it, Iggy. I mean we've all had the temptation. They use some very bright people in MI5 and Army Intelligence. They are plausible, very convincing and use all that slippery charm the Brits have when they need it. I've been tempted myself. I mean, who wouldn't be? The chance to play God, pull all the strings.' Eamon sips water from a bottle. He watches Davin closely; he looks for a sign, a twitch, any slight movement. There is nothing. Eamon continues in the same vein. 'I don't imagine Iggy, that money would be what drives you. I wouldn't have my doubt either about your commitment to the Movement – I never have – after all, we've been together in this right from the start. And I imagine you'll have had the doubts, the fear that maybe we were on the wrong track – who hasn't been terrified at the violence, the ruined lives? At times, you wonder if you've made a pact with the Devil. Those times when you begin to think about how we might alter the course of the war, maybe make some concession, reveal we were open to negotiations but on strict conditions. I know all that went along the back channel, but it is much more effective coming from right inside the Movement, from the man at the top table. Easier to be so much more effective behind the scenes. Yes. I can see that, Iggy.'

Eamon stands up and moves around the room. He is sweating heavily; he uses his handkerchief to mop his face and neck. And Iggy Davin remains silent, impervious to his words. Which does not entirely surprise him, he knows this is the early stages, that it will take time to loosen Iggy.

'I suppose right now you're trying to buy some time, which is very understandable. You are counting on the Brits coming for you in one way or another. That they'll contact us and try to do a deal, maybe an exchange of prisoners, except that isn't nearly as important a bargaining point, not since the early release programme. Or perhaps you think some of the loyal followers who would follow you anywhere will make an effort to get you out.' Eamon stands behind Davin. He places his hands on Davin's shoulders, feels them slimy with sweat, he leans forward and says softly. 'But of course you know that won't happen, Iggy. You know from your own experience that we have had this operation planned well in advance, that we have you in a very safe house, under heavy guard. So I'm wondering, Iggy, why you are holding out, what you hope to gain. I mean, it's not like the old days.' Eamon squeezes his shoulders, like an old friend, reassuring, calming and leaves his hands there for a moment longer before he removes them. 'We don't automatically execute informers any more. You know that. Once we have a detailed report on your activities, I'm fairly certain that we can come to some arrangement. After all, we're nearly there. What would be gained by killing you now, Iggy?'

Davin does not flinch, he is still and silent, almost inanimate, only his slightly heavy breathing indicates he is alive. Eamon looks at the battered face, like a boxer after a bad beating. He wants to avoid any torture, the controlled violence perfected over the years. He knows there is the visceral bloodlust against informers, which needs to be contained. Iggy Davin broken and beaten half to death is not going to be any use to them. Eamon forbids any further physical persuasion; he insists that they clean him up; they give his face some attention to stem the bleeding, to protect the cuts, they put ice on the black eye and the bruising. They fix his glasses with Sellotape and return them to him.

Through the night, they take it in turns to question him. Eoin and Breda work him over, then Donal and some of the Internal Security Unit. Eamon spends time alone with him. And Davin utters not a word. Eamon is a skilful interrogator, he sticks to his questions; he is difficult to divert from his line of questioning, and by his memory and infinite patience succeeds where physical methods have failed. Now, as he contemplates the impassive bloody features of Ignatius Davin, he feels out of practice, rusty, unsure of how to proceed. The old comradeship for Iggy, the sense of the lost hopes Eamon had, clouds his brain, he stumbles, and he is not as forensic as usual. After a short time, he hands him over to Eoin and Breda and Donal. They take it in turns to play the good and bad cop. Eamon returns as the voice of infinite understanding, the most reasonable person you could hope to meet, a technique that has worked well for him. They alternate between questions, never letting up, continuing through the night and into the next day. When Davin shows signs of falling asleep, they force him to his feet; make him stand on his toes, leaning only on his fingertips against the wall.

During a break, he says to Donal, 'He's holding out because he's trying to protect somebody, help them get away. What about his family? His wife and daughters? Maybe he is also waiting for the Brits to find out he's gone. They will have an emergency plan to get him out if at all possible. Maybe he's counting on that.' They are on their own while Breda and Eoin continue with Davin's interrogation. 'We're due to move him as soon as it's dark. Maybe we should do that now?'

Donal is silent, as he has been for the past twenty minutes. He hunches over a laptop, clicking on and off, taking emails. Eamon nudges him, meaning news of O'Dowd. Donal shakes his head. He stands around uncertainly, almost flat out with fatigue. He is keeping going only by the adrenalin, the fuel of all their hatred for what Davin did to the Movement during his long years of treachery. And most of all, Eamon thinks with the fear ripping through him again, by their failure to find any trace of Sean O'Dowd.

'I wonder are we right to keep on at him about the informer? Maybe if we hit him with the fact we know about the other matter that might break him.' Eamon realises he is talking to himself, that he is so tired he is not concentrating.

'Eamon,' Donal says, with none of his normal lightness, 'maybe we let him see this.' He shows him a laptop. 'It came in a few minutes ago.'

'Can we verify it?

'That we can indeed, boy.'

Eamon nods grimly, motions to the others to look. In silence, they too nod their agreement.

Iggy Davin breaks his silence for the first time since his accusation. He looks wildly at Eamon. 'Are they safe?' he shouts, he tries to get up and then realises he is strapped to the chair. 'Are they all right?' he is screaming. The pictures of Davin's wife and their two daughters, young women in their twenties, Eamon guesses, being held in a room, guarded by two figures in balaclavas holding guns, sitting by the TV set with the BBC News 24 channel on, the time and date clearly visible.

'Yes, 'Eoin McDonagh says. 'They're safe, well away from harm, with our people. Nothing need happen to them.' He pauses, looks steadily at Davin. 'As we've done that for you, we think you owe us an explanation, Iggy, a long, detailed one.'

Eamon has never seen Iggy look so wary, so scared, so terrified. He appears lost, vulnerable; his Achilles heel is his family, as it is with most of us, Eamon thinks, and understands why Iggy went to such lengths to protect them, keeping them out of sight, creating an armed fortress around his farmstead.

Over the following hours, Iggy talks, almost without a break. They move him to another safe house. He sleeps during the drive. They keep his hands tied. Eamon fears he may have some plan to commit suicide. He thinks it unlikely but it is best at this stage to assume he will. Iggy gives them chapter and verse, sheds light on many of the murky operations that went wrong, he names names, and apportions blame, as they try to sort out the facts from the deliberate distortion, because he will do that, instinctively, it can't be helped. What they do not want him to do is stop, to give him time to reconsider. Whenever Davin flags, they keep him supplied with food, bars of his favourite Kit Kat, packets of biscuits, mugs of tea, plates of sandwiches. They give him a meal heated in a microwave. The more they feed him, the longer and more detailed he becomes. It is as though now the ordeal of living two or three lives is over there is the relief of confession, the release from having to make decisions. There is a catharsis in the non-stop talk, starting with his recruitment in Magilligan Camp. 'Where my first benefit to the Movement,' he says flatly, looking at Eamon, 'was to escape, with you. With of course help from inside. I insisted you come with me. Not to save your neck, but for cover. We were in it together, Eamon,' he adds enigmatically.

Eoin McDonagh breaks it up. 'Names, Iggy,' he snaps. 'Who handled you? Where did you meet? How did you make contact? Methods of contact? Dead letter drops, where and when? Who was your go-between? Did you have a back channel? I want the lot.'

To Eamon's surprise, he gives them that as well.

Eamon takes a break, tries to catch twenty minutes rest in a chair in another room. He knows he has not finished with Iggy. Until they have O'Dowd, they have to keep Iggy talking.

CHAPTER 25

PRELIMENARY STATEMENT BY IGNATIUS LEO DAVIN
(APPENDIXS 1-6 ATTATCHED)

My name is Ignatius Leo Davin. I have been a member of Oglaigh na hEireann since 1972. I served as a member of the Army Council at different times and was elected Chief of Staff on two occasions. My last position was Chief of Staff.

I confess that I was a paid informer for the British security services from 1981. It happened during my time in Magilligan Camp, where they approached me about becoming one, as we all were. I did not agree to anything then, but I left enough of a hint to suggest that I might change my mind. On that basis, I was able to secure some internal assistance to make an escape with my long-time friend and colleague, Eamon Delaney.

During the past year I became concerned that in the lull that had come about due to the Ceasefire and following the Good Friday Agreement – both of which I supported and continue to so do – some members of the Movement were taking a close interest in my past career. As well, I was receiving reports that Michael Donnellan, under sentence of death for his treachery to the Movement while Officer Commanding of the London Brigade, was funding a splinter group of dissidents who did not agree with the path the Movement was taking. I believe this group called itself the True IRA.

While I was considering how to tackle this problem, I was informed that an emissary from Michael Donnellan, who by then was living in Spain, along with his long-time henchman, Hugh O'Neill, had been sent to make contact with Eamon Delaney. You will know that Eamon Delaney resigned from the Movement following the disaster of the operation Golden Boy, an operation for which he was responsible. Since then he has supported the Movement in many ways, financially, administratively. This attempt by Michael Donnellan concerned me, as it led me to believe he was seeking to recruit respected former members of the Army Council to the TIRA. I therefore decided to eliminate the emissary before he could contact Eamon Delaney. He was held, and questioned by members of the Internal Security Unit. They were able to extract a confession from him that he was to give a message from Donnellan to Delaney, suggesting a meeting, the location was not known. I decided in the interest of the safety of the Movement that the man should be killed. He was disposed of by means of a drug overdose, administered from his own supply of Phenobarbital, which he was taking to treat the onset of Parkinson's disease. This brought on a heart attack, recorded by the coroner as the cause of his death.

Following that, I decided to send Eamon Delaney and his wife Mary to see if they could establish a link between Michael Donnellan and Flash Gordon (Fernando Griffin), who was alleged to be running drugs from Galicia into Ireland. It was my belief that this drug money was funding TIRA. Of course, I was very concerned that Donnellan had knowledge of my role as an informer for British intelligence. That was the ulterior motive. I also wanted to bring Eamon with me, to test him, to find out how much he knew – if indeed he had had any contact with Michael Donnellan. When I was satisfied he had not, I sent him to Santiago de Compostela, where I knew that Griffin was in the habit of staying on his visits to collect consignments of drugs on the coast of Galicia.

Why did I become an informer? It was not because I was blackmailed, or because I volunteered, or for money. No. I did it for the long-term benefit of the Movement. When I realised that we were never going to win the war against the British by continuing our campaign of violence – something I became aware of back in the mid 80s – I saw we could do so by becoming part of the political process. After all, is not the history of every revolution that eventually the fighters become the politicians? My problem, and I know I was not alone, was how to control the membership, how to persuade them that the violence far from helping us achieve our aims, was doing the opposite? For many months, I agonised about my decision. I could not openly voice my opinions. Even to allude to that way of thinking was to risk expulsion from the Army Council, and I knew I had to remain a member if I was to have any effect on making the changes. I therefore decided the only way I could achieve the changes needed to drag the Movement into the real world of politics, to make us a legitimate party, was by remaining an informer for British security. In that way, I could influence policy.

It is my conviction that I was right to do this. I also claim that far from costing the lives of members of Oglaigh na hEireann I was instrumental in saving many more. That as my influence grew, I was in a position at times to get the British to alter their policies. It was my reports of the changing mood on the Council and amongst the membership, which encouraged the British and their lapdogs in Dublin, to make moves towards us for talks. I further contend that the efforts by Michael Donnellan and others to incriminate me are not because they have the best interest of the Movement in mind – rather they have been put in place in order to cover their own illegal drug running.

To return to the operation in Galicia. No, I did not have any help from British intelligence. By then they were preoccupied with al-Qaida and their problems with the possibility of suicide bombers attacking London. I had been downgraded to more or less personal security. However, I did have contacts with ETA, the Basque separatist organisation, and as a quid pro quo, they were able to offer some back up in Santiago de Compostela and in Arousa, where Eamon made contact with Griffin and provided me with confirmation that Griffin was conspiring with Michael Donnellan.

Of course, I was suspicious that he had met Donnellan. I had, however, to be careful not to show too much of my hand. I questioned both Eamon and Mary on their return. Although I had my suspicions, I did not have enough conclusive evidence or proof to make me act. That, I now realise, was my biggest mistake. I decided instead to keep them under surveillance. Well, you know the rest.

I knew my time was running out, that somebody was closing in on me. I didn't get out because my efforts to contact my controller were not successful, or not in time.

I understand that in return for my full cooperation, in giving details of my recruitment, training and methods, information on my controller and other handlers in British Intelligence over the twenty-five years when I worked for the British, you will release my wife and two daughters and allow them safe passage to live abroad. They have never known anything about this. I always kept my work well apart from my family.

Eamon reads the statement for a third time. Copies have been distributed to Donal, Breda and Eoin. 'Okay?' He looks at them. 'We'll send the details in the appendixes for closer examination by hand. Meantime I am sending this to the Council.' They nod in agreement.

By now, Eamon is so tired he has to fight to keep awake. He calculates that he has not slept for over thirty-six hours. They have moved Ignatius Davin to a third safe house, to await the verdict from the Army Council. Eamon is not sure what their decision about him will be. He has asked for a media check, including the Internet, radio, TV and the newspapers, including the English ones to see if there are any reports about Davin, any of those cryptic items that hint something is amiss. There is nothing. Iggy is no longer in play, he thinks. Or they are keeping quiet because it suits them. He finds it difficult to believe the British do not know that Ignatius Davin, their mole on the Army Council of the IRA, has vanished. Maybe they have no need of him, at least not in the way he was regarded in the years of the war; that he's a busted flush as far as the Brits are concerned. But he knows that Iggy has not been in contact with his controller to get him out. He can't figure this out, what Davin thinks he can achieve with his confession. Does he expect to live, to be spared because of his support for the GFA? And he knows that is it. Iggy is trying to tie them into a double knot. Pull one way we are exposed to the dissidents. Pull another way by letting Iggy live and he stays in play as the operator pulling the strings on the Nuclear Option.

These they passed on and the word has come back, as Eamon was sure that it would, to keep the knowledge in the tight circle of himself and Donal. The possible threat of an attempt on Paisley's life is sent via the back channel to the security forces and they have increased his level of security.

'That gives us some breathing space,' Donal says. His face is grey with fatigue, the bags under his eyes like large bruises.

Eamon reads the transcript again. 'We have to get to O'Dowd,' he says to Donal. 'That is why Iggy coughed up so soon. He is buying him time. I reckon they are close to completing the arrangements. He is relying on that and when it does it will change everything, get him out of here. That's why he's made no effort to contact the Brits.'

'We were told,' Donal says, 'the Security people have cancelled all of Paisley's engagements, put some story out that he has a bad cold and is confined to bed.'

'All the more reason to get on so.' Eamon yawns, sips his tea with distaste, his mouth feels metallic. 'Leave me with him.'

'Why did you keep doing it, Iggy?'

For a long time Ignatius Davin says nothing. He is no longer interested in the plate of food, his mug of tea remains untouched. The swelling on his face has gone down slightly; the cut beneath his eye is less conspicuous, only the black eye indicates how badly he was beaten.

'I wanted the outcome to be as it is now. And when I got it, I couldn't let go. The power of information, Eamon. That sense of control you get with the power when you have all the information. Whoever relinquishes power without a fight, without being forced out? It is hard to let go.'

'But what were you hoping to achieve? You had got all you wanted.'

Again, Davin is silent. He reaches for a biscuit. 'You'd want to make sure things go on. If they didn't, well there was always the chance to influence events. And I needed to have manners put on a few people.'

'Revenge.'

'Sure. We have a fair share of people who broke and continue to break the rules.'

'That was it, Iggy. The power? So you could play God with the Movement? That if you decided you didn't approve of the way we were going, you could intervene?' Eamon looks at him almost with incomprehension for a moment. 'You believe you and only you know what is right for us?'

Davin looks at Eamon with a flash of his old arrogance; the defiance is there in his eyes. 'You'll miss me, Eamon. You'll mess it up.'

'You haven't told us everything Iggy.' After he says this, Eamon looks at Davin. He lets the silence lengthen and waits as he tries to gauge the effect it is having on him. Davin gives him his baleful glare. Eamon suspects that Davin is inclined to get up and attack him and all that stops him is the pointlessness of such a move.

Eamon says softly, 'You've not mentioned a word about the arrangements you made with Fernando Griffin to send Sean O'Dowd to meet the Serbian arms dealer in Trieste.'

Davin retains his composure, his set expression. It is impossible to detect from his movements what reaction this is having on him: he is as still as a Buddha.

'Because of that, we've had to take some unpleasant decisions as a result.'

'You lied about them.' Davin growls in his most intimidating voice.

Eamon's anger rises slowly up in him; he struggles to keep it under control. 'You better start to tell me.' He pauses. 'About Sean O'Dowd, Fernando Griffin and Borislav Josaniv.'

'You're a liar. You don't keep your word. Why should I tell you anything?'

'The deal is still on, Iggy. All that's happened is that we've delayed it. You start and we'll keep our side of it.' He pauses. 'Because you know what will happen once the word is on the street and your family are not under protection. We don't have to do a thing.'

'I wanted to keep the channel open for arms. We can't trust those bastards, ever. So we give them decommissioning but we make sure we have our supply lines open if we ever need them. I knew Flash Gordon was messing around with all and sundry. I wanted some contacts. Sean O'Dowd was like you, out of play, the ideal man to use.'

Eamon has to admire his convincing tone, he remembers the old Iggy, who could make you believe anything if you were not aware of his skill.

'So why do we need a sniper's rifle, special bullets, with a night vision and laser sights?' Eamon thinks Davin flinches but he's not sure.

'Part of the list of stuff available. Things have moved on since the days of Semtex.'

'And Borislav Josaniv? Is he the new arms instructor or the sniper?'

Davin does not answer. Eamon is sure now that they are close to setting up the attempt, there is no other reason for Davin to prevaricate, string things out like this. If they do kill Paisley Davin will reckon somebody will spring him once the word is out and that will be as soon as it happens. With a sudden new gush of fear, he realises that they don't even have to kill Paisley – the attempt on its own will be enough to trigger things.

Eamon resists the urge to smash his fist and boot into Iggy Davin. He gestures hopelessly with his hands. 'Okay Iggy. Have it your way. The deal with the family is off. I am going to let the news out about you now and we'll withdraw all protection of your family.' Eamon gets up and he thinks Iggy is going to do it, that he is prepared to throw his wife and daughters to the mercy of the mob. They'll tar and feather them at the very least, shave their heads, beat them up. Eamon feels the nausea inside him at the thought that he is reduced to this, that he is prepared to let it happen. He walks slowly to the door, where he turns and says to Iggy. 'I'll give you ten minutes to think about it, Iggy, and that's ten minutes more than you deserve.'

CHAPTER 26

The guards around the house change while Breda and Eoin are asleep in chairs in the next room. Donal looks at him as Eamon shakes his head.

'You're right, boy. I reckon they are close to getting everything in place, and Iggy is waiting and hoping.' Donal says eventually.

Eamon nods. He is trying to think where Iggy would stash the gun, the instructor, Sean O'Dowd and the sniper. They will want somewhere secure to practise, to enable whoever they have recruited to become familiar with the gun and the conditions. It is a risk though. Does the night-vision work in dense sweeping rain with a strong wind? He supposes it must, they will have considered all those before parting with any money. Where will they make the attempt? As Paisley arrives or leaves Stormont? He can't think how they might penetrate the security around the place, but he knows also that gaps and weaknesses appear when you start to look closely for them. It is possible for somebody to find a spot in the grounds, to operate from there. One thousand metres allows for a lot of distance. 'We're like bloody bats, Donal,' he says, 'we have no idea where they'll try or when. I wonder if Michael is falling into some fantasy world?' And is reassured when Donal shakes his head. 'One thing Michael has always been is a realist. He won't waste time if he doesn't believe there is something in it.'

Eamon realises he has been trying to dismantle the case, that he does not want to accept that Iggy Davin is not only an informer but prepared to countenance and perpetuate more murder and misery.

'We can't keep this just to ourselves,' Eamon says. 'We need help. What about Eoin? He's one of the smarter boyos. He's close to the feel of what's running around.'

'He might be boy, he might be,' Donal says in his slow fashion. 'But he's also close to the edge. He might not be so sure about the GFA if he thought it would come unstuck.'

Eamon thinks about this and walks outside. He realises he hasn't had any fresh air for a day or more. He breathes in deeply, shivering in the chill of the night. He looks at his watch. Three o'clock and it seems impossible to believe that a few weeks ago he was in his bed and asleep every night at this hour. He goes around the field, past the dark house where no lights are visible, and is challenged quietly and allowed to pass.

The walk clears his mind. Back in the house, he shakes Donal who has nodded off. 'I'm going to speak to Eoin and Breda,' he tells him. 'We have to take the risk, the alternative is worse.'

Donal stops yawning and sits up straight in the chair. 'You know the orders. Keep it quiet.' He stands up and stretches a leg and his back as he considers it. 'Okay. I suppose we have no choice.'

Eamon wakes them and gives them a moment to shake off their sleep before he ushers them back to Donal. Briefly, he tells them what they know. As he does so he watches Eoin closely, keeps an eye on Breda. Neither show much emotion, save for Breda who pulls a cigarette from her packet and sucks smoke deeply.

'We have to get to O'Dowd. It would help if you have any idea who might be the sniper?' He looks at both of them. 'See if you can think of anywhere that might be used.'

'Let me work Iggy over,' Eoin says in a hard tone. 'We've been too soft with him. I know a few of his weak areas.'

'We don't have the time to do that.' He pauses and says deliberately, 'What we can do is to remove the protection around his family. I've told him that is what I'm going to do, if he doesn't talk.' Eamon pauses again. 'I'm going back in to see if his love of his family has overcome him yet.'

There is silence at this apart from Breda's heavy inhalation of smoke and equally loud exhalation. 'That's the choice, is it?'

'I can't think of anything else,' Eamon admits. 'We haven't the time to beat it from him, it would be like digging a hole with a pin, and the drugs won't work for a few hours.'

Eamon goes back to Iggy's room. 'Right Iggy, what's it to be? Are you going to talk or do I let your family off to fend for themselves?' He knows it is the wrong question, that he has failed to make any impression on Iggy but he can't think how to do so. There is no answer. Davin stays like a chained bear, immobile, sullen, only his baleful glare indicates what he is thinking. Eamon waits, counts to sixty and leaves. At the door, he says to the two men on guard. 'Watch him all the time and definitely no visitors unless they have my authorisation. If he wants the toilet, let him use the bucket.' 'Fine, Eamon.'

Eoin paces around the room. He clenches his fists balling one into the other hand. Eamon sees how powerfully built he is, how the tension has cranked him up so much that he is certain he was right in vetoing any more physical persuasion by Eoin, he thinks he could easily kill Iggy. After a ten-minute circle of the floor, Eoin says slowly, 'There is one place we might try. It's a long shot but it might be there.'

He goes to his car and returns with an atlas. 'Long ago, when I was under Iggy's command, he took me here. His ace in the hole he called it.' He spreads the map on the table and prods a finger. 'There. On the coast of Derry facing the Atlantic.'

'What is it?' Donal says.

'One of Iggy's investments, as he calls them.'

'Okay,' Eamon says slowly, 'Iggy owns the land?'

Eoin nods. 'I'm sure he does. It belonged to one of the old Anglo-Irish families. When they sold up, Iggy bought it.'

'Another place of his,' Breda says bitterly. 'Jesus, the man owns half the bloody country.'

'We need to search it, for that we'll need people we can trust. It will be under heavy guard, I'll bet.'

They split up and go in two cars. Shadow drives Eamon, Donal and Eoin, while Ciaran and Breda and two of Eamon's men take the other vehicle. Shadow leads them. He drives at high speed, he takes corners that Eamon is convinced he won't get around, until after a mile or so Eamon starts to feel safer, he trusts his skill with a car. Close to daybreak, Eoin says, 'Slow down, this is the main entrance. Keep going until I tell you to stop.'

Eamon sees grey stone walls, a closed metal gate, a long curving drive flanked by trees and then they are past it, by high hedges. They go up a hill, round a bend on a country road.

'Okay, pull in over there. Right,' Eoin says to Eamon when they have parked in the gateway to a field, 'If my memory is right what we are looking for is here.' He takes the Ordinance Survey map, which he folds into a square and shines a pencil torch on it. 'This is where we are. The place is there. Beyond that, over here is a farmhouse and outbuildings, a barn and a couple of sheds. The farmhouse is a good one, you could live in it all right. If he has people using the place, that is where they'll be.' He looks around the group. 'Right, we'll need to fan out and move in pairs across the ground. I'll lead with you, Eamon?' Eamon nods. 'Make sure you go slowly, and if they stop you, tell them you are with me. I'm known as one of Iggy's men, it is not that unusual for me to be doing a wee job for him.' He takes a deep breath and says, 'I hope.' He pauses again for a moment and then as crisply as before says, 'Right Shadow, go to the gate, take a look around, see if the house looks as if somebody is living there, any cars. There used to be an old building they used as a garage, open on one side. Then let Donal know and come back to the cars and wait.'

In the faint light, Eamon follows Eoin. They crouch down while Eoin sweeps across the undulating field with his binoculars. A few cows bellow in the distance. 'Good grazing land,' Eoin mutters. 'There's dead ground over there to my left. And just above it that copse. See? I reckon he'll have somebody there on patrol.' The rain comes down again, sweeping in a brutal gust across the field, and drenching them. 'Okay, let's go while this lasts.'

In the dense rain, Eamon struggles to see Eoin who moves quickly in a crouch across the sodden heavy grass. They make it to the hollow as the shower eases. Eamon lies down while Eoin goes ahead, slowly but not furtively. He sees a man come out of the trees and challenge him, a gun pointing while Eoin raises his hands. Eamon can't hear them but he surmises the man knows Eoin when he lowers his hands while he talks. And not for the first time, the suspicion crosses his mind that Eoin might be leading them on, that perhaps he should have sent somebody other than Donal and Breda with them. Eoin beckons him across as the man leads them through the copse, beneath the trees dripping heavily, and out into another field. Ahead Eamon sees a grassy hillock. At the top, the grass is bare; the area is muddy as though the cattle congregate here.

'All right,' Eoin says to the man, his gun in his back. 'Nice and easy now. Hands behind your back and keep very quiet.' The man drops his gun, places his hands behind his back and Eamon slips a pair of handcuffs on him while Eoin winds tape across his mouth and eyes. 'You won't be left for long,' he says to the man.

They carry on across the field, dipping down into hollows, squelching through the mud, before climbing up to drier ground. The rain continues to come in heavy bursts, but Eamon is immune to it.

Eoin nudges him. 'We're there,' he breathes.

Eamon fingers his gun. His hands are deep in his jacket pockets, his head tucked in against the strong breeze that is bringing more rain in from the sea. He shivers and clenches his jaw to stop his teeth chattering. They move cautiously toward a corrugated iron shed that is open on two sides. Eoin whistles softly, he speaks indistinctly and a figure in a cap emerges from the shed. The man looks unsure. He holds his gun at the ready listening while Eoin speaks. He moves closer as he talks and without warning, with a suddenness that catches Eamon, Eoin fells him with a punch to his stomach and a boot in his ribs. As Eamon reaches him, he hears Eoin say, 'Sorry Seamus, one day I'll try to make up for it.' He has his knee in the man's back, pins him to the ground, while he takes handcuffs from his pocket and forces his hands behind his back, then gags and blindfolds him with stretch tape. He pulls him to his feet and steers him to the top of the mound. 'Where is it?' Seamus, doubled up in pain, nods towards a water pump and stone trough.

There are cowpats, some of them fresh, littering the area of bare earth. Eoin goes down on his knees and feels under the trough, he pulls some bricks away and removes a big old-fashioned heavy metal key. He motions Eamon to him and says, 'Send a message to the others to spread around here. We have to go in there and then we'll try the farmhouse. Better get Ciaran to come in with me.'

'I can manage it,' Eamon says sharply. He rings Donal and gives him Eoin's instructions.

Eoin lifts the sods of grass and stones from the top of the mound. The rain has eased again. In the early morning light Eamon sees a heavy metal door with a key hole, laid flat across the top of the mound. Eoin struggles with the stiff lock, it takes him some time to get it working. 'This is heavy, give me a hand.' Eamon helps him and he struggles to lift the thick solid steel door. When it is open, Eoin shines his torch down a vertical shaft; the bottom looks a long way down. There is a metal ladder fixed into the concrete wall. 'I'm going in. Follow me as soon as we have somebody to watch the area,' Eoin says.

Eamon struggles to hold his footing on the first rung. Once he feels secure, he climbs down gripping the cold wet slippery metal rungs, smelling the damp mouldy air. The rain drips off his head and down under his jacket collar, his trousers and socks are drenched. At the bottom, he stops to get his breath. He sees a door to his left and ahead of him a tiled passage, at the end there is a room where Eoin is. The bunker is L-shaped, he realises, with rooms off each corridor.

'What the hell is this place?'

'It belonged to the British. They built it as a bolt hole for the local government and civil servants in case of a nuclear war.' Eoin shines the torch on two tiers of bunk beds, a couple of metal desks and office chairs. There is a small electric cooker, a sink, a cupboard on the wall. 'They say they could live here for three months if they dropped the bomb,' Eoin whispers. He flashes the torch. 'Somewhere in here is the armoury.'

'What's in the other room?'

'A radio room and a couple of more bunks. They could hold up to twelve people, on duty 24 hours a day in shifts.'

Eamon goes to the radio room, tries the door and is not surprised to find it locked; the lock is secure, the metal door solid. Eoin hands him the key ring.

Inside he sees the electrical sockets and plugs, the twin metal bunk frames, the small toilet portioned off and tries to imagine being down here with eleven other people after the nuclear bomb has been dropped. He sweeps the torch along the floor, over the cream coloured brick walls, up on the ceiling, along the steel girders. There is nothing to indicate an arms store. But he knows there won't be because if this is it, Iggy will have concealed them very carefully. He walks back to Eoin.

'You think this is the place?'

'It's here all right,' Eoin says harshly. 'Iggy wouldn't waste guards on it if he had nothing to hide.'

'The British must know about it. They will search it from time to time.'

'I bet they do. But this is Iggy's land now. He told me they offered the owners the right to buy the site when the defence ministry wanted to close it down, so they did. A fucking black joke isn't it.' Eoin breathes deeply. 'We have to find it, because we won't have much time to nail those fuckers in the farmhouse. They'll be getting up soon.'

Ciaran joins them and the three of them split the bunker between them, going over every section with minute care, delicately touching the surface, using the torches to look for any indication of a hiding place. Eamon's knees and back are stiff; his joints seem to be seizing up in the damp. In his sodden clothing as he scratches around on his hands and knees on the floor, a murderous rage at Iggy Davin takes hold of him. Blindly he pushes it down, he uses his fingertips to probe the walls and ceiling and along the floor, seeking a strip cut in the lino covering, a bump too small to feel underfoot. He is almost at the stage of thinking this is not the place when Ciaran says, 'Here.'

Underneath the radio operator's desk, he lifts the lino with his knife. Beneath it is a steel plate covering a hollow in the concrete floor, where there is a padlocked steel case. 'Be careful,' Eoin warns them. 'That will be booby-trapped. It may even have something that triggers an alarm in the house.'

'Is this it?' Eamon says. 'It looks like a rifle case.'

'That's it all right. We'll come back for it.'

Eamon is relieved to get back to the top to take in some fresh air even though the rain is sluicing down and he is soon as sodden as he was earlier. Breda and Eamon emerge from the shed. They have the second guard from the copse trussed up.

'They come over here to collect the guns between eight and nine every morning.' Breda says. 'We have just over two hours.' They shelter under the corrugated iron shed, where the two guards are sitting with their backs to the wall.

'Anything else?' Eoin asks her.

Breda shakes her head. 'They say all they do is keep guard, two on and two off, twelve hour shifts. They've been here for ten days, been told they could be here for three weeks. When they're not on duty they sleep in the farmhouse over there.' She takes a cigarette, lights it and says, 'Something is not right about this. It's all too casual. Those two are not happy, they grumbled about things, how they are doing these stretches, and then get treated like shit by the guys in the house.'

'How so?' Eamon asks.

'They have to share a room, the food is lousy and there is no booze.'

'So what? That's normal procedure on something like this,' Eoin says sharply.

'Sure it is. But the others in the house don't follow the rules. They drink every night. One of them gets through a lot of vodka. There are four of them. That's all they would tell us. Shadow says there are two cars and a jeep in the shed. He couldn't see any guards around the farmhouse or in the grounds.'

'What time do they change over?' Eamon asks.

'They come off at nine, back on again at nine tonight.'

'We haven't much time,' Eoin says. He has taken over the command and direction of their group. He takes a moment as he thinks while Breda smokes and they huddle beneath the corrugated roof listening to the rain hammering on it.

'We need to get across to the house. We can make it on foot in about ten minutes from here. Johnny, you get back to Shadow, take the cars and watch the front entrance and gates but unobtrusive, mind, nothing obvious. I'm sure they will have somebody inside the grounds watching the entrance.'

They make their way across the fields to the farmhouse and edge their way forward, sending Ciaran and Connor, Eamon's other man, ahead to see if the way is clear. At the end of a field of stubble, Eoin calls a halt by a hedge. 'The farmhouse is on the other side. We need to go around the house, two at the back. Connor, over there with you, near the hedge on the side of the house, by the vegetable plot. Watch the conservatory door in case anybody tries to come that way. Eamon and Ciaran make your way to the outhouse on the side. Get by the garage, check the cars are still there. You can see the front door from there. Donal and Breda take the back door and windows. I'll come as a messenger from Iggy. I just need to get the door answered and we'll take it from there. Everybody got a gun? Okay, well be prepared to use it if you have to.'

The farmhouse is a solid building of stone, with ivy around the door and under the first floor windows. There is a lawn with flowerbeds in front and along the side, where the conservatory juts out. Eamon looks for chimney smoke, for a curtain twitching but there is no sign of life. He and Ciaran make their way cautiously towards the front and get in beside the outhouses, where he sees the couple of cars and a mud-spattered jeep. Donal and Breda are circling around towards the back door. He sees Johnny doubled in two sprinting across behind the buildings towards the far side. Eoin is already at the front door, knocking gently.

Eamon finds his mouth is dry and he is shivering again. Ciaran crouches on one knee as they watch the door. Eoin presses a bell a second time. There is no answer. He holds a finger up and beckons. 'I'll go,' Eamon says. 'I know O'Dowd, maybe one or two of the others.'

He straightens up and walks quietly and quickly to the house. Eoin says softly. 'There is no reply, so they have gone out or left or they are still asleep.' He looks at Eamon. 'Yeah, fucking odd, but I think we'll have to chance it and go in.'

Slowly he tries the door handle and pushes. The door is locked. Eoin takes a credit card and slips it behind the Yale lock, fiddles for a few seconds and when the catch is released, he pushes the door open. Eamon notices the mortise lock and wonders why that is not in use. Inside the hall is deadly quiet and he is wondering if the house is empty, if they are too late or at the wrong place. It is no surprise that Iggy has guns cached in the bunker: it does not follow this is the training site for the sniper.

They walk carefully, slowly, as quietly as possible, down a passageway to what Eamon assumes is the kitchen. On the way he sees another room, empty, apart from packing cases, piles of old newspapers and stacks of vinyl records, some of them scattered across the floor.

Eoin looks at him and nods. Quickly he opens the kitchen door. The heat hits Eamon. The room is in darkness, the blinds closed. Dimly he makes out a stove and beside it in a chair, a large man is asleep, his mouth open as he snores. In another chair, a second man is also asleep while a third is flat out on a settee. Eoin holds three fingers up, then holds one finger and nods at Eamon to look around. The stink of cigarette smoke and stale drink is everywhere. There are two bottles of vodka and a bottle of Bushmills and glasses and lager cans on the table. Eoin circles around the room and gets behind the chair. Eamon takes his gun and waits as Eoin checks the door leading off the kitchen, sees it is to a storeroom. He stands with his back to the wall and snaps the lights on. 'Don't move Sean. Nice and easy now.' His gun is jammed into O'Dowd's neck.

The big man continues to snore. Eamon keeps his eyes on him and on the other figure curled up on the couch. O'Dowd rubs his eyes. He looks as if he is still drunk, a bewildered expression on his face, he tries to get up and stops as Eoin's gun presses into his neck. Eamon is trying to see any weapons. He is wondering where the fourth man is located, he prays he is outside covering the entrance and drive. As he straightens up, the snorer wakes with a start. For a moment he seems puzzled, baffled almost, then quickly realises what is happening. With a roar, he takes a gun from the side of the chair. Eamon fires, sees the bullet hit the man's chest, followed by a spurt of blood. The man continues to struggle, tries to stand and Eamon fires again and the twitching body is still.

By now the third figure is awake and on his feet. 'Hands over the head and keep them there,' Eoin says. He looks across at Eamon. 'You okay?'

Eamon nods. He realises that the gun is still pointing at the dead man, that his hands are shaking, that he is close to throwing up. There are running steps in the passageway and Breda and Ciaran come in.

'All okay here, now?' Breda says.

'Yeah,' Eoin says. 'Where are is the forth guy?'

'We are searching the grounds for him. We got the two upstairs. They gave in, had no fight in them,' Ciaran says.

'Take a good close look upstairs, around the house,' Eoin snaps. 'This looks a right fucking sloppy set-up so it does. He might be as drunk as the rest of them and sleeping it off somewhere else. But get him. We need them all.'

Eamon is wondering at the ease of it all, how the house was not secure, the guards bored and disaffected. He remembers that O'Dowd took to the drink in a big way, that he has been an alcoholic for the past few years and not the type of operator Iggy would use from choice. Is Iggy's influence reduced to using the dregs of the Movement to mount this operation? If that is so, he thinks, we might have a chance.

While Ciaran searches the house, Eoin ties O'Dowd and the man to chairs. He looks at Eamon. 'Good shooting,' Eoin says and Eamon can't decide if he is being complimentary or sarcastic. All he knows is he feels sick: that he has done something he was sure he would never have to do again, to kill a man. Connor and Seamus remove the dead man to the boot of Ciaran's car.

O'Dowd looks dreadful, his eyes heavy with sleep, his face boozer-red and veined, he has the shakes and is anxious to talk. He tells them that the dead man is Borislav Josaniv. The other man, who has not uttered a word, works for Josaniv. 'He doesn't speak any English. We call him Milo. All I know is Iggy sent me to meet them,' O'Dowd says. 'I flew to Trieste and then went to Croatia, where I met yer man in a place called Rijeka, a port. From there we went into the hills and did the business. You know how it works, Eoin. I had a list of stuff Iggy wanted.'

Eamon by now has recovered somewhat. 'Where is the sniper?' Eamon says harshly.

'Him,' O'Dowd says. 'He doesn't drink but he never left Borislav's side, so he kipped on the settee every night.'

'We want every last detail, Sean,' Eoin says. 'What are you here for?'

'To train yer man in local conditions. They used the local area farmland for practice. They set up a firing range out in the fields.' He points to the land outside.

They return with him to the underground bunker. Ciaran goes in first, and then O'Dowd follows him down, a rope around his neck, another around his legs. 'No fucking heroics, Sean, or we'll leave you hanging here,' Eoin says.

Eamon stays on top with Donal. They agree that Donal will go with Shadow to report to the Army Council. 'What about the body?'

'It's on the way. We'll dispose of it.' Donal says. He looks at Eamon. 'Are you sure you're all right? You look like death.'

'I'm fine, just dog-tired.' Eamon is inclined to tell Donal how he feels but he stops himself in time. There is work to do. Later on, he will have to try to come to terms – again – with another dead man and a family who will never know what happened to him.

When O'Dowd has defused the lock on the case, Eamon goes down to look at the rifle.

'It's a Lapua Magnum, with .338 calibre bullets, the British Army snipers use it,' O'Dowd says. 'A night sight that is removable so if he wants to use it in other spots he can.' He points to what looks like a pair of binoculars. 'The latest laser range finder. And a range of up to a thousand meters.'

'Does it work in any weather?'

'We were getting a hit at about six hundred metres even in heavy rain. There is an adjustment for the wind as well. My job was to mark out the sightings on the way to the target, at 100 metres, 200 metres. He used range-finding binoculars and they'd radio the information down to me. I also had to put up on bushes and trees strips of cloth so he could gauge the wind. He started out shooting at 100 metres, then 200.

I never saw him miss once. He treated the gun like a child, cleaned it every day before he used it. They are very professional. They know their job, all right. Borislav was the trainer. Milo did the shooting.'

'When?' Eamon asks.

'I don't know. Borislav said he wanted at least two weeks to train him in these conditions. Then he was ready. I was to send word to Iggy when that was the case and wait to hear from him.' O'Dowd waits as though he is hoping what he has told them has found favour.

Eamon is not convinced he is telling them everything. They take the case back to the car. 'Where did you go for the training?'

Eagerly O'Dowd says, 'I'll take you there.'

'We are still looking for O'Dowd's buddy,' Breda says.

'We have to find him,' Eamon is desperate. 'Iggy may be the leader, but he won't be on his own. This is too big for one man, even for Iggy. Maybe Iggy is working with the Loyalists who want shot of Paisley as well.'

'That could be the case,' Eoin says. 'But we have the gun and we have the sniper and we've killed the armourer and trainer. They are not going to be able to mount another operation like this again, not in the near future.'

Eamon can't help himself. 'If I know Iggy Davin, he'll have a back-up plan. He always had in the past.' He hesitates. 'Why was the security around here so lax?'

O'Dowd shrugs. 'I don't know, that was organised by Iggy.'

Eamon is not satisfied with this, he feels he is missing something. Or is he right in thinking Iggy no longer has the men at his disposal that he once commanded. He says eventually, 'Okay. Take us to the training area.'

The jeep is not in the garage. 'Is that what you use when you go to the training area?' Eoin says.

Suddenly O'Dowd looks very frightened.

'I knew he wasn't telling us everything,' Eamon says fiercely.

'He'll fucking talk now,' Eoin says. Eamon waits as Eoin takes O'Dowd into a shed. They split up with one group going back inside the house to search it again, while Connor and Ciaran spread out to see if the jeep is hidden in one of the sheds or in the copse beyond the vegetable garden or around the estate. Shadow reports that nobody has left by the main entrance. Eamon is perplexed by the operation, so sloppy and amateurish that part of his mind is wondering if this is a decoy of some sort, that the real sniper is hidden somewhere else.

'There is a liaison guy who comes every day. He's probably already at the site,' Eoin says when he comes back. 'O'Dowd is sure that the other guy, Danny Carlton, has gone there to wait to meet up with him.'

'And then they'll be off,' Eamon says. 'How far is this place?'

'About three miles across the fields. You could make it on a foot but they always used the jeep.' Connor says. 'There's a good tractor over there. We could send that after a car, in case we need it.'

O'Dowd, his face covered in blood, both his hands wrapped in towels, is frogmarched to the car. He mutters directions through swollen lips. Despite the rain and the muddy fields, the track is not too soft. Driving carefully, Johnny gets them about two miles of the route, skidding and sliding at times. Once they have to get out to push the car out of a muddy rut.

When they climb the steep field, and get to the brow, about eight hundred metres away, Eamon sees a small shed down in the hollow on the other side.

O'Dowd nods. 'They used that as the target area. They had a body figure he used to aim at.'

'What's in the shed?'

'I don't know. I never went beyond there once I'd marked out his distances for him and set the wind directions. My job was to wait and watch this end. Danny went down there and watched.' He points to a clump of trees. 'He has a butt just beyond there. They dug it out themselves. You'd never know it was there even with the binoculars on it. He used to shoot from that.'

Eamon and Eoin run across and get into the butt. It is narrow, with barely enough room for two people. 'Very professional,' Eoin mutters. He uses the binoculars. 'No movement down there. No, hold on, I think that is the jeep.' Eamon looks and can't see anything except the nondescript stone building.

'Which way does the liaison guy come?' Eamon says.

'He makes his way here by another route.'

'So Danny is here waiting for him? Unless he has heard about Iggy and isn't going to show up.'

'He was here yesterday – I don't think O'Dowd is lying,' Eoin says.

Eamon still has the binoculars trained on the building. He thinks he sees a movement, a door opening a fraction. He raises the glasses and goes beyond the building. 'Here comes our man, I guess.'

He hands the binoculars to Eoin. 'That's him for sure.'

Quickly they start down the hill, leaving Breda and Johnny with O'Dowd. Eamon and Eoin head down one side, Connor and Ciaran go on the other side. By now the rain has passed over, they are in bright sunlight.

When they reach the shed, they get down and Eoin crawls forward. Eamon has the binoculars on the building. His breathing is heavy and so loud he is sure they can hear him from inside the shed. Eoin waves to Connor and Ciaran to circle around the rear.

Eoin crawls to the shed very slowly. At times Eamon loses sight of him. He notices the shed door opens a crack, a man looks out warily and quickly retreats. Suddenly Eoin is on his feet and charging at the building. Eamon gets up to follow him. When they reach the door, a man comes out with his hands in the air, a look of terror on his face. They hear the sound of a 4x4 and the revving engine, followed by a crack of shots, and when he gets around the building, Eamon sees the vehicle rocking and swaying as it heads into the trees.

'What's through there?' Eoin says roughly.

'A track through the woods and out to a side road.'

Ciaran and Connor run around from the back. 'He's gone. He was waiting in the 4x4. We tried to shoot the tyres and the fuel tank,' Ciaran says.

Eoin nods, 'Okay let's see what yer man has to say for himself.'

They question Danny Carlton, who is like O'Dowd, eager to tell them what he knows.

'He goes by the name of Lance, that's all I know. He has an English accent. He brings the money every week for me to buy the grub and the booze and fags. He and Sean would talk above there,' he nods towards the brow of the hill above them. 'They say he was from Iggy Davin.'

'With an *English* accent?' Eamon can't disguise his surprise.

Danny Carlton shrugs. 'You don't question, Iggy, you know that.' They take him inside the shed where there are two boxes of groceries on the floor. Carefully Eamon sifts through them, two packets of tea bags, a jar of coffee, two litres of milk, a box of eggs, bacon and sausages, packets of sliced salami and ham and one of cheese slices, a bag of oven chips, a couple of sliced pans, a bottle of vodka, a slab of cans of lager shrink-wrapped. It could be a week's groceries for anybody. They go back and search the farmhouse and the bunker again. There is nothing apart from the gun the dead man tried to use, that and some clothing in the bedrooms. There are no papers, no passports, no money, nothing to indicate who they are or that they have ever been in the house. They take the sniper away for questioning by a Serbian immigrant Eoin uses to do some heavy work for him.

'Well,' Eoin says as he and Eamon get into the back seat of the car, 'Who'd have thought we'd go to so much trouble to save the Reverend's life, eh?'

Eamon nods. He can't work it out still, he finds it difficult to comprehend how badly organised Iggy is at this end of the work and he's still not sure that this is not some sort of decoy. I'm too tired to think straight, he thinks, but despite his difficulty keeping his eyes open, he knows they have not finished yet.

CHAPTER 27

For the past month, Hugh has walked to the kiosk in Sol to buy the *Irish Times*. He has read the reports about the disappearance of Ignatius Davin, the alleged Chief of Staff of the Army Council. There is speculation that he is dead. Alternatively, that Irish or British Intelligence are questioning him: that the IRA have him, or they have killed him. He can't be located; nobody is certain where he is, apart from the fact that somebody is holding him incommunicado – or he is dead. When Hugh asks Michael, he tells him that Eamon and his followers are keeping Davin under guard in a safe house, under interrogation. Michael can't or won't tell him any more. Things are quiet at work. People pay their rents to Michael Donnellan. There is little for Hugh to do.

He has been to Seville with Jésús to check that Griffin is still alive. Hugh takes a macabre pleasure in the sight of the filthy unkempt figure of Griffin, locked in a stifling stinking room in the apartment of the shitting donkey, as he and Jésús call it. By now, Griffin seems beaten, he does no more than ask plaintively when they will release him; he seems worn down, past resisting, all the fight and belligerence is gone. To keep him quiet, Jésús's friends dose him regularly with Tamazepam. Jésús tells Hugh he suspects Griffin is addicted to it by now.

On their next visit, he and Jésús again drive down to Seville, they take the almost broken Fernando Griffin and threaten him with his life, make the suggestion that it is about time he returned to Colombia or Cuba, anywhere other than Europe. Late at night, they hand him two thousand euros in a wad, openly, standing under one of the few street lamps working. They watch him as he stumbles away from the apartment in Las Tres Mil, where he has been a prisoner for over a month. He looks wildly around him, starts to walk quickly, nervously. There is a patch of waste ground, with few lamps, dimly lit, full of potholes and stray dogs. '*Adios señor,*' Hugh says softly.

Jésús laughs. 'How long will he last? You want to make a bet?'

'*Coje lo que quieres, dio Dios. Coje lo qui quieres, y págalo.*'

Jésus whistles quietly, almost admiringly. 'You know what it means?
Hugh translates. 'Take what you want, said God. Take what you want and pay for it.'

For the first time since he arrived in Spain, Hugh has time on his hands and is bored. He works out in the gym, hangs around the gay bars, picks up men, has sex, goes home. Some days he stays in the apartment drinking and watching gay porn. The drinking always leaves him feeling ill for a couple of days. To his surprise, in his boredom, he finds he has started to smoke cigars.

He continues to have the weekly meeting with Michael over dinner. He has the feeling that Michael has little interest in anything: now that his quest to oust Ignatius Davin has been accomplished, he has lost his purpose in life. Hugh again gets out his passports, checks his emergency supply of currencies. He goes over his plans. Should he go to Greece, France? Maybe he ought to make for Latin America, Argentina, Brazil. Even Jésus seems to have found other work. He is busy getting ready for the season, when he takes his Flamenco band around the tourist resorts, playing for the *extranjeros*, the *guiris*.

Things come to life again with the news that Ignatius Davin has been exposed as an informer for British security. There is no comment from the British or Irish governments. The *Irish Times* devotes four pages to the event. It is reported in some detail in the Spanish press. Much to Hugh's surprise he learns that Ignatius Davin has been allowed to go free, that as the war is over, the IRA have no desire to execute him. Over the *fabada madrilèna*, he discusses it with Michael Donnellan. Who is not happy. Who has been in touch with Eamon Delaney to tell him he regards the release of Ignatius Davin as foolhardy, cheap politics. Who knows what he will get up to now?

'Eamon tells me he opposed the idea, was all for giving him the treatment, a bullet in the back of the neck. But the "politicals", as he calls them, argued that it would simply give further ammunition to the Loyalists, who are looking for any excuse to stall the setting up of a new power-sharing Executive of the Northern Ireland Assembly. It was done to show magnanimity. Magnanimity! How much fucking *magnanimity* did Iggy fucking Davin ever fucking show to anybody? The man is a fucking mass murderer. He needs to be executed.'

Hugh has never seen Michael Donnellan so angry. Never before, in all the years he has known him and worked for him, has he heard him swear so much.

Nothing more is said. Their life resumes. Michael goes back to business, Hugh is once again sent off to do jobs: he travels with Michael, babysits him as he does his shady deals. After a time Ignatius Davin drops out of the news. Hugh continues to look through the *Irish Times* and never reads a word about him. He teams up with Jésus, who is back from his tour of the tourist coastal resorts now the season is over. Hugh realises it is a year since they set up the whole thing, since he first went to Santiago de Compostela. However, he is happy to be busy, work fills his days, helps him to keep his drinking in check, although he continues smoking cigars.

Michael takes him on another visit down to the office in Toledo. Hugh is pleased because they usually have lunch in a local restaurant where the speciality of the house is partridge. After they order, Michael says, 'I've found out where Iggy is living.' Hugh feels the old tightening of his scrotum, the sweat on his neck. He fumbles for his cigars and lights up, even though he normally never smokes before a meal.

'On the Meath-Louth border. He has gone to ground, lives like a recluse, sees nobody.'

'Well maybe they were right when they decided to leave him alone.'

'He won't stay like that. It's not in his nature.' The wine and water are placed on the table. Hugh puts his hand over his glass.

'Just water, Michael. I'm driving.' But it is not that, it is because he has the urge to down the bottle and then another until a form of oblivion overtakes him.

Michael pours his usual quarter glass of red wine and sips. 'He can't be left, Hugh. You know what will happen. He'll become the focus for any discontent. He still has a fortune at his disposal. Believe me, I know. I've had it checked out. One thing he is good at is making money and above all else, hanging on to it.'

Hugh says nothing. He savours the partridge, mops up the sauce with bread, drinks a couple of glasses of water. He orders a flan; they have a *café solo* each. And they do this in silence, apart from some desultory conversation about work, a project Michael has invested in, some new holiday homes being built in Murcia.

Afterwards they stroll around the walls of Toledo, going through the narrow streets, past the tourist shops with their array of swords and daggers and suits of armour, around by the cathedral, by the beggars who squat with outstretched hands. Michael drops some euros into most of the palms. Close to the tiny Mezquita del Cristo de la Luz, they perch on the city wall under the shade of some trees. The tourists come and go, take photographs.

'Have you ever wondered why Flaherty was carrying around a bomb when he saw Godfrey?'

'It's a long time ago, Michael. Wondering and worrying about it isn't going to bring God back. I've moved on. That was then, this is now,' Hugh says tightly. He sucks deeply on his cigar and inhales. Down below, the battlements and the old gateway are quiet, a few people move along.

'I had an order for your execution. The plan was to expose you for the video, take the propaganda benefit, make the point that we could more or less do what we wanted where we wanted – which by the way was not true – to raise morale and to get the British press on the Government's back to embarrass them. The fear was what would happen if the Brits picked you up afterwards, hauled you in and got you talking. You were both a real prize and an enormous risk in propaganda terms. However, the pragmatic Army Council, under the firm hand of Ignatius Leo Davin, decided that once used, you were expendable. The plan was to give you a bomb, send you somewhere sensitive and detonate it from afar. In other words, you were to be a suicide bomber, but an ignorant one. The claim would be made that you volunteered for a job and it went horribly wrong. What I was supposed to have done was lock a briefcase to your wrist and send you into New Scotland Yard, where the bomb would be detonated. You can imagine the message – nowhere is safe. There were a lot of reasons I wasn't going to do that, Hugh. As well as the personal contact, my high regard for you, and the knowledge it was never our policy to sacrifice people without their agreement. There was the fact that I couldn't believe that the Army Council endorsed that policy. It is my conviction that was a plan conceived by Iggy himself, for his own survival. By then I had my suspicions about him, was close enough to getting the proof to make it stick. Anyway, when Flaherty turned up at my house, after leaving a trail across London that was so obvious even a boy scout could have followed him, I locked the briefcase on his arm and sent him off on a mission. Then I let you go.'

'Like hell you did, Michael! I had to half kill a guy to get out of the bloody club.'

'A mistake. But do you seriously think you'd have got far if we were really guarding you?'

Hugh shrugs. 'I don't know. I was pretty nifty, fit, and I was bloody desperate.'

'Sure you were, and you might well have got away. The point, Hugh, is that I did not carry out the order from Iggy Davin. By one of those bizarre coincidences, Flaherty spotted Godfrey without you and well…' Donnellan shrugs his shoulders. 'Davin wanted you dead. Apart from the risk, he was furious when he found out you were gay. Couldn't handle it, that added to the pressure he exerted.'

'Now you want me to kill him?'

'Yes. It is the final act, Hugh. You owe it to yourself, and to Godfrey. Davin is scum, he needs to be exterminated.'

'If I do it, I want something from you.'

'What?'

Hugh says, 'I want my pension, and the apartment on the Costa del Sol. I'll continue to work but I want to be able to go when I want.'

And Michael Donnellan smiles in agreement.

CHAPTER 28

A year later, to his surprise, Eamon finds Ignatius Davin still haunts him – he can't forget about him. He is convinced he did the right thing in making a strong case before the Army Council for the Movement to spare Davin's life. After two days and two nights of often-acrimonious debate, the vote, in the end, is unanimous. They will not execute Davin in the time-honoured manner the Movement uses to kill informers, by a bullet in the back of the neck, but decide to spare his life. He knows this is for pragmatic reasons. The secret about the Nuclear Option has remained. There was no attempt to assassinate Paisley because they had stopped it. Ignatius Davin has maintained his silence, claiming that all he wanted was to secure a supply of arms, as an emergency measure, that he had no knowledge whatever of any plot to assassinate anybody. When they confront him with the evidence of Sean O'Dowd and Danny Carlton, he denies it has anything to do with him. The Serbian sniper will only admit that Borislav Josaniv hired him, that he is a contract killer.

The reasons are both political and practical with the practical reasons the most important. Iggy Davin could not now tell his paymasters anything that they did not already know – after his twenty years of treachery, Iggy was privy to the most secret of the Movement's machinations. Moreover, if he is in the hands of British security he is somewhat hampered if he tries to resurrect anything. Give it a few years and he will be lost and forgotten. Part of the deal hammered out during those two long nights is that Davin is to go into exile. Those of his property and bank accounts they are able to lay hands on are confiscated. The dissent concerns the multitude of rumours flying around about properties that Davin owns in England, in the USA, in Australia and New Zealand and secret bank accounts in offshore tax heavens. The political reasons are the chance to demonstrate the Movement eschews violence, and, of greater importance, to minimise Davin's influence. The official line they put to the friends of the Movement in the media is that Davin has not been a figure of any real importance at the heart of the Movement for a number of years. Nor do they want to offer any further ammunition to the Loyalists, even though they know there will be accusations of blame and of gangsterism and racketeering.

The Brits break their silence. Stories in the media hint at the exposure of an informer at the highest level of the IRA and after a day or two of further tantalising hints, they name Ignatius Davin and give a full, detailed account of his roles in the Movement, highlighting his years as Chief of Staff, the most senior position in the IRA. Just as predictably, the Democratic Unionist Party, led by the Reverend Paisley and his allies, grabs the story and begins a round of interviews on TV and radio to voice again their allegations about the unsuitability, of what they always refer to as Sinn Fein/IRA, participating in the still suspended Northern Ireland Assembly. Eamon along with Mary and their friends simply ignore the hypocrisy of these sentiments, as Loyalist paramilitaries continue to inflict violence and murder on each other in their many gang wars, and in some cases to murder innocent Catholics. They note how little of that is reported in the media.

The main concern is to get Ignatius Davin out of the country. By means of the back channel, the Army Council inform the British that Davin is theirs to remove and interrogate.

Eamon, having won his case, the Army Council depute him to tell Davin of the decision.

Davin is calm and composed after two months of confinement, of moving continually from one safe house to another for fear of an attempt by the British or by dissidents, loyal followers of Ignatius Davin, of whom there are still a few in the Movement, to release him. He has lost a little weight, his face, though still scarred, has healed from the bloody mess it was when Eamon began his interrogation. The security of his wife and daughters, the assurances he has of their safe life in exile has had the desired effect on him. Eamon senses they have squeezed everything they can from him – all the methods he used, the safe houses, the names of his contacts and how they operated, the codes and the phone numbers. He has given them a list of his banks and property, although Eamon is sure somebody as canny as Davin has managed to keep hidden by some means a proportion of his wealth. Even then, Eamon remembers, he wondered how much his family really mean to Iggy. If his concern for them, his fears for their well-being, so realistic when confronted with the scenes of their captivity under armed guard on a laptop, was perhaps no more than or part of the excuse he needed to confess. After all, Ignatius Davin, master interrogator, must have known he could only maintain his silence for so long. His calculation was to buy time before the assassination went ahead and to do that he was prepared to risk the lives of his family.

Davin prowls around the bare room where he is under twenty-four hour guard and does not answer Eamon when he tells him of the plan.

'Surely to God you know what will happen to you if you stay in Ireland, anywhere in Ireland?'

Davin turns and glares at Eamon but remains silent.

Eamon continues, 'I suppose you want to see the family again. We handed them over to the British three weeks ago, once you were talking sense. All I can tell you is they are not on this side of the water.'

Davin thinks about this. 'You're certain they want me?'

'Of course they want you. They'll mine you for every last nugget of information you can give them.' Eamon adds sardonically, 'That is if you have anything left to tell them.'

Davin grunts, he sits on the single canvas deck chair in the room. There is a mattress on the floor and a sleeping bag, the only furniture in the room, with its windows boarded-up inside and out. Davin's thumbs rotate, his hand resting on the now diminished belly.

Eamon takes this as a yes. 'All your assets – at least those we could get hold of – are now in our hands, confiscated. But I'm sure your British masters will reward you with a generous pension and a lump sum.'

Davin remains silent; the ursine bulk sits immobile, unmovable; it is impossible to know what he is thinking.

That was the last time Eamon saw him. Despite the gap, he is unable to rid his mind of Davin. Of the reasons for his treachery. If he genuinely believed that a negotiated settlement was the best the Movement would get? Where was the old Davin, with the moral certainties that any method they used were justified to win the war? The conviction, firm purpose, that this time the Movement would not sell out as Michael Collins had done in 1922 and Eamon De Valera some years later? Was the assassination attempt a serious miscalculation by Iggy? Had he lost his usual cool perspective, his astute judgement? Did his mind go a little under the years of secrecy and the sense of omnipotence?

Of course, Eamon tells himself repeatedly, that is too simplistic, that Iggy is far more cerebral about the direction of the Movement than the straightforward hard man image he cultivated. When they talked privately and argued intensely, as they used to do, they kicked around the possible ways the Movement might go forward, a form of power-sharing government was one option. They both knew that in all probability the Movement would have to settle for a deal of some sort, that however much they believed otherwise, they were never going to bomb and intimidate a million Unionists into a Catholic dominated island of Ireland. No doubt, Eamon also realised, once Iggy is exposed, that his views on the matter are logged somewhere in British intelligence files for their analysis.

Their business continues to expand. By now, Eamon has more or less withdrawn from the day-to-day running of the B&Bs, where they have appointed one of the housekeepers as manageress to run them. They have moved from their first home and now live for most of the year in the cottage in Greencastle. However, Mary remains very much in charge of the business. Charlotte finally came to her senses about Bobby and kicked him out. Bobby, following his incarceration by some of Donal's men, does not argue when Charlotte, flanked by Mary and Eamon breaks the news to him. She moves away from Limerick and buys a house in Letterkenny. She and Liam are regular visitors to Greencastle and to Eamon's surprise, he finds himself playing and enjoying the role of godfather to the little boy. When Mary teases him after Charlotte and Liam have left one day, Eamon says dryly, 'Of course, after all the press call me one of the Godfathers of the Movement.'

It takes Eamon some time to square Michael Donnellan, who is furious at the decision to release Ignatius Davin. Donnellan wants him executed, nothing else will do and it takes Eamon a long time to convince him of the reasons for the decision to allow Davin to go into exile. Eamon, in an attempt to mollify him, calls it a form of British imprisonment. 'After all, Michael,' he says in one of the lengthy meetings they have in Marbella in a holiday apartment lent to Eamon and Mary by Donnellan, 'being without power is worse than death to Iggy. He'll hate farming or whatever it is he does to pass his days now.'

'That is the point, Eamon. The devil and idle hands.'

'He's busted, Michael, finished. We couldn't understand why the security around the farmhouse where they had the sniper was so lacking. Turns out Iggy was scraping the barrel to get people to do the work, so those who were there were not the best.'

Donnellan does not answer.

To try to placate him, Eamon goes on, 'Did anybody tell you how they were hoping to assassinate Paisley? They had rigged out the storehouse they used for target practice like a helicopter. He was going to fire once when the door was open, a bullet ricocheting around inside a military helicopter, particularly an armour-piercing high calibre one is a lethal weapon. If he missed, he was going to shoot out the rear rotor blades. Even if Paisley survived, the damage was done.'

Mary and Eamon's life resumes the pace and pattern it had before Eamon was called to the fateful meeting with Iggy Davin.

Until the day he has been dreading, arrives. He has known viscerally that it was bound to happen at some time. Word comes to him that Iggy Davin is back in Ireland, that he has moved to a fortified smallholding, land he owned in Co Meath in the south. Eamon takes it to others to demand why Davin has been allowed to return from his exile. And he is not reassured when they tell him it was Davin's wish, that the Movement regard him as a busted flush. The implication being that it is Davin's choice. Eamon does not pursue it any further.

By now, the slow painful process engrosses them as the politicians try to gain any advantages they can as they move, like two enormous tortoises, towards the power-sharing executive. Eamon wonders why the fate of Ignatius Davin matters so much, why his memory stays with him, why he can't help but feel that Davin is in some manner the victim of his times. This gives him sleepless nights; he is irritable and he and Mary have many rows and arguments, most of them trivial and his fault.

A farmer taking his milk to the local creamery discovers a corpse by the side of a small narrow, little-used road outside a village near Slane in Co Meath. Ignatius Davin is dead with three bullets in the back of his neck.

The next day on TV Eamon watches the installation of the Reverend Ian Paisley as First Minister of the Northern Ireland

Assembly, along with Martin McGuinness as Deputy First Minister.

Not long afterwards, such is the rapport between the First Minister and the Deputy First Minister, the press and the public refer to them as The Chuckle Brothers.

CHAPTER 29

Hugh lies on the bed in the tiny bedroom. The hotel is packed; there is a concert on at the local castle, a wedding in nearby Navan. There are no rooms available within a fifteen-mile radius, so the receptionist told him as she showed him the tiny room, with a shower room off it. Hugh nodded and said, 'I'll take it.' The roof slopes, he has to stoop when he walks around the bed and remain so in the shower room.

He goes over his plans again. He takes the Uzi pistol and slowly checks it before returning it to his small suitcase. He has a shower and descends the steep stairs to the tiny reception area, where a young woman inquires about a room. 'We have nothing. I'm just after letting the last room off a few minutes ago.' The receptionist is apologetic. When the woman leaves, the receptionist says to Hugh, 'She's the third person asking for a room.' Hugh does not answer.

The hotel is on the main street, half way up the hill. At the bottom is the castle. Hugh walks uphill along unmade pavements covered in loose gravel. There is a crossroads at the top, signposts to Newgrange, Drogheda. He notices the four large four-storey houses, one on each corner of the crossroads. He is waiting for information about the whereabouts of Ignatius Davin. Apparently, he lives a nocturnal life, is never seen during the day and only on rare occasions at night. An electric fence topped with razor wire surrounds his land and guard dogs patrol his small farmstead. There he lives with his wife and daughters, although that has not been confirmed.

Back in the hotel bar, Hugh orders bacon and cabbage with parsley sauce from the bar menu, and a pint of Heineken. There is a large family group eating at one end. A single woman takes a seat at another table. As Hugh eats, he hears the barman telling some English tourists perched on bar stools, about the four houses at the crossroads. 'The lord of the castle below had four daughters who were always fighting. After the mother died, he couldn't get any peace on account of the four of them being there and there always being holy war in the castle. They had him scalded. So what does he do but he builds the four houses the same and gives one to each daughter and then enjoys the rest of his days in peace and quiet. Well, that's the story I prefer anyhow,' he says, as the tourists laugh.

After he has eaten, Hugh takes another walk, this time downhill to the bottom of the main street. There is a pub with a big TV screen showing a football match. He goes in, orders a pint and takes a seat. After about ten minutes, a man slides in beside him. 'Great match, isn't it? What do you think of that fella Rooney? Is he the next George Best?'

Hugh smiles, he does not reply. The man persists. Hugh says in very broken English. 'Excuse please, I do not speak English.'

'Game ball,' says the man. 'Are you here for Newgrange or the concert?'

'For Newgrange,' Hugh says, and keeps his eyes on the screen.

The man insists on shaking his hand, he wishes him well. He leaves Hugh and heads for a group sitting at the bar.

Hugh waits and watches about thirty minutes of the football but he does not touch his beer. Walking back to the hotel, he passes the Church of Ireland, there is a padlock on the gates, inside the grass is overgrown; there is an air of dereliction about the building. A car pulls in beside the kerb. A man and a woman sit talking; they glance across at Hugh. Is this it? he wonders. He tenses, prepares to fight, because the waiting for the word about Ignatius Davin is vague, the usual wink and nudge from Michael Donnellan. He sees that the woman is waving the *Irish Independent* from the window as he passes by and speaks. 'Can you tell me the road to the concert?'

Hugh approaches the car, bends down to look in and says in his Spanish accented English, 'I can for a ticket, *señora*.'

The woman laughs, she nods, as though listening and noting his instructions. 'Tonight', she says and gives him the newspaper. Hugh tucks the paper under his arm and watches them drive away. In his poky room, as the traffic roars up and down the hilly main street, Hugh reads the directions on the sheet of paper; he takes the Ordinance Survey Ireland maps for the counties of Meath and Louth, opens them on the bed and locates the small farmstead. He checks his watch; he lies on the bed and waits.

Back in Madrid, Hugh resumes his work. He continues to buy the *Irish Times*. On the fourth day after his return, he reads that a body has been found outside the town of Slane. That it is believed to be that of Ignatius Davin, formerly Chief of Staff of the IRA. That he was executed in the usual manner the IRA use for informers, by three bullets to the back of the neck. He reads on that the IRA has denied any knowledge of the murder; they state that it was not sanctioned or carried out by any of their members. The Loyalist politicians claim this is further proof, as if any were needed, that IRA/Sinn Fein continue to act outside the law, it proves they are not fit to join any democratic government while they retain the means of executing those who fall out of favour. The Garda announce a massive search to find Davin's killers. It remains in the news for a further three days, getting smaller and smaller, until they no longer report it.

Acknowledgements

I would like to thank Alison and Walter Cummins, Lyn Clarke, John Drew, Mike Gerrard and Thomas E. Kennedy, who read the manuscript in various forms. Their careful reading highlighted the many errors and typos and their ever-positive criticism improved the novel considerably.

—Thomas McCarthy